PRAISE FOR PAUL McAULEY:

'Science fiction has seen fashions come and go, but there are still a few out there who keep the faith, and McAuley is one of the best'
Independent

'McAuley matches the best of his American rivals in zest and scope'
Guardian

'McAuley [has an] acute ability to get under his characters' skins and convey a rich sense of place'
The Times

'Paul McAuley is better than most of the established giants in the field'
Lisa Tuttle, *Time Out*

'Complex and rich . . . vividly imagined, strongly plotted, a constant surprise'
New Scientist

'McAuley is one of our most versatile and talented SF writers. He's created space opera in the grand tradition'
Publishers Weekly

400 BILLION STARS

PAUL McAULEY

First published in Great Britain in 1988 by
Victor Gollancz Ltd

This edition published in Great Britain in 2009 by
Gollancz
An imprint of the Orion Publishing Group
Orion House, 5 Upper St Martin's Lane, London WC2H 9EA
An Hachette UK Company

Lines from *Buddhist Scriptures* selected and translated by
Edward Conze (Penguin Classics, 1959),
copyright © Edward Conze, 1959, are reproduced by
permission of Penguin Books Ltd.

10 9 8 7 6 5 4 3 2 1

A CIP catalogue record for this book
is available from the British Library

ISBN 978 0575 09003 3

Typeset at The Spartan Press Ltd,
Lymington, Hants

Printed in the UK by CPI Mackays,
Chatham, Kent

The Orion Publishing
are natural, renewable
from wood grown in
manufacturing proce
environmental regula

www.orionbooks.co.uk

1
Camp Zero

They took away Dorthy Yoshida's clothes and gave her a cut-down gee-suit, doped her and fitted her into a dropcapsule, flooded it with impact gel and sealed the hatch. And then they shot her assbackward out of orbit.

For a long minute she was falling free. Oxygen hissed in her facemask and meaningless indicator lights blinked centimetres from her face through the distorting gel, but it all seemed like something she was watching on a trivia show. She knew that her detachment came from the tranquilliser, but that didn't matter either. She was floating beyond it all.

And it was good to be alone at last. Despite her implant, she had never been entirely free of the emotions of the crew and other passengers in the ship's cramped quarters, forever colouring her thoughts and seeping into her dreams like bad gas. A not-inconsiderable reason why she had wanted to become an astronomer at the end of her contract with the Kamali-Silver Institute had been the opportunity it afforded for escape from the seething energies of civilisation, the storms of emotion that broke upon her day after day, eroding her resources as steadily as the sea erodes the land. The weeks in transit had been as exhausting as a year in any city. So the minute of freefall was a drop of nirvana: salt crystal or snowflake, she dissolved in it.

Then the retrojets cut in. The impact gel gloved the length of her body . . . and relaxed. For a moment she was weightless again.

A jerk!

And another!

The dropcapsule groaned. Something working behind Dorthy's cloudy detachment told her that it must be entering the atmosphere. They'd explained the sequence of events while she was being prepared for the descent, and she tried and failed to remember what came next as her weight began to build again, counter-balanced by the resistance of the gel. The dropcapsule vibrated, its thin skin plucked as it ploughed the upper air. Interference patterns raced through the gel, rocking Dorthy's body, shattering the constellations of indicator lights. Below her, below the ribbed floor, the capsule's ablation shield was growing hotter, burning red, burning gold, burning white, flowing backward and flaking away. All Dorthy felt was her increasing weight, seemingly centred between her breasts, pushing down on her heart, pressing her against the rigid cushion of gel. She couldn't breathe: her cheeks were drawn back in a ghastly rictus: her eyeballs were flattening in their sockets.

A shocking moment of freefall. She sobbed for breath, but already the weight was building again.

Something shattered. A whole patch of the little lights turned red.

And then it was over. One by one, the red lights returned to their benign green blinking. Dorthy's weight fell away, became something less than Earth-normal. She could feel the capsule swaying as it traced slow, wide figures of eight, a Foucault pendulum suspended beneath the blossom of its parachute. There was a peremptory crackle and then a tinny voice said something in her right ear.

At the same moment the chemical shutter that shielded her from her Talent seemed to dissolve. It was as if an unfocused incandescence had sprung through the walls of the dropcapsule, qualified here and there by hard flecks of intelligence, scattered gems burning in the mud of the world. Dorthy was enmeshed in the routine boredom of the drop controller whose attempts to make contact were nagging in her ear, in the seething flux of the hundred minds all around his.

This is worse than the ship, she thought, and then she felt something stir beyond the horizon. A nova flare boiling up, bending its blinding beam towards her. It was too much. She could feel too much and, turned inside out, pressed raw against the fire, she couldn't shut any of it out. Through a red fog of panic she tried to remember the calming ritual of her exercises: but the light was too much. Like a dropcapsule on too steep a trajectory, like Icarus, poor moth, she burned across the burning sky.

And went out.

2

*

For a long time, Dorthy hung at the shifting border between sleep and wakening just as she had sometimes hung just beneath the surface of the sea, the sea warm as blood off the Great Barrier Reef. It was possible to float facedown, the tube that connected her to the world of air piercing the flexing silver skin just above her head, the blue underwater world spread below: but she had to be careful. Too deep a breath would send her up and as her weight left the water she would roll, sun dazzling through her mask and the snorkel dipping upsidedown, turning her next breath into a choking gush. And if she breathed too shallowly she would sink towards the rounded masses of coral and the patrolling fish, leave the silver skin for stretches of bare bright sand shelving away into unfathomable darkness.

(A door opened somewhere, bringing an odour not unlike that of the flensing yard. A voice said patiently, 'Not yet, Colonel. No, I don't. Perhaps a reaction to the tranquilliser they give for the descent, perhaps the allergen inoculations, perhaps something else. I will tell you when she is awake, I promise, but it will not be for a while.' Dorthy tried to open her eyes but the effort was too much; she sank from silver into darkness.)

Before she had been sent away there had always been the smell of the flensing yard, and the circling white flecks of the seagulls beyond the flat roofs of the apt blocks that showed you where the yard was. There, the huge cymbiform carcasses, stripped of hide, were attended by great, slow gantries that sliced and rendered the blubber and muscle. Later, smaller cranes picked among the bones like brooding carrion birds. That was where Dorthy's father worked.

Sometimes he took Dorthy to watch the whales swim into the chute from the bay where they had been herded. The water in the concrete channel was so shallow that she could see the rolling eye, so small for so huge a creature, of each whale that passed, could almost touch, had she dared reach beneath the bar of the catwalk's railing, the seaweed and barnacles that crusted the scarred hide sliding by. She had to wear a poncho because sometimes a whale would vent a fetid oily spray. Dorthy didn't like that, and she didn't like the moment when the electrodes closed and sent a brief fierce shudder through the long body. The stench then was like burning water. She would jump, too, and her father would pick her up and smile at her:

3

this was a joke, to him. That was where her Uncle Mishio worked. Dorthy was afraid of his scarred, one-eyed face.

The stench of rendering blubber hung over the yard and the little town all summer. Everyone was hoarse within days of the opening of the whaling season, and the apts became stifling because the windows couldn't be opened. But it was the smell of money. The town was a company town, and the flensing yard was its only industry.

Dorthy's father brought a little concentrated cloud of this stink home each night, and slowly lost it to the hot water of the bath Dorthy's mother had already drawn for him. Dorthy and her small sister, Hiroko, had to be quiet while their father lolled in steamy water, nibbling tidbits his wife had prepared as he watched the trivia stage, before leaving to meet Uncle Mishio at one or other of the bars. Dorthy's mother wasn't Japanese; in marrying her, Dorthy's father had earned his family's grave and continuing disapproval. As if in expiation of this unhealed rift, he had become fanatical in practising the old, orthodox ways, the ways of life before the Exodus, and his wife had become a martyr to his fanaticism – perhaps that was the point, although Dorthy only realised this years later, when her mother was dead and her father ruined by drink, bad company, and worse luck.

The little apt with its concrete walls hidden by paper hangings, its concrete floors strewn with *tatami* matting, the brightly painted Shinto altar in one corner, the charcoal stove with its perpetually bubbling teapot, beside which Dorthy's mother squatted as she stirred a fish stew – and the two dozen other apt blocks, the little row of shops and bars, and the large houses of the yard engineers and managers on the hill that rose above the little town, the ocean on one side and the bush on the other, sealed by the blank blue sky that was only occasionally cracked by the remote howl of an air-car . . . Dorthy's Talent had taken her away from all that, just as it had taken her away from her research out beyond the orbit of Pluto. So quiet out there. No mind but her own, and the sun shrunken to merely another bright star among the myriad others.

Dorthy woke to darkness that smelt of antiseptic, a sharp tang that overlay another, half-remembered odour. Her first thought was that she had failed again (once with bleach, once with a sharpened table knife, once she had tried to drown herself in the spherical pool at the weightless heart of the Institute). Pressure lay tightly across her shoulders, became apparent over her body when she tried to move. Not the Institute, that had been years ago. Was she still in the dropcapsule?

Then the little room flooded with light.

A face swam in her blurred vision. Dorthy twisted away from it and something stung her arm.

Sliding under silver. Sleep.

After the Institute it seemed to Dorthy that her Talent had always been with her, but in her early childhood it had been latent, untrained and unfocused, and she had not recognized it for what it was. After all, no child likes to think it is different.

Always it had been in her dreams. Sleeping, her mind ranged out among the lights of other minds, like the quivering scintillae she could call up by pressing her closed eyelids, like the stars, each quite separate and all unaware of each other. And sometimes, awake, she knew what other people were going to say next, sometimes sat through whole exchanges that had the stale inevitability of a trivia rerun.

But Dorthy seldom remembered her dreams, and she was too young to know that her persistent *déjà vu* was anything other than normal. It was not until she had been contracted to the Kamali-Silver Institute that she began to realise just how different she was, and what it meant. So the first time her Talent manifested itself in public, no one realised what had happened, not even Dorthy.

She was six. She hadn't been going to school long, but she already knew that she didn't like it. There were plenty of Japanese children, but they kept away from her because of her mother, scornfully called her little half-and-half when they talked to her at all. And for some reason Dorthy couldn't understand, most of the other children disliked the Japanese, and included Dorthy in their dislike. So Dorthy stood out, not of one world or the other. She became a target.

Most of the non-Japanese, the *gaijin*, were only mirroring their parents' prejudices, and limited themselves to taunts and name-calling, but one girl, Suzi Delong, took especial delight in tormenting any Japanese small enough. This particular time she was electrified with anger, her thin elbows and knees jerking as she held Dorthy with one hand and pinched her arms with the other, all the while raining down accusations that all Nips smelled, that they should go away and give real people a chance, go back to where they came from and leave everyone alone. Suzi's face grew redder and redder; her accusations became more extravagant, an unstoppable flood that Dorthy didn't know how to begin to deny. Her whole body flushed with misery and indignation as she squirmed in the other girl's grip, and tears began to prickle behind her nose.

And inside the prickling, a picture formed. Dorthy didn't know where it came from, but she heard herself speaking from its luminous centre.

'Well, your mother is playing a game right now with Seyour Tamiya. They're playing a game with no clothes on!'

Then the picture was gone and Suzi was fleeing knock-kneed across the playground. Dorthy rubbed the smarting places on her arms and was satisfied to be left alone. But one of the teachers must have heard about it, for Dorthy was taken to see Seyoura Yep, the school principal, at the end of classes.

Seyoura Yep was a tall pale woman who sat upright behind a desk with a glass screen in it. Dorthy stood before the desk and watched as the principal wrote on the glass with something not quite a pen. She wrote for a long time before at last setting the instrument down with a small precise *click*; then she folded her long white hands together and asked what the problem was.

Dorthy's teacher began to explain over Dorthy's head and all the while Seyoura Yep stared at Dorthy. Dorthy felt hot, then cold. It seemed that something was her fault – but hadn't Suzi started it all? After all, Suzi had picked on her, and all along her arms were little paired bruises that proved it. But she was too young to dare question the arbitrary authority of grownups, and here she was in the principal's office, so she must have done *something*.

At last Dorthy's teacher finished her explanation. Seyoura Yep sighed and leaned forward over her knitted fingers. 'Well, we mustn't tell tales, must we? Suzi's parents are having trouble, d'you understand, girl? You mustn't upset her.' She wrote on the glass and pressed a switch: a slot unreeled a little tongue of paper. Seyoura Yep tore it off and said, 'Show this to your parents. And don't do it again. All right?'

Dorthy took the paper and looked at her teacher, who told her to run along. As the door slid shut behind her, Dorthy heard Seyoura Yep say flatly, 'These Nips. Still living the Age of Waste, most of them. They're almost as bad as the Yanks.'

After Dorthy's father had read the note, he unbuckled his belt and formally beat Dorthy three times across the bottom. But it didn't hurt very much and it was worth it, really, because after that Suzi left her alone. Dorthy forgot all about the picture that had come from nowhere until the second time her Talent manifested itself, two years later.

The second time began with a dream.

One of the children in the apt complex, a boy not much older than Dorthy, had disappeared. His parents went from door to door asking about him and then two of the yard police came and made a lot of noise as they looked in all the apts: but they didn't find the boy either. The next day the grown-ups forbade their children to play outside. The women called to each other like startled birds, asking after the latest news, and the men squatted in little groups in corners of the walkways, over a *go* board or a shared bottle, talking in low voices. It was midwinter, the end of June, a traditional time of unrest in the town. The whale herds were trawling the oceans half a world away, and the flensing yard, almost the whole town, was closed. Everyone in the apt complex feared that the boy's disappearance was an early symptom of yet another pogrom against the Japanese. Many remembered the last, not twenty years before, and the relatives they had lost in it.

That night Dorthy had her dream, although she didn't remember it as such. She found herself standing beside her parents' sleeping mat in cool darkness, her head swollen with a blinding headache, her mouth thick with a blubbery taste. Memory of the words she had spoken as she had jerked out of her trance was like an echo in her brain.

The old vats in the yard!

It was a measure of the community's anxiety that this slender and unlikely clue was taken seriously. A party of men broke into the yard. Most were chased out by the police, but two found the lost boy huddled in a corner of the disused storage tank into which he had fallen, the hatch an unreachable two metres above his head.

That night, Uncle Mishio came around to discuss what should be done: he alone of Dorthy's father's family was still on speaking terms. Dorthy listened to their voices, a rising and falling cadence interspersed with the chink of china upon china, as she lay in her parents' bedroom, where she had slept fitfully all day. She felt hot and cold again, felt once more a hopeless undefined guilt.

The voices went on, and at last she fell asleep. When her father woke her, the room was filled with grey dawn light. He reeked of rice wine, and Dorthy began to cry in confusion because she had been sure that she was going to be punished.

Her father wiped his mouth with the back of his hand and said, 'You may be something special, daughter. Understand me? To-morrow we go to a place in Darwin to see.'

Her Uncle Mishio clapped a hand on her father's shoulder, his seamed face twisted around his single live black eye. 'Go up, girl! Away from the world!'

And behind him, Dorthy's mother pushed back a stray lock of hair and smiled tremulously, lines deep around her mouth. That was how Dorthy always remembered her mother after her death, a tired woman on the edge of things, worn down by her husband's bluster-ing, a frail vessel of love.

So that was how Dorthy's life had been decided. After the tests, she was accepted into the research program of the Kamali-Silver Institute, escaping the confines of her rigid upbringing, the rundown apt block, the miasma of the flensing yard that hung over the little town strung along the barren West Australian coast. Yet, waking now in a hospital room fifteen light-years from Earth, she smelled once again something very like the sad corrupt odour of her early childhood.

The room was almost in darkness. For a while she lay quietly and wondered at the evil dreams she had had. The glittering net of minds and the singular *other* rising above the horizon, a quasar compared to the dim Pleiades of the human camp.

A cold mantle spread over her skin. There had been no dream. It had all happened. She was down. She was on the surface of the conquered planet.

She sat up. The pressure over her body that before had held her was no more than a sheet that slipped lightly to her waist. She fingered her unfamiliar sleeping tunic, discovered a drip-tube, patched to a vein in the pit of her left elbow, throbbing with slow peristalsis. Amber constellations glittered above her head, at the foot of her bed: the checklights of diagnostic machinery.

A door opened. Silhouetted in the glare, a man said, 'Come now, Dr Yoshida. You must lie down and rest.' He gently forced Dorthy back, drew up the sheet, and palmed a syringe.

Dorthy felt a brief tingling in the muscle of her shoulder. Her eyelids slid down like weights and she murmured, 'I had a dream . . .' and then the surface closed over her and at last she truly slept.

When she woke the doctor was there again and she asked quickly, 'What time is it?'

The man, slightly built, thick black hair swept back from his pale thin face, smiled. 'Ship time or local time? Truth is, there is not much difference at the moment. It is just after seven in the morning, or just after dawn. So, take your pick. How do you feel?'

'All right,' Dorthy said impatiently, although it wasn't true. A kidney-shaped headache pressed inside her skull and her skin prickled with dry heat. She remembered the sudden hypersensitivity of her Talent, the overwhelming incandescent intelligence. Something out there, something deadly. When she tried to sit up the doctor deftly helped her.

'Be careful, now. Your body sustained a massive systemic shock; for a couple of days it put you out. You should have told them about your implant.'

'I thought they knew.' She was thinking: *two days!*

'Someone upstairs was careless, and the mess, as usual we clear it up. There was a reaction between the tranquilliser they gave you for the drop and the medicine your implant secretes. This I have determined.'

'A reaction?'

'Very severe. But you are healing.' He reached up to fiddle with diagnostic equipment above her head and added, 'I am Arcady

Kilczer, by the way. Welcome down, Dr Yoshida. Now you are awake I can take a proper look at you, yes? I will start with your respiration.'

As the doctor worked on her with the faintly brutal detachment of his profession, Dorthy wondered just what would happen now. As soon as she had landed, she should have gone out to one of the islands of life in the planet-wide desert, one of the holds, done her work and come back. The Navy had promised her that that was all she had to do. Had everything been delayed? Or had they gone ahead anyway, found out what she had been sent to discover, found out just what had transformed this world? Almost certainly, it had been the same aliens that had colonized the asteroid system of another, nearby red dwarf star . . . but no one knew what they were, or even what they looked like. Here, civilisation seemed to have died out (but again she remembered the nova-bright flare that had briefly touched her); but among the asteroids the alien civilisation was insensately hostile: the enemy.

Dorthy asked the doctor if he knew anything about the expedition, but he shrugged as if it were of no consequence. 'Duncan Andrews went back out once it was clear you would not be available for a little while. He is an impatient man, all over the camp you could hear the argument he had with Colonel Chung. She did not want him to leave without you, but he said that specimen collection was overdue anyway and got his way in the end. One up for us.'

'Us?'

'The scientists. Oh, I am qualified medical technician, that is how I started out in the Guild, but now my real job is nervous-system tracing, a little like you I think. When I am not fixing sprained fingers and bandaging cuts, that is – and bringing you out of a coma, of course. They promise to send down an autodoc, then perhaps we work together. Please now, don't blink.' He shone a light in her left eye, then her right.

'When will Andrews be back?'

'Soon, I hope. Hold out your arm – no, the other. Already you have enough holes in the left.'

Dorthy obediently clenched and unclenched her fist. 'Don't look,' Kilczer said as he slid the needle into a vein.

But Dorthy had become inured to needles during her years at the

Institute. She watched her blood rise in the cylinder of the syringe with equanimity and asked, 'Do I pass?'

'I must check your titers. You are hungry?'

'I'm not sure.'

'You have been on a drip long enough. Time you got something into your GI tract. I will go over to the commons while this is running.'

When he had gone, Dorthy swung her legs over and stood. A rubber hammer seemed to hit her at the base of her skull. Her sight washed red. 'Wow,' she said out loud, and paced up and down the small space until the dizziness had passed. There was a set of coveralls and a pair of boots in a locker, together with the minuscule kit she'd been allowed to bring down. She took it all out, and when Kilczer returned, bearing a covered bowl, she was sitting on the bed pulling on her boots.

He said with mock severity, 'I hope you're not being premature,' but Dorthy sensed his relief: she was no longer his responsibility. She stayed long enough to eat the sugary gruel he'd brought, and Kilczer watched her eat with an almost proprietary air. 'When you are done,' he said, 'I expect Colonel Chung will wish to have a word with you.'

'Let her find me then,' Dorthy said. If she had to speak with the base commander, she would have to tell her about what she had seen in the moment before she had passed out in the dropcapsule. And she couldn't face that, not yet.

'It would not be a good idea—'

'I want to look around. I'm not some instrument package. She wants to talk to me, fine. She can come find me.' She finished fastening the snaps of her boots.

Kilczer said, 'I do not think you are quite ready to begin to chase bug-eyed monsters.'

'Really, I feel fine.' *Except it hurts like hell when I smile, and I'm scared to death of what might be out there.*

The base disappointed Dorthy. She had expected something exotic, or at least something shipshape, battle-ready and defensible. Instead, she found herself in the middle of nothing more than a scattering of cargo shells, long, ribbed-metal cylinders half buried in the friable ground, all windowless and seeming to be eerily deserted. A concrete blockhouse stood foursquare in the centre of all this, *Camp 0° 15' S, 50° 28' W* stencilled over its armoured entrance. A faint pervasive stink of something rotting, rich in ketones, hung in the dry air; glotubes strung from high poles shed a harsh light. The sky was impenetrably black but for a rouged edge, a glow as of an immense but distant conflagration.

Dorthy struck off in that direction.

The level but unpaved street came to an abrupt end beyond the last cargo shell, and then there was nothing but a level stretch of sand and tumbled rock. And the sun.

It was balanced just above the horizon, a ball of sullen red flecked with a string of cancerous black spots, so big it overfilled her vision, so that when she squinted at one side of the flickering rim she couldn't see the other. Her first thought was that it filled half the sky, but really it was much smaller, its diameter a sixteenth, a twentieth, of the horizon's circle? Still, it was huge, a cool MO red dwarf star on the flat end of the Hertzsprung-Russell diagram, constant in its unhurried smelting of the elements. Dorthy raised a hand towards it but felt very little warmth, for all that it was only two million kilometres away.

Sunrise: this was the greatest achievement of whatever had transformed this world, for, like any potentially habitable planet of a red dwarf star, this world huddled close to the feeble fires, well within the radius of captured rotation. Like Earth's Moon, one face should have been perpetually turned to its primary, the nearside at best a howling scorched desert, the farside a starlit icecap where oxygen ran like water. Yet the world was rotating. Slowly to be sure, but it was sufficient to maintain bearable temperatures over most of the surface, was enough to prevent most of the atmosphere and all of the water being locked away on the farside. To see the sunrise was to realise the magnitude of the achievement. To look around was to wonder why anyone would bother.

Dorthy drew a breath, made a face at the stink, and walked on, her boots crunching on gritty sand, adding to the criss-cross muddle of other bootprints and vehicle tracks. Nothing grew here, nothing at all. A dead landscape unshaped by any human need or desire, subject only to the random fluences of erosion. And therefore, to the human eye, featureless. It was not, of course. The implacable physical laws were fixed here as everywhere else: so that each rough boulder had on its lee side a tail of sand, and a shelf of sandstone was splitting in paper-thin wedges, each a virgin page laid down by a season's silting in some lost lagoon, untouched by the scribbled spoor of life. There had been no life here before the enemy came.

Most worlds consisted of such landscapes, Dorthy thought, as she followed the vague track through a field of boulders (most no bigger than her head, some as large as herself, some few as big as a house), if they weren't, like Jupiter, failed suns. Emptier in a way than the blooming buzzing vacuum of space. She had long ago become convinced that because the universe was largely useless to human purpose (although who knew what other concerns there might be?), because of that, humans had only a small place in things, could never aspire to any grand role. In the six hundred years since first touching another world, they'd explored a bubble of space less than thirty light-years across, a hundred stars in a galaxy of four hundred billion, a dozen habitable worlds and half of those only marginally so. All energy used by all humans who had ever lived was surpassed by a single second's output of a star like Rigel or Vega, was as a raindrop to the storm of energy produced by a quasar. Like all that energy, fleeing untouched to the utter ends of the universe, this red-lit desert was innocent of utility.

As if in refutation, the track led around a pocked hillock and dipped into a cairn that had been turned into a junkyard. Tipped crates and mounded plastic sacks of rubbish, junked equipment already pitted by the sandblast of erosion: the singular ugliness of civilisation's entropy.

And row after row of dropcapsules, the ribbed metal of their conical shells scorched by the fire of their single passage. Some were tipped, revealing the flaking ruins of their ablation shields, and parachutes were still attached to a few, tattered orange tents that stirred and shifted in the errant breeze like the random lifting of the wings of mortally wounded birds.

A woman crouched beside one of the capsules, flensing away a section of metal skin. The pea of irradiance at the tip of her cutting torch was cruelly dazzling in the sombre dawn, threw her shadow a long way across the ground. As Dorthy approached, the woman switched off her torch and pushed up her dark goggles. Her grin was a bright flash in her brown face. 'They let you up already, Dr Yoshida?'

'Does everyone in the camp know about me?'

'It's a small place.' She rose from her squat. A tall, lanky woman, two metres to Dorthy's one and a half.

'So I'm beginning to understand,' Dorthy said.

The woman's laugh was rough and low, like the purr of some great cat. 'Jesus Christos, be here a few days more, honey, you'll *know* it.'

'Can you tell me, why does the air smell so bad?'

'Huh? Oh, that's the sea.' The torch dangled casually in her hand. Behind her, cooling metal ticked.

'What do you mean?'

'You don't know?'

'I'm just starting to look around.' Dorthy kicked grit. 'This is my first alien world, if you don't count Luna and Titan.'

'Alien world . . . yeah, I like that. Well, go see if you want. Just follow the track on down past the heliport. I guess everyone should see it just the once.' The dazzling light of the torch flared as the woman turned back to her task.

Her vision bedevilled by afterimages, Dorthy walked on. The sea? She'd been brought up beside the Pacific Ocean, had returned to it after her tenure at the Institute because diving reminded her of the lost, loved, languorous sensation of freefall. So she walked on through the junkyard, followed the track as it climbed a rubble slope. Once she glanced back, but saw no one.

Beyond the rise, a couple of thopters and a single lifting body squatted on a crude pad of resin-sealed sand. To one side was a cluster of antenna towers and a parabolic bowl, its receiving dish aimed at zenith. A hut nuzzled its support struts. Then there was nothing but a rutted track through dusty rocks.

Five minutes later, she reached the shore.

The sea stretched towards its level horizon like a bowl filled with cold blood, mottled with drifts of scum like porous icebergs. Wave and wind had conspired to accumulate the scum along the crusted shelf of the beach, a winding line of dirty white nuzzled by slow waves, quivering faintly in the breeze. There was a slow constant crepitation as stiff bubbles subsided. And the smell . . .

14

There had been a creek that received wastes from the flensing yard that couldn't be discharged into the ocean because they would panic approaching whale herds: the local people had called it Bubble Billabong. The smell here, a thin stink as of old sewage and rotting vegetables, undercut with a whiff of something foully metallic, was not as bad as Bubble Billabong's, but small wonder Dorthy had been reminded of her childhood. She wondered if the scum served a purpose, then smiled at the thought of creatures reeking of the pits of death. What would humans smell like to them?

She walked a little way down the shore: boulders, loose shifting slopes of pebbles, banks of foam shivering in the breeze. The sun was still balanced above the rocky horizon; elsewhere, a few stars wavered weakly in the dark sky, spots worn through the backing of an old mirror. An alien world, yes, and eight light-years away humans and aliens were fighting and dying around another red dwarf star, like this one so insignificant that despite its proximity to Sol it had no name, only a catalogue number.

The enemy. Here their civilisation was supposed to have died out, suggested by the simple fact that the Navy had been able to establish a base camp on the surface. But remembering the searing instant before she had fainted during her descent, Dorthy was not so sure. Despite the enhanced sensitivity caused by the reaction of the tranquilliser with her implant, it seemed impossible that something could reach around the curve of the planet to touch her. What creature, what mind?

As she meditated on this, her sense of being watched became more and more distracting. At last she looked around and said, 'You might as well come out.'

After a moment, the doctor, Arcady Kilczer, stepped from behind a house-high boulder a hundred metres away, silhouetted against the vast circle of the sun. As he came towards her he called out cheerfully, 'I should have known I could not hide from a Talent.'

'Why are you following me?'

'Colonel Chung is worried about you wandering around so soon after you leave your sickbed.'

'Worried about my Talent, you mean.'

He leaned against a ragged sandstone pillar, hugging himself across his chest; he had rolled down the sleeves of his tunic, turned up the collar. He asked, 'You see that as a difference?'

'Why not?'

'Are you doing it at this moment?'

'Reading your mind?' Dorthy smiled. 'It's a lot of trouble to go to when I can simply ask you what I need to know.'

'I am an honest man, Dr Yoshida, it is true, but I am not sure if I am as candid as you wish.'

'Perhaps you'll tell me about the sea, anyway. Why is it like this?'

'The water is full of photosynthetic bacteria, one species, millions of them in each drop. They grow crazily in the day and mostly die off in the night. That is what causes the smell. But they are the chief source of oxygen on the planet, so we must put up with them. You wish to know more, you must ask Muhamid Hussan, he is our expert on them.'

'And are the holds like this?'

'The remote probes are classified, and Duncan Andrews does not tell what his people or Major Ramaro's team discovered out there.'

'Not even a rumour . . . ?'

'There is rumour about almost anything, in the camp. I expect Colonel Chung will tell you all you need to know, and soon you will see for yourself.'

'What are you, her errand boy?'

In the incarnadined light, his angry blush was a dark mottling on his cheeks. 'Sooner or later, you must talk with the colonel, Dr Yoshida.'

'I'm not a package. As I believe I've told you.' Most of her own anger sprang from the realization that she couldn't walk away from the problem. That was how she had got through Fra Mauro Observatory, walking out on one budding relationship after another; but here she knew that eventually she would have to explain about what she had sensed, what had touched her.

'Please, all of us scientists must live with the military,' Kilczer said. 'They brought us here, after all. Duncan Andrews may get his way in the field, but we must endure the camp, for now. You have privilege because of your Talent, but I hope we do not suffer for it.'

Dorthy shrugged. 'I didn't want to come here in the first place.

16

And I want to get back as soon as possible, so I don't want to waste time with some jumped-up administrator. Okay?'

'To be sure, I came here because I wished it. Look all around you, there is enough to keep a thousand of us busy a thousand years. That bacterium: it possesses twelve enzymes and three structural proteins, a lipid membrane and the photosynthetic pigment, and that is *all*. It grows and divides and produces oxygen but it does not appear to have any genetic material to code the information to do this. Does not use sulphur or potassium or half the other elements any ordinary organism would need. It was not tailored, as we manipulate organisms to our needs; it was built, Dr Yoshida, designed and built by experts, and we do not know who they are. There are around two dozen scientists piffling around Camp Zero when we should be all over the planet. But the people who run things from orbit will not do it that way in case some of our technology falls into enemy hands or flippers.'

'Or tentacles.'

'Whatever the case,' Kilczer said. 'Anyway, the Navy uses dropcapsules instead of shuttles because they are frightened that the enemy might capture one and get into orbit, fuel cells instead of catalfission batteries, and we are standing on a world whose rate of rotation was spun up somehow without melting the crust as it should have. Crazy people the military, yes, but we must live with them and get by on what crumbs they throw us.'

' "Let not ambition mock thy useful toil." '

'Huh?' He rubbed his hands together. 'Ah, I see, you quote to me. Well, believe me, I am not wishing to stab any backs. None of us are. At least we are down here. Marx's beard, this wind gets into my bones. I am going to find a jug of coffee and perhaps swim in it. You come, too?'

Dorthy sighed. 'Why not? There's nothing out here for me.'

'Fourteen enzymes now, Dr Yoshida. See, the ones that survive the darkness develop two more on the capsule wall at sunrise, one a kind of all-purpose degrader, the other to take up the resulting carbon skeletons. They're losing those now. Perhaps we'll lose the smell as well.'

'I don't know much about biology,' Dorthy said.

Muhamid Hussan smiled and patted her hand where it lay on the plastic tabletop. She drew it back as he said, 'But it is interesting, yes? Such a specific system, a pure unicell culture, indefinitely self-sustaining with minimal input. We have been here for much less than a planetary day. There is much to learn.' His soft hoarse voice was hard to hear above the noise of the commons. In one corner half a dozen people were watching a trivia tape of the fighting at BD twenty, a newscast brought by the ship that had also brought Dorthy. Elsewhere Navy personnel drank and laughed and yelled at each other with a kind of hysterical bonhomie, drowning out the earnest talk of the little group of scientists that had gathered around Dorthy. Beside her, Arcady Kilczer said to Hussan, 'How do you know the stink isn't going to get worse?'

'I don't.' Hussan clutched air either side of his curly black hair. 'I can but hope, eh?' His eyes were hidden by archaic tinted glasses. Now he leaned across the table and Dorthy saw her face doubly reflected: she looked awful. Hussan asked, 'Did this communist tell you the most interesting thing about the bacteria?'

'Jesus Christos, Hussan, you're boring the hell out of her, just like you've bored the hell out of the rest of us.' This was the tall, dark-skinned woman Dorthy had met in the junkyard. She smiled at Dorthy and asked, 'What do you think of it all, Dr Yoshida? Crazy place, right?'

'I suppose so.'

'I might as well be on Mars,' someone else complained, 'for all the difference in geology. I want to look at those holds. I've a bet with the imaging crew that they're volcanic, not impact—'

'And how will you collect if you win?' Hussan asked. 'When they're upstairs and we have no ladder back until this thing is wound up.'

Dorthy asked, 'Is that true? There's no way to get into orbit from—'

Kilczer told her, 'Not with what is down here.'

'But I was told that when I finished I'd be able to go back.'

'They sure sold you one,' the lanky geologist said with gloomy satisfaction, as if it were some kind of dubious achievement.

'Maybe they send down a shuttle,' Kilczer said. Then, 'Where are you going?'

'To find Colonel Chung. I think I'm due to talk with her.'

'You can't just—' He followed her through the crowd, into the thin cold air outside. 'You cannot simply walk in there,' he said.

'That damned sun hasn't moved. It's like time has stopped.'

'Oh, a couple of degrees, I think. It will be over the tops of the cargo shells by tomorrow. The command centre is in that direction, by the way.'

Dorthy turned. 'You don't have to follow me around.'

'How do you feel?'

'Angry.'

Kilczer pushed back hair stirred by the breeze. 'You really were not told that it is a one-way trip down? What did you think the dropcapsules were for?'

'By the time they put me inside I was so high on that tranquilliser I didn't even remember where I was going. And listen, I don't need to have my hand held. Okay?'

'Of course,' he said, and turned away. Dorthy had gone only a little way when he called to her. 'Come and see me when you have finished with the colonel. Good luck, now!'

But Dorthy didn't even look back.

Inside the concrete blockhouse of the command centre, Dorthy was escorted to an elevator that dropped in near freefall for ten seconds. The force of deceleration almost knocked her over, and her escort, a stocky Polynesian rating with a reaction pistol strapped at her hip, supported her impassively. 'I suppose I'm still not quite over getting down to the surface,' Dorthy said, embarrassed, but the rating didn't reply, not even a shrug, and led her on down a bare corridor. Open doorways let on to dark rooms; behind one of the few that were closed, Dorthy heard the hiss of a printer as she passed. How far did all of this extend? She visualized level after level of honey-combed passages and rooms extending through the bedrock – but to what purpose? Anything on the planet was potentially vulnerable, no matter how deeply it was buried.

The rating keyed a door and ushered Dorthy in. Behind a desk, a burly sergeant waved her to a fragile plastic chair, nodding in indifferent acknowledgement of the rating's salute as she departed.

'Colonel Chung wants to see me,' Dorthy said.

The sergeant made an annotation to the desk's screen and without looking up said, 'That's right, Dr Yoshida. In a while.'

Dorthy sat wearily, her headache a constant pulse now. She had learned enough about the Navy's hurry-up-and-wait routines to know that any protest was useless. Well, an astronomer must cultivate patience if nothing else. Her anger that she might be locked down here with everyone else, despite all she had been promised, had evaporated. What she felt now was fluttering anticipation. The Navy could do anything to her, anything at all. The sergeant was still ignoring her. She tried to reconstruct that blinding instant of contact during her descent, phrasing and rephrasing a description until at last the sergeant turned off his screen and showed her into the next room.

Colonel Chung was a small, fine-boned woman with crew-cut grey hair and all the aura of a clerical computer. Her office was almost empty, nothing in it but a desk and two chairs and a cot with a metal locker at its foot. The only personal touch was a jade figurine perched at the edge of the desk, which Colonel Chung fingered as she asked politely if Dorthy would take tea.

'Thank you, no.' Dorthy wanted to come straight to the point. 'What about the expedition?'

'The expedition, yes. I'm sorry you were incapacitated. Duncan Andrews will return in two days; he'll take you out then.'

'Can't you fly me out to him?'

'We have only a few aircraft, Dr Yoshida. Dr Andrews's expedition has already tied up too many of them – although we hope for more supplies soon. I'm afraid that you'll have to wait here. I'm sorry there isn't any way to expedite your case.'

'All I want to do is finish what I was brought here to do and leave. And I understand that even that might not be possible. How will I get off this world, Colonel Chung?'

'I am sure that orbital command has the matter in hand.'

'But you don't know. Come on, Colonel. I might be young, but I'm not fucking naïve. Perhaps I had better speak with Admiral Orquito.'

'I don't think so. I am acting under his general orders, after all, but even I don't know all the details. Nor do I want to. Caution, Dr Yoshida, is our watchword. I hope you will come to appreciate that.'

Dorthy's headache was a knife-blade prying behind her forehead. Beyond it, the colonel's malice glittered like light on insect wings. She didn't want to go after that terrible, bright intelligence, didn't even want to follow the Navy's plan. All she wanted was the empty solitude from which she'd been dragged, quiet contemplation undisturbed by frenetic human affairs. But she saw herself wasting weeks taking one cautious programmed step after another when she knew better. She said, 'I have a right, I believe, to talk to the admiral.'

'We are in a state of war down here, Dr Yoshida. There is only a single channel to orbital command, for coded, authorized communications, no more.'

'I see.' She didn't have to be told who authorized the communications. 'Well, I wouldn't like you to risk anything, Colonel. Don't even stir from this tomb of yours.'

'We have to proceed carefully, Dr Yoshida. We have only a foothold on this planet and as yet we haven't identified what owns it. If anything still does. Dr Andrews believes that the enemy died off here after they planoformed P'thrsn.'

'P'thrsn?' It was like a cross between a spit and a sneeze.

Colonel Chung allowed herself a brief smile; Dorthy could guess why. After all, Dorthy knew almost nothing about the planet (*Security*, they had told her when she had asked. And, *You'll only be there a couple of days.* And, perhaps for the twentieth time, *Don't worry. You'll be well looked after*), so if she wanted to know something, she had to ask. The colonel was appreciating the irony of feeding information to an empath, and Dorthy sensed the flicker of her small satisfaction as she explained, 'While you were . . . out of circulation, a remote probe found writing at the hold. In a kind of city, in its centre. The people out there have made a few tentative discoveries, and the name of this world is one of them. They also believe that they know what the enemy calls itself: the Alea. That at least is easy to pronounce.'

' "Give airy nothings a name, and a local habitation." '

'I am sorry?'

'Shakespeare.'

The colonel's shrug implied that she had never heard of Shakespeare, and neither did she care, reaffirming Dorthy's longstanding opinion that all Chinese were cultural barbarians. 'Your job has still to be done, of course, and I appreciate its urgency,' Chung said. 'If descendants of the enemy still live here, then perhaps we can learn enough to bring the war at BD twenty to an end. At present we do not know how to communicate with the enemy; we do not even know what they look like. And the cost of the war grows each day; suppressing the enemy may yet bankrupt the Federation. I trust that you agree it would be better to negotiate for peace if we could find some way of engaging the enemy in a dialogue. And you may help find the key for opening that dialogue, Dr Yoshida.'

'I'm flattered. Colonel. From what you say, do I understand that the expedition hasn't found any trace of the enemy? The Alea.' The word hummed in her mouth.

'There are . . . possibilities. With your help—'

'Well, it's possible that I may have discovered something already,' Dorthy said, suddenly dry-mouthed. But she might gain some small advantage if she gave Chung this. 'When I was in the dropcapsule the tranquilliser I'd been given neutralised the secretions of my implant.'

'Dr Kilczer told me of a reaction.' The colonel's gaze was averted from Dorthy, intent on the figurine. An old man or an old woman, Dorthy saw, bent double beneath a loaded wicker basket.

'Well, that meant that my Talent was operating.' Dorthy paused, picking her words carefully. 'It was operating with unusual sensitivity, too. I could visualize the minds of all the people in this camp, and I also saw something else, something a long way off but so intense it burned brighter than all the camp. I think it was focused on me.'

'This wasn't, then, a human mind.' Still the colonel did not look at Dorthy.

'I don't know what it was. But certainly it wasn't human.'

'That's to be expected, surely.' Beneath the colonel's seeming calm Dorthy detected something else. Dark, formless, coiling.

'Perhaps. But it means that there is *something* out there, and I'd suggest that all effort be put into finding out *what* it is. I only saw it for a moment – then I passed out. But it was somewhere over the horizon beyond the camp.'

'From your descent trajectory that would put it to the east of us, unless it was in the sea. Let me show you, Dr Yoshida.' The colonel pressed an indented tab and the clear surface of the desk flickered, then glowed with a ragged map composed of overlapping rectangles: holos taken from orbit. Here and there were black strips, areas the survey had missed, but the map was mostly complete, red and riven with canyons, peppered with craters. The colonel tapped a dark circle the width of her hand. 'We are here, right on the shore. Now . . .' She pressed another tab and more than a dozen green dots flicked on, scattered more or less along the equatorial line. The colonel tapped one with a long fingernail. 'This is the hold where Andrews and Major Ramaro's team are working. It's in the same direction as the thing you say you . . . sensed? Is that the correct term?'

'It's as good as any.'

'There are four other holds in that direction.' The colonel tapped them one by one. 'Do you know how far away this phenomenon was?'

'No. My Talent doesn't work like that.' She saw that the colonel didn't really believe her. Or didn't want to believe her. She said, feeling a sliding touch of desperation, 'But if I'm to find—'

'You are a valuable resource, Dr Yoshida. We don't wish to sacrifice you. If there is any danger, we will have to alter our plans.'

'Thank you,' Dorthy said coldly. It was as if a great gulf had opened between them, and on her side Dorthy had the sensation of slowly sinking.

The colonel switched off the desk and clasped her hands, her long nails meshing with a dry, ragged scratching. Dorthy curled her own fingers to hide her close-bitten nails. The colonel said, 'In any case, orbital command is of the opinion that the enemy civilisation has certainly collapsed here, and may well have died out completely. It is the only point on which they and Dr Andrews are able to agree. You are here . . . well, to test that idea. To eliminate possibilities, not take off on some tangent.'

'And what if orbital command and Dr Andrews are wrong?'

'You must talk with Dr Andrews. I'm sure you'll have a lot to discuss. But understand, Dr Yoshida, that this operation is under my jurisdiction. I must proceed carefully.'

'Oh, I understand, all right.' Dorthy rose from her chair and for an instant her headache cleared and a touch of the other woman's feelings came to her, as a scent will rise and fade on an erratic breeze. In a way, Colonel Chung was as scared as Dorthy, and as helpless. She knew that she was completely in the hands of orbital command, and for some reason that was terrifying. But scarcely had Dorthy registered this when the breeze died, the scent faded. All that was left was the certain knowledge that something was very wrong.

It seemed, then, that there was nothing Dorthy could do until Duncan Andrews returned to Camp Zero. She tried to tell the doctor, Arcady Kilczer, about what she'd sensed in Colonel Chung's thoughts, but he shrugged it off, tried to turn it into a joke by pointing out that everyone was a little crazy, down here on the surface. This only infuriated Dorthy.

'I'm paranoid, is that what you're saying?' Her headache, diminishing, pulsed in her temples.

'Of course not,' Kilczer said mildly, not looking up as he fiddled with a woven copper sensor from one of his neural tracers. 'It is our situation, that is what I mean. Cut off as we are, the unknown over every horizon, one would expect nothing less. I handle a large' – carefully, he slid the delicate flexible sensor into its protective nylon sleeve – 'a large and regular traffic in psychotropic drugs.'

'And because of my Talent I'm bound to be affected.'

'Remember, you said that, not I. Please. You might be correct in your suspicions. I hope you are not. But I can do nothing about it in any event; I am under Colonel Chung's command.'

'Are you going to tell her about this?'

He bent over his machine, trying to fit the sleeved sensor inside the crammed casing. 'No,' he said, 'of course not. Unless I am asked. Wait until Duncan Andrews returns, that is my advice.'

Dorthy looked down at Kilczer's narrow hunched shoulders, the white nape of his neck exposed below the edge of his black hair. She had a sense of a door softly closing in her face; yet in his refusal to ally himself with her, Kilczer had held out a thread of hope. 'Can Andrews do anything?' she asked.

'He is the only one of us down here who can.' Kilczer turned in his chair. His eye sockets looked bruised; he had been working hard, Dorthy thought, forgetting, because it was the kind of thing she hated to remember, that she had been in his care until only a few hours ago. 'Wait for Andrews,' Kilczer advised. 'And meanwhile do not worry about what you think you saw or sensed. It may mean nothing.'

Easy for him to say: he could never understand the intimacy of her Talent, a touch deeper than any lover's caress, the way she had, for a moment, fallen inside Chung's mind and brought back, like a remote sampling of the ocean depths, the undefined dark touch of the woman's fear. But she could do nothing by herself and so she took Kilczer's advice, kept quiet, and waited. After all, Andrews was supposed to be returning very soon.

But she had to wait five days; and when at last he did arrive, it was in the middle of a sandstorm.

Dorthy spent the interregnum working with the geo-chem crew, helping set up drilling rigs to take deep cores that, the layers prised apart and fed into neutron density counters and isotope separators, yielded some history of the planet.

In every core from every site was a layer of volcanic ash, compressed into a thin dark line, marking the millennium-long pangs which had followed the spinning of the once tide-locked globe and the bombardment with ice asteroids which had created the shallow seas. Near the shore, striated fossiliferous sediment above the ash provided a reasonably accurate dating guide (and incidentally clocked the lengthening days: in ten million years or so the world would be tide-locked again). The best guess was that the planoforming had occurred roughly a million years ago.

And only a little way into the fossil record was a discontinuous hair-thin layer of minute chondrules and fused impure metal flakes, indicating a secondary bombardment with nickel-iron asteroids. There was a hypothesis that the secondary strikes had been intended to enrich the metal content of the impoverished crust – some of the plant and animal species in the holds had relatively high concentrations of metals in their tissues – but it didn't explain why the enrichment had followed rather than preceded the establishment of a beachhead of life on the planet.

Dorthy was not particularly interested in these problematical findings, but the physical labour brought a blessed surcease of thought. Each evening, exhausted, she sank gratefully into deep untroubled sleep. Arcady Kilczer let her use the bay in the medical centre, away from the close, claustrophobic common dormitories. Dorthy was still suffering from flashes of enhanced empathy, but Kilczer couldn't do anything about it. Although he deepscanned her implant, it was beyond his power even to find out if it was functioning properly. 'What is it, anyway?' he asked, puzzling over the image, shades of red from dusky rose to deepest purple, on the screen.

'It's derived from a fluke, a parasite of the blood system,' Dorthy told him. '*Shistosoma japonicum.*'

'On Earth you have such things still? I understand that it is a strange world. Well, your implant is dribbling a rich pharmacopoeia, but I can't tell if it is doing it properly. Serotonin, acetylcholonine . . . and what is this peak, I wonder.' He thumbed the wiggling line of a printout.

'Some kind of noradrenalin derivative. I don't know much about it. I'm an astronomer, not a biochemist.'

Kilczer smoothed back black hair. 'All I can say is that it is not dying. Let us hope that this is just a residual effect. Your attacks, they are increasing in frequency?'

'Two or three a day, no more, no less. I try and sleep a lot.'

'That I notice. Also, people are beginning to say that you are too remote, Dr Yoshida. That and the fact that you will go out to the hold is causing some resentment among the other scientists.'

'I don't give a damn what anyone thinks! All I want is off this planet. I didn't ask to come here. And when I was brought here, against my will, my implant was screwed up and no one can fix it, and I'm left sitting on my hands waiting for this Duncan Andrews character. Look, it *hurts* if I have an attack when there are a lot of people around. You wouldn't understand that, but it does. So let me alone, huh?' Her forehead burned with anger; her eyes pricked with tears. She took a deep breath, another.

Kilczer said mildly, 'I know I do nothing. For this I am sorry. I have asked orbital command's chief medical officer for advice, but she knows as much about it as I, which is nothing, really. Your implant is copyrighted, and we can hardly trek all the way back to Earth to pay our consultation fee to get the gene dis. I could give you a tranquilliser, but a tranquilliser set this off in the first place.'

'I'm sorry, I didn't mean to be hard on you, but it's frustrating, you know?' Dorthy smiled unsteadily. 'I'm used to having my Talent under control. More or less.'

'Duncan Andrews will be here soon. You will do your job then.'

'And suppose when I've done all I can, they don't let me back upstairs? What then?'

Arcady Kilczer shrugged. 'What can I say? Doubt even Colonel Chung knows whole story.'

Dorthy remembered that glimpse, the pit of shadowy fear behind the colonel's neatly ordered consciousness.

Kilczer suggested, 'Perhaps Duncan Andrews can put in a word for you. He has influence.'

'Perhaps,' Dorthy said, not believing it at all. By now she'd heard too much about Andrews, his vigorous infighting with the hydra-headed Navy administration, his fabulous wealth and concomitant longevity (one rumour had it that he was more than a century old, older than the Federation). The scientists didn't resent *him*, out there at the hold. Instead, they venerated him for having made the whole scientific arm of the expedition possible, made him seem to be an unlikely combination of Einstein and Beowulf. Dorthy knew too much about human fallibility to believe even half of what she'd heard, but despite herself she began to lay some hope that he would sympathize with her plight and contrive to call down a shuttle as reward for her corvée. In the meantime, she minimised her external irritation by avoiding people as much as possible, and calmed her internal fears by hard work and long runs across the tumbled landscape outside the camp.

She went to bed early and fell asleep almost at once, exhausted by the work at the drilling site; yet without chemical aids, which Kilczer refused to prescribe while her implant was recovering, she woke early to the constant red light of the sun, still rising by imperceptible degrees above the crumpled eastern horizon. The camp, fixed to the diurnal rhythms of Earth, was quiet, deserted. Dorthy had cut down a pair of coveralls to leave her arms and legs mostly bare, and she ran in these, sandals ploughing dry dusty grit, slapping across shelves of rock, muscles stiff at first then loosening, their sheathed pull liquid and easy in the slightly lower gravity. Despite the apparent size of the sun, this long morning was cold, and in the chill dry air her sweat evaporated quickly so that she never grew hot as she ran, following part of the rim of a huge crater that lay several kilometres south and east of the camp, skirting huge half-buried boulders, impact ejecta like the boulders around the camp, ancient sandstone laid down in some vanished primeval ocean when the planet had yet to lose its natural rotation, leaping from ridge to ridge where strata had been thrust up and turned over. Part of the planoforming seemed to have involved bombardment with ice asteroids: this crater was a remainder of that period, a secondary strike from the vast impact that had created the basin of the sea. A million years, imagine. She shied away from the thought of the burning intelligence – a million years ago there had been no humans, only rare, scattered groups of habilines moving outward from the drought-ridden African plains: in a million years what would there be? – and ran on until cold air began to work knives deep in her lungs, gentled to a jog on her way back to the camp and hot coffee before work and the grateful surrender of self. She hardly spoke to the rest of the drill crew, suborned navy ratings, but they easily accepted her presence, more so than most of the scientists. Kilczer was right; they were beginning to resent her.

Two days after her recovery, orbital command sent down a cargo shell. Most of the people in the camp made their way to the shore of the sea to watch its descent: the white parachute cluster suddenly blossoming high in the dark, star-pricked sky to ragged applause and foot stamping. The drill crew covertly passed around a flask of liquor someone had illegally distilled from the thin ration beer; Dorthy took a swig when her turn came, knowing enough etiquette not to wipe the flask's neck, the raw yeasty stuff burning her gums, making her choke. A woman slapped her back; someone else told her that her palate needed to be educated, this was a fine vintage, almost a week old. Dorthy discovered she didn't mind this gentle banter. More applause staggered around her and she turned to see the parachute gently collapsing far out across the scummed water. The huge ring of the lifting body roared overhead, circling wide as it headed towards the floating shell. As Dorthy tramped back to work with the rest of the crew, she passed close to a group of the scientists. Muhamid Hussan caught her eye, then turned and said something to the tall, stooped meteorologist beside him. A touch of Hussan's contempt came to Dorthy, but she discovered that she didn't mind that either, and hurried on to fall in step with her companions, the liquor a warm glow in her throat, her belly. If not for her implant she would have drunk to maintain that glow. Instead, she worked as hard and as well as she could, which was how she had earned the respect of the rest of the crew. And slept. And ran. Sometimes she felt that she could have run forever, away from the camp, from people, from her responsibilities, running easily through the constant red light, trailing dust like a comet-tail across the dead, dry land.

Then, the fifth day into her routine, as she began the long circle out from the camp towards the crater, she saw that the huge disc of the sun, lifted by half its diameter above the horizon now, was glowering through a shifting tawny haze. A thin breeze clawed the scape of sand and rocks, and the air seemed colder, fresher; as she ran, Dorthy slapped her arms across her chest to get her circulation going. The breeze rose, gusting. When she had climbed the ridge of the crater's rim, wind whipped around her. Stinging sand grains peppered her bare arms and legs; she had to squint against the stronger squalls.

Kilometres away, the far reaches of the crater were hidden by roiling orange and brown clouds that seemed to lift higher even as she watched, the sun a bloody smear within their shroud. Sandstorm. She turned back, and when she reached camp found that ratings were stringing ropes from cargo shell to cargo shell. The air was laden with fine dust; the glotubes had each gained a grainy halo. Dorthy changed and went to the commons for her breakfast. The planetology team leader was already there, gulping down coffee in between taking huge bites out of a spiced roll (crumbs clung to his unkempt beard), and he told her that a blow was coming on, they had to secure the equipment.

By the time Dorthy reached the drilling site, the wind was keening, whipping ropes of sand across rock. Now the whole eastern sky was a high dark cliff rising out of rolling cloud, its fluted shifting face stretching up and up, thinning as it rose, to merge with the general overcast. The sun was hidden within it; everywhere hung a shadowless chthonic twilight.

Dorthy helped half a dozen others lower the drilling rig, a task that took over an hour because the wind kept warping in unpredictable directions, threatening at times to topple the whole structure. After the proton drill itself had been covered, they had to abandon the rest and make a run for it. Once Dorthy fell and fetched up against a boulder, scraping a cheek badly and getting a mouthful of grit. She staggered up, spitting, and ran on after the others, buffeted by wind. In a way it was exhilarating. The wind was a vast impersonal force, capricious and utterly powerful, and she was but a mote within it, her fate insignificant.

The network of rope guides had been completed by the time Dorthy and the rest of the drill crew reached the camp; the glotubes shone weakly through the murk. Dorthy showered, rinsing an amazing amount of grit from her hair, and crossed to the commons to get something to eat. The sky had closed up: a dull bronze ceiling. Unstable columns of dust whirled and collapsed about the cargo shells.

The wind mounted and mounted. Every time someone came into the commons, a gust of sand and dust blew high across the crowded room. At last the wind was a constant howl, no one stirred. Dorthy sipped green tea and watched for perhaps the tenth time a rerun of a newscast, for once happy to be submerged in the crowded commons, a bubble within the storm. Sunken. Safe. On the trivia stage, the diagram of the J-shaped attack profile of a singleship was replaced by shots of a pitted siding of rock, a tumbling chiaroscuro of shadow and red highlights that suddenly blew apart with soundless violence. Something flew at the camera and with a flash the view changed to show from a more prudent distance an expanding, fading fireball. An announcer listed estimates of enemy casualties and suppositions of the asteroid's function: it had blown itself apart as the singleship approached, by now a familiar tactic. So far not one of the enemy had been captured – not so much as a drop of blood (if the enemy had blood) had been found on the fragments of wreckage retrieved at hideous cost. Almost as an afterthought, the voice added that three singleships had been taken out in the action and *flick* the trivia stage now showed views of Rio de Janeiro, crowds swaying along wide sunny avenues beneath arching palm trees. Sovereignty Day, a week before Dorthy had left the Solar System, finally caught up in the war.

For a long time BD twenty had meant little to Dorthy; for most of the people of the worlds of the Federation it was a remote irrelevant affair, safely quarantined by interstellar distance. It had begun quietly enough with the loss of an unmanned probe. These often disappeared, and before it had ceased transmitting it had established that the star it was approaching had no planetary system, only a broad belt of asteroids that might have been a failed attempt at a couple of Earth-sized worlds. The data lay undisturbed for twenty years, until a graduate student, searching for a thesis subject, ran a preliminary check on some of the other telemetry sent by the probe, and found that the asteroid belt was combed through with pinpoint neutrino sources, many of them moving counter to the general orbital motion. Only nuclear interactions generate neutrinos: stars are excellent sources; so, too, are fusion and fission power-plants. A manned expedition was sent out. And limped back a month later, half its members dead, the ship's hull riddled, the life-system devastated. There was something hostile around Bonner Durchmeisterung +20° 2465.

Dorthy had been in the midst of preparing for the practical part of her thesis research, but like everyone else in the fastness of Fra Mauro Observatory she followed the reports, listened to the rehashing of opinions in the bars and cafés, sometimes even chimed in with her own ideas. Many people were bitterly puzzled that the first truly intelligent aliens to be found should be so immediately, unremittingly hostile, but the astronomers shrugged it off. The Universe was at best a marginal place for life.

To Dorthy it was a confirmation of what her childhood experiences had taught her, that things are not what you make them (that old legacy of lost American optimism which had once dominated half the Earth), no, things are simply what they are, neither good nor bad. The potential for evil is not in our stars, but in ourselves. Possession of her Talent had taught her, too, that any discovery, any seeming advantage, is at best a two-edged gift.

She was devising the instrumentation for her experiments when a second expedition was repulsed at BD twenty. It seemed that it was to be war. Cargo bodies were fitted with phase graffles, survey ships were armed, liners were sequestered from the Guild. There was even talk about building battleships. But no one was too alarmed. The aliens (which by now everyone was calling the enemy) didn't appear to possess knowledge of the phase graffle, were limited to sublight speeds. For them, travel from star to star would take years, not a few weeks. It was unlikely that the conflict would spread beyond their own system.

In the middle of all this, Dorthy left on her solo expedition, a long, slow swing through the Oort cloud to study hydrogen condensation beyond the influence of the solar wind. For the first week, as she passed one landmark orbit after another, she scanned all the news beamed to her in daily, five-second maser squeals, but things began to slide when she started work. Messages from Earth piled up in the files for days before she found time to clear them, and she lost interest in the newscasts. The first she knew of the discovery of a planoformed world circling yet another insignificant red dwarf was when a priority message dragged her from her experiments. She had been selected to join the exploration team. Selected? She'd been shanghied, press-ganged, kidnapped! Three days after the message reached her, a cargo vessel matched orbits with her singleship, swallowed it whole, and took her, reluctant Jonah, back to Earth.

It was because of her Talent, of course. It was a bitter irony that because she had refused to use it after leaving the Kamali-Silver Institute, she had lacked the political clout with which the other mature Talents had avoided the draft. In her lowest moments Dorthy thought of her Talent as a separate entity, a parasite riding her for its own purposes. Well, now look where it had got itself. A shanty camp set in a miasmic wasteland, and the certain prospect of danger. She remembered the burning glimpse and shivered, sipped her tea: cold.

She fetched more, and sat half listening to the drone of the trivia, to the idle chatter of the half-dozen scientists at the other end of the long table who clustered around a triple-layered chessboard (a fashion spreading across the Federation from Novaya Zyemlya). The tall meteorologist was saying wearily, 'No, I don't know how long it will last. Go look at the satellite pictures and make your own guess – it can't be worse . . .' He fell silent, because almost everyone in the commons had fallen silent, too. The bland voice of the trivia announcer echoed emptily in the sudden hush.

Dorthy turned and saw that a burly, red-haired man, the centre of the thinning haze of sand and dust, was shoving the door closed.

As he stalked through the maze of tables, voices resumed the threads of conversation. One or two of the Navy personnel held their hands up, palms out, and the man touched each in turn, cracked a white grin when someone said something to him; Dorthy couldn't hear his reply, but two of the ratings at the table got up and hurried out, pulling up facemasks as more sand blew through the briefly open door.

The red-haired man pushed on through the crowded room, towards the treachers.

Now the trivia was showing the presidential address, a tiny figure against the huge backdrop of the flag of the Re-United Nations, the various globes of the nine worlds arched above, amplified words clattering over the packed heads in the *Quadrado de Cinco Outubro*, the great buildings on either side white and sharp against the vivid blue sky of Earth.

'The same old bullshit,' a voice remarked close to Dorthy's ear. When she looked up, the red-haired man grinned.

At the other end of the table, the scientists around the chessboard were staring at him.

'You'll be Dr Yoshida,' the man said, and pulled out a chair and sat opposite her, setting his glass carelessly on the scarred plastic tabletop. Amber liquid splashed: foam ran down the sides. 'I'm Duncan Andrews. You'll have heard of me, no doubt.'

'Nothing but.' The feeling behind the words was a tight ball of astonishment.

He laughed. 'Don't believe any of it.' Sand was caked in his cropped red hair, in the lines that scored his freckled forehead. He leaned forward. His eyelashes were pale, almost invisible; the pupils of his eyes were a transparent blue, that of the left marred by a fleck of brown. 'How are you now? Recovered?'

'Thank you.' An urge to tell him all swept over her, almost sexual in its intensity. Her sides tingled; sweat started in the hollow at the back of her neck. She asked, 'How did you get here?'

He raised an eyebrow. 'Flew.'

'In this storm?'

'Yeah, I know. I thought I could run under it, but it moved faster than my estimate. Flying by radar the last hour, thinking that at any moment the vents of the jets would clog. But here I am. Well, what d'you think of P'thrsn?'

'I—' She looked away from Andrew's blue gaze, saw Arcady Kilczer making his way across the crowded room. What she wanted to say clashed at the root of her tongue with reflex banality. She stuttered, 'It, it isn't w-what I thought it would be like. I'd like to see more.'

'You will, as soon as this blows itself out.'

She began, 'I want to tell—' as Arcady Kilczer said, 'I do not need to make introductions, I am correct? What possessed you to fly in this weather, Andrews?'

Andrews turned his easy smile on Kilczer. 'It wasn't like this when I started, or I wouldn't have tried. Tell me, is McCarthy around? I brought a little present for the biology team.'

'That is so?' Kilczer's hand went up to his chin. 'Good. Good! Where—'

'The Navy'll be unloading it for you.'

'I had – I mean, they will not realise perhaps how important. I think I find McCarthy, yes?' Kilczer started away, turned back and said, 'And thank you!' before hurrying on.

Andrews drained half the beer from his glass, made a face. 'Damned artificial piss, a pity we are not allowed anything stronger. Well, Dr Yoshida, I hope your Talent survived the ride down.'

'More or less.'

He raised an eyebrow.

'I get flashes when it breaks through despite my implant. When I was coming down from orbit, the tranquilliser did something to it. I saw, I mean, through my Talent I sensed all the minds in the camp, and more, out beyond the horizon, something—' She started, because he'd clamped his hand around her wrist. His touch was cool and dry.

He said, 'Wait a moment, now. Start from the beginning. A tranquilliser did something to your Talent?'

Dorthy's throat and cheeks warmed in confusion. Andrews let go of her wrist and picked up his glass of beer, but didn't drink, watching her over its rim. Dorthy explained, 'I have an implant living in my hepatic portal vein that secretes various agents to inhibit my Talent. Once training and treatment have opened the Talent, you see, its operation is quite involuntary; to have it all the time would be like never being able to close your eyes, never being able to sleep. In fact, the damage caused by an uncontrolled Talent is a lot like that caused by chronic sleeplessness, or loss of REM sleep as caused by alcohol addiction, for example. Hallucinations, fits, lesions in the medulla oblongata, eventually death. So I have the implant to keep my Talent in check, and when I need to use it I take a counteragent that knocks out the production of the implant for a while. You know the tranquilliser they give you, for the descent?'

'Certainly.' That wide white easy smile. 'I could have used a double dose.'

'It was a reaction between that and my implant which activated my Talent. I sensed something, way out beyond the camp, something—' She faltered before memory of that light.

'This was one thing? Or many?'

'I don't know. It was like a hundred minds compressed into a single, incredible intelligence, but I suppose . . . I'm sorry. It wasn't like anything I've ever come across.'

'And would it be too much to ask if you know where this incredible intelligence is located?'

For all his easy smile, she sensed his hungry need for this knowledge. 'I don't know,' she told him. 'To the east, I suppose. Colonel Chung showed me that it could have been any one of half a dozen holds.'

'This is interesting. I have just had a brief conference with Colonel Chung and she did not tell me anything of this. She knows of it? What was her reaction when you explained this to her?'

Dorthy told him.

'Ah. That is to be expected, I suppose. To the east.' Andrews drained his glass. 'You know that the hold we are investigating is to the east of Camp Zero?'

'So Colonel Chung said.'

'How loquacious of her. Well, don't worry, Dr Yoshida. All this must be sorted out between the colonel and myself. What I want you to probe is far less dangerous. The plains herders, that is all.'

'Herders?'

'I suppose you wouldn't know. This security is a foolish business at the best of times. In this camp it is everywhere, like the smell of

35

the sea. Though that, I think, has blown away for the moment.' He stood. 'Come on, I'll show you something. You have protection against the sand?'

'A scarf. What—'

'You'll see. It's what I brought back.'

Dorthy followed him among the tables, pulled her scarf over her nose and mouth, and tied it at the back. Andrews donned a facemask and opened the door on keening wind and flying sand.

There was a taut rope plucked by pouring air, and Dorthy clung to it with both hands, the ends of her scarf whipping around her face. She squinted through narrowed eyelids, not daring to look up from the ground where skeins of sand snaked past her boots. She sensed rather than saw Andrews ahead of her, his dry matter-of-fact maleness seeming to stream out on the wings of the storm. She ducked after him under a knotted intersection and a curving metal wall loomed, drifts of sand with spuming crests billowing against it. Andrews pressed a shoulder against a section and it grated in. Dorthy almost fell through after him.

'Jesus Christos, close that—'

'Hey, Duncan! You should see the scan on this—'

'Loaded, just loaded with heavy metal complexes. The proteins don't chelate them – look here, chromium in the backbone of this thing. Structural, yes?'

'So you find reproductive equipment, my friend. To begin with, it seems haploid, if this cell really is dividing. How do I know? Occam's Razor – have you anything better?'

'What did you hit it with anyhow, Andrews? Nothing to mess up its blood chemistry, I hope. It's weird enough as it is.'

In grey uniform coveralls or white smocks, the dozen scientists clustered around benches cluttered with instruments and glassware. Dorthy recognised most of them: all were part of the biology team. The woman she'd come across in the junkyard was pipetting a straw-coloured liquid, drop by drop, into a rack of tubes. Arcady Kilczer was jacking leads to a display unit. Talk echoed in the bare, high-ceilinged space, undercut by the whine and susurration of the storm. Beyond the biologists, something slumped within a mesh cage, its hide the dirty white of a corpse, glistening in the harsh light. There was no obvious head or tail. Bristles protruded from the joint of each ring segment and each bore a pair of stubby flippers. In the central segment a ridged flap pulsed intermittently over a moist hole the size of Dorthy's head. Weird cross between decapitated walrus and slug, it was perhaps two metres long.

Andrews told Jose McCarthy, the dark-complexioned section leader, 'We used nitrous oxide, simple as that. Hell, it has an oxygen metabolism. Maybe it'll have a headache, but its blood chemistry will be unaffected.'

'Headache, indeed.' Arcady Kilczer turned from his instruments. 'This creature has no head, unless you count the third segment back, where its mouth is. You see the scans here? Very nearly, each segment is autonomous. Each has a nerve ring, but there is no spinal cord, only a few interconnections between each ring. Perhaps these nodes are ganglia, perhaps not, I tell you later. Hardwired, is my guess. How does it behave?'

'It eats,' Andrews said, grinning, 'and that's about all it does.'

'Let's worry about integrating all this stuff tomorrow,' McCarthy said, twisting one end of his drooping moustache. 'For now we let everything run, people.'

'It may be recovering,' Kilczer said. 'How much did you give it, Andrews?'

'Enough to keep it quiet during the flight. I didn't want it moving around.'

'I'm not sure I want it moving around now. Hello, Dr Yoshida.' Kilczer smiled at Dorthy and turned to fiddle with one of the displays; a smeared line sharpened to a set of tightly packed peaks.

Dorthy stepped back as someone brushed past, bearing high the long extensor with which he'd just snipped a sample of hide. She felt a tingling sensation of expansion and thought *not now*, because that was how her attacks usually started.

Andrews told her, 'This is one of the critters they herd. The plains herders I was telling you about. What do you think?'

' "A most poor credulous monster." '

He ignored this remark. 'All the damn thing does is eat and move on to the next patch of food. In my opinion it's gene-melded, like the bacteria in the sea.'

'These plains herders eat things like that?'

'To be sure. Maybe it's their idea of prime beefsteak; it is certainly

37

not mine. The herders live on the plain that surrounds the central part of the hold, little groups of them with a herd of critters. A dominant female and her ten, twenty consort males. They are what you will probe for me. If there's anything left of the enemy down here, in the holds, the herders are it. Except for your singular apparition, of course. We must talk more on that soon; in view of my working hypothesis it is damnably inconvenient. I am trying to open up exploration on this world. If the Navy thinks that there is something dangerous down here, they will want to go the opposite way.'

'I didn't say it was dangerous.' Dorthy didn't want to think about it, asked, 'How can you be sure the herders are the enemy?'

'Were once the enemy,' Andrews said, then pointed towards the cage. 'Look there, it moved a little. I think it's coming out of it. What was I saying?'

'Why you thought—' Dorthy was watching the hulking seg-mented creature as well, beginning to feel confined by all the activity around her. There was a strange raw stifling scent in the huge echoing space. Something from the creature?

Andrews said, 'The herders have no technology, no tools beyond a broken branch or woven baskets, but they do have fire – Are you all right, Dr Yoshida?'

'A touch of claustrophobia. Do you smell anything?'

Andrews flared the wings of his large nose. 'No, I don't think so.'

'A warm, salty smell? It seems . . .' Dorthy shook her head. She felt a wrongness, unnameable but growing stronger. As if she should be somewhere else.

The creature rolled one end of its body from side to side, then was still again. Kilczer said, 'I have coordinated motor firings now. There it is again.' As the creature jinked, pushing one blunt end high, striking at the cage's rigid mesh.

Dorthy felt a pressure across her forehead, tightening like a noose. The raw smell was worse, searing her nostrils; everything seemed to be muffled in syrup, slow and distorted. The lights wavered, took on haloes, multiplying. She heard someone say dis-tantly, 'That's it. It's coming out of it now,' and someone else, 'Jesus Christos, is that its mouth? Are we getting that on record?' Then sound and light slowed and blurred like a stalled recording, and a channel seemed to open between *here* and somewhere else. Dorthy strained towards it and for a moment saw light – pure blinding light. Then it was gone, the afterimage like a silvery ceiling through which she sank into enfolding darkness.

Dorthy awoke to soft red light and the constellations of the diagnostic machinery above her head and at the foot of her bed. She swung her legs over and, the metal floor cold beneath her bare feet, padded out into the larger medical bay and drew and drank two glasses of water. The timetab on her wrist told her that it was almost twenty-four hours since Andrews had taken her to see the critter. Her head still ached, but she no longer felt the tingling expansion of her hypersensitive Talent. The attack had passed.

By the time Arcady Kilczer came to check on her, Dorthy had dressed and was sitting on the edge of her bed, reading the book she had brought all this way. 'I was hoping you would be up and about,' he said, smiling. 'I am in the middle of my preparations.' But he started to check the diagnostic machinery anyway.

'All I need is something to eat,' Dorthy told him. 'Where can I find Andrews?'

'Oh, he left a few hours ago, but soon you will see him, I think. You know that you slept around the clock after you passed out? Was it another of your attacks?'

'Unless someone hit me over the head. I think I was getting something from that thing Andrews brought back.'

'You make jokes. So I know you are better.'

'No, this is true. For a moment it was as if I was back in the dropcapsule, bright, too bright to see what it was . . .'

'The creature is a loose collection of reflexes. Is not centrally organized. You say it is like the phenomenon that knocked you out in the dropcapsule?'

Dorthy shrugged, submitting as he took a blood sample. 'There's nothing wrong with me.'

'This we will see.'

But there wasn't.

This time Colonel Chung raised no objection to having Dorthy flown out. 'Dr Andrews has assured me that all is secure at the hold, and we have two more thopters now. An autodoc will be coming down tomorrow, so Dr Kilczer will fly you out. Dr Andrews wishes him to investigate those creatures.'

'The herders. But I thought—'

'Dr Kilczer's instruments will be a valuable supplement to your, ah, Talent. Besides, you may suffer one of your attacks.'

Dorthy felt an empty, airy sense of falling. 'Kilczer's instruments can do far less than I can.' The bubble of hope that had been buoyed by her trust that Andrews would reward her service softly collapsed. Obviously, the attack she had suffered in front of him had devalued her usefulness, and so had diminished the likelihood of his helping her escape the planet. *Trapped*, she thought. Trapped.

Colonel Chung knitted her fingers together, touched them to her chin. 'I merely relay Dr Andrews's wishes. If you disagree, you must tell him so.'

'By then it will be too late. Kilczer will be wasting his time coming out with me. Truly, Colonel.'

'If that proves to be so, I will also wish to speak with Dr Andrews. I hope that you will keep me informed.' There was a pause, and then the colonel added briskly, 'Good luck, Dr Yoshida. Good luck on your mission.' And, surprising Dorthy, she stood, and offered her hand in a gesture of benediction.

2
The Hold

The thopter flew low over the desert landscape.

Within the still air of the bubblecabin, Dorthy Yoshida watched empty vistas trawl past. Slopes littered with rubble, draws silted with fine dust, the softly eroded circles of meteorite craters. All was carmine and cinnabar in the soft light of the huge dim sun, but the running circle of the thopter's spotlight revealed, like the illuminated panels in Ernst's *Day and Night*, fantastically fluted cliffs of delicate cyans and yellows, pillars veined with glittering quartz and feldspar, sculpted sand dunes dusted with a mica shimmer. In another light this world might be beautiful, but under the baleful eye of the red dwarf it was merely sombre. Nowhere was there any trace of life. It had been transformed, yes, but only up to a point.

Startling her, Kilczer said, 'Less than an hour. Do you think that is it, ahead?' It was a long time since he had spoken, apart from routine reports into the transceiver, the springs of his small talk drying on Dorthy's brooding silences. She blamed him as much as Andrews for her betrayal, and felt quite alone, having considered and rejected Colonel Chung's tentative offer of an alliance. Stay aloof, stay clean. Rise above mere human nonsense, petty intrigues, and quarrels, remember solitary silent contemplation of the lucent universe.

Now she leaned forward and saw that the horizon had grown a dark rim. 'That's the hold?'

'The beginning of it, I think.' Kilczer held the stick in one hand while with the other he reached up and fiddled with the loran indicator.

Dorthy said, ' "The ground indeed is tawny. With an eye of green in't." '

'Again this is Shakespeare, yes?'

'I thought I was about the only person who read him anymore.'

'On Novaya Rosya we know him. Sometimes his plays are staged, even.' Kilczer expected her to ask about Novaya Rosya. When she didn't, he said, 'Why would anyone want to live on a world like this? Is worse even than my home.'

'Perhaps I'll be able to tell you why soon enough,' Dorthy said tartly.

Kilczer shrugged, pretending once more to be intent on flying the thopter, which was flying itself really. He didn't need to be an empath to sense Dorthy's icy hostility.

Dorthy turned away from him and attended to the landscape once more. The desert began to give way to scrubby growths of leafless black-branched bushes, and, slowly, the bushes yielded to a parched-looking grassland (if that was grass down there, deep violet in the light of the sun, blue-green in the thopter's spotlight) studded with small flat-topped trees. A spare open plain that reminded her of the Outback: but she didn't want to think of that.

Ahead, the land was rising, tree-clad slopes broken by cliffs and canyons vanishing upward into cloud. The thopter's motor hummed at a lower pitch as the machine beat higher in the thin air, following a narrow winding canyon. Dorthy saw a herd of huge creatures lumber off between low trees, and Kilczer turned the thopter towards them, swinging so low that tree branches whipped in the pulsing downdraught of the vanes. Dorthy glimpsed half a dozen long-haired creatures the size of elephants, plodding along in single file, stocky hind legs and longer forelimbs, long flexible snouts . . . Kilczer said something in Russian and heeled the thopter hard around. The restraining straps bit into Dorthy's shoulders and then they were over the line of creatures again.

'Megatheria,' Kilczer said breathlessly.

Dorthy craned to look down. She saw that the forelimbs were armed with long recurved double claws; because of these, the creatures had to walk on their knuckles. A broad dark stripe crested each shaggy back; the snout was pinkly naked.

'Megatheria,' Kilczer said again. 'It cannot be parallel evolution. But how—'

'You know what they are?'

'Think I know. Giant sloths, lived on Earth perhaps a million years ago.' He kicked the stick forward and the thopter picked up speed as it lifted away.

'A million years,' Dorthy echoed, remembering the line of volcanic ash compressed in the drill cores, the vanishingly thin meteoritic layer just above. A million years.

Their uneasy silence settled again. The land levelled out, a high forest plateau. Ahead a huge lake spread out towards the mountains. Kilczer followed the shore, checking and rechecking the loran. And then Dorthy saw a small blister of orange at the edge of the water. 'The camp,' Kilczer said unnecessarily. Dorthy felt his relief.

They circled and hovered a little way above the level ground, released the cargo net before descending. The thopter touched the ground and promptly hopped up again before finally settling. Kilczer swore, and switched off the motors; on either side, the vanes collapsed. Dorthy saw two people hurrying forward; then Kilczer popped the hatch. Cold air scented with the familiar tang of pines rushed in. Kilczer sneezed.

On the ground, Duncan Andrews, grinning hugely, shouted, 'You made it at last! Welcome to the front line!' His companion, the black, rough-haired biologist, Angel Sutter, was pulling netting away from the jumbled pile of supplies. 'Come on,' Andrews said, clapping his hands together, 'let's get this stowed away.'

So for the next half hour Dorthy heaved plastic-crated equipment and sacks of supplies with Andrews, Kilczer, and Sutter. All the while, Andrews kept up a steady enthusiastic chatter, telling them that everything was fine, they'd have no trouble here, it was a goddamn paradise, that the twins (he neglected to explain just who they were) were goofing off following some herders and collecting specimens. Kilczer asked about the megatheria, but Andrews shrugged the question off. 'Of course, of course. Most of the known worlds and a few we don't know about were plundered to set this place up, but that's about all I know.' And when Kilczer started to ask another question, he added, 'Really, you must ask the twins. They know all about that stuff,' and went on to explain that they were supposed to keep to a schedule, but it was so tight that there was no way they could manage. 'So the hell with it. We decide what's important out here, not the crackbrains upstairs. Don't you worry.'

He was even more hyped up than the first time Dorthy had seen him, a friendly frazzled giant dominating them all, even stately Angel Sutter. Dorthy smiled politely and heaved a small crate on to a slightly larger one beside the inflated orange dome. She leaned on them, looking across kilometres of black water to where mountains rose from their reflections, curving away left and right, dense cloud obscuring their peaks. She felt the dislocation of reality that all travelling works, the submergence of identity to motion so that everything strange is unquestioningly accepted: the carpet of violet tendrils that covered the ground, already worn in dusty tracks around the orange dome of the bubbletent, the daytime stars and the sun's vast cancerous disc, the dense tangled forest beyond the meadowlike strip that hugged the contours of the shore. Three weeks ago, she thought, I was on Earth, at Galveston . . . but that no longer seemed real either.

'Mind, now.' Duncan Andrews set a huge crate down and straightened, feeling the small of his back with one hand. 'Christ!' He towered above Dorthy, radiating a hot smell of maleness. 'I guess that's neat enough. I hope nothing is broken, is all. There will not be any more runs up from Camp Zero for awhile. I used up my small reserve of goodwill with the colonel in persuading her to let you and Arcady come here. I honestly wonder why she bothered to uncrate her precious flying machines. Here we are, anyhow.'

He called to Sutter and Kilczer and they all trooped inside the bubbletent, stood together in a little chamber as acrid, cloying vapour jetted over them from all sides. Kilczer coughed into his fist. Andrews winked at Dorthy as the vapour was sucked away, said, 'You'll get used to it,' and flung open the inner door. The central chamber was piled with equipment, on the floor, on benches, on an inflated chair that sagged beneath the weight. Dorthy looked around, wrinkled her nose at the smell of stale food and old sweat.

'You'll get used to it,' Andrews repeated, more briskly. 'How are you feeling?'

'I'm all right.'

'I hope so. It could be rather unfortunate if you keeled over out here, especially if you were anywhere near the herders. As well as eating their critters, they are fearsome hunters. Dangerous. We are not supposed to shoot even in warning at one, you see. It could be misconstrued as a hostile act.'

'I'll be ready for it next time,' she said.

Angel Sutter, seated on the edge of the overloaded chair, pulling off her boots, looked up and said, 'You'd better be, honey, because they're serious about these regulations. When I was told about it I asked – joking, you know? – should I struggle if one starts eating me? Know what the guy said back? "Don't even make it belch." Cute, really cute. Remind me how to get coffee out of this thing, Duncan.' She waved a hand at the treacher and while Andrews bent over the control panel she smiled at Dorthy and added, 'I only got here yesterday. Duncan flew me up. I've been waiting for this a *long* time.'

'There you go.' Andrews handed a cup to Angel Sutter, held out two more; after Dorthy and Kilczer had stepped up to take them he picked up his own, raised it in salute, sipped and made a face. 'Maybe you could drop down in front of one, Dr Yoshida. No, I will call you Dorthy, you will not mind, I hope. Drop down in front of one, a discreet distance away of course, and I reckon I'd have a valid excuse to shoot. We wouldn't want to lose our only empath now. That way we'd get a herder to study at least, instead of snooping out in the bushes like a pack of dirty old men. We're out here, but we have a lot of rules to observe. So if I shout at you, don't take it personally. We are all of us a little on edge.' He smiled at Dorthy, at Arcady Kilczer.

'I won't,' Dorthy sipped at her coffee: sweet, milky. She set it on the edge of a bench, beside the innards of some ailing machine.

Andrews drained his own cup, crumpled it and tossed it into the hopper across the tent. He brushed his large hands together. 'Now, I propose to fly up to the rim to see how Ramaro's remote-sensing crew is getting on. You'd both like to come?'

'Of course,' Kilczer said, brushing back black hair. His smile was wider than Andrews's.

'I'd rather rest, if it's all the same,' Dorthy said.

'You'd see the keep, get an idea of what we are up against.'

'She's tired, Duncan. Leave her be.' Angel Sutter winked at Dorthy. 'Don't mind it. He has the delusion that he runs everything.'

'As a matter of fact, I have the feeling that I'm the centre that cannot hold. I'll be back in a couple of hours, unless Ramaro comes up with something good. He's trying to figure out the murals, Arcady.'

45

'So are a good number of people in orbit.'

'To be sure, but I can't talk to them.' Andrews told Sutter, 'Two hours, I promise. Settle in, Dr Yoshida. Dorthy. Get some rest. We'll let you do your thing tomorrow.' He gave her another smile and strode into the little airlock, Kilczer following without a backward glance.

'Jesus Christos, he is *not* to be *believed!*' Grinning, Angel Sutter rubbed her broad flat nose. 'He thinks nothing is running properly unless he's there with his hands deep inside it. But he gets things done, I'll give him that. We wouldn't be here if he didn't push the Navy. He might not be much of a scientist, but he's surely on our side.'

'So now I know who to blame. Look, where do I sleep?'

'Blame? Oh, right, you were caught in the draft.'

'Kidnapped. That's the way I look at it. Really, I—'

'Oh, hey,' Angel Sutter's expression changed to one of concern. 'I guess all this is sort of confusing, you reading minds and all.'

'I'm not doing it right now, not really. All I want is to rest awhile.'

'Sure, sure. Right here, look.' Sutter held open a flap of one of a row of cubicles. Inside were a cot and a shelf, nothing more, but Dorthy was grateful for at least an illusion of privacy. She picked up her sack and pushed past Sutter, let the flap fall.

Despite the exhaustion of the long thopter ride, Dorthy was too jazzed to sleep. After she had unpacked, she sat on the edge of her cot, the one book she had brought with her open on her lap. Its familiar rhythms, as precise and stately as a court pavane, began to soothe her, but she had not been reading long when the flap twitched aside and Sutter said, 'Hey. How are you feeling now?'

Dorthy looked up and the woman grinned (white teeth in a very black face) and stepped inside, the flap falling behind her, sat on the cot beside Dorthy and plucked the book from her hands, began to look through it. 'This is writing, poetry, right? What is it, English? You speak English?' She looked at the cover. 'Huh. Shakespeare. What do you call this thing?'

'A book.'

'Yeah? Listen, sorry if I seem too curious, but I figure we've got to get along, thrown together like this.'

'The sooner I'm out of it, the better. You know I didn't ask to come here.'

'But you might as well make the best of it, right?' Sutter held out the book and Dorthy received it back gratefully. 'Don't mind Duncan Andrews, by the way. Unlike you and me he's regular Navy, as regular as anyone can be anyhow. He's okay, as long as you don't argue with him too much. He really thinks we're here to subdue the natives, get what we can from them, and take off to finish the war at BD twenty.'

'He's Navy? The way people were talking about him in Camp Zero, I thought—'

'Sure he's Navy. Captain no less, came in from the Guild survey arm like a lot of the people out here. Matches rank with that tight-assed Chung, that's how he gets things done. Now *she's* seconded from the Democratic Chinese Union Security Force, who knows *what* she thinks she's doing here. Andrews, though, is on our side in a way, but that's only because we happen to need what he wants. When it comes right down to it he orders us around just the same as upstairs does.'

Dorthy thought about it. It had never been really clear who had precipitated the chain of events that had ended with her being removed from her research and being transported here. It was quite possible that Andrews had pushed the idea until it had turned into action. On the other hand, he was so casually dismissive about her Talent . . .

Sutter said, 'I listen to all the scuttlebut, both when I was upstairs and when I was kicking my heels at Camp Zero. You need to find out anything about him, I can tell you at least three conflicting stories. Did you know he's on agatherin?'

'I had guessed as much. The first son of an Elysian duke, after all. Besides, he behaves as if he is. A mixture of authority and impulsiveness, invincible confidence . . . I've met that before.'

Sutter rubbed her nose. 'I guess you would move around in strange circles like that.'

'Because of my Talent?' Dorthy smiled. 'I'm a scientist like you, an astronomer. I'm not like Giles Riahrden or Kitty Flambosa-Brown.' But for a year she *had* moved in those circles, to support Hiroko (but Hiroko had returned to the ranch in the desert, leaving only the cryptic message that had puzzled Dorthy ever since), and to earn the credit she had needed to support her studies at Fra Mauro. Prostituting herself. She said, 'You wouldn't expert people like that to end up here, would you?'

Sutter shrugged. 'I guess not.' Then, in a completely different tone of voice she asked, 'You really can read minds?'

'When I have to. At the moment, no. I have an implant that stops my Talent working, unless I take a counteragent.'

Sutter meditated a moment. 'And you'll be able to read the minds of these herders?'

'Probe them. No, I don't expert any real difficulty.' The nova reaching up from the horizon, reaching through the walls of the dropcapsule. The transferred claustrophobia of the caged critter and the subsequent searing flare. And now she was supposed to set her naked mind against the unknown. She thought, no difficulty? I'm as scared as hell. But she couldn't admit it – any weakness would bring unwelcome solicitude. She had long ago developed her armour, and pity would corrode it. So she forced a smile and told Sutter, 'As a child I used to practise on animals. You'd be surprised at what goes on in their heads.'

Sutter laughed: rough metal dragged across crumpled velvet. 'Most of the time I can't imagine what's going on in the heads of other people. Say, come and eat something. No sense in waiting for Andrews and Kilczer. I'll bet they won't be back for hours yet.'

It was true. Dorthy ate and then took a long shower in the cramped toilet facilities before retreating to her cubicle. She lay awake a long time, the welcome ambush of sleep a long way off, listening to Sutter moving around outside, the chink of glass on metal as the biochemist set up her equipment, the faint sound of a Mozart quartet. And when she awoke with a start, the timetab implanted in the skin beneath the knuckle of her wrist telling her that it was 0726 in the morning, the two men had still not returned.

As Dorthy sleepily sipped scalding black coffee, Sutter tried to assure her that there was nothing to worry about, but Dorthy sensed the agitation beneath the woman's serene surface. She asked, 'Can't we just call him up and find out—'

'It isn't that simple. We're operating under radio silence here, in case something is monitoring us. Can't talk to Camp Zero, can't even communicate with groups in the field. All we're allowed is a two-second coded squirt to orbital command each time it's above the horizon – even that is lasered, so that there can be no chance of interception. Don't worry about it, honey, they'll turn up.'

Dorthy finished her coffee while Sutter fiddled with a proton resonance probe, getting ready for her first samples. She was supposed to analyse the photosynthetic pathways of the plant life in the hold and develop specific inhibitors that might be introduced into the asteroid habitats of the enemy around BD twenty. Dorthy watched for a few minutes, then announced. 'I think I'll take a walk outside.'

Sutter looked up. 'When I've finished this, I'll come with you.'

'No, no. I just want to walk.' What she wanted was to be left alone.

'It's really against regulations, but what the hell. I can't tie you up, can I? Take care though, okay? It's supposed to be safe, that's why this was chosen as the first campsite, but *I* don't know what's out there, I've only been here a day longer than you. Listen, take some sample bags, pick any plants you see small enough, make a note of where you found them, okay?' She poked around, drew out a handful of bags, and pushed them across the bench. 'And be *careful*, huh?'

'I will,' Dorthy said, and escaped through the lock.

The carpet of interlocked violet tendrils gave slightly under each step, so that her progress was almost soundless. She stooped and plucked a strand; it was actually three close-woven tendrils joined at regular nodes that each sprouted three feathery leaves. This complexity stirred her sense of wonder: all unknown to humankind this had evolved (somewhere else, not here) to gather energy from the sun, in some unimaginable landscape. . . She dropped the strand, for certainly Sutter would have a sample of it, and walked on, skirting the edge of the dark water that stretched away, perfect Euclidean plane reflecting the distant mountains and the sun and the dim daystars. The carpet of tendrils ran right up to the edge of the water, interrupted here and there by tall, hollow-stemmed plants that, lapped with translucent scale-leaves, stood twice as high as Dorthy, knocking together in the faint breeze. There were no insects, no sign of any animal life at all. It was as if she were strolling through some pristine parkland . . . and perhaps that was what it was, abandoned yet self-perpetuating. She glanced back and saw that she had left the dome far behind: an orange blister near the shore, alien. As she was, here.

The tidy edge of the lake curved towards the distant point where the far shore swept near, a narrow channel of dark water between. Dorthy struck off instead towards the margin of the forest, the trees a sort of conifer, broad needles clustered around each branching node of the crooked close-woven branches, bark as fine-grained as human skin, roots humped or widely splayed: not from Earth. She wondered if they were from some other known planet, Serenity perhaps, or Elysium . . . The creatures she and Kilczer had seen from the thopter, megatheria, *they* had been trawled from Earth, at any rate. And how many other worlds had been ransacked to stock this place she wondered as she picked her way among the trees, her boots sinking deep in the carpet of brown needles that lay everywhere between clutching roots. Nothing grew beneath the trees: the forest was as neat as an orchard, the light so dim that she could not distinguish one colour from another, the atmosphere as oppressive as that of the converted freighter which had brought her to this world, two dozen human minds continually impinging upon her own. She felt an absurd sense of being watched that nonetheless was real. Her skin prickled and she turned to go back. And saw the creature, less than a dozen metres away.

Bigger than a man, it crouched in shadow beside a humped tree root. Dorthy glimpsed a narrow long-snouted face within a loose hood, a lithe black-furred body – and then it fled, crashing noisily among the trees, was gone. Whether it ran on two legs or four Dorthy didn't see, because she began to run at the same moment, once tripping over a root and sprawling headlong in dry prickling needles and scrambling up with her heart pumping hard and running on, out into the bloody light of the huge sun. The tent was a fleck of orange far down the shore, a period between the margins of dark forest and darker water. Dorthy ran hard towards it over the soft ground, and as she drew nearer she saw that once more two thopters were parked beside it. Andrews and Kilczer had returned.

*

'A herder,' Duncan Andrews said. 'That's what it was, all right. A loose hood of skin around its face?'

'I thought it was some sort of clothing.' Dorthy clutched a cup of coffee with both hands. Even so, the black lake inside trembled.

'No clothing, not so much as daub of mud? A hood of skin, and dark fur? That's a herder, all right. Well, now.' Andrews sat on a tall stool, leaning an elbow on the cluttered bench as he slowly and methodically picked at the edge of his coffee cup, dropping the shreds of plastic inside the diminishing bowl. There were loose dark pouches under his startlingly blue eyes and a deep line either side of his narrow lips drew his mouth down, yet for all his seeming exhaustion he was preternaturally alert. He said, 'There are crazy things happening, all right. No herder has been seen in the forests up here before. That's partly why I chose this site. Christ, I wonder if they're watching us.' He tossed the cup at the disposal hatch – it tipped the rim, throwing a dribble of brown liquid as it spun to the floor – and scrubbed at his hair with both hands before clasping them atop his head. 'You read anything out there?' he asked Kilczer.

'Nothing that big.' Kilczer was bent over the flickering display, his narrow shoulders hunched. 'Man-sized or larger, there is nothing. But machine only works at close range.'

Andrews looked at Dorthy. 'Maybe your Talent would be better; that scanner is based on it, after all.'

'It only works at close range, too. Usually.' Dorthy sipped scalding coffee.

'Just go over it again,' Andrews said, 'You saw just one?'

As Dorthy recounted the incident again, it came to her that the creature, the herder, had been frightened too. They'd run from each other, alien from alien. Yet memory of the glimpsed cruelly thin face within loose folds of skin, the huge deepset eyes, the lines of the long body blurred by shadow, was still unsettling. Somewhere out there. She realised how insubstantial the tent was, a bubble sunk deep in the bloody light of the sun.

Andrews rasped his stubbled cheek with a spatulate thumb, sighed loudly. 'Goddamn, if we had the people out here . . .' Abruptly, he jumped up and peered over Kilczer's shoulder at the screen, paced around the bench and studded the treacher for more coffee. Pulling the cup free, he said, 'Maybe now I can get more resources out here, anyway. The lights and now this. Things are changing.'

'Lights?' Sutter asked. She lounged like some potentate in the deep bubblechair.

Andrews sipped noisily. 'At the keep. That's why I didn't come back last night.'

Kilczer turned from his machine. 'It seems that the city or whatever it is in the caldera turned itself on.'

'The keep,' Andrews told Dorthy. 'In the middle of the caldera there's a complex construction of spires and winding ramps, more a kind of vertical maze than anything else. We don't know what it is – it certainly isn't a city. I guess with the moat it could be defensive. Perhaps they sank that low before they died out. It happened on Elysium, after all.' He settled on a stool. 'Anyway, there's a team surveying it with remotes. Maybe they set it off, maybe it's a cyclic thing, but lights came on yesterday, some kind of phosphor. For what purpose we don't know yet, but Ramaro is working on that. And now a herder wandering around up here. It makes a kind of sense. Dorthy, how do you feel about going to read the mind of one of those things?'

'I'd like to get it over with.'

'Good.' He clapped his hands together, grinned. 'That's good. How about you, Arcady?'

'I would prefer to sleep,' Kilczer said, smiling.

'I wish we had the time. Anyway, you slept up at the base, slept when we flew back: you can't spend your life asleep. Listen, Angel. While we're gone you check out the forest, see if you can spot more herders. My guess is that there'll be more. What we need is an aerial survey, but that'll have to wait awhile. Don't wander too far into the forest now.'

'I don't intend to put even one foot in its shade. You crazy?'

'Come on, put your stuff in the back of the sled and you can outrun anything out there.' He grinned. 'At least, I think you can. If you want to complain about the lack of help out here, I'm not the person to talk to. I've been doing a lot of it myself. Dorthy, let's get your kit and go. Arcady, you need a hand with your monitoring equipment?'

As Dorthy packed she heard Angel Sutter's voice rising and

falling in protest, Andrews's bluff unflappable rumble undercutting it. Then Sutter laughed and as Dorthy came out of the cubicle she was saying, 'Up and down the shore, then. But I don't even want to do that. I suppose you're going to tell me that if something *does* attack me, I don't shoot. Shit.'

'That's entirely up to you,' Andrews said mildly. 'It is not a regulation I made. Come on Arcady, Dorthy. Good luck now, Angel.'

'Oh, sure,' the woman said. But she was grinning: Andrews had charmed her just as Dorthy had hoped he would charm Colonel Chung on her behalf.

The tent shrank beside the shore of the lake. The lake shrank within the contours of the forest.

As the thopter rose, turning wide over black water, Dorthy, in the cramped space behind the seats occupied by the two men, leaned forward and yelled to Andrews, 'Aren't we supposed to be going down to the plain?'

'Eventually. But first I must check out events at the rim camp. This damned radio silence makes it hard to keep track of what's going on, and a lot is going on up there right now.'

Kilczer said, 'Wait until you see this, Dr Yoshida. Is incredible.'

'Come on, Arcady,' Andrews said. 'Don't give anything away. And don't worry, Dorthy, we'll get your job done. The herders don't keep our kind of hours; we'll find some that are active enough for you at any time.'

Dorthy subsided. Argument was pointless. Besides, she didn't want to fall out with Andrews. He was supposed to be on her side, her ticket home.

The lake narrowed. Soon they were flying between steep tree-clad slopes, following a twisting river that widened once where a waterfall poured into a foaming pool, narrowed again, enclosed now by steep rock walls hung with masses of vegetation. Fierce random air currents buffeted the thopter as it beat up the river's course, the vegetation that clung to the rock thinning as mist thickened in the air. Rivulets of condensation ran the plastic of the cabin's bubble; the spotlight's beam was milkily blurred. Andrews switched on the cabin heater and leaned over the stick, watching the radar set as much as the limited view outside. Kilczer hunched in his seat, nervous and tired.

Behind them, Dorthy picked through various conversational openings and gambits that would lead to the necessity of her leaving as soon as her job was done, rejecting each in turn as being too obvious or too phatic. Twice, she glanced across at Andrews, wanting to exchange even a banality about the riven landscape below, but he was intent on flying, nursing the stick gently between his big hands, constantly working it with delicate motions as if urging on a live and nervous steed. Dorthy, who had once or twice ridden horses on the coast after her contract had ended, after her final confrontation with her father (but forget that, it was all over, done with, nothing left but the mystery of Hiroko's riddle, the note she had left when she had returned to the ranch from which Dorthy had rescued her), was on the verge of asking Andrews if he had ever ridden, if they had horses on Elysium, when a flock of wide-winged shapes shot out of the mist, spiralling above and below the thopter like so many wind-driven leaves. An adrenalin spike rammed through Kilczer's consciousness while Andrews calmly pushed the stick forward and the thopter shot above the creatures, which all turned in one motion, wingtip to wingtip, and vanished into the mist.

'They don't understand about aircraft,' Andrews said, pitching his voice over the noise of the motors as he allowed the thopter to glide back to its former path, the river just visible through scarves of mist below.

Dorthy rejected one reply, tried to think of something else to say. A minute later, it was too late.

No more trees. The river was a braided torrent split by great boulders. The canyon, little more now than a deep channel, split, a minute later split again. Then it was gone and the thopter was beating through blood-tinged mist over a scape of tumbled rock as bleak as anywhere on the Moon. And then everything dropped away.

The thopter swooped out from a great cliff that curved away left and right, dropping steeply to humped foothills. Beyond, the land fell in irregular terraces cloaked in dark forest, thinning to a great sloping plain in which, centred like the pupil of an eye, was a circular lake.

Only the upper rim of the sun peeped over the misty peaks of the rimwall of this vast caldera; everything within was a confusion of shadow and dull embers of half-light. Except for something in the very centre of the lake.

Dorthy leaned forward as the thopter began to climb again, squinted across Andrews's shoulder at the great multiple spire, wound with constellations of blazing red sparks, which thrust up from still black water.

'What is it?'

'The keep. See why I had to come back? It was dark a day ago.'

'Is crazy place.' Kilczer was also intent on the panorama, his edginess subsumed by consummate fascination.

Andrews said, 'We're maybe twenty kilometres away. This is as close as we get, for now.'

Twenty kilometres. The size of the basin doubled, tripled, in Dorthy's perception: the spire must be taller than the Museum of Mankind in Rio, wider at its base than the Galveston spacefield, no mere building but a small mountain. Then it was lost from sight as the thopter turned parallel to the cliff's sheer face and, just as a bird lifts in flight before sitting on a branch, swooped up and settled on a bare stretch of rock that nestled in a wedge broken into the cliff's bubbled strata. A pair of bubbletents glimmered in the shadow there.

Even before the thopter's vanes had stopped beating, someone had reached the craft and swung down the hatch at Kilczer's side. After he had stumbled down, Dorthy followed, and the man who had opened the hatch held out a hand in old-fashioned courtesy. She ignored the gesture and stepped down carefully to gritty lavic rock. Less than ten metres away was the edge. The tip of the keep glittered across kilometres of misty air.

Andrews came around the curve of the cabin, grinning. 'Luiz, how goes it? Dorthy, Dr Yoshida, this is Major Luiz Ramaro. He's running this part of the show.'

'Dr Yoshida. Welcome.' The man, not much taller than Dorthy, and not much older either, his belly making a comfortable swag over the belt of his coveralls, executed a quick bow and then openly scrutinized her. Dorthy stared back, refusing to be intimidated. A round coffee-coloured face with a snub nose and small, live black eyes, like currants in a glazed pastry. A duelling scar seamed his left cheek. After a moment Ramaro nodded as if something had been confirmed and turned away as Andrews asked how the drones were doing, whether there had been any other activity, if any power sources had been found.

'Please, please,' Ramaro said, smiling, 'Give us time, Andrews. No, there are no detectable power sources. The lights seem to work like glotubes, releasing stored quanta, although these are but molecule-thin coatings. As for why they have come on now – we are still working on that problem. But let us get out of the wind. Seyoura, you must be cold, no? Andrews, you are staying here long?'

'If we could stay in contact by radio I wouldn't have come up here at all. No, we're on our way to catch up with the twins, down on the plains. Dr Yoshida is going to read the minds of the herders. If they have minds, of course.'

Major Ramaro glanced at Dorthy, his look both shrewd and amused. His voice was dismissive. 'So that's your Talent. I thought as much. Well, good luck, Andrews.'

Dorthy felt a prick of anger but said nothing. Nothing she could say would make any difference, she knew. Clearly, Ramaro was a Greater Brazilian of the old school; the duelling scar identified him as belonging to one of the aristocratic families. Women, to them, were little more than a precious asset, breeding stock, an attitude that dated from a couple of centuries before when most of the women and girl children had been killed by a tailored plague during one of the succession wars. After that, women had been bought and sold and fiercely protected in Greater Brazil, no more so than by the aristocracy, who had squandered vast sums to enrich and extend their bloodlines. Women had been given rights of property disposition and general civil liberties less than forty years ago in Greater Brazil, years after the establishment of the Federation of Co-Prosperity between Earth and the old colonies founded by Russia and the United States of America, and men of the aristocracy like Ramaro were the last bastions of old prejudice.

The little major led them to the nearest bubbletent, cycled them through the lock. Beyond, the dimly lit circular space was crammed with racks of monitoring equipment; half a dozen technicians crouched over screens, their faces livid in relayed blood-red light. Ramaro served Andrews, Kilczer, and Dorthy with coffee, and with elaborate courtesy pulled a rollerchair over for Dorthy – and, after she was seated, promptly ignored her.

Dorthy sipped black coffee, watched an unattended screen that showed the keep rearing out of its still moat, lights twisted around its many pinnacles like necklaces of fluorescent rubies, and listened as Andrews and Ramaro argued about what the keep was for, whether its builders were still alive. Kilczer stood a little to one side, his coffee steaming untouched in his cup as he watched the two men, nodding slightly as Andrews mentioned the herder Dorthy had seen in the forest, reiterated his belief that the enemy had degenerated on this world, that the herders were their barbarian descendants.

'As your ancestors descended to barbarism after traffic between Earth and Elysium ceased, five hundred years ago?' Ramaro smiled, his eyes almost disappearing behind his rounded cheeks. 'My opinion is that the enemy are hiding,' he said, as much to Kilczer as to Andrews. 'Hiding, or waiting to be recalled from sleep. Perhaps even now they are being awakened, and the lights are a part of the process. It is possible, Andrews.'

Dorthy wondered if he'd been told about the burning intelligence she'd twice glimpsed, but kept quiet. This wasn't her argument. And besides, she had taken an immediate dislike to Major Luiz Ramaro.

Andrews said, 'Possible, if you can explain why they would do such a thing. Transform a whole world and go to sleep? Why? This isn't a colonyboat, taking years to travel from star to star.'

'We must remember that they are alien.'

'That's hardly a basis for speculation, now. It explains everything and nothing.'

Ramaro shrugged. 'What is certain is that there is an entire planet to be searched, most of it poorly mapped, almost all of it untrodden, untouched. We need half a hundred teams such as this to make any impact on the problem.'

'I've told the people upstairs just that so many times . . .' Andrews scratched at his stubbled chin. 'And suppose the herders *are* coming up here. What do you say to that?'

'It is my opinion that they are animals only, intelligent as an ape or a dolphin, no more. At most they might be caretakers, servants, awaiting their masters. Wherever they are.'

'It's opinion like that which keeps research here at a minimum,

Luiz. As long as upstairs believes that there may be a chance of stumbling across something inimical, they withhold the resources we need. If we suggest that all is clear, they will commit themselves to a full survey, believe me.' Andrews leaned a hip negligently against a console. 'Well, whoever of us is right, it appears we will learn a great deal from the herders. One way or another.'

Dorthy, her anger finding sudden focus, said, 'You assume I can probe these creatures to a greater extent than I can probe human beings, Dr Andrews. Besides, you don't seem eager to put it into practice.'

Andrews raised a bushy eyebrow. 'I'm sorry, Dorthy, all this must be dreadfully boring. But I just want to check that things haven't overtaken my plans.'

Ramaro said, slightly turning away from Dorthy (whether from deliberate insult or unconscious dismissal she couldn't tell), 'You should give up your lakeside camp, scenic though it is, and come up here. We learn new things every day, every hour, and it will save you considerable commuting time.'

'Ah, now, I have a fondness for that camp,' Andrews said, smiling. 'It was where we started out, after all. Besides, there is the biological program to consider. The ecosystem is as finely balanced as the optics of one of your probes. I do not think we should abandon that aspect of our research.'

Snubbed, feeling the tingling that heralded one of her attacks (or perhaps it was simply anger: she hoped so), Dorthy set down her coffee and went over to one of the technicians to ask where the bathroom was. After she had used it, she splashed cold water on her face, dabbed it around her forehead. Strands of her black hair had come loose and she tucked them inside her barrette, bent again and rinsed out her mouth, rinsed away the bitter taste.

When she returned to the dimly lit space outside, Andrews turned from his study of a sheaf of holograms spread on a bench, sections of intagliated wall or floor, Dorthy saw. Kilczer held one up, tilting it this way and that. 'Sorry,' Andrews said.

'You and Major Ramaro have done?'

'He's over there, checking out the telemetry of a remote probe that's thrown some sort of fit. Look, I can take these with me. I really do want the herders checked out.'

'Don't worry, I'm not about to throw some fit of my own. I just want to get it over with, get back to my own work. All this seems a little unreal.' As she said it, she felt a sliding sensation of disquiet, as if the tent, with all its consoles and benches and personnel, had slid metres across the windy shelf of rock towards the abyss. Suppose, she suddenly thought, suppose Andrews is wrong, the herders aren't anything at all to do with the enemy. What will orbital command do with me then, send me home or set me looking elsewhere?

Kilczer was saying, 'To me also this is unreal. Now that I am here it is less real to me than when I was waiting at Camp Zero to come out.'

'Oh, it's real, all right,' Andrews said. 'Now, Dorthy, I'll sort out Ramaro and then we will go. A promise.'

He crossed the room and bent to confer with the major, who twice snapped a glance towards Dorthy before returning his attention to Andrews's earnest chatter. 'They argue all the time before,' Kilczer said, 'but they are very alike, I think.'

'Obsessed,' Dorthy said.

Kilczer shrugged, and began to collect the holograms together.

At last Andrews finished talking with Ramaro, brushed his forehead with his thumb in lieu of a salute, and returned to Dorthy and Kilczer. 'All set,' he reported. 'Let's get both of you down to your work.'

As the cleft tilted away and the thopter circled out over the gulf towards the pass, Dorthy felt the intimation of her Talent's wild onset recede, contract to a fuzzy point. Somewhere, she imagined, just out of reach, was a switch that would completely extinguish it: if she could find that switch she would throw it. She leaned back, trying to settle her legs comfortably in the confined space. In front, Andrews gripped the stick and studied the radar as they dived veils and veils of mist. Beside him, Kilczer dozed fitfully. Dorthy felt, faintly, the sliding texture of his uneasy dreams.

After a while, once they had crossed the pass and begun to follow the course of the river as it wound through the rocky landscape, Andrews said over his shoulder, 'You're an astronomer, Dorthy, is that not so?'

'That's what I like to think.'

His laugh was a single bark. 'I suppose all of this would seem pretty small to you. I used to know one of your sort pretty well; he was fond of pointing out that life is a chancy, anomalous thing in this Universe of ours. You believe that?'

'It's a fairly common attitude, I guess. After all, how many stars have suitable bands of temperature – high enough for life but outside the radius of trapped rotation? How many of those stars have planets inside that band, or last long enough for life to have evolved? How many of those planets have life? Yes, I think it's a rare sort of thing, despite the number of stars. There may be four hundred billion in this Galaxy, but more than half of those are brown dwarfs, so small and faint that even those in the neighbourhood of Sol weren't detected until the late twentieth century. And most of the rest, like this one, are little better.'

'The old Drake-Sagan equation, to be sure. But one thing they overlooked is the way life spreads out, turns back entropy, increases order to its own system. Look around you—' He gestured one-handedly. Beyond the bubble of the canopy, dark trees hung with feathery creepers dripped in the mist, sliding past as the thopter descended. 'Here we are on a planet that not so long ago wasn't rotating, too close to the sun up there, trapped. Yet something spun it up, dropped a few hundred ice mountains on it and fired up a couple of dozen volcanoes to enrich the atmosphere, seeded it with a brew of life. That's something, isn't it? Sure, I know all about Seyfert galaxies and black holes and white holes and quasars and all the rest, but that's simply a lot of fireworks going off because of chance accumulation of matter. But give us another million years and maybe we'll be creating the right sort of star systems out of the energy that's shooting out of the hearts of colliding galaxies. Hell, we'll change the Universe to suit us if it comes to that. We've only just begun, I suppose is my point. With knowledge of how the enemy planoformed this world, we can spread faster. It'll be exponential. We won't have to search out the few worlds that we can live on; we could transform ten or twenty within thirty light years right now! You can forget the limitation of K5 to F0 – anything'll do for a million years or so. You know, back when Elysium was founded, in the bad old days of the Russian and American empires, before the Interregnum, my ancestors were just one group who wanted to run their lives their own way, one group of many sent to Elysium to be out of the way. Another thousand years, any group that wants it can have a world of their own. And it will spread. Exponential, do you not agree? This Galaxy, the Magellanic Clouds, the local group . . .'

'And if we find more of the enemy? Or something else?'

'Then we fight them or join them. What else is life about? Evolution, do you see? It does not pity the slow or the meek.'

'And if we happen to be the meek?' She felt a faint contemptuous amusement that someone could hold such ideas so strongly. They burned in him.

'The enemy is like a test. We'll win out at BD twenty because they don't have the phase graffle. They have to fight on their own territory, they have nowhere else to go. And here? They have gone to pieces, it seems. Do not worry about it, Dorthy.'

'It wasn't quite what I meant. Suppose there are even more powerful civilisations out there: Empires, Galactic Clubs, call them what you will. We go out there with our phase drives and our little weapons and scant knowledge. And we could be swallowed. I'm content to watch the stars from a convenient viewpoint, not storm them.'

'It's not a view I hold with, now. My father, he'd agree with you. Sits at home, overseeing our part of the Combine, never stirs from the castle.' 'A great stone pile about three hundred years old, draughty, inconvenient, lashed on two sides by the sea – the west curtain wall will subside in a decade or so if nothing's done – and nothing in any direction for five hundred kilometres. That's his world, and he could be anywhere on any one of them. We own two houses on Earth, another on the Tallman Scarp on Titan, a beach house on Serenity. He's never seen any of them. He trusts his staff and myself to get things done. And you know what? It works. In a slow, inefficient, ramshackle way. But it works. He's a century old, you understand; he was forty when Earth came along to free the old colonies from the centuries of barbarism we'd tumbled into. Actually, for my family it wasn't so bad, but then, we were rulers of our little part of Elysium. Oh, I don't remember too much, I was only five when the Federation was set up, only ten when Earth more or less forced a central government on Elysium, and forced all the agatherin growers to join the Fountain of Youth Combine. There, I've given away my age. Did you think I was older or younger?'

'You're very enthusiastic,' Dorthy said mildly.

He glanced back, grinning. 'That's kind. I suppose that I am. I have drive, do you see. A thousand years ago they would have called it sublimation or some such nonsense. My father couldn't understand why I dropped out of the Guild (we have a very big investment in the Guild) and joined the Navy at the first intimation of trouble out at BD twenty – he said that he was quite prepared to have another child if I really felt that a member of the family had to enter the military – doesn't understand what I'm doing out here. My mother does, a little, but then she does leave the castle, on occasion.'

'And what are you doing, out here?'

'Taking you and Arcady here to the herders, of course. Wake up, Arcady!'

The neurobiologist stretched as well as he could in his seat, yawning. 'We are soon there?' he asked, and when Andrews told him that they were not he subsided again, his head sagging sideways. His profile was limned against the great circle of the sun hung above the dark forest (no mist now) that reticulated away towards the sweep of the plain. It was perhaps halfway up its climb to zenith, dominated the whole sky. A whorl of sunspots flecked off centre, holes into which worlds could sink without trace. It was so dim that Dorthy could watch it for minutes at a time without having to blink or look away, imagining that she could almost make out the granulation of its photosphere.

'Here we go,' Andrews said.

Dorthy looked back at the landscape as the thopter banked left, braced herself against the back of Andrews's seat. The forest was failing. Rifts of scrub reached far into its dark quilt; dry gullies scored it, red rock seeming to glow in the red light of the sun. The land was flattening out. Ahead, the plain stretched towards an intimation of the desert.

Andrews was checking the radar display. 'They were right around here,' he said, 'but they've moved. I'll go higher, see if I can pick their crawler up on this.'

As the thopter's vanes briefly beat faster, Kilczer asked, scrubbing his eyes, 'Who have you lost?'

'The twins. Our biology team. They're following one bunch of herders. Marta has this idea that she can work out their social behaviour.'

'And do they have any?' Dorthy asked.

'Fucking mostly,' Andrews said evenly. 'The boss female controls the group by choosing which males fuck her, and the males fuck each other, too, to establish their dominance. Rather like the Navy.' He glanced at the radar, edged the thopter a little higher. 'How are you going to be, reading their minds, Dorthy? We haven't any real medical facilities out here if you collapse again, and I'd hate to have to fly you all the way back to Camp Zero when things might be starting to break.'

'I'll try my best not to inconvenience you.'

'Hell, I didn't mean it like that,' he said impatiently. 'You will be all right?'

'If I'm prepared.'

'I will see to it,' Kilczer added. Dorthy bridled at his interference, but bit back a reply. Let it pass, let it pass. Just so she could do her job and go.

'That's good,' Andrews said. 'Well, I think I've found them. Thank God they haven't moved far, otherwise it might have taken days. Here we go.'

The sun filled the cabin with light dull as clotted blood as the thopter tilted, circling lower. Dorthy glimpsed, far off, a crawling line of dirty white and then, nearer, the boxy shape of a tracked vehicle moving through the scrub. Andrews flipped the stick and the thopter beat low, swirling dust all around, turning neatly and settling to the ground even before the vehicle had stopped.

Jon Chavez, the ecologist, was a tall, slender man, his finely carved brown face framed by glossy black hair that swung and bobbed as he animatedly told Andrews, 'They've been coming out of the plain for two days now. We lost track of our original group when they went up into the forest. Maria's still pretty upset – now she has to figure out a new set of names for the herders in this group. We think they're headed for the forest as well.' He gestured at the dark line rising in the distance out of the flat land.

Marta Ade, a lively woman as tall and slender as Chavez, her skin as glossily black as his hair in the red light, chimed in, 'The first group had stopped to rest, and all of a sudden started up towards our camp, we were lucky to get everything out in time. Jon was running around bare-assed naked throwing equipment into the back of the crawler.'

'She thinks it was funny,' Chavez said, smiling.

'Well, it was,' Ade insisted.

'What about this bunch?' Andrews asked. 'Will they stop?'

'I'm sure they will, but I can't say when. There's what's left of a lake ahead. Maybe then.' Marta Ade turned to Dorthy. 'They don't have any set periods of rest and activity. Something to do with the extended day and night, I suppose, since they didn't evolve under these conditions.'

'At least, we're pretty sure they didn't,' Chavez added. 'After all, who can say where they came from, what it was like?' He turned, hands on hips, to look out across the parched plain towards the gleam of water, like a copper coin flashing at the hazy horizon.

Dorthy asked, 'How close can I get to them?'

'I don't really know.' Ade smiled. 'I wouldn't try under a hundred metres. I can run fast, but once, when I got too close to a group, perhaps seventy, eighty metres, some of the males almost had me.' She held a hand out, pink-skinned palm downward, and joggled it. 'I was like that for the rest of the day. Very hairy, my dear. Still, you don't have to worry about the critters, they aren't anything but eating machines. If you're standing on a clump of vegetation they might try and snatch it from under your feet, but that's all. Just thump them on the snout and they'll turn away. That's how the herders control them, more or less.'

'Have you still not seen any children?' Andrews asked.

Ade shrugged. Ritual scars marked the taut black skin over her high cheekbones. 'In the other group there were two males who maybe were immature – or could simply have been a different variety, freemartins perhaps. There is one sort, I *think* it's a different species, maybe the size of a vervet monkey, grooms the female and whichever male is her consort at the time. Could be a pet or a symbiote, just possibly could be a very very young child. But nothing in between that and the full-sized male.' She grinned at Dorthy. 'If you see a birth while you're out there I'll come running faster than I ran from those males.'

'Perhaps they lay eggs,' Chavez said. 'Like birds, they have a cloaca, no overt genitals.'

'Except we've never seen an egg,' Ade said. 'Plenty of sex, but no results, as it were. Perhaps it's seasonal, maybe they're going up into the forest to do it. There is something of an axial tilt to the planet, after all, though it doesn't mean much at the equator here. But there has to be a definite rainy season, or there wouldn't be all those big dried-up gullies at the edge of the forest rise. Dig down in one of those and you'll find water. We're in the middle of the dry season, that's all.'

Kilczer asked, 'And that is why they are moving their herds, perhaps? Because the plain is dried out?'

'It isn't that dried out. The stuff that substitutes for grass has taproots that go very deep, stores a lot of moisture down there. It comes right back up after it's been cropped.' Chavez scuffed his boot-tip in the dusty earth. 'A few days and you won't know a herd of critters has been through here. It's very good fodder, too. We could live off it, just avoid the old growth, is all. Lousy with heavy metals. The critters eat the lot but the rest of the fauna just nibble the tips.'

'The herders, on the other hand, are strictly carnivorous,' Ade added.

Chavez grinned. 'Don't you know it?'

Dorthy looked from one to the other. The way they stood close together, each watching the other, sly covetous glances, adding to each other's explanations . . . she understood why Andrews had nicknamed them the twins, felt a faint pang of jealousy at their obvious paired closeness. Lucky, to be able to cleave to each other in the random sundering Universe. Dorthy had never really loved anyone except her mother – and she hadn't realised that until the poor woman had died, worn out by her husband's constant demands, themselves sprung from a well of loneliness, the loss of his family's love.

Andrews was telling the twins about the lights that had sprung on at the keep, about Dorthy's encounter with a herder in the high forest. 'I'm becoming convinced that we've triggered something by our presence,' he said, beating his arms across his chest. It was still cold, here at the equator in the middle of the morning of the long, long day. 'This migration, the lights, something's under way, all right. Slow perhaps, but it is happening. You must all be careful now. I don't want you triggering an incident that will give the Navy an excuse to pull us out. Colonel Chung would love that.'

'*We* are the victims of a hostile incident,' Chavez said.

'It was as if the campsite has become the local version of the *Avenida das Estrelas*,' Ade added, trilling a light, breathy laugh. 'Really, Duncan, you should have seen us hopping about.'

Andrews chuckled politely, then, abruptly businesslike, suggested that they unload Kilczer's equipment. 'Be careful, please,' the neurobiologist said as, one after the other, Andrews handed down the crates. 'Is very delicate.'

'Well, I hope it all works. I've got my neck on a line over this. Now, here you go.' Andrews held out the two small sacks that contained Dorthy's and Kilczer's personal possessions. Hanging in the circle of the open hatch, his hands caught casually on the jamb above his head, he said, 'I'll come and find you in three days, so don't go too far.'

'That would depend on the herders,' Chavez said.

'Look now, with this radio silence I'll have a hell of a job finding you if you stray too far. In three days we will rendezvous here, no matter what the herders do, so you will lock your compass to the loran coordinates.' Chavez began to protest, but Andrews shook his head. 'That's the way it will be,' he said firmly. 'I don't want to lose you.'

'All right,' Chavez said, after looking at Ade.

'Things are tough all over,' Andrews said. 'Take care of those two, now. I'll see you all in three days.' He swung inside the cabin, slammed the hatch. They all stepped back as, either side of the cabin's transparent bubble, the thopter's vanes flexed. Dust blew and the thopter leapt into the air, turning even as it rose. Dorthy watched it dwindle with the empty feeling of having been marooned.

'Come on,' Ade said briskly, 'the herd is getting away. Let's load up and go.'

*

The crawler groaned and jounced as, in its lowest gear, it trailed behind the slow-moving herd of critters. Chavez, at the controls, ignored all but the largest obstacles, grinding up steep slopes and slipping down the reverse faces, smashing through the dry scrub. Red light fumed through dust that continually powdered the windscreen, flicking away after a moment's contact with the charged surface. Ade sat in the swivel seat beside her lover; Dorthy and Kilczer in the small bunks directly behind, clinging to the stays.

'There is something I must ask,' Kilczer said. 'Coming here I see something I believe impossible, creatures that resemble an extinct form of sloth from Earth. Am I perhaps mistaken?'

'Hell no,' Chavez called back. 'Duncan Andrews didn't tell you?'

'Once I ask him, but he said you knew more about it. I meant to ask him again, but the opportunity—'

'He just brushed it off,' Dorthy added, 'said something like we hadn't seen the half of it.'

'Well, you haven't,' Ade said.

Chavez inclined his head. 'There are cohorts of flora and fauna gathered from a dozen planets, all mixed up into this crazy ecosystem. We can recognise some: Earth, Elysium, Ruby, Serenity. The others we don't know. The herders and the critters belong to the same cohort. Blue oxygen-binding pigment in the blood, high heavy-metal content.'

'But nothing from Novaya Rosya?' Dorthy caught a touch of Kilczer's excitement as he bent forward on the narrow bunk, clutching the back of Ade's seat.

'Not that we've found,' Ade told him. 'Maybe in the other holds.'

'Show him the list, Marta,' Chavez said.

As Kilczer flicked through, light from the screen glowing on his face, Dorthy asked, 'So they collected a menagerie together to populate this world? But why didn't they simply colonize Earth or Elysium instead? It was a million years ago, nothing would have been in their way. Why go to all this trouble?'

Kilczer glanced up and said smugly, 'This is what I ask you, remember? You said you would find out.'

'My theory,' Ade said, 'is that the enemy evolved on a world of a red dwarf, can't take high light intensities.'

'It is true, the critter Duncan Andrews brought back, its hide is sensitive to ultraviolet,' Kilczer said. 'But any such world would be like this one before it was planoformed, one face fixed to its sun. Not good for life. And the lights in the hold are very bright. Red, yes, but bright.'

'So maybe a red giant.'

'Impossible,' Dorthy said. 'Any red giant is either a star like Sol that's run off the main sequence, so it'll have expanded and destroyed any worlds in the habitable zone, or it's a big star on the way to becoming a white dwarf. And big stars don't last long enough to evolve life on any of their planets.'

'She is an astronomer,' Kilczer said. 'Is best not to argue.'

'So I had better leave it to you to find out the truth, right?' Ade smiled at Dorthy, who smiled back. It cost nothing, after all.

They followed the herd for a long time. Dorthy tried to read her book, but the jouncing of the crawler made reading impossible. She lay on the hard bunk, half listening to Kilczer discuss ecology with Ade and Chavez, and woke suddenly, the aching metallic taste of exhaustion in the back of her throat.

The crawler had stopped: that was what had woken her. Chavez leaned back in his seat, stretching. Ade was studying a screen that relayed a view from the camera-eye of a remote, and after a while announced that the herders were setting up camp: they had stopped at the shore of a small lake, perhaps to let the critters take water. 'So I suppose I should try to do my stuff,' Dorthy said, more casually than she felt. 'How long will they stay there?'

'Two hours, maybe, or maybe twenty.'

'Two hours would be long enough,' Dorthy said. She took out a single tablet of the counteragent that would release her Talent from its chemical thrall and washed it down with acidic orange juice. The crawler's treacher was more rudimentary than the ones at Camp Zero or that in Andrews's lakeside tent, stretching only to simple beverages and a dull two dozen or so variations on protein mixes and vegetable purees.

Kilczer, chewing on a concentrate bar, watched Dorthy take the tablet with the air of a priest officiating at a rite of communion. Dorthy turned away from his solemn gaze as she chewed her own bar of concentrate hungrily (time had flown in the deceptive unvarying light; it was a long way after the spurious noon of Earth, of Greater Brazil). There were twenty minutes or so before her Talent came into its own and she sat back on the bunk to wait.

And woke again, her mouth dry, and her Talent was there, a more brilliant illumination than the smouldering light that fell through the windscreen. She could sense Kilczer's careful thoughts, like slabs of ice moving in stately procession down a smooth river, as he prepared his sensors; Chavez's thoughts a heavy stream of quicksilver with a sullen undertow of exhaustion; Ade's light darting intelligence: three separate melodies that only slightly impinged one on the other, a taste of the cacophony of civilisation from which Dorthy had fled into the serene silence of space.

Even as Dorthy crossed dry ground towards the distant gleam of the lake, the sense of the human minds behind her was like a distracting light just outside her field of vision, Kilczer's most of all as he followed her at a discreet distance, his equipment bumping awkwardly at his hip.

Packed sand, sinuously grooved as if water had once flowed across it, crunched under her boots. Here and there clusters of plants thrust up fleshy spikes with close-packed scale-leaves, black in the red light. Some were as high as her waist. From which world, known or unknown? Rounded boulders of all sizes cast a confusion of shadows. She climbed the shallow face of a dune, sand crumbling under her hands. Beyond, a thin weave of groundcover carpeted the bone-dry ground. She could make out movement by the lakeshore now, but she was too far away to sense anything. Kilczer's presence nagged at her attention: flickering sideways light, a fleck of grit in her eye, the electronic hiss of a receiver between stations.

Dorthy steeled herself not to look back and walked on with a fluttering in her stomach. Not fear, but anticipation. Also stilled was her curiosity: she was like a blank page waiting to be filled, like the smooth sheaves of sandstone she'd seen on her first walk outside Camp Zero, blamelessly unblemished.

Closer now. She could make out individual shapes in the dull industrial light, stepped more slowly. The lake was a wide circle of still water ringed by denuded ground over which the critters, a hundred at least, rowed on ludicrously small flippers, slow and desultory. One or two were curled up, dead perhaps, disregarded. A clump of flat-topped trees stood a little distance beyond, and within their shade a fire sent up a thin unravelling thread of smoke. That was where the herders were, Ade had said, the female and her harem of males.

Stooping low, Dorthy moved forward a few metres more, reluctance growing with each step, but still not precisely afraid. There was a tall growth of pulpy wood grooved like coral and she settled in its shadow, sat crosslegged and began the ritual of clearing her mind, swelling her abdomen and straightening her back, concentrating on the tidal rhythm of her breath, feeling it gentle within herself as she sank from her silvery sense of self.

There were as many ways of preparing and focusing as there were Talents. Some were able to do it with the slightest concentration, visualizing some object or simply imagining the space between their eyes, using their Talent as easily as opening an eyelid. Others, like Dorthy, needed to go deeper. She had found the practice of *Sessan Amakuki*, Zen meditation, the most helpful technique, sitting zazen 'outwardly in the world of good and evil' as now, cold sand hard under her buttocks and the dull glow on her eyelids disregarded, 'without thought arising in the heart,' no, no thought of her own, but there, there, dim flickerings of the other. Out, out. Not the quick skimming glance of empathy but a detached lingering absorptive examination, there, there at the *Samadhi*, the still central point of undisturbed purity, perfect vacuum where entropy flattened out. Not watching: becoming.

There.

Like sparks crawling over a charred log, sluggish and slow as the movements of their charges: the thoughts and beings of the herders. Most were sleeping; others lay almost inert, sodden with exhaustion but pricked by a distant dim yearning. Higher, a dizzy glimpse of a skein of stars. Higher. It was a geas laid upon her, perfect fusion of act and will. Higher to the winding stars, to . . . It slipped from her as she tried to understand it, it was like trying to catch a current of air. There, and not. Higher, and stars. Higher . . .

. . . and Kilczer crashed into her ken, his hand bruising the thin bones of her shoulder, his voice hoarse with outrage and fear. 'Please stop now this craziness. What is it you think—'

'I . . .' She shook her head. She was lying on dry mud as

something scraped past a few metres away. One of the critters, the bristles that ringed each segmented joint working back and forth, the little flippers scooping the hard ground. Others were around them and the crusted edge of the lake was only a dozen metres away. How had she . . . ?

'You just started crawling towards them,' Kilczer hissed. He was looking around, every nerve alive with panic. 'Bit by bit. You wish to be eaten?'

'I thought . . . I thought I was climbing? No. I wanted—' Whatever it was slipped from her, leaving only a sense of loss. Her Talent was fading, too. She glanced at her wrist, the black numerals woven into her skin telling her that it was an hour since she had started reading the herders. She shivered, afraid now. Never before had she gone so deep, had been drawn so far from herself. Calm, calm. Find the centre. She took three breaths, the first shudderingly deep, the second calmer, held the third a moment before letting it go. The sense of her body flooded back as if she were rushing into the tips of her fingers, her toes. Her left thigh pulsed with a fading cramp; she was very thirsty. Crumbs of sand clung to her dry lips.

'Come on.' Kilczer said grimly. 'We must crawl back. Slowly. I do not want to have to run and leave you behind.'

Beyond them, the critter heaved half its bulk into the edge of the water and subsided. Ripples spread out across the stagnant lake. Dorthy said, 'The herders have a drive, a need; they need to go up. Something about stars, or the lights of the keep. They see it, dimly.'

'Talk later. Now we go back.' The forms of his thoughts jarred and jostled, whirling like melting icebergs on the hot dark river of his fear. Dorthy, afraid too, nodded agreement.

They crawled a long way, back to the place Kilczer had left his equipment. Halfway there Dorthy's thigh knotted again and she had to rub the clenched muscles to relieve it. Kilczer sprawled on the ground beside her, warily watching smoke rise from inside the distant clump of trees. She asked 'Did your machines pick up anything?'

'Will take a long time to find out. Not like you, direct input. Must guess, find a baseline.'

'That's my problem, too.'

'Still we do not know if they are the enemy?'

'If they are, they're good at hiding it, or very far gone in dissolution. One thing's certain: they are nothing like the thing I glimpsed when I was in the dropcapsule. All I have is a compulsion, a need. I don't fully understand it. Not the need, but why it's there.' She straightened her leg, bent it. 'I can go on now.'

When they reached Kilczer's abandoned equipment, as he packed it up, he asked, 'Need is all you get? I tell you, there must be something more, the way you act.' The last catch snapped home and he stood, hefted the case, and slung its strap on to his shoulder. 'We walk now. Run maybe, if they come after us.'

Dorthy glanced back, was surprised to see how far they had come. 'They won't,' she said.

'This is something you learn from your probing?'

Dorthy sighed, fell in step as Kilczer started back across gullied sand towards the distant crawler. Beside which, she saw, the orange dome of a bubbletent had risen. She felt the dull comedown that always clamped over her after using her Talent – the result of reduced serotonin levels, but knowing what it was didn't help. 'I don't know,' she said. 'There was something, but I don't know what it means.'

'That compulsion to go up? You mean you read them for an hour and that is all you find?'

Dorthy stopped, and Kilczer turned to face her. 'Look,' she said, 'I didn't ask to come here, something I have to keep reminding people about, it seems. I've tried once, it doesn't mean I won't be successful if I try again. Perhaps I was straining too hard at something and got caught up in it. That happens to us, sometimes. Now that I know what to expect, though, I might be more successful the second time.' She walked on quickly, deliberately outdistancing him so he wouldn't have a chance to reply. She was angry now, angry at Kilczer, angry at her failure. Behind her anger was the unsteady conviction that if she didn't discover something she would never return to the isolation of her work. The Navy, and Duncan Andrews, had been maddeningly vague about what they wanted from her, but it was certainly more than a recounting of the obscure desires of the herders. Dorthy had once been marooned for several days on a small sandy island when her skiff had broken down, and each contrail in the pure sky had been a broken promise that had engendered afresh a sense of disappointed betrayal. She felt a touch of that as she hurried towards the camp ahead of Kilczer.

Inside the bubbletent, Chavez and Ade were setting up their equipment on folding trestles; a few pieces of inflatable furniture were scattered about, a mattress had been unrolled, and the treacher was set up beside it. Ade looked up as Dorthy, doused with the acrid scent of the sterilant, stepped from the airlock, and said, 'Oh, my dear! It didn't go well?'

'No,' Dorthy said. 'No, it didn't go well.' She sat in one of the chairs, its plastic wobbling under her weight.

'I watched you for a little while, but you stayed so still I'm afraid I gave up. Where's Arcady?'

'Bringing his equipment.'

'Oh,' Ade said, understanding that something had happened out there but not sure how to begin to ask what it was; she was a little afraid of Dorthy, of her Talent.

'I didn't realise we were setting up camp,' Dorthy said. 'What if the herders move on?'

On the other side of the circular space, Chavez looked up from the microscope he was assembling. 'We can always catch up with them. They don't move fast, and they leave a clear trail. Anyway, *we* have to rest, and try to catch up on our schedule. I've set a dozen or so traps for the smaller, more elusive fauna. Perhaps you'd like to help me with them, later.'

'I'll pass,' Dorthy said, 'if you don't mind.' She wanted to be left alone, but at that moment feared solitude. She saw the indicator light over the lock door change from green to red. Kilczer had arrived.

'I don't mind at all,' Chavez said. 'Are you going to do your thing again?'

'Jon,' Ade said with gentle remonstration, 'can't you see that she's tired?'

Kilczer came through, coughing. 'We stay here long?' he asked, looking about.

'Long enough to get some sleep anyhow,' Chavez said.

'Then I work on my recordings. Perhaps my machine got something, at least.'

Dorthy saw Ade and Chavez exchange glances, but neither said anything. For an hour she sat with her back to the others and tried to pin down what she had garnered from the herders; no more than three minutes of recorded talk, in the end. As she worked, she nibbled a tasteless concentrate bar and sipped bad coffee, more from habit than appetite. Across the tent, Kilczer hunched over his machines; at the other end of the trestle, Marta Ade watched a monitor, flicking restlessly from one remote to another as she spied on the herders, while beside her Chavez worked on his dissection of some small animal, muttering into his recorder, occasionally jumping up to slice a section from some organ and scrutinise it briefly under the microscope.

Once Dorthy had finished, she found that without the distraction of her work the flickering involuntary glimpses of the others' emotions, last gasp of her Talent's emancipation, were increasingly irritating. Finally she asked, 'Where do I sleep?'

'Huh?' Chavez looked up from his dissection. 'Oh, better go in the crawler. You and Arcady take the bunks, okay?'

'No,' Dorthy said, 'it isn't.' All three looked at her, and she felt a cold sharp pang, anger mixed with envy. She said to Kilczer, 'You know I have to sleep alone, especially after I've used my Talent. I'm still coming down. Why can't you sleep here? There's plenty of room. I need to be alone.'

'That is luxury here. Unaffordable.'

Ade glanced at her lover and said, 'Besides, I'll be working late. These herders have no sense of time whatsoever. Or have I already told you that?'

'You managed at the other camp, didn't you?' Kilczer added.

'When there was only one other person, when I hadn't just used my Talent.' Dorthy knew that she was being unreasonable, but didn't care, safe within the smooth cold armour of her anger. 'If I'm to be successful, I need to rest. Alone.'

'You will be successful, a second time?' Kilczer asked mildly.

'What did you find out with your machinery?' she shot back.

'I admit I need more time also. Without a baseline it is difficult. Neural activity is low, I think they must sleep, although none showed dreaming activity as in spiked alpha waves. Poor candidates for the enemy, I think. This vague talk of stars and needing to climb mountains, it is not enough.'

'Look,' Dorthy told him, 'animals don't have plans or aspirations. So that's *something*.'

'No, no,' Kilczer said. 'It could be no more than simple migration drive. Look into mind of zithsa or monarch butterfly if you do not believe this.'

Ade looked up from the monitor, shook her head, and returned her gaze to the screen, her round, dark, pretty face underlit by relayed red light.

Kilczer took a deep breath. 'Dr Yoshida, we have to show that these herders are either no more than clever animals, or that they are the descendants of the creatures which planoformed all this world. And this we must do quickly, yes? There are a hundred people down here, a thousand more in orbit. All may be in immediate danger if the enemy is here, hiding, perhaps, as that glimpse of yours suggested. So we must find them, or find what happened to them. We find nothing today, so after we sleep we must try again. And if we find nothing again I must decide nothing is to be found, we waste time here. So we sleep and then we try again. Yes?'

Dorthy stood. 'That isn't what I was told—' she began, and felt weak tears prick her eyes. 'I'll try again,' she said, 'after I sleep.' Something rose in her throat; she swallowed, swallowed again, turned quickly towards the lock, afraid that Kilczer or one of the twins would see her tears.

As she unfastened the flap of the inner door, Chavez said, 'We're all tired, people. A hundred? There should be ten thousand down here at least. Go ahead and rest, Dr Yoshida. Sleep. Arcady will sleep here, this time.'

He really did mean it kindly. Dorthy nodded, not trusting herself to speak, and before anyone said anything else she ducked into the lock and sealed the flap behind herself. Escaped.

She was awoken by Marta Ade. 'Come, my dear,' the woman said as Dorthy yawned and stretched, 'please hurry. We are on the move again. The herd has left us behind.' Without waiting for a reply, she hurried out of the crawler, the hatch whining shut behind her.

By the time Dorthy had dressed and stumbled outside, the bubbletent had been deflated, an orange pancake that Kilczer and Chavez were rolling up on the dry uneven ground. Dorthy helped

Ade stow neatly packed boxes of equipment, helped her carry the treacher into the crawler's cabin and plug it in. Within fifteen minutes, the crawler was bucketing along the stripped swath left by the critters; within half an hour it was in sight of the dust cloud raised by the herds; in ten minutes more it was trailing the ragged vanguard.

The herd didn't stop for thirty hours.

They all four took turns to drive the crawler. Dorthy enjoyed her spells at the controls. As she wrestled the ungainly but powerful vehicle across dry washes and gravelly ridges she felt that she was at one with it, extending into every corner of its trapezoidal hull, its churning tracks and hard-worked suspensors; the nagging sense of the others in the cabin receded. Otherwise she clung to the stay of one or other of the bunks or sat in the swivel seat beside the driver, watching the monotonous landscape crawl past, unable to read, unwilling to talk, the unvarying red light of the huge sun like some bore that had long overstayed its welcome. Once they stopped to snatch sleep for a few hours, Ade and Chavez outside, under the crawler, Dorthy and Kilczer on the bunks inside; Dorthy was too tired to complain about the arrangement, was too tired to care.

And then they were off again, on one side the slope of the caldera rising into pink-tinged cloud, on the other the dark plain stretching to the level horizon. Once they passed, in the near distance, a herd of big slope-shouldered antelope that Chavez said came from Ruby. And once something the size of a small groundcar, with a high domed shell and broad massive tail, shot across the path of the crawler, forcing Kilczer to swerve. The vehicle ploughed through scrubby bushes, stiff branches rattling its sides, before he pulled back on to the stripped tail. 'Glyptodon,' he said to Dorthy, who sat beside him in the other swivel seat. 'Extinct Earth animal.'

Behind him, clutching the edge of the bunk, Chavez called out, 'The enemy seem to have collected plants from the Arctic Circle, animals from South America. Who knows why, eh?'

'I see why that one became extinct,' Kilczer said, 'with such poor instinct to run before vehicles. We also see megatheria. All animals brought here are herbivores?'

'Surely,' Chavez said. 'There are perhaps twenty thousand herders in this hold, each one the size of a small lion. That's a lot of carnivores to keep fed; even with the critters, they don't need competition.'

Ade added, 'As for why herders prey on other creatures when they do have critters, or why they have critters when they prey on other creatures, we don't know. We've barely scratched the surface here.'

When Ade was not driving she crouched over her monitor. Her probes quested wide either side of the herd as it moved across the dry plain, and a few hours after the glyptodon had thrown itself in front of the crawler they picked up a hunting party of herders. The crawler stopped and all four people gathered around the monitor, glad of the break from the monotony of travel.

The herders, three of them, had brought down an antelope; now they were butchering it with long stone axes they had flaked on the spot. The unfortunate creature was still alive, panting into the dust and spasmodically shivering as the herders stooped over it and stripped ropes of muscle from its hindquarters, hoods of naked skin flaring about their narrow faces. At last they discarded the bloody axes and shouldered the meat and began to lope at an angle towards their still-moving herd. Behind them the ground around the antelope cracked and heaved up as creatures like cat-sized moles, with scaled hides and massive, humped forequarters, broke surface.

'By the beard,' Kilczer breathed, avidly watching the final dismemberment of the antelope, 'I no longer feel safe walking about out there.'

'Those things only come up after a kill,' Ade said.

'At least, we think so,' Chavez added, returning to the controls.

As the crawler's motors shuddered into life Dorthy turned from the monitor, looked out at the sombre landscape beyond the windscreen. The herd was a distant crawling line hazed by dust. Animals, she thought, seeing again the herders' cruel, crude butchery. Animals.

The path of the herd slowly bent towards the edge of the forested slopes. The vegetation became thicker: if not lush, at least less threadbare. Again and again the crawler bumped across dry streambeds. No dust obscured the herd now; the ground was increasingly marshy. Then there was a vast swath of green rushes, long stems bending in the wind. The critters hadn't eaten these, had simply trampled a path through them. The crawler followed. And then Ade, who was driving, cut the motors.

A dry lake bed stretched out, hectare upon hectare of ochre mud crazed into huge plates. Here and there boulder-strewn mounds rose from the dried mud like boats stranded by the tide. Close at hand to the north, low cliffs bordered the lake bed, cut by a wide canyon from whose mouth spread a fan of gravel; in the opposite direction the herd could be seen less than a kilometre away, gathered around one of the mounds.

Ade looked at them through field-glasses for a while, then announced, 'They've stopped. What do you all suggest?'

Chavez, gripping the back of her seat, looked out of the windscreen over his lover's shoulder. 'I think we need to rest,' he said. 'And I'd like to set more traps. Besides, we must think about turning back soon, to keep our rendezvous with Andrews.'

'I agree,' Kilczer said, behind Dorthy. 'I would like another chance to take readings. What of you, Dr Yoshida?'

'Whatever,' Dorthy said, feigning indifference because she knew that another attempt to probe the herders would only confirm what she already knew, that they were not intelligent enough to be the enemy.

So they made camp, choosing one of the rocky islands as a site in case the herd should break in their direction. The crawler was winched up the steep slope, Ade and Chavez doing most of the work, lithe and limber, coordinating their efforts with little more than looks. Chavez pulled off the top of his coveralls, and Dorthy guessed that if the twins had been alone Ade would have done the same. While Kilczer unpacked the bubbletent, Dorthy walked to the point of the little island, scrambled atop a huge boulder, and watched the herd through Ade's field-glasses. Beyond it was a distant white-flecked line of dust; presently this grew larger, and soon Dorthy could make out the individuals moving within it.

The others were unloading crates of equipment from the crawler. 'There's another herd coming,' Dorthy told them. 'Perhaps bigger than the one we've been following.'

Marta Ade snatched the field-glasses and jogged off towards the point. Dorthy and Chavez and Kilczer followed. 'It's a big herd,' she said, watching through the field-glasses. Her elbows stuck out like wings. 'Could be more than one group, though I've never seen that before.'

Kilczer asked, 'What will happen when it meets our group?'

Ade shrugged. 'I don't know. I had thought that each kept to discrete territories. Oh well, wrong again.' She handed the glasses to Chavez. 'Take a look. I must send my remotes out there.' Then she was off, running among boulders towards the canted crawler.

By the time the camp had been set up, the two herds had begun to mingle out on the lake bed. The new, larger herd of critters had three discrete groups of herders within it, Ade said, hunched over her monitor. Chavez had brought her half a dozen concentrate bars in lieu of a proper meal and she nibbled at one, the focus of the others' attention in the sparsely furnished dome as she gave up staccato comments and speculations.

Feeling confined, Dorthy went outside and stalked around the perimeter of the island, kicking at driftwood that marked the vanished waterline, climbed the boulder at the point again and stared across the cracked mud towards the mixing herds, no more than a distant blur of white. Feeling a deadly tiredness – she hadn't slept six hours in the last forty-eight – she clambered off the boulder and went back to the bubbletent to find out what was going on, whether she had to try out her Talent again.

'They are all setting up camp,' Ade told her. 'Four separate ones, each at a corner of a square with the island in its centre.' Over her shoulder Dorthy saw a dozen dark shapes sprawled around a flickering eye of orange flame, blurred by smoke. 'The herder groups keep separate,' Ade said, 'but their critters are all mixed up as if it didn't matter who owned what. It doesn't make sense. I haven't seen any interaction between the groups of herders at all.'

Kilczer, lounging in the embrace of an inflatable chair, said, 'Perhaps we go out now?'

Ade stretched hugely. 'I wouldn't advise it. Half the males are off hunting, and I don't see how you could hide from them out there. There's not a scrap of cover. But if you want to risk being eaten, go ahead.'

'When it is safe to observe, they do nothing,' Kilczer grumbled, 'and perhaps they do something now, and we cannot go near.'

'Life is tough,' Chavez said, slotting another slide into his microscope.

'I will wait and see if I get a chance,' Kilczer said.

'And I'm going to sleep,' Dorthy told him, and went out again.

The crawler hulked over its elongated shadow on a slope of sand, its metal flanks dully gleaming in the perpetual twilight. As she crossed to it, Dorthy felt frustration sink into the black pool of her exhaustion. She undogged the hatch in the crawler's sloping rear, crawled in and endured the sterilising blast, then opened the inner hatch and stepped past the motors and their archaic fuel cells. Red light poured through the wide windscreen. She found the switch that polarised the glass, then pulled off her boots in the glimmer of the checklights, tumbled on to a bunk.

She was awoken by the sense of Kilczer somewhere close, a moment later heard the inner hatch hum back. She pulled the bunched pillow closer, feigned sleep as he came in, bringing with him a sour whiff of sterilant. He didn't switch on any lights. She heard the rustle as he swung into the bunk opposite (so close she could have reached out and touched him), sensed his disappointment and frustration sullenly flickering within the shroud of his tiredness, a black tide flowing across her own mind.

Again she slept, and dreamed (or was it Kilczer's dream?) of a vast plain beneath a starless night sky hazed by frozen banners of luminous crimson, against which a great moon was rising, its full disc banded with blurred magentas. Shaking back folds of skin, she raised her head and howled long and high before moving on through the dense black-leaved bushes, their pungent coppery scent stinging her nostrils but not masking the salt trace of her prey, a twisting trail she followed at a loping run . . . And abruptly she was climbing a great ruined tower, a stair of broad steps winding widdershins between roughly dressed walls. Her claws rattled on old, cold stone. Behind, though she could not look back, something was climbing after her. Above was safety, but as she climbed the thing gained on her, its shadow thrown huge on the curved wall. Then she was somehow standing atop the tower, clutching wet stone and facing into a howling gale beneath a sullen sky in which a single star shone, a lonely fleck of light that suddenly flared brighter, a spark, a lamp, a searchlight that threw her shadow across the floor, mixing it with the shadow of the other. She turned just as the gale ripped loose the tower, and reeled as it reeled into the sky.

And awoke.

The crawler rocked back from a steep angle, its suspension groaning. Dorthy caught the side of the bunk as it tipped again. Something slammed into the windscreen. Glass cracked, then burst inward. Beyond the sagging frame, bristle-ringed segments scraped past. Cold air, the stench of aldehydes. Kilczer swung his legs over the side of his bunk just as the crawler lurched and he almost fell, catching himself on a pipe above Dorthy's bunk; in the same moment Dorthy lost her grip and her head banged hard against the hull behind her. For a moment her sight washed with black.

'Stay there,' Kilczer said hoarsely. 'I go out, find—'

And then the cables holding the crawler to the slope parted. The vehicle slipped sideways, its rear slamming against a huge boulder and splitting open. There was a roar as the casing of a fuel cell burst. Flames blossomed over the motors, the hatch.

Kilczer grabbed Dorthy's arm, helped her stand. 'I can walk,' she said, and bent to shove her feet into her boots before stumbling forward, broken glass grinding under each step. Kilczer used his elbow to smash out knifelike shards still stuck in the frame of the windscreen. Thick smoke rolled through the crawler's cabin, enveloping them. Outside, things were moving slowly past, humping over sand and rock. Kilczer lifted himself on to the dead console, reached around and pulled Dorthy after him; as they went through the broken windscreen she fell on top of him. Half a metre from her face, something huge dragged past, spraying sand.

Kilczer stood, pressing against the blunt nose of the crawler. Smoke crimped out of the windscreen above his head, black banners rippling up in the thin breeze. Dazed, Dorthy crouched at his feet, watching without comprehension as critters heaved past, their blind snouts weaving to and fro, some half-climbing their fellows before falling back.

'The tent! I do not see it!' Kilczer pounded the crawler's hull. 'By the beard—'

The crawler rocked again, slipping farther down the slope as three critters hit it simultaneously, trying to crawl over it with idiot persistence. Turning, one brushed Dorthy and she was knocked backward. Kilczer caught the collar of her coveralls; her knees suddenly unjointed, she held his arm gratefully. At her back, she felt the hull of the crawler growing warm; the critters were widening their path around it now, some slithering down the slope to join the tide of their fellows on the dry mud of the lake bed. Smoke slowly obscured the vast disc of the sun.

'We must go,' Kilczer said in her ear. 'When fire reaches intact fuel cells they blow all at once. Hold on to me now.' He hooked a hand under her arm and they staggered forward, narrowly missing a critter, stopping to let another heave past. Kilczer pulled and Dorthy drew in a breath, with the last of her strength ran forward through a gap, choking on cold air and the stench of the critters, gaining temporary shelter of a rocky outcrop. Kilczer clambered up, reached down and more or less lifted Dorthy, her coveralls snagging and tearing free. She pushed down with palms and heels, working up the tilted slab of rock on her buttocks until she reached the top. Below, the backs of the critters humped past. Beside her, Kilczer began to cough, his chest heaving. At last he managed to say, 'Still I think I sleep. Is there sign of the twins?'

Obediently, Dorthy lifted her head. Her sight washed red and she almost fell, felt Kilczer grab her wrist. 'I'm all right,' she said. But everything seemed disconnected.

'That was quite a knock you took. Concussion perhaps. Stay still now. Nothing we can do.'

'I was dreaming,' Dorthy said, as if it were an explanation for the chaos around them.

'You and your damned Talent,' Kilczer said. 'Can you use it to find the twins?'

But all Dorthy could sense was his helpless fear.

He pushed up on to hands and knees at the slab's ragged crest. 'Look at this around us,' he said angrily. 'How many critters are there?' Then, more subdued, 'The tent has gone. I see only critters.'

The critters were still passing their haven, ten minutes later, when the remaining fuel cells in the crawler blew, a series of sharp explosions that threw rolling plumes of fire into the jostling herd. The critters on the lake bed around the island continued to move forward as if nothing had happened; on the slope above, mutilated carcasses were slowly trampled into the sand as those behind pressed on.

'Now there are not so many,' Kilczer said. 'At least, I think not.'

Somewhere beneath the choppy surface of her confusion, Dorthy was beginning to be truly afraid. She wrapped her arms around herself, hunched in the dull, chill sunlight, watched the slow procession below. It was true: there were fewer critters now. After a while only one or two hitched past her perch: then at last only the trampled corpses remained, sprawled around the burned-out hulk of the crawler.

Kilczer told Dorthy to stay where she was and clambered down, vanished among the boulders. He was gone almost an hour. Dorthy shivered but otherwise did not move. The blow on her head had dulled her will. Time did not pass: it simply was.

Then Kilczer returned, scrambled up beside her. A rifle was slung over one shoulder; tied to his belt was a bag of torn orange fabric in which small shapes bulged. 'The twins,' Dorthy said. 'Did you find—'

'I found Ade; and buried her. No trace of Chavez, but if he got away, I am sure he would now look for Marta. The tent and all in it more or less gone, too. Not much food, no transmitter. How are you?'

Dorthy was thinking about her book. She had had it a long time and now it was gone, a loss that for some reason hit her harder than the deaths of the twins, made everything that had happened real at last. She said, 'I'll do my best. I can walk.'

'Walk where? Nowhere to go. We wait here, perhaps Chavez—'

'He's dead, Kilczer. Face it, we are alone here, stranded, and we can't stay. There's no water or food. We have to go up, do our best to find the lake, Andrews's camp.'

'Andrews may find us,' Kilczer said. But he did not believe it.

'You know he might look, but we'll probably not be found. We're more than a hundred kilometres from the rendevous point, and he doesn't know which direction we took.'

'No more talk.' Kilczer rubbed his pinched white face. 'You are right, unfortunately. Walk through the wilderness, well, I do not like it, but I suppose we must.'

*

The critters had left a broad trail across the dry, crazed mud, leading up the alluvial fan and on into the canyon that split the cliffs. Every so often as Dorthy and Kilczer climbed, they passed the corpse of a critter, white hide torn and trampled, blood a drying black jelly pooled around it on the sand.

'They are being pushed hard,' Kilczer said. 'See, they do not even eat plants, simply trample them.'

Dorthy said nothing. She still felt a strange remote clarity, but felt stronger than she had when perched on the rock, was no longer afraid but simply hungry and thirsty. During one of their frequent rests, she and Kilczer chewed a little of the emergency chocolate he'd rescued from the wrecked tent. The sweet bitterness left her thirstier but was reviving. Savouring the last crumbs, Dorthy squatted on her haunches and sifted a handful of sand through her fingers. Grains clung to her skin. Mica flecks. Quartz. Realisation of the enormity of their isolation was slowly settling around her, like a cold cloak. For all her brave talk it seemed impossible that they could climb up to the camp beside the lake, live off the land without succumbing to allergic reaction and histamine shock or simply dying of exhaustion and exposure . . . yet Camp Zero was five hundred klicks away across empty desert. There was no other way.

Kilczer sprawled a little way off. One outflung hand rested on the stock of the rifle; with the other he scratched at his swept-back hair, looking off at the low cliffs, nervous, on edge. Sand caked his uniform coveralls down the small of his back.

Dorthy said, 'I'm rested now. Let's get on.'

He stood slowly, then bent over and coughed into his fist, afterwards spat on to the ground. 'I could drink much water, if we had it.'

Dorthy licked her cracked lips. 'Marta Ade said something about water underneath a dried-up riverbed like this one.'

'That was different place. Besides, how do we get at it?'

'We dig with our hands. Come on, it's worth trying.'

She knelt and began to scoop away handfuls of sand and pebbles, and after a moment Kilczer joined her. They dug for fifteen minutes, Kilczer in the end using a knife to loosen the freezing subsoil, Dorthy scooping it out. The pit grew, a metre deep, twice as wide. There was moisture, but not enough to collect. Dorthy sat back, sucking at a torn fingernail.

'No damned good,' Kilczer said in frustration.

She said, 'There's an old trick I remember reading about. There are plants over there in the lee of the cliff that the critters missed trampling, see them? They must tap into this.'

'To be sure. But the chance of allergic reaction . . .' He brushed his hands on his thighs, switched off the knife and put it away.

'But what are we going to eat? Sooner or later we'll have to try them. Anyway, didn't one of the – didn't Marta Ade say that the plants were edible?'

'Weird proteins, high metal concentrations. But I suppose we die anyway if we do not eat.'

'That's the spirit.'

Dorthy uprooted a handful of soft succulent. Dark juice oozed over her fingers, but when she made to lick it off Kilczer caught her wrist. 'Wait. Use this.' He wrapped a scrap of orange cloth around the broken stems, squeezed. Clear liquid blebbed the weave; Dorthy bent and sucked. The moisture sank into the parched cavern of her mouth, bitter but welcome. When no more would come she handed the cloth to Kilczer, who tried with a fresh handful. 'Not too much now,' he said. 'Just in case. Come on, we go. When we are tired we stop. How are you, Dr Yoshida?' He squinted into her face. 'Your pupils are both the same size, so no concussion, I think.'

Gingerly Dorthy touched the pulpy skin at the back of her head. 'I'll be all right. Come on, let's go before we stiffen up.'

Walking became an automatic process. After a while Dorthy could only concentrate on the next step, on placing her boot in the waffle print Kilczer had left moments before. They rested more and more frequently, each time sucking a few drops of moisture from a plant stem, no longer thinking of the possible reaction their immune systems might raise to the alien proteins, aware only of their unslaked thirst.

The canyon narrowed, its walls growing higher. Still they followed the trail left by the critter herd. No more bodies now; Kilczer said that the weakest must have been weeded out. As Dorthy followed him she felt a dizzy sense of expansion, glimpses of Kilczer's thoughts like oxen plodding around and around a water lift. The forest-ringed lake with the mountains rising beyond; the nightmare parade of critters; Ade's smashed body, her face receiving a handful of dirt; the lake again; a dim glimpse of a naked woman turning towards him in a shadowy room. She accepted these images as a page accepts ink, too tired to think about them. Her legs ached to the bone now, and if Kilczer had suggested they stop she would have fallen on the spot. But he plodded on grimly, in more pain than she, and she shared his grim resolve, too muddled to be able to realise that it was not her own.

And there was something else.

It was weak at first, scarcely distinguishable from Kilczer's fragmented thoughts, but growing clearer with each step. Watchfulness, a hesitant fear, skittish, fading and returning, but each time returning more strongly.

And then an image, two strange spindly things creeping forward, their distorted shapes radiating menace, danger. Dorthy stopped, and after a moment Kilczer turned to her.

'There's something watching us,' she said.

He unslung the rifle and looked about cautiously. 'Your Talent is working? Where is it?'

'Somewhere up ahead, high, looking down on us. No, wait.' She whirled just as the creature bounded from shadow at the top of a gravel slope, starting a small avalanche as it crabbed down on all fours. Dorthy and Kilczer stepped back and it reared on its hind legs, its arms extended as if in desperate entreaty. A middle pair of vestigial limbs were clasped across the swag of its black-furred belly. Its hood of skin flared around its narrow face; beneath the snout, black lips wrinkled back from ridges of sharp-edged horn.

For a moment Dorthy was overwhelmed. Then sand spat up metres to the left of the herder, which gyred and sinuously ran, on all fours again, twisting around humped boulders as a second shot blew fragments of stone. Gone. Dorthy came to herself just as Kilczer caught her arm.

'I'm sorry, I missed,' he said. He meant it. Drops of sweat stood on his white forehead. 'It will do no good going after it, the way it ran.'

'A herder.'

'To be sure.'

86

His dissonant thoughts frustrated her attempt to locate the creature. She said, 'I don't think it meant to harm us. It was trying to protect something.'

Kilczer said halfheartedly, 'I suppose we could look around up there.'

They did not have to search very hard. Above the scree slope, the cliff was split by a high crevice, and wedged deep within it was a blunt-ended shape encased in something like dried leather. Ridged and wrinkled, it was a good metre taller than Kilczer. Dorthy sensed nothing in this enigmatic form, not even the simple knowledge of self that all but the most primitive of terrestrial animals possessed. It might just as well have been a seedpod or a suitcase.

'I will be damned,' Kilczer said, pushing back lank hair. 'I swear this.'

'You know what it is?'

'I make a guess. What is Portuguese for the transitional form between larval and adult form of an insect?'

'A chrysalis. Or a pupa.'

'On Novaya Rosya we have bees, you understand? I have the beginning of a glimmering, Dr Yoshida, of what this is about.'

'I'm not going to read your mind to find out. Look, that herder might be coming back. Oughtn't we to leave this?'

'I just want to see . . .' Kilczer took out his knife, pressed the stud. The bright blade hummed. As he reached forward, the tall shape chittered; Kilczer calmly withdrew the knife, moved it forward again. When the blade touched the thing's skin, the pod jerked and twisted forward, the chittering suddenly loud in the confined space. Kilczer knocked into Dorthy as both fled, tumbling and sliding down the scree in loose falls of grit and sand. Kilczer fetched up against a boulder, coughing weakly. Dorthy picked herself up gingerly, flexing each of her joints in turn. But nothing was broken.

'*Yoi-dore kega sezu*,' she said. 'Drunkards break no bones.' After a moment she began to laugh. 'It couldn't have hurt us. We're crazy . . .'

Kilczer grinned and began to slap dust from his coveralls. 'A defensive reaction, of course. Well, I think we leave it. I have a feeling we will find more.' He shouldered the rifle, turned to look up the canyon. 'Come on, Dr Yoshida. We had best get away from here, I think. That nursemaid may come back soon, and I am not so good a shot with this rifle.'

'It's a reaction rifle, and you're handling it as if it were a laser. Allow for windage, and don't hold, it so tightly. Squeeze the trigger when you fire, don't jerk it.'

'You have used one of these?'

She'd once gone on a hunting expedition in the Philippines Preserve as part of her job, nursemaid to a wealthy neurotic, when she'd been whoring her Talent. She said, 'Maybe you should let me have it. I might have a chance of hitting something, at least.'

'In all this wilderness I feel better if I carry it. I promise to take your advice.'

As they walked on, Dorthy felt a little more alert, residue of the adrenalin surge from her panicked flight. She tried and failed to detect the herder that had surprised them, then asked Kilczer, 'Are you going to tell me what you suspect? Do you think that that thing was the chrysalis of a critter?'

'Ah, that indeed is the question.'

'And what does it turn into?' Then she understood. 'A herder? But that's crazy! The herders *eat* critters!'

'As that mythological character, Medea, who ate her children. But the herders have so many of them. You might call it a kind of population control. It would explain why there were no immature forms of herder to be found. Rather, why we did not recognise them for what they were. Just wait until I tell Andrews and McCarthy about this!'

'We have to get back first.'

'That is what we do,' Kilczer said, 'through all this damned wilderness.'

'I would have thought you'd be appreciating it; as a biologist, that is.'

'I am specialist in nervous system activity, with original training as a medical technician. I pick up some biology when I am on Earth, but I am no xenoecologist. On Novaya Rosya all sensible people stay in cities and farm domes, only rogues and insane persons such as zithsa hunters roam outside. I came out to this place because it is necessity, as no one was willing to bring a herder to Camp Zero. But had I known I would be walking through it, I would have thought again.'

'I wish I had the choice,' Dorthy said.

They went on, following the trampled trail left by the herd of critters up the gentle winding slope between high rock walls. The sun peeped huge and swollen above the canyon's rim, its apparent immobility mocking the passage of time. At last Kilczer slowly and carefully laid down the rifle and sat on a water-smoothed stone. Dorthy more or less collapsed beside him, lying for a long time without thinking, simply breathing hard and feeling blood throb in her feet. Blistered, she was sure. The light boots she wore were not made for hiking.

After a while Kilczer got to his feet and cast around, pausing now and then to cough drily. Dorthy sat and watched him as he wandered a ways up the canyon, wandered back.

'I think the herders and their children leave this road, went up the slope there.' He gestured at a steep shelf of rock that slanted to the rim of the canyon. Above it could be seen a dark line of trees; they looked like pines.

Dorthy worked off her boots, wincing as she pulled them over her swollen ankles. 'How far do you think we've gone?'

'At most I say fifteen klicks. How do you feel?'

'I don't think I have a concussion. I've certainly worked up a good set of blisters, though.' She looked at her timetab; it was over twelve hours since the herd of critters had smashed through the camp, twelve hours since Ade and Chavez had been killed.

Kilczer, still standing, tapped his fingers impatiently against his thigh. 'I suppose we can stop here for a time.'

'We have to pace ourselves, or we'll peg out like those critters we passed farther down. Have you any idea when the herd might stop?'

'Perhaps not until it reaches the keep. I suppose we follow their trail, the herders must know where to go. Well now, you wait here, I will take a look at the top of the slope there. Here, take this.'

He tossed her the knife and turned away before she could protest at his transparent, foolish bravado. Beneath it, she knew, he was deeply fearful of the strange wilderness into which he had been thrown; like a shipwrecked mariner, he clung tightly to the flotsam and jetsam of civilisation that had washed up with him, the rifle and orange bag of oddments. Dorthy could have told him that now it was better to rest, and that anyway she knew more about survival than he did, but she was too tired. She watched him climb the long slope; he moved very slowly, and twice stopped, in the even red light a small black figure splayed against the smooth rock. When at last he disappeared over the edge, Dorthy hobbled over to an untrampled cluster of plants and strained juice from their stems; not even a full mouthful. Afterward she prodded her lips with her forefinger, gingerly traced the hot swollen skin there. A reaction, probably. Well, it had to come sooner or later. She was too tired to be anything but resigned to whatever happened, and she sprawled on the sand and waited for Kilczer's return. But he was gone a long time. Two alternate fantasies vied in her head: that he'd run into a maverick herder and was lying wounded and helpless, perhaps even dead; or that he'd run off, left her because he thought her a liability. After half an hour of this her panic was quite real, and when at last she saw him begin to crab his way down, his arms full of something, relief and happiness flooded her. Here, at least, being alone was unbearable.

Part of Kilczer's load was a bundle of dry fragrant branches with brittle brown ruffs of needles that he had gathered in the forest above the canyon. He and Dorthy broke these up and built a fire, which he ignited with a catalighter fished from his sack of booty. The branches burned with fitful yellow flame, a cheerful homely bubble sunk in the well of sombre alien light. Kilczer set a flat stone in the centre of the fire and turned to the other thing he'd brought.

Long-bodied, blunt-headed, covered in fine, lapping scales that shimmered in the firelight, it was a little like a cross between an armadillo and a rabbit. Dorthy wondered if it was a relative of the subterranean scavengers they'd seen out on the plain. Certainly the blunt claws on its powerful forelimbs were adapted for digging, and it lacked eyes, long fine vibrissae springing instead from above its snout.

'I pull easily on the trigger as you said,' Kilczer told her a little boastfully. 'Two shots.' He took back the knife and set to butchering his kill.

Dorthy was slow to realise what he intended to do with it. 'You're going to eat that?'

'I try it. We cannot live on sap.' He stripped back the hide with an abrupt motion, connective tissue tearing wetly. Bending over the flayed corpse, he began to slice away the thick muscle bunched over the shoulders, laying slivers on the hot stone. As he worked, he told Dorthy, 'It probably is not poisonous for us. I think I remember it from Chavez's catalogue, something from Serenity. The biosphere there is compatible with Earth's. No nasty glucosides or cyanogen complexes such as Novaya Rosya animals have. Similar amino acid composition, energy-storing molecules very like ATP and NADPH, complex sugar acids on a phosphate backbone to carry the genetic information. This beast has only four limbs; creatures with six, like the herders, have high heavy-metal concentrations in their tissues, use a copper-binding protein in their blood to carry oxygen instead of an iron-binding one as we and this animal use. Blue blood, not red.'

But in the red light of the sun, the blood on his hands was black.

'I thought no one has ever killed one of the herders. How do you know all this?'

Kilczer laid more slivers on the stone within the fire. The first were beginning to sizzle and curl; he flipped them over. 'Creatures like the herders, I said. Chavez had catalogued perhaps a dozen such, all small. That was why he laid the traps. And you forget the critter Andrews brought back to Camp Zero.' He reached forward and with the point of his knife lifted a sizzling slice; droplets of grease burned orange as they spattered. 'Wish me luck,' he said, and took it into his mouth, made a face.

'How is it?'

His jaw staggered. 'Tough,' he said, chewing. 'But not so bad. Like a muddy sort of pork, perhaps. You do not eat if you wish not. In fact, it might be best, in case there are side effects.'

But the smell had reached Dorthy; her empty stomach clenched. She burned her fingers getting a sliver of meat off the stone, burned her lips as she ate it, but the greasy fibres brought saliva flooding from beneath her tongue, began to silence the clamour of her starved cells. Kilczer allowed half a dozen small slices each. 'Any more and we risk an instant reaction, if one is coming; we lose all the goodness we have eaten.'

A silence fell between them. Eventually, Kilczer took out a

holocube and watched its two-minute cycle over and over with yearning hopeless nostalgia as the young woman smiled and whispered hoarse Russian endearments. Dorthy had no such comfort; that book was lost. *The world will wail thee, like a makeless wife.* Exhausted, she lay down on the hard ground and fell into a fitful strung-out doze.

She awoke when something cool and small touched her cheek. Another splashed her forehead; a third hit her eye and made her blink. Raindrops. For a while she lay with her mouth open, letting random drops soothe her lips. The embers around the flat stone hissed and smoked; after a while Kilczer sat up, cursing.

It was raining heavily now.

They picked up their scattered possessions and found partial shelter under a low overhang. Dorthy's feet had swollen, and she had to slit the sides of her boot to get them on. Rain sheeted down steadily beyond the lip of the overhang; water dripped down Dorthy's neck.

'First we nearly die of thirst; now we drown,' Kilczer grumbled. 'Where is this rain from?'

Dorthy was trying to remember something. Something about desert washes and rain. Flash floods. She tugged at Kilczer. 'We have to climb,' she said. 'Come on.'

He pulled back, hunching his shoulders. 'You are crazy. Wait until this stops.'

'We're in a riverbed, you idiot!' Dorthy shouted. Surprise widened on his face, and then he understood.

The slope of bare rock ran with rippling sheets of water; time and again Dorthy's thin-soled boots slipped and she had to throw herself forward to stop herself sliding back. Her breasts and hips and knees were bruised, her coveralls sodden. Kilczer, laden by the rifle strapped sideways on his back and the orange sack at his hip, climbed no faster. They were less than halfway up when Dorthy heard an ominous rumble. The rock beneath her fingertips vibrated and she clung tighter, turning her head against cold slick hardness. Raindrops rolled her eyelashes, bejewelled her vision. The vibration was a roar now, so loud that she was unsure if she was hearing it or feeling it with the length of her body. Then a wall of water surged around the bend in the canyon, metres high, one side purling in white foam as it struck the wall (and rocks crumbling into the deluge threw up their own cascades of foam), dropping lower as the other smooth crest came on, forever falling at its feet, a great grinding torrent of tawny water.

All this in an instant. The next, Dorthy was clinging by her hands as her legs, awash to the knees in spume, were knocked loose. Kilczer, a little higher, reached down and grabbed the neck of her coveralls as the current pulled at her. With all her strength, she pushed up, pain shooting through her arms, kicked away from the water, now only the roiled surface of a deep, strongly running river.

When they reached the top of the slope, Dorthy collapsed forward on matted vegetation, uncaring as rain hammered her slicked hair, her soaked coveralls. Curtains of rain blew across the open ground; beyond, trees bent before the wind. The sun was a vast smear in low black cloud.

Kilczer bent and lifted her, and together they staggered forward, feet sinking to the ankles in flooded tendrils, gained the shelter of the trees. The dense canopy more or less screened out the rain, but trickles still found their way through, pattering on the sodden carpet of needles, running down the smooth-barked trunks, rebounding from the humped roots over which Kilczer and Dorthy kept tripping in the near darkness. After the third fall Kilczer simply lay there, and began to laugh. Dorthy sat on a wet tree root, wiped her face. 'What's so funny?'

'If I knew no better, I think someone is really out to get me.' His laughter became a choked cough. She heard him draw a rattling breath, spit. 'This is crazy. A crazy thing.'

Dorthy leaned back against the tree trunk. Water trickled down the back of her neck, but she was so wet that it didn't matter. 'They knew,' she said, after a moment's silence.

'Who?'

'The herders. They turned their . . . their children out of the canyon in time, and that chrysalis was lodged high up – the flood won't touch it.'

Kilczer coughed. 'This is teleology. Instinct, coincidence. That is all. Not intelligence. You get your Talent working properly, you prove it, then I believe. But truly I think the herders did not build this ecology, they are simply part of it. My readings showed this. Not intelligent, or perhaps a little more than an unmodified chimpanzee. Andrews was wrong. They are not the enemy. They are not even the barbarian descendants of the enemy.'

'I don't know if they are or aren't, not yet. But there was something—'

'Ah, yes. You feel it, I know. Your wonderful Talent, so much better than my machines.'

'It isn't magic!'

'Dr Yoshida, you must understand—'

She was gripping the smooth tree root with both hands, she realised, and let go. Her palms tingled. She was very tired. 'It isn't magic,' she repeated.

'We should rest,' Kilczer said, as if he hadn't heard her; and what with the soughing of the wind in the branches above and the sounds of water seeking by many ways the common lowest level, perhaps he had not. After a while he added, almost shyly, 'It is very damned cold. Perhaps we should share our warmth?'

Dorthy hugged herself. 'I'm all right. Please, let's just rest a while.'

But for a long time, cold and afraid, she could not find sleep. Again and again the events of the long day passed through her mind, the knife-edge by which she had survived. She nodded and immediately awoke, opening her eyes to near darkness, dim shapes of trees receding into shadow all around. Kilczer was huddled nearby. She remembered the glimpse she had had of the herder in the forest beside the lake, felt the depth of silence at her back. There was nothing there, she told herself, nothing but the sounds of the rain. And it was the lulling sound of rain, persistent and as innocent of meaning as white noise, familiar despite the infrequency with which she had heard it during her strange childhood, that at last loosened her grip on her buoyant fear, let her sink into sleep.

It was still raining when Dorthy awoke; or at least, water was still finding its way beneath the canopy of branches, pattering on to the deep carpet of dead needles. But it was lighter, and she could read the black numerals in the skin of her wrist: 0743 of some irrelevant morning in Greater Brazil . . . perhaps halfway to noon here.

Kilczer slumped against a loop of root a metre away, his face hidden by the fallen shadow of his long hair. His breath sawed raggedly in his open mouth.

Dorthy shivered, crossing her arms over her breasts and rubbing the wet cloth of her coveralls over the ladder of her ribs, then stretched to relieve the cricks in her back, yawned. A tightness around her mouth tugged, then broke; bitter fluid spilled from her lips and she spat, rubbed at raw skin where blisters had burst. She found a still pool cupped in the hollow where a root bent, and drank. Water was no problem now. But, when she was done drinking, she realised that she was hungry.

She relieved herself some distance away, quickly and nervously, then went back to Kilczer and without thinking woke him the way her mother had always woken her, stroking the skin behind the ear. He stirred, caught her hand, and drew her down so that her face was centimetres from his. 'So it is real,' he said, and let go.

Dorthy drew back, shaken. Kilczer got to his feet, moving slowly, rubbed his tangled hair with the knuckles of both hands. 'Can you walk?' he asked. 'My legs have turned to stone, I think.'

Her blistered feet were numb inside her boots, but otherwise she felt all right. Those early mornings, running along the ridge of the crater beyond Camp Zero. She said, 'You'll find that will wear off once you've been walking a while. You pushed us hard yesterday.'

'I am eager to get back to civilisation.' He picked up the rifle, the orange sack of oddments. 'You look as bad as I feel,' he said. 'Come on.'

They stumbled out of the forest, and Dorthy saw what she had missed in the darkness of the rainstorm: a smashed track that scarred the broad margin between the edge of the canyon and the eaves of the forest, scored down to bedrock in the middle, merely muddy at the margins. It was still raining, but the rain was no more than a thickened mist drifting through the air. High above, a deck of tattered black cloud pulled apart to reveal an airy chasm filled with the coal-red fire of the sun. Kilczer crossed the track left by the herd to look down into the canyon, and Dorthy followed. Black water ran quickly between the rock walls. No path there.

As they tramped beside the track, Kilczer asked, 'What did you mean, about magic? About your Talent?'

'What do you know about the way my Talent works?'

Kilczer was carrying the rifle on his shoulder, one arm hooked over it. He looked over the arm. 'Do you want me to tell about the quantum correspondence effect, or how you translate synapse firings generated by it into your own sensorium? Or perhaps I tell you about the limitations, for instance your inability to access long-term RNA memory. My machine at least detects the amount in storage, and the location. I could talk an hour on each.'

'I'm sure that you can.'

'So you see I know it is not magic.'

'But you *behave* as if it was, don't you see? As if it is a magical gift that I have, a gift that you lack. Perhaps it wasn't conscious, but I know that you expected me to instantly find out all about the herders, just by squinting my eyes a little and concentrating. Duncan Andrews felt the same way, and he should have known better, too. The problem is that those creatures are like nothing I've encountered before. I don't know whether or not they're intelligent; I don't even know how to begin to make sense of them. If I found nothing at the first attempt, it doesn't mean that there isn't something there.'

'Perhaps. But you see no blazing light of intelligence in the herders as you described you have seen twice now. Reading them did not knock you out.'

'No, it didn't.'

'So,' Kilczer said, 'perhaps that is a different thing, something we have yet to find, something that is nothing to do with the herders. Perhaps it and not they are the enemy.'

After four paces, Dorthy said, 'You really think that there's a hidden civilisation here?'

'Have you not already discovered something suggesting it? Look around you. Think of the technology in the asteroids around BD twenty. They have spaceships, all crazy kinds. Habitats, weapons. This is classified, but it will not matter if you know it: the enemy has a way of creating a self-sustaining plasma ball. Travels fast, a quarter the speed of light. That is what takes out so many of our ships, down in the gravity well of BD twenty. But here, in this hold? At best this is some kind of park, abandoned, the owners dead or elsewhere. At worst, it is the ruins of something grander, as Duncan Andrews believes. I do not. Think, Dr Yoshida. If those herders are the enemy but have degenerated, why has the keep awakened as it has? Major Ramaro is right. The enemy *is* here, somewhere.'

'I don't know.' Dorthy walked a little more. 'Why are you so fired up by this anyway?'

'For the opportunity to discover, not for the hiking, that is certain. It is a great honour, to be asked to join this expedition, although I know you do not think so.'

'But you wanted to come, all you scientists did. For all you grumble about the Navy's restrictions, you all want to be here.'

'Nervous-system tracing is my life work, Dr Yoshida. I can do it with humans, but many do that; or with animals, but there are only a number of simple themes to describe. I spent six months on Elysium, studying the aborigines – that until now was the highlight of my career. So when I am asked of course I come here. Nowhere else can I study intelligent aliens – when we find them.'

'And so of course you have to believe that they exist.'

'And you hope all there is, is the herders, so you go home quickly.' But he said this with good humour, without rancour. Whatever he was thinking was now completely opaque to Dorthy. Her Talent was biding its time. Perhaps the intermittent seizures had passed: she hoped so.

They walked for an hour without speaking, the constant rain filtering out of the air uncomfortable only when wind blew it across the canyon into their faces. Sometimes the clouds opened enough to glimpse the rising uplands of forest that they had still to climb. Five days, six days to reach the lakeside camp?

Then the canyon bent away sharply, and the track they were following became a path smashed through the forest, trees ripped out of the ground, broken foliage half buried in the mud churned from the needle-covered ground. When the land opened out again it was on to a long, rising meadow of the tendrilled groundcover that had carpeted the shore of the lake. The herd had widened its path here, trampling a great swath through the violet vegetation. And not far from the edge of the forest were the remains of a great fire.

The charred circle still smoked here and there, where patches of glowing charcoal clung to the undersides of great boles that had been roughly heaped together. Kilczer kicked a smaller log over and it rekindled. Blue fire sizzled in the misty drifting rain.

Kilczer held his hands out over the flames. 'Those herders are strong, all right. We would need a small truck to haul trees this size out of the forest.'

Dorthy felt warmth rise up, caress her wet face. At her back, a breeze beat the sodden cloth of her coveralls. 'How do they light fires, anyway?'

'They carry sparks around, smouldering stuff wrapped in clay. That is what Ade told me.' He was looking at the meadow and the forest that bordered it, the land rising ahead, vanishing into cloud. 'Cannot have been more than a few hours ahead of us when they left here.'

'What would you do if you caught up with them?'

'We, Dr Yoshida. Why do you always talk as if you are not here? You wipe yourself from existence.'

Dorthy, remembering her mother, said nothing.

Kilczer clapped his hands together, began to poke around in the ashes. On the far side of the fire he picked up a long bone: a lump of meat surrounded the strange, pronged joint, blackly sticky with ashes, which Kilczer brushed away before he shoved the end into the fire. Fat sizzled. Yellow sparks danced through the blue flame.

Dorthy didn't like to think about where the meat had come from, but ate gladly enough, her jaw staggering on crisp fat. Kilczer pulled up a twining length of groundcover, tasted it, spat it out. 'Pah. I think we must be carnivores, like the herders. Next time we rest, I go hunting again.'

'I wish you'd let me take the rifle. I really am a fair shot.'

Kilczer said nothing for almost a minute. Then he pushed back long, wet hair and muttered, 'I wish this rain would stop,' and started to poke around the charcoaled circle once more while Dorthy squatted by the fire watching the scraped bone burn. Once Kilczer said something in Russian, then was quiet, picking over the ashes. After a while he came back, dropped the things he'd found in front of her. One was a metal shard, another a half-melted plastic beaker. A fragment of muddied orange cloth. A length of braided wire.

Kilczer kicked at the burning log until sparks flew higher than his head. 'I wondered why there was so little left,' he said. 'Why is it they carry our stuff with them, you think?'

Dorthy didn't point out the obvious conclusion, that he was

wrong about the herders. Instead, she suggested, 'Shall we start again? I'm more or less dry now.'

Kilczer picked up the wire as if to keep it. But, after scowling at it, he dropped it into the flames and turned away. 'Come on,' he said roughly, and started without waiting for her.

They had been walking for two hours or so, the open ground steeper now and studded with boulders and stands of tall woody ferns, when Dorthy was hit by stomach cramps. She crouched with Kilczer holding back her hair, bringing up half-digested lumps of meat, then thin bile, and finally nothing but strings of clear sticky chyme. Her stomach clenched wetly on emptiness; she felt a dismal humiliation. When at last she could stand, red light beat in her eyes, mixing with the dizziness mounting in her head. The vast sun had been revealed by a widening rift in the black clouds. A few hundred metres on, weaker spasms hit her, but now there was nothing at all to come up. She sat on the ground as everything tilted around her, leaned her head against a boulder, concentrating on nothing but her breathing and the cold gritty contact of stone against her brow and cheek and jaw. All around, the silence of the alien land.

Kilczer sat on soggy groundcover a little way from her, his face a dirty white. 'It was a chance,' he said, 'eating that stuff.'

Presently he managed to stagger off into the ragged margin of the forest, and returned dragging several long, broken branches. He cut away secondary spurs with his knife and flensed wet bark from the dead, dry wood inside, a crumbling punk that he laid in a nest of brown fern fronds before applying the catalighter. Fronds crackled, crumbling as they were quickly consumed; then wood caught, sending up thin resinous smoke. Dorthy collapsed beside it, grateful for the heat that shook into the air before her face.

'We rest,' Kilczer said. 'Is not a bad fire, considering.'

'I'm not going anywhere,' Dorthy said, and for a moment managed a smile.

The fire was their focal point in the next two days. Whoever was stronger would stagger off and search out fallen branches and dead ferns, carefully arranging this fuel around the hearth to dry before use. The fire's bright light was as welcome as its heat, and it came to seem to Dorthy that if it died so did all hope of survival. Both she

99

and Kilczer developed itchy rashes, diarrhoea, shivering fits, boils: the reaction of their bodies to the alien molecules of the meat. The rain over, the sun again dominated a dark unclouded sky. Kilczer's racking cough returned as the air grew drier, but otherwise, perhaps because he had already lived for long periods on other worlds, he wasn't as badly affected as Dorthy.

To pass the time he told her something of those worlds: Elysium, Serenity, Novaya Zyemlya, of the expedition to the binary white dwarf system of Stein 2051, in the days when he'd been more medical technician than scientist, before the Guild had allowed him to develop his interest in neurobiology. And he told her about Novaya Rosya, a world once Earth-like, which half a million years ago had suffered a massive cosmic bombardment that had destroyed all but one per cent of its biosphere. Now only the poles were habitable. The rest of the surface was covered in a water and hydrocarbon mixture, a steamy soup at perihelion of the planet's eccentric orbit, covered with waxy floes at aphelion. Kilczer recounted secondhand tales of the hunting parties that tracked zithsas in their continual migrations, spoke with nostalgic longing of his home in the domed city of Esnovagrad, and of his partner. He showed Dorthy the little holocube whose loop she'd seen him watch over and over since the disaster: a surprisingly young woman, as young as Dorthy, at least fifteen years younger than Kilczer.

'We make contract only two years ago,' Kilczer said. 'Before that I was too much on the move. After I settle to my work on Novaya Rosya we will be able to have a child, I will be important then. You may know, there is a large research centre in Esnovagrad, almost as big as the Kamali-Silver Institute, where I help develop the machines.'

'You worked at Kamali-Silver?' Dorthy wondered if he'd been there when she had.

But he hadn't.

Kilczer did not ask much about Dorthy's life, and for that she was grateful, fobbing off his few questions with the near-truthful repertoire she had long ago developed. His curiosity was only phatic anyway. He was more interested in talking about her Talent, something Dorthy didn't mind so much – she had become used to describing its every nuance at the Institute.

As the pools that had collected here and there in the forest dried up, Dorthy and Kilczer had to resort to straining plant sap through cloth to obtain moisture. Dorthy's lips blistered afresh. Between fits of delirium, she sat as close to the fire as she could, shivering and wondering vaguely if the illness would damage her implant, perhaps even kill it, allowing her Talent to flower to full and final glory.

It didn't.

Once she awoke to find Kilczer gone, the fire died back. She piled handfuls of needles and dried fern fronds on to the warm ashes, managed to kindle weak flames that she carefully fed small bits of wood. The fire was life, the light of life countering the sullen red of the sun's huge disc – close to noon now. It was warmer, although Dorthy in her sickness didn't recognise it. She huddled beside the fire, feeding it and fighting to stay awake. To sleep was to risk losing it. Of course, Kilczer could easily rekindle it with his catalighter . . . but suppose he didn't return?

He came back hours later, the carcass of a brown-pelted animal held over his shoulder by its paddle-like tail. He walked slowly, head down, his face gaunt under a thin beard and long matted hair, white skin blotched by raised weals. He sat on the other side of the fire for a long time before telling Dorthy where he'd been: as far as the end of the long ride through the forest, to a large pool that fed the river in the canyon. That was where he had shot the creature, which he proposed to eat.

'A little, at least. This is four-legged, maybe from Earth or Ruby or Serenity if I am lucky. You recognise it? No? Well, I eat it anyway, and see what happens. Before you try it we must be sure it is all right.'

Dorthy had gone beyond hunger, simply shrugged and looked away as Kilczer went about the unpleasant rigmarole of butchering the carcass. He skinned a leg and skewered it on a fire-hardened stick, broiled it over the glowing wood in the centre of the fire. He ate only a few mouthfuls, then promptly fell asleep. Despite her best intentions, so did Dorthy.

She woke to the smell of cooking meat. Kilczer was hunched over the fire, licking his fingers. Dorthy rolled over and crawled forward, and he handed her a hot, greasy sliver.

When they had eaten as much as they could, they left the fire to smoulder to death and set off again. The track of the passing herd was almost obscured by new growth, a path of a lighter shade of violet woven into the luxuriant carpet.

They reached the pool after three hours, almost midnight by Earth time – but Dorthy had lost all sense of time to sickness and the constancy of the soft red light. She knelt at the mossy shore and scooped up water and drank, then rubbed her face, her matted hair.

Kilczer had finished drinking a while ago. He sat on a boulder, looking at the far end of the pool where water poured down in white foam from a narrow neck between high rock walls. Growths like indigo geodesic domes, some taller than Dorthy, studded the swerve of the shore, and stands of reedy plants, with flowering structures of filmy white spiralling a dozen metres into the air, waved like banners in the cool breeze. The carpet of moss on which Dorthy knelt was a red as dark as dried blood, stippled with nodes of faint luminescence like reflections of the day-stars in the dark sky; the water of the pool was clear all the way down to the clean sand bottom. It was a place of sombre alien beauty and Dorthy sat back, enjoying it.

At last Kilczer said, 'We'll rest another day, but we must go on. If we follow the canyon I think it leads to the lake where the camp is. You think maybe the herd has reached it yet? You do not see, but they took a path off through the forest behind you.' He kicked at the side of the boulder on which he sat, as if it were a recalcitrant mount. 'Andrews must have forgotten we exist, I think, busy up there in the keep.'

Dorthy pushed wet hair from her eyes.

'Tomorrow we try to cover ten klicks at least. Are you able to do that? We have a long way to go yet before we are out of this damnable wilderness. I hope to hell they have not moved the camp, or we have to climb all the way up the rimwall mountains. I mean, I come to find out things here, but this is taking things too far!'

'Tomorrow,' Dorthy said, hoping to appease his restlessness.

'Tomorrow and tomorrow and tomorrow, as your favourite writer has it. Whenever tomorrow is. Look, I will hunt something for us to eat, perhaps another of those flat-tails. You wait there?'

'I'll come with you. Really, I think I'm better,' she said, and was rewarded with his smile. Never since the time she had crouched in the Australian bush with her sister while their father and his cronies had searched for them had she felt so close to someone.

The canyon, narrow and deep, meandered through the rising forest, the river at its bottom thrashing white water over boulders. As Dorthy and Kilczer climbed beside its edge, little streams from sources higher in the rocky, wooded slopes crossed their path and fell in brief arcs before being torn to pieces by the wind. Once they saw a flock of black shapes floating high on the updrafts in the canyon, double-vaned wings metres wide; once some great beast crashed away from them deeper into the dark forest. Dorthy glimpsed a long hairy flank disappearing into shadow among the pines; it must have been at least as big as the crawler. But for the most part the forest was deserted, as if they really had strayed into some carefully tended park. The few animals they saw were small and quite unafraid. Kilczer shot at everything with a tyro's enthusiasm, even at six-legged creatures, which if he killed he threw over the canyon's edge. 'Target practice,' he would explain, and Dorthy, knowing that the azide tape in the rifle held perhaps a thousand shots, a large number to be sure but still finite, in the interests of peace said nothing. After all, the lakeside camp couldn't be many days away now. Still, after each meal she saved as much excess meat as possible by drying thin strips on a heated stone; they chewed the resulting jerky as they walked.

It took six days to reach the site of the lakeside camp.

There was a high waterfall shrouded in billowing clouds of mist that drenched Kilczer and Dorthy as they toiled up the long slippery slope beside it, pushing through vegetation more luxuriant than any they'd previously seen. They really had lost the herd's trail now, even though Kilczer had insisted on casting about at the base of the waterfall, wasting half a day before giving up.

At the top, they had to pick their way through rock-strewn dense forest that grew right to the edge of the wide smooth sleeve of water which swiftly flowed towards the lip of the waterfall. Trees clutched porous blocks of stone with crawling humped roots, trunks sometimes bent at right angles at the base as they jutted up. The dense canopy filtered most of the dim red light so that it was difficult to distinguish a step down to level needle-strewn ground from one into a water-filled pit.

Then the forest fell away. Dorthy and Kilczer emerged on to a wide violet-carpeted shore, the calm black lake stretching away towards the distant cloud-capped mountains of the rim-wall. Dorthy realised with a terrific sense of relief that she had been here before.

But no orange blister punctuated the long curve of the shore. The camp was gone.

Neither Dorthy nor Kilczer spoke as they walked on. There was a churned area scraped bare of vegetation, a hollow half filled with water, half a dozen tracks worn into the ground-cover, fanning away in every direction. Nothing else.

Dorthy sat on the springy ground while Kilczer kicked around the muddy site disbelievingly. Eventually he sat down, too. 'We just have to go on,' he said.

'What do you think happened?'

'I don't know. I suppose Andrews pulled Angel Sutter out of here. It would be his style to concentrate everything at the keep when things started to change there. Him and his fucking lights!' He pulled at his hair, looked under the crook of his arm at Dorthy. 'How are you feeling?'

'Disappointed would be putting it mildly.'

He laughed. 'Your reserve is intact, at least.'

'Poor Arcady. You are still trapped with me, out in the wilderness.'

'I am in no mood for joking, believe it. If I had fucking Duncan Andrews here now I would be a step away from strangling him! Disappointed!' Abruptly, he stood and walked to the edge of the water, thumbed out his cock and began to urinate. Ripples spread across the black water, distorting his reflection.

Dorthy looked away. During the days of illness it hadn't been possible to conceal their natural functions from each other, and afterwards Kilczer had been increasingly casual about it; still, heat rose at the back of her neck, along the rims of her ears. This coarse edge was something she hated: a dissipation of the cocoon of privacy about the secret core of self, an assertion she was too afraid to make.

Kilczer zipped up and walked back, picked up the rifle. 'There is no utility to sitting around here. We—'

104

Dorthy looked around, because he had half raised the rifle to his shoulder.

The herder stood at the margin of the tangled shadows under the forest canopy, stooping so that its humped shoulders were higher than its head. Large eyes glinted in the shadows cast by its loose hood of skin. Dorthy felt a chill where a moment before the heat of embarrassment had been. And felt something prick in the still centre of her mind, as elusive and dangerous as a knife-blade seen point on, as complex as the eight-dimensional twistor equations that describe any given point in space-time. For a moment she almost had it, but her Talent was too subdued, and it was too strange . . . She closed her eyes and straightened her spine, tried to expand the still centre where her Talent focused; but the feeling was like mist, hung always at the same elusive distance no matter which way she went. And the mist began to fade. When she opened her eyes again, the herder was gone.

Behind her, Kilczer let out a breathy sigh. 'We had better go,' he said, and he said it so softly that only now was Dorthy scared; for in all the long dangerous trek, no matter how much he had felt it, Kilczer had never outwardly shown fear before.

Later, they camped amid tall rustling stems near the edge of the water, screened from the ominous shadows under the close-packed trees. For once Kilczer did not suggest going off to hunt, but watched as Dorthy deftly wove the hollow reeds together to make a kind of narrow platform, squatting on his haunches less than a metre away. They had stayed close to each other as they walked the long curve of the shore between the lake and the forest.

'That looks comfortable,' he said, nudging the platform with his boot. 'Where did you learn such a trick?'

'My mother used to weave mats.' Her death. And then that one terrible night with Hiroko under the huge sky of the Outback. Dorthy said, 'I'll do one for you, if you like.'

'Let me try it,' he said, and sat gingerly on the woven stems, then smiled and swung his legs up. His hand brushed Dorthy's and it was as if a switch had been thrown, meshing the gears of desire in her belly. She grabbed his hand and they drew each other down. His knees got in the way as she tried to climb beside him; one of her palms sank in mud beside his head, the other was still in his grip, gripping him. She kissed him, stubble scraping her chin, and his arm came up around her, lifted her on top of him as his other hand let go of hers, reached down between them, pushed into her coveralls, his thumb slipping in her wetness as she tried to get his coveralls open while still kissing him, mashing his dry lips apart until her teeth ground his. His tongue pushed into her mouth as his cock pushed into her cunt and a moment later he came as she did, a long shudder that after a moment started to turn into a cramp. But didn't. She relaxed on top of him, sudden desire still scraping a hollow in her chest, between her breasts. Discharge of their fear and desperation, a definition of the bond that had slowly grown between them. Her heartbeat mixed with his.

'By the beard,' he said, and chuckled, pulled his hand from between them and found her wrist, his grip totally encircling it. 'I didn't think—'

'You thought I was too reserved? Was I?'

'You know you were not. You are okay?'

'Move your knee. That's better.'

'Suppose one of the herders came upon us when—'

'Don't,' Dorthy said, and quickly kissed him to stop his talk. She didn't want to talk, never had wanted to talk, in the aftermath of sex. In her worst moments she saw it as a biological reflex, something to be satisfied and no more; in her best as a mutual act of trust and gratification. But always she stopped short of exploration. All the spilling of hidden emotion, little inconsequential secrets and confessions; that was the part she hated. It reminded her too much of her childhood work at the Kamali-Silver Institute. She had made a rule once, never to sleep with anyone more than three times. In the mores of Greater Brazilian-dominated Earth, emerging from a long dark period of repression, that was still regarded as unusual, even perverted – even if she rarely slept with *anyone*, anyway. But if men took advantage of her because of it, she also took advantage of them. Besides, things had been different at Fra Mauro Observatory, more cosmopolitan. The people from the colony worlds, most of which had fallen into barbarism after having lost touch with Earth after the mutual near-destruction of the USA and USSR, barbarism only fifty years past, liked to mock the more staid students from Earth, and were not a little shocked by some of the attitudes of men towards women, would have been horrified if they had known that in some parts of Greater Brazil women were still openly sold into marriage. Dorthy preferred the views of the colonists, knowing well enough that it was in part a rebellion against her father's strictness. But what mattered was herself, what she needed. Which, sometimes, only sometimes, was sex. What she didn't need was the urge to spill the self afterward, more messy than the act itself. She had been bombarded with other selves for too long, at the Institute and during the year she had worked to raise the funds for her studies at Fra Mauro. *Whore.*

'I think,' Kilczer said, his mouth muffled against the side of her neck, 'that we have more or less wrecked your lovely bed.'

'I'll make another.' She pushed away from him, and avoided his grasp when he tried to pull her back. Don't get too close. 'I have to wash,' she said, 'that's all.'

When she came back he was standing, looking out in the direction of the forest. Dorthy began to bend reeds. 'Are you worried about us getting back?' she asked him.

'Please, we do not talk about that now. I am tired.' He stepped out of the way as she wove stems together. She had unsettled him, and she smiled as she worked; she didn't like being cast to type, even though it was often convenient to play the retiring neurotic Talent. Almost all the trivia shows had a character like that. Kilczer said, 'Several years ago, now, I was on Elysium, I think I tell you a little bit of this already. I camped out in the wilderness, alone, and I like it then no more than I like it now, even though I had brought all the necessary comforts; but was to advance my work, you understand. Here we make our own comforts, yes?'

Talk, talk. Always binding all time to the present moment. Dorthy worked on with her back to Kilczer, plaiting bundles of stems and weaving a single loop at either end to hold them together, while he told her about the grass plains of the Outback of Namerika on Elysium, the aborigine villages and their strange inhabitants, who stood stock-still whenever a human approached them – you could kill an abo that way, the local people used to say. Kilczer explained that he used to watch the aborigines from a distance, but never saw anything that hadn't been described many times before. No one knew if the aborigines were properly sentient or not, and despite the six months in the field with his instruments, clumsy forerunners of the compact setup he'd lost to the herd of critters, Kilczer hadn't been able to form any positive conclusions either.

Tugging a loop tight, Dorthy asked, 'Don't some people say that the aborigines once built cities on Elysium?'

'It is legend only,' Kilczer said with sudden scorn, 'worked up from wishes and a few ambiguous geological formations. In just the same way, it is claimed that there was once a civilisation on Novaya Rosya, destroyed half a million years ago when a big asteroid struck the planet. I tell you that already, I think. Certainly it destroyed almost all of life, but as for anything else, well, zithsa hunters claim they sometimes see man-shaped creatures in the lowlands. Mist demons, the hunters call them, and say that they are the ghosts of the fabled lost race. I say they are half vodka, half imagination. Zithsa hunters are crazy kinds of people anyway. We wish not to be alone in the universe, Dorthy, and this drives people to invent things that are not really there. Even on Earth there are stories about ancient technologies. Atlantic or some such place.'

'Atlantis,' Dorthy said, pulling the final knot through. For some reason she remembered the hair-thin geological layer which marked the unexplained bombardment with nickel-iron asteroids. And at the same time felt a tingling touch as of uncontrolled expansion of her Talent . . . but after a moment it all faded.

She lay on the completed reed platform, and Kilczer looked down at her. 'You look good enough to eat,' he said.

'There's some jerky left, if you're hungry.'

He knelt at the edge of the platform, stems crackling under his weight. 'I am not that hungry. Tomorrow we go hunting, perhaps.' He lay down and put his arms around her; after a moment she hugged him back. 'That was a nice idea you had,' he said.

'I thought that we both had it, at the same time. Don't talk, it isn't necessary.'

'You do not like to talk . . . afterward?'

'Actually, I feel a little guilty. After all, you're married.'

'Married . . . ? Ah, my partner. No, it is not the same as on Earth; we bond not for sex but for child, or perhaps children. Your customs on Earth are too strict, I think, that is why there is so much strife, so much restlessness. When I work for a few weeks down on Earth, in Ascension, a woman who also worked there one day killed her husband. In jealousy of another woman, it was said. I remember the words, "husband," "wife." A very bad custom, I think, that makes things like that happen.'

'Perhaps.'

'But this does not relax you, it is not the problem, I think.' He pushed up on one elbow, his face over hers. 'You do not like to talk about yourself, I have noticed. We come through all this together, and still I know little more about you than was on your file.'

'What was on my file?' She couldn't help stiffening defensively.

'Hardly anything. What is it like, Australia? Like Elysium, it has an Outback, I think, but no more the aborigines.'

'I haven't been there in years.'

'Not even to see your family?'

'I don't— My mother's dead. My father . . . well, he's a drunk, mostly. Spent all my earnings on a ranch in the Outback, went to pieces after my mother died.' Her uncle there, too. Uncle Mishio. She didn't want to think of him, or of her sister. Poor Hiroko, the brief riddle of her farewell message.

'You do not have to say, if you do not wish it.'

Dorthy kissed him and felt his lips relax in a smile. She suggested, 'You talk, if you want to, I don't mind.' Even though she did. But they were close now, as close as they could be, and she felt that his talk was an outlet for the pricking of his fear.

'All I try to say, before, was what started me on this road, I think. I wonder if I would be here now if I had not wasted day after day lying among dry grass with heavy binoculars growing sweaty in my hands while I watched the really rather boring to and fro of the aborigines among their round mud huts. You know, I see how people live, and it is as limited as the abos. For all the exploration, all the expeditions, how many people ever look up at the stars, how many wonder what is out there? My first day here, I walked away from the place where they were setting up Camp Zero, much machinery around a great hole they dig for the command centre. It was night then, the sun had not risen. And it was so very cold. Lights were blazing everywhere and people were shouting and banging away at girders and panelling. It was not how I thought it

109

would be. So I walked away from it all, over the ridge so the lights were just a glow against the dark sky. There is a crater . . .'

'I know,' Dorthy said. She felt sleepy and comfortable, closed her eyes against the red light.

Kilczer said, 'I sat down on a boulder at the edge of the rim, the air so cold it was like little knives in the back of my throat, no light but the stars above and the little pinlight of my suit heater. Sat there for maybe two hours looking at the stars as if I had not seen them before. Not so very different from Novaya Rosya or Earth, we have not come all that far. When I return, Colonel Chung spits blood, thought the enemy had got me. I think she is a little paranoid.'

'So I gather. Was it her idea to dig the command centre so deep?'

Kilczer stiffened slightly. When he spoke, Dorthy knew that he was not telling the truth. 'On orders from orbital command it was built. I do not know what they think they protect themselves from.' But he knew all right; yet what he knew Dorthy couldn't quite tell. Something final . . . But it slipped away. He was in the Navy, she remembered: of course.

'You sleep?' Kilczer asked.

'Nearly.' But she lay awake a long time, trying to grasp what he was hiding from her, the same thing she had glimpsed in Colonel Chung's mind. A danger, some dark, final deed, and the buried command centre was connected with it.

When they awoke, Kilczer started to make love to Dorthy again; but she resisted, pushing away and declaring that she was ready to get on, they had a long walk ahead of them. The sudden desire she had felt was quite gone; and besides, the little maggot of hidden knowledge within his otherwise unblemished candour nagged at her.

So she stood and suggested that they both take a swim. 'I feel absolutely filthy, and we might not get another chance.'

'I think not. We do not know what lives in the water.'

'Well, there are no large carnivores on land, except for the herders, so why should there be any in the water?' She pulled down the top of her coveralls, undid the halter that cupped her small breasts, kicked out of the coveralls' legs and walked into the cold black water. Her toes gripped rotting reed stems and oozing mud. When she was thigh-deep she threw herself forward, gasping at the water's cold embrace but doggedly swimming out a few metres before turning, treading water, and calling to Kilczer to come in. But he refused, almost sullenly, and shied away from the water she playfully splashed at him.

It was too cold to stay in long. She clambered ashore and began to blot herself dry with her coveralls, aware now of their rank smell, of the dried sweat of many days walking, of her illness. The drops of water that clung to the down of her arms gleamed like blood, like smooth dull flecks of ruby and carnelian, in the light of the huge, dim sun that hung high above the black lake, hugely mirrored in it.

'There's nothing out there,' she said to Kilczer. 'You should try it. Invigorating.' She rubbed her hair, and Kilczer politely looked away from the upward tug of her breasts.

As she pulled on her coveralls he said, 'I will hunt breakfast,' and was gone before she had finished dressing, ashamed of his fear.

Slowly she fastened the snaps of her boots, then shook back wet hair and started to braid it, beginning to be annoyed by Kilczer's presumption. He thought that making love had settled something between them, but like most women Dorthy knew that the act was only a part of a greater whole, a synthesis she had always resisted. Never more than three times? She had enjoyed most of her partners only once; half of them she hadn't even stayed the night with. Admittedly it was not a great number. But she knew well enough why she had resisted Kilczer's waking advances; not to sink into the other, not to have to open up. But here she was with Kilczer every minute, in a way she had never been with anyone before, and he obviously expected her to reciprocate his openness. Well, she wouldn't, she decided, and where the hell was he anyway? She pushed through the reeds, looked up and down the margin between forest and water, and saw no sign. Scared of creatures in the water that weren't there, and then compensates by running off to waste shot at creatures that probably weren't edible anyway, she thought. But this articulation of her annoyance only made plain her need for his company.

It was more than half an hour before he returned, empty-handed. They broke camp and set off, each chewing a stick of jerky. Kilczer kept asking Dorthy if she was all right, and his well-meaning solicitude irked her; that and the burning itching sensation, growing as she walked, that always preceded her period. No doubt brought on by their lovemaking. She trailed sullenly behind him, and after a while he gave up trying to talk with her and walked silently ahead, the rifle slung on one shoulder, the little orange bag bumping his left hip.

In this fashion they walked for a dozen hours, stopping only when Kilczer brought down a fleeing creature something like a dog-sized antelope with horny ridges protruding either side of its blunt head, each knife-edged blade as long as Kilczer's arm. But it was six-legged, and they left the carcass untouched.

The shore here was rocky, a shelf of granite undercut by the slow-lapping water, scrub growing in whorled declivities and hollows. The forest was shrunken to a distant dark line. Ahead, the rimwall, which they would have to climb to reach Colonel Ramaro's camp, rose into a bank of haze.

They camped in the lee of a cairn of huge boulders, chewing more jerky for their supper; even after soaking it in water it was barely palatable. Hunger scraped at the bottom of Dorthy's stomach, and little cramps were starting lower down; she went off, tore a strip of cloth from the sleeve of her coveralls, and bound it between her legs, hating this necessity. Men have it so easy, they don't know.

When, later, Kilczer reached out and put an arm around her shoulders, she told him matter-of-factly that she was bleeding.

'I don't mind that,' he said gently.

'Well I do,' Dorthy said, and moved out of his loose embrace.

Kilczer rolled over and sat up, kicked at the little fire she had built; sparks flew up, whirling constellations. Flames staggered blue and white across grooved fragments of driftwood. Once he looked across at her as if he were going to say something. But he didn't. They settled down to sleep separately.

The next day was much the same, although Dorthy managed to shoot a large animal that had been watching them from the top of a shallow rise.

Kilczer had wasted a dozen shots without even scaring it before giving in to Dorthy's requests to try. The stock fitted snugly into her shoulder, against her cheek. She sighted carefully, allowing for windage, gently squeezed the trigger. The smack of the recoil was like a congratulatory pat as, far across shelving rock and scattered scrub and boulders, the ungainly animal collapsed as if its legs had all at once been cut away.

Kilczer accepted the rifle without word and they trekked over to Dorthy's prize; she counted just over six hundred paces, easily half a kilometre.

Her shot had hit the animal's flat head just behind one of its large, slightly bulging eyes; there was very little blood. Its four legs were long and many-jointed, a swollen body slung between them like the belly of a spider. Except for the ruff of reddish fur at the neck its deeply wrinkled hide was naked. Jaws like those of a mechanical digger gaped to show many flat-topped teeth.

'This is not mentioned in Chavez's catalogue as I recall,' Kilczer said, as he slowly circled it. 'It is perhaps from Earth?'

'I don't know much about creatures that were living a million years ago, but I don't think so.'

'Nor I.' He examined it for a while, cut into its hide, dipped his finger into the blood and tasted before pronouncing it edible. He cut thick slabs of muscle, marbled with fat, from its haunches, and these they broiled on flat rock in the centre of a fire; Dorthy ate tentatively at first, then with avid appetite. The meat was delicious, slightly sweet but juicy and fibrous. She ate until she could eat no more and lay back, feeling something close to contentment. 'All I need now is a good *pinot noir*,' she said.

'I am sorry?' Kilczer was shading his eyes as he looked at the sweep of shore that they would have to follow around the lake.

'Red wine. A glass of that, and maybe a baked avocado to follow. What's wrong?' Because he had scrambled to his feet, still shading his eyes.

'I see smoke, I think.'

Dorthy stood, too. Far in the distance, the forest crept down to the shore. Something seemed to float above the trees there, as small in the distance as her thumbnail, difficult to make out against the dark, star-flecked sky.

'Could it be a camp? Andrews? But why would they need a fire?'

'Perhaps a camp, but perhaps not people,' Kilczer said.

They watched the little distant cloud for some time, but it did not change. Eventually Dorthy lay down, the hardness of the rock not much alleviated by bundles of scrub, and said, 'Come get some sleep.'

'You are right; we must get nearer to see,' Kilczer said, and lay down heavily beside her. After a while he snuggled closer, and Dorthy put an arm around his waist, slowly stroked his side. He turned his head, and they kissed.

This time it was slow, a slow building rhythm that climbed a little and stopped, climbed again. Dorthy felt as if she were edging towards a great drop, moved her hips to clasp him deep within herself. There, the edge, there, *Oh*. She fell, softly fell. Oh. Oh. Kilczer thrust, thrust again, gasped. She pulled his heavy head down, and they slept.

She woke with a start from a dream of running in red light across some vast plain in pursuit of something, something . . . but the dream was already fading. There was a burning edge to her bladder and she went off to relieve it. Still bleeding. She retied the clout and pulled up her coveralls, looked along the shore to the distant forest: the smudge of smoke was still there. Kilczer slept on undisturbed, his face untroubled and innocent in the perpetual red light; her Talent was quiet, she could sense nothing. Tired, too tired to speculate about the smoke, she lay down beside him again, and slept.

The smoke was still there when they started off again. Kilczer suggested that it might be a forest fire. 'Too big to be a campfire, I think, but it could have been started by one.'

They walked on. The shore curved back on itself and the rocky margin narrowed, vanishing in a tangle of muddy backwater creeks and boulders and crooked trees. Dorthy and Kilczer thrashed through this as best they could, but it was not easy to pick a path through the dense growth, and again and again they were forced to wade scummed ponds that painted their legs up to the thighs with black mud. At last they gave up and turned to strike farther inland.

Kilczer said, 'We turn back towards the fire, or perhaps it is farther from the water than I thought.'

'Suppose it *is* a forest fire?' Dorthy remembered the swift fierce conflagrations of the Australian coast.

'We take the chance.'

'In case it is Andrews.'

'To be honest, I do not think so. But we must see. If it is a forest fire we can always jump in the lake, yes?'

'I'd rather take a boat ride.'

'I will see what I can do.'

As the land rose it became drier and less rocky; soon they were walking between low, spaced trees, easily picking their way among roots that humped and crooked over the needle-carpeted floor. The nodes of the tree branches seemed different, more swollen. Some were dusted with a powdery stuff that Dorthy and Kilczer kept knocking into the air as they pushed their way through; it made Kilczer cough.

Eventually he plucked the soft tip of one of the branches and examined it as he walked. 'Now look here,' he said at last. 'Like little flowers in there, spore-producing bodies. The rain perhaps triggered them, or the sunlight. I wonder if they do this every day. Planetary day, that is.'

'Does it matter?' Dorthy ducked under a low, spreading branch, stepped over a gnarled hoop of root.

'Remember the bacteria that produce most of the oxygen, in the sea? They were bioengineered. I am wondering if these trees were, too. Adapted, at least.'

'But what's so special about bioengineering? They did it all the time in the Age of Waste.'

'After the Age of Waste, in fact, but before the war and the beginning of the Interregnum. But people then did not build up organisms from nothing but an idea. Spores . . . I wonder how far they blow. It could mean that each hold is not genetically isolated; it would explain why the remotes found no difference in the ecological systems of the holds they sampled, no genetic drift. Well, for the plants at least. But the animals are the same also, I think. Perhaps all the junk has been deleted from their genetic codes.'

'Civilisation could have crashed only a thousand years ago. Or it could still be here. What junk, anyway?'

'About half the genes we carry in our cells do nothing. Some of it is parasitic DNA, riding our chromosomes simply to be reproduced by division of our cells. Internal viruses if you like, never expressed, cryptic. Some of the rest is vestigial, no longer with a function. Cut it all out and the potential for mutation plummets. That is why I wonder if everything here has either been built or modified. Engineered. The star up there will not vary its output for hundreds of millions of years, so no climatic changes to shake up the ecology. Maybe that is why the enemy chooses red dwarfs, do you think? They are taking the long view. Think of all the red dwarfs in the Galaxy, Dorthy. What percentage of radiating stars? I do not count the brown and black dwarfs, they are no more than very large planets for all purposes. What is it, fifty, sixty per cent?'

'More than eighty per cent, if you don't count the substars. Eighty per cent in the spiral arms anyway, more in the halo stars above the plane of the spiral arms.'

'More than a hundred billion stars like that one up in the sky, then. Of course, many are short-term variables. But still . . . And planets around red dwarfs will have no native ecology, easier to seed after you have planoformed them.'

'As long as you know how to spin them up, overcome the captured rotation. But I suppose there are any number of theories.'

'One for each of the scientists down here, I expect. Andrews makes the most noise, but we all have our own ideas, that is only natural. Well, I was hoping we could make the field small.'

'Narrow it down. I'll do my best, if we ever get out of this.'

Kilczer pushed aside a branch and was enveloped in a cloud of dusty spores. He beat the air in front of his face, and when he had finished coughing he said, 'I hold you to that. Come on.'

Still climbing, they began to circle back towards the shore, towards the fire. The forest opened out and patches of sky were visible through gaps in the canopy, glimpses of the huge soft sun. Dorthy mused on red dwarfs and other suns, trying to imagine the bubble of explored space within the great turning wheel of the Galaxy, a diatom in a lake, a jellyfish hung in some dark sea, the smallest atoll in Earth's wide oceans. A few dozen suns in the triple-armed swarm of four hundred billion. Lost in reductive, recursive calculations, she didn't notice that Kilczer had stopped, and almost bumped into him.

Ahead, through layered pine boughs, thick skeins of smoke rose against the dark sky.

The ground dropped away abruptly, trees gripping the rim of the steep slope with gnarled roots as they leaned over it. Below was a wide river valley, black water looped in its broad bottom. The trees on the flanking slopes had been felled, their stripped trunks lying in criss-cross patterns, and great fires burned along the bank opposite, sending up black columns of smoke. Even at that distance, the herders moving among them were plainly visible.

'I hope you're not going to tell me that *this* is some kind of instinctive behaviour,' Dorthy said, fighting her own instinct to crouch down, get out of plain sight.

Kilczer clung by one hand to a tree as slim as himself, shaded his eyes with the other. After a minute he said, 'There must be thirty or forty down there. I see no critters. Surely these cannot be them, cannot have changed so soon. It has been, I forget, only eight days or nine since they started their migration.'

'There were other groups before the one we were following,' Dorthy said, remembering her glimpse of a herder in the forest on the day of her arrival at the lakeside camp. Had that been newly changed?

'Of course, that I forget, too. Do you see, there at the water edge?'

Dorthy leaned against him, sighted along his pointing arm. Three small, regular structures drawn up at the silted edge of the river.

'Boats,' Kilczer said, pushing himself away from the tree. His uneasiness had been cancelled by sudden electric excitement: he saw a way out of the wilderness, a chance for action. He said, 'I told you I try to get you a boat,' and started down the slope, moving with crabwise caution among the trees.

Dorthy followed, not at all affected by his sudden exuberant confidence. At bottom, he still believed that the herders were animals, and with the rifle he had proven his mastery over the animals they had encountered. When they reached the edge of the cleared part of the slope Kilczer stopped, looking through a screen of branches at the muddle of fallen trunks beyond, the slow river and the herders moving on the other side. Dorthy crouched beside him and took out the little dispenser from the breast pocket of her coveralls, popped a tablet of counteragent into her palm. Kilczer turned at the tiny *click* of the dispenser mechanism. 'What is it you do?' he asked, and when she raised her hand to her mouth he lunged. But she jerked back, pressed the tablet into her mouth, swallowed.

117

He caught her wrist. 'Crazy, you are! Last time you did this you went into a trance. I cannot carry you out of here if things go wrong.' His hair had fallen over his face and he shook it back, glared at her.

'Let's hope there isn't anything to go wrong, then,' Dorthy said. 'It will take a while to work, anyway.'

Kilczer let her go, turned to look across the river. Most of the herders were working around one of the huge fires, banking it with earth. Two or three on the near bank were squatting over half-finished planks. 'Stone tools,' he muttered. 'Not so very advanced. Those fires, now, perhaps for making charcoal or rendering down wood. Resin to caulk the boats, maybe. But why do they want boats?'

'In half an hour or so I'll be able to tell you,' Dorthy said, kneeling beside him.

'If you can understand them. If you do not go into fugue again. What the hell. I do not need to know why they build boats, all I know is that I want one. It is another week to hike around the lake to its source, longer if the way is difficult. In one of those boats we could get across in a dozen hours. Look at that stuff on the far bank. That is I think cloth.' He pointed.

'I can handle a sailboat. But those don't have masts.'

'Not yet. But I do not wait for them to build masts. Look there, at the stern. Raised rowlocks, that is the word? There on the platform, long oars. Those creatures must be strong. Do you think we can handle them?'

Dorthy touched his arm. 'Let's be patient. I'd rather spend a week walking around the lake than be caught by those things.'

'There is only one pass through the rimwall into the caldera. We must reach it ahead of the herders, if that is truly where they are going.'

'That's the only positive thing I got, at my last attempt.'

'So, then. They build boats to cross the lake, perhaps. They do not wish to walk through the forest, perhaps it is not even possible.' Kilczer looked sideways at her. 'You should not try this now.'

'I can't stop it; neither can you. If you'll let me, I'll prepare as best I can. If I know their intentions it can't hurt our chances, can it?' She didn't want to go down there at all; that was why she had taken the counteragent.

Kilczer shook his head, then smiled, the expression somewhat grim in his gaunt white face. 'No, I do not suppose. You are right, I should not go off as I did. Better to mark our moment.'

Dorthy saw then that nothing she could say would dissuade him from trying to steal one of the boats, and she began to feel really afraid, a cold dread weighing down her stomach. She said, 'I understand the impulse. I still think you're crazy, though.'

Kilczer lay down in a crackling litter of branches, peering down the slope and taking account of the herders' activities with something of the precise observational manner of old. Dorthy sat zazen, feeling her heart and breath slow. Nothing but alpha rhythms, self sinking through silver into darkness, darkness in which she dissolved as the lights of other minds began to flicker through the veil.

Kilczer's analytical but edgy thoughts were a close distraction she must look through to discover the others. Down there were not separate entities, it seemed, but minds linked to a single purpose, like waves marching across the silver sea or like the fish that patrol coral reefs, glittering shoals turning in unison in a welter of precise tail-flicks, like an impulse down a nerve, all one nerve, turning again. Dorthy saw their common vision rise up: the tower, to the tower! This time she knew that it was another voice. She spoke out of her still centre. 'They're getting ready to move on, to the keep. It's urgent, I don't know why . . .'

'What will they do when they get there?' Kilczer's words were an echo of the thoughts that rose like the bulging heads of dolphins from the complex currents of his emotions, fear and curiosity, resolve and impatience, everything running into everything else. No longer a calm surface but a fragmented three-dimensional mirror. Dorthy had to look past it now, not through it. Out, out to the unified purpose working at separate rhythms. *Ittaikan*, she thought. The bond of belonging.

Yet within the apparent unity individual thoughts flitted, swelled, and shrank. Briefly glittering edges of self as dangerous as the grinning barracuda that would sometimes sweep through a shoal's synchronized school.

Dorthy said, 'They're not herders, or not like the ones out on the plain. Something else. Only a little time, coming together, moving on towards the keep. It's difficult, not clear.'

119

'Please, stay calm.' Through the darkness she felt the hard grip of his hand on her wrist.

She opened her eyes. For a moment everything in her inner vision ran into everything in her outer.

'Can you move?' Kilczer asked. 'They are all on the other side of the river now, dragging tree trunks. To build another fire, maybe.'

'I know. There's something by the river . . .'

'They are all on the other side,' he said firmly. 'Come, now.'

The litter of felled trees and stripped branches made the going difficult in the red half-light. Dorthy concentrated on her footing; it helped keep out the welter of Kilczer's emotions, the ominous swell of the herders' single purpose. Several times Dorthy and Kilczer had to crouch down when the herders on the other side seemed to turn towards them, but Dorthy knew that they were intent on the task of stacking the huge tree trunks and digging an outflow channel to collect the rendered resin. Each time she crouched behind Kilczer, she pushed at the earth with her own hands in unconscious imitation.

'Come on!' Kilczer said, tugging at her, and she followed. The river was close now, the boat nearest to them shivering a little in the wash of the slow current. No more than a large dinghy really, crudely clinker-built, its square stern crowned with a platform on which rowlocks raised on crude poles each supported a great oar. Dorthy's split boots sank in ooze; then Kilczer gripped her waist and boosted her up. She caught the edge, pulled herself higher.

And when the herder that had been sleeping inside reared up she kicked back, sprawling half on mud and half in cold water, its panic meshing for a moment with her own, then exploding apart as Kilczer brought the butt of the rifle around and slammed it into the herder's narrow head so that it fell back into the well of the boat. He looked around, his thoughts frantic and shattered, picked up a discarded stone adze as big as his doubled fist and brought it down just as the herder began to struggle up again. It uttered a hoarse bleat and crumpled, black blood welling through the dark pelt behind its loose skin hood.

'We go, we must go,' Kilczer said urgently. Dorthy splashed into the water, lifted herself into the boat (tipping one way as she pulled over the gunwale, the other as she tumbled into the well, almost landing on top of the stunned herder and recoiling in revulsion) while Kilczer sawed through the hawser with his knife and vaulted in after her. She saw what he wanted even before he said it and clambered on to the stern platform, unshipped one of the huge oars, longer than herself, used it to push the boat out into the current. The other herders were scrambling down the bank; a few were running ahead, overtaking the boat as Dorthy pushed down again, the oar grounding on what felt like gravel, the boat's prow shimmying as it was caught in the river's flow. Kilczer was binding the stunned herder's arms and legs with a sleeve he had torn from his coveralls.

Some of the herders were wading out into the river now, their loose hoods flaring about their faces. There was something wrong about their foreheads, but Dorthy didn't see clearly because something flew at her from the bank and she ducked as the chunk of stone flew past end-for-end, splashing into black water. Another tipped an edge of rough planking and spun over the side. Kilczer grabbed the rifle and snapped off a dozen shots, spume fanning across the water in front of the advancing herders, who scrambled back in confusion.

Dorthy leaned on the oar, trailing the long blade to steer at the end of each stroke. Ahead, the banks rose up on either side, and she saw herders working there, throwing ropes across to each other, weaving a slack cradle that trailed in the currrent. She shouted a warning to Kilczer as the boat bore down on it, understanding what the herders were about to do even as they pulled back and lengths of rope lifted into their path, shedding strings of water drops. Kilczer raised his knife and waved its buzzing blade through the strands. Once, twice. Most parted immediately; the rest gave way as the boat brushed through them amid a small hail of stones. And then they were past, and the lake was ahead of them.

Kilczer took the oars, having to lift on tiptoe at the beginning of each stroke because the poles that supported the rowlocks were as high as his shoulders. Dorthy cradled the rifle, dividing her attention between the dark mouth of the river among the trees that ran down along the shore, dwindling with each stroke of the oars, and the herder as it huddled in the well, up against the prow, its arms bound behind it. It was still dazed by Kilczer's attack.

'We did it,' Kilczer said exultantly, as he laboured at the oars. 'We show them, do we not, Dorthy?'

'We did,' she said, catching the edge of his jubilation. After all, they had lifted themselves out of their fate, if only for a moment.

There was no sign that the other herders were chasing them, and after a while Kilczer shipped the oars and came forward, took the rifle from Dorthy. 'What do you make of our friend here?'

'He's still more or less unconscious.'

'A male, you think?'

'They were all male.'

'Indeed. There is something funny about his head, you see? The forehead is swollen. Hydrocephalic. This is no normal herder.' Kilczer nudged the creature's legs with the tip of the rifle barrel. The feet were long, and arched high, the heel protruding back from the ankle, the three toes splayed and tipped with broad claws. The black fur had a luxurious shimmer in the red light, as if each fine hair had a translucent, refractive tip. Kilczer said, 'Perhaps this one is like you saw in the forest when you arrive. They must be coming up all around the edge of the hold, herds of critters, all of them changing.' For a brief moment his vision of a horde of these creatures moving on the black spire within the caldera overwhelmed Dorthy. 'Look at it, a scrawny specimen, is it not?' Beneath the flow of his thoughts, an undertow of revulsion. He asked, 'Is your Talent still functional?'

'Of course.'

'See what you can get out of it when it returns to consciousness,' Kilczer said, and handed back the rifle, returned to the oars.

The rocking of the boat and the regular creaking as Kilczer pulled and feathered, pulled and feathered, was lulling. Dorthy didn't know precisely when the herder came round, but gradually became aware of its attention burning upon her. When she looked up the beast tried to scrabble back, jerking its legs. Beneath the bulge of its forehead its large eyes widened, membranes sliding sideways across black balls slit by a horizontal pupil: a panic reaction, she understood, and moved back, too, felt Kilczer take hold of her shoulder. The boat drifted, leaning a little in the current.

'I'm all right,' she said. 'It's scared of me. Of us.'

'Anything else?'

But the steady bright flame of its panic seared everything away, even the compulsive vision of climbing towards the tower of the keep. 'It thinks we're going to kill it,' Dorthy reported. 'No, worse than that, kill everything. It sees us bringing the sky down. That's as near as I can explain it.'

Kilczer pulled twice on the oars, then said, 'It must have got that from its parents, us coming down from the sky. But I wonder how they knew?'

'It's all mixed up with its fright. I can't see anything too clearly.'

'You must try,' Kilczer said.

So, while he rowed, Dorthy sat zazen at the edge of the stern platform, her attention focused inward where the mind of the herder flickered like a reflected candle flame at her still centre. As Kilczer fell into the steady rhythm of rowing, the distraction of his thoughts lessened. She began to make out shapes, loci of being, behind the creature's fear, each separate and starkly isolated like strange chess pieces on a great featureless board. Its mind held only a few experiences, a little learned knowledge, yet below the surface, shadowy areas to which Dorthy had no access hinted at as yet untapped reserves of wisdom. Its sensorium was a flickering screen above this deep core of memory, something like the mind of a recent amnesiac but with none of the sudden random associations such a mind possessed.

Surfacing, Dorthy opened her eyes. They were a long way from the shore now, turning towards the great inlet, kilometres distant, that fed the lake. Long low waves slapped the hull as Kilczer rowed steadily. The sun stood close to noon, a sullen lid to the dark sky, and at last the air was warm. After a while Kilczer stripped off the top of his coveralls, the action sending a flare of panic, followed by curiosity, through the herder.

'I think it wonders why you wear a false hide,' Dorthy said.

'It is still scared?'

'A little less. But I'm not learning anything useful, except it has reservoirs of knowledge it hasn't tapped yet. Do you suppose they could be programmed into its brain somehow?'

'Instincts, you mean?' Pulling on the oars, Kilczer grunted. He had wrapped orange cloth around his blistering palms, tied an orange strip around his head to hold back his lank hair. This, and the scruffy beginning of a beard, made him look like a skinny bedraggled pirate.

'More than that. The herders could have been born, if that's the right word, only a few days ago, yet they were cooperating on building boats so that they could reach the keep. I don't think it has language yet, beyond a few signs and gestures maybe, but when the herders were working together it was as if they were all parts of a whole.'

'Hardwired knowledge. So they may later develop a language?'

'Given the right stimulus.'

'Like the writing in the keep.'

'Perhaps,' she said, seeing a concatenation of speculation run through his mind like a whirling collision of ice floes, familiar and almost comforting after the shadowy spaces of the herder's mind.

'I begin to wonder,' Kilczer said, as she knew he would, 'if our presence has perhaps sparked off all these changes. Andrews told me that trapped neutrino analysis suggests that there has been no powered activity in the keep for thousands of years. Then we arrive here, the invaders, and the keep turns itself on, and instead of more mindless herders the children turn into this new sort of male with a compulsion to get to the keep. Perhaps they summon the enemy, do you think? In which case—'

'We must get to the keep before them, and warn Andrews.'

Curiously, Kilczer didn't mind this demonstration that his thoughts were open to her. He was not a particularly private person. 'Absolutely,' he said. 'And the more you find out from our friend here, the better.'

'I'll try. Keep rowing and don't try to think.'

He did his best to comply.

But after trawling the shallows of the herder's consciousness, mirrored in the directionless space of her centre, Dorthy was little wiser about its intentions. The enigmatic areas of knowledge were like shadows glimpsed far down in the sea, even their boundaries uncertain. In clear light were only the isolated flickerings of the creature's brief existence: the trauma of its birth (or, more properly, its rebirth) from the chrysalis, a painful struggle into light; flashes of solitary hunting, more alive in its muscles than in its head; and the work at the river, urgent yet somehow peacefully contented

124

cooperation, the blissful tightness of belonging. And over and over, as a tongue returns to a nagging broken tooth, the sign that gripped its being, touched everything that it did: the vision of the keep rising out of its black lake. How could the herder know about that?

Dorthy mused on these few lacunae while the sun dropped warmth on her head and shoulders and Kilczer laboured at the oars. Her Talent was slowly fading. With its last residue, she became aware of the herder's thirst, spreading across the surface of its fear like oil over water. She took the coveralls top that Kilczer had discarded and trailed it over the side of the boat until it was soaked through, then tossed the heavy bundle in front of the herder.

It watched her suspiciously, nervously. Then its feet pushed against the ridged sides of the boat, claws splintering green wood, and it moved its shoulders, jerked them up against the prow until it was sitting at a seemingly impossible angle, its legs bound beneath it, its tiny, weak, vestigial arms, too short to reach its muzzle, clasping and unclasping across the muscled, heavily furred keg of its chest. Suddenly it dipped its head and caught the cloth in its muzzle. Dorthy was distracted for a moment by Kilczer's sharply renewed attention (although the steady aching rhythm of his rowing didn't falter). The herder mouthed the cloth, watching her from beneath its swollen brow.

'See if it is hungry,' Kilczer suggested.

'It isn't,' Dorthy said, but pulled out a strip of jerky anyway, tossed it over. The herder eyed it, Kilczer's top still dangling in its mouth, then looked at Dorthy. Then with a smooth toss of its head it threw the sodden cloth at her; she caught it one-handed, the garment's remaining sleeve slapping her face. The herder tossed its head again and subsided. It was thinking of the tower again, but with a kind of qualification, a wistfulness Dorthy didn't quite understand.

Her Talent, now that the implant had recovered from the counter-agent, faded quickly. Soon all that she could sense was that faint wistful longing, no longer specific, mixed with Kilczer's steadfast stubborn determination as his body protested against his hours of labour at the oars. Dorthy offered to take over for a while, but she wasn't tall enough to work the oars properly. Sprawled on the decking at her feet, picking at the chevron marks left at the edge of

125

each plank by the stone tools of the herders, Kilczer smiled at her efforts. Behind him, huddled at the prow, the herder was watchfully still.

Dorthy sat down, too. 'I'm sorry,' she said.

'You will not worry. I manage it.' His bare chest and white, bony shoulders glistened with a fine sheen. He rolled over and leaned at the edge of the platform, reaching down to scoop water to his mouth, splash it over his face. Then he looked sideways and asked, 'Does our friend there need another drink?'

'I can't tell anymore.'

'Ah. Well, never mind.' Kilczer sprang up and briskly took hold of the oars again.

'You should rest,' Dorthy told him.

'We are in the current from the river that feeds this lake now, do you not see how we are drifting?' He bent to examine the bindings on his hands, then adjusted his headband and feathered the oars, began to row with long slow steady strokes, each bringing the boat a fraction closer to the broad mouth of the river, the shore on either side near enough now for Dorthy to be able to see the trees that ran down to the edge of the water, the white boulders piled up along the shore. The clear, dark water was beginning to be clouded, and soon Kilczer had to pull close to one of the banks, where the current was weaker. Now the water was the colour of the milky tea favoured by native Australians. A cold breeze blew down upon them; ahead, high above the stepped pine forest, the bare rimwall rose into cloud tinged pink by the vertical sun.

More and more often, Kilczer paused between strokes, rubbing at his brow. Once he stopped altogether to cough into his fist, a deep, dry, dragging cough that went on for more than a minute. But he shrugged off Dorthy's concern and resumed rowing.

In the midstream of the river – for they were between the forested banks of the river now – swift currents humped and swirled. The low trees shed dark shadows in which anything might have been watching. Kilczer rowed on, his strokes slow and laborious. At last he said, 'I will rest a little, I think.'

'Perhaps we should leave the boat. We've done the worst part, crossed the lake. You were right, by the way.'

He pulled, feathered the oars, pulled. 'I was lucky, we both were.

No, we stay with this boat we fight so hard to take. I would not trust our friend there, in the forest.'

'We could let it go.'

'No, I do not wish that. Perhaps you try to find out more from it.'

'I've done my best. There's hardly anything *to* find out.'

Pull, feather. Pull. Kilczer was angling towards the rocky shore, where dark trees leaned over huge boulders. He said, 'Deep down there is knowledge, you said.'

'But I haven't access to it. You know that I can only see what it's thinking. Equivalence is electrical, not chemical.'

'This knowledge is waiting to be released, yes? Our friend is only a few days old, at least in its present form. In a few days more . . .' He pulled heavily on the port oar and the boat hit something. Dorthy looked around, saw the herder crouch low as fans of needle-leaves scraped over the bow which had lodged against a tree leaning horizontally across the water. Kilczer unshipped an oar and used it to pole the boat parallel to the trunk; Dorthy tied the severed hawser as best she could to one of the main branches.

Kilczer stretched, working his arms. The herder watched him, crouched now beneath a bower of pine branches. 'Do not think of escaping, little monster,' Kilczer said, and picked up the rifle. Claws scraped wood as the herder hunched lower. 'Ah yes, you understand. Dorthy, you can watch our friend if I rest?'

'Of course,' she said, and when he lay down she began to massage his shoulders, working the tense muscles until they loosened under her fingers. 'That is good,' Kilczer said, as she kneaded him. His cool, somewhat waxy skin, the ladder of his bony back: her thin white lover.

Presently he slept, his head cradled on his crossed arms, face turned sideways, half hidden by tangled black hair. Dorthy sat beside him, the rifle on the planking by her hand. In the bow, the herder was still, its large eyes pools of unfathomable shadow. Perhaps it slept, too.

Hours passed. Dorthy watched the river run past, red light glittering on the reticulations of its skin, her anxiety dissolving in its ever-changing unchanging now.

Once, a raft of vegetation moved past, performing a stately waltz in the grip of the swift central current.

Once, a flock of flying things burst from the trees on the far bank, circling the boat – the herder's glance flicked up – before swooping away downstream. The herder watched them go, then subsided, a mass of dark fur, its face almost hidden within the shadow of its hood.

Some time later Kilczer stretched, then sat up, scrubbing at his eyes. 'How long did I sleep?' he asked.

Dorthy glanced at her timetab. 'Four hours or so.'

'I did not mean it.' He stepped to the edge of the platform and pissed over the stern, his back to Dorthy and the herder. 'We will go on. You can sleep now, Dorthy. I watch as I row.'

'I'm all right. I've done nothing.'

'Nonsense,' Kilczer said cheerfully. After wrapping the binding around his hands, he returned to the oars. When Dorthy had untied the boat he swung it out and resumed his steady rhythm.

The banks on either side rose higher, near vertical rock walls hung here and there with black vegetation, shingle beaches at their feet and at their tops pines etched against the dark sky. The red sun shone directly into the canyon. The river threw a loop around a gravel bank. As the boat rounded the bend, Dorthy heard the roar of falling water, and then saw the great waterfall half a kilometre upstream, smashing down from a lip as smooth as glass into the churning bowl. A touch of the billowing mist that boiled around the foam where it fell kissed her face. Kilczer grunted behind her, feathered the starboard oar, and turned the boat into a little cove. Wood scraped on gravel and he poled down until the prow grounded. The herder shifted, looked around, its hood flaring.

Kilczer pulled on his coveralls top (one arm bare), picked up the rifle, and handed it to Dorthy, then fumbled in the sack of orange fabric, came up with his knife. 'Cover me,' he said, shouting to clear the roar of the waterfall, and jumped into the well of the boat.

The herder tried to stand, kicking its bound feet. Its claws drew long weals from the unseasoned wood.

Kilczer bent and slashed the binding around the herder's black-pelted legs. 'Damn you, come on! Stand!'

The herder pressed its back against the prow, convinced, Dorthy was sure, that it was about to die, its hood of skin flared out fully around its face. Kilczer reached to grip the angle of a bound arm and the herder kicked out: Kilczer danced back, staggering, the small of his back slamming into the edge of the stern platform. Dorthy jerked up the rifle, her heart pounding.

But the herder subsided, watching them both warily.

'You would think I was going to kill it,' Kilczer said. 'The rifle, please.'

'As long as you *don't* kill it.'

'Of course not,' he said, and sent a single shot into the sky. The flat *crack* was hardly audible above the pounding of the waterfall. The herder twitched, then was still again.

Dorthy felt a spasm of angry impatience and snatched at the rifle. Surprised, Kilczer let her take it. 'You get out of the boat now,' she told him. 'Go on.'

'What – What are—'

'Just go!' After a moment he picked up the orange sack and jumped ashore. Dorthy aimed at the lapped planking in front of the recalcitrant herder's feet and loosed a close pattern of shots. The herder began to scramble up as chips of wood flew around it. Dorthy fired again, the rifle butt slapping and slapping her shoulder, saw, with a pang of almost physical relief, water well up around shattered planking, then quickly turned and jumped into chill, waist-deep water, waded to the gravel beach where Kilczer stood. The boat was beginning to settle, stern first. A moment later the herder sprang over the side, lithe despite having its arms bound behind its back, splashed into the river up to its thighs. It looked downstream, then at Dorthy, at the rifle she casually held. Stolidly, as if resigned, it plodded out of the water.

The boat began to slide away from the shore, only the oars and the stern platform showing above the water as, turning, it moved into the central current. One oar drifted free, spinning. Soon it and the boat were out of sight.

'"A rotten carcass of a butt,"' Dorthy quoted, '"not rigg'd, Nor tackle, sail, nor mast; the very rats instinctively have quit it."'

'I am sorry to lose it,' Kilczer said. 'The way will be harder for us now.' He was looking at the tumbled slope of shingle and boulders that rose to the top of the cliff, a couple of hundred metres above.

Dorthy could sense the herder's distress. She asked, 'Can't we just let it go?'

'And let it find its friends? Let it tell them in which direction we are going? That I do not believe a wise course of action.'

'But we can't take it all the way up to the keep!'

'That is the way it wishes to go, is it not? Or would you prefer to shoot it here?'

'Arcady, of course not. But I don't know if we can trust it all the way up.'

'We do our best.' Kilczer looked at the herder. 'Up, now.' He pointed. 'Up. Understand? Dumb beast, this is. It respects the rifle at least. I will take the lead, Dorthy. You make sure our friend follows.'

The way was easy at first. Tumbled boulders formed an irregular giant's staircase, the gaps between them packed with sandy gravel. Feathery sprays of vegetation, dark and tough as old leather, grew from cracks and provided convenient handholds. Pools of water had collected here and there, rimmed with a froth of bubbleplants that popped wetly underfoot. The herder clambered clumsily in front of Dorthy, elbows sticking out for balance; its hands were still bound behind its back. Leading it, Kilczer kept glancing around to make sure it followed, his white face luminous in the violet shadow. Once, when the herder stopped, he yelled at it, made as if to throw a rock. The herder didn't flinch, but when Kilczer tossed away the rock it lowered its hooded head and began to climb again, its claws scratching on rock, deeply scoring packed gravel.

Higher up, loose scree made the going more difficult. Dorthy's feet kept slipping because she found it hard to balance while carrying the rifle, and she scraped the palm of her free hand raw. Then the top surprised her, a wide pocket of lush grass surrounded by pine trees. The waterfall flickered no more than a hundred metres beyond trees that leaned over the edge of the drop, water falling as smoothly as silk, the sound of its continual impact terrific, shaking the air and the ground. The wind generated by its fall shook the stiff needle-clusters of the trees; clouds of spray fine as mist blew up, drenching everything.

Kilczer stood at the far edge, in a gap where a tree had fallen away. Mist blew around him and he coughed, pounding at his chest with the flat of his hand as if to drive out something. A little distance away the herder looked at Dorthy, standing up to its knees in the grass.

Kilczer turned, shook back black hair, still coughing. After a moment he said, 'I suppose we can rest a little while,' then began to cough again, bending over his fist.

'Let's get away from here,' Dorthy said, shouting over the waterfall's roar. And then the herder's intention struck her and she started forward, yelling, 'It's going to—'

It did.

Head down, hood fully flared, the herder charged across the grassy space. Before Kilczer could straighten up it smashed into him and they both tumbled over the edge.

Dorthy reached the gap in time to see them hit a clump of trees far down the sheer rock face, spinning apart, dwindling and vanishing into the boiling mist. She shouted after them in despair, shouted Kilczer's name over and over, shaking as mist drenched her, her voice swallowed in the indifferent roar of the waterfall.

At last she looked away, her throat raw, breath driven from her. She had dropped the rifle and bent to pick it up, saw in the grass three trails, darker where stems had bent over: Kilczer's, the herder's, and her own. It was only then that she realised that she was alone.

She prowled the edge of the small clearing for a long time, watching the strong foaming currents of the basin at the foot of the waterfall, the dark water of the river running swiftly between high rock walls. Wind plucked her wet coveralls. Over and over she rehearsed the informed intuition she'd felt the moment before the herder's charge. She couldn't remember if she had sensed anything before then. Perhaps the herder itself hadn't known what it was going to do before it charged, and certainly it was comforting to believe that, because it meant that even with her Talent she couldn't have prevented it.

But something she couldn't quite pinpoint suggested that this might not be so. She remembered the enemy around BD twenty, the way they always committed suicide when capture seemed inevitable; every crippled ship or englobed asteroid blew all its power sources in a single surge, very often taking their would-be captors with them. The enemy, the enemy . . . but surely the new male herders, hacking crude boats into shape with stone implements, lacking even the rudiments of language, couldn't be the enemy. The enemy . . . Whatever it was, it evaded her, but thinking about it kept her mind off the terrible instant when the herder had collided with Kilczer, the way his head had snapped around, white face vivid, the moment before they both plunged beyond the edge, the moment before his death. For he had to be dead, she told herself, as she stared downstream. She had seen his fall, and nothing could survive that, let alone the churning currents at the foot of the waterfall. But still she prowled, half expecting Kilczer to appear at the top of the track, smiling wearily, his black hair plastered back from his high forehead.

More than two hours passed before Dorthy turned reluctantly and quit the little clearing. The forest sloped upward as she left the roar of the waterfall behind. Her soaked coveralls clung to her chilled skin. The trees were widely spaced and pools of red light sank between them, on to a carpet of fallen pine needles or clumps of dark-leaved plants that sometimes took advantage of these little glades.

She stopped in a larger than usual clearing where pocked black rock, some crumbling outcrop, thrust up as high as the trees around it. She cast down the rifle and lay beside it in warming sunlight on the soft layer of needles and fell asleep almost at once, a deep dark sleep with no remembered dreams.

When she awoke, she felt a warm weight on her belly, and thinking it was Kilczer's hand reached out for it sleepily. Short fur pricked her fingertips and she opened her eyes, then scrambled to her feet. The creature dropped and uncoiled at her feet, long-bodied with fur a lustrous red shot through with gold, large black eyes that looked at her as if in reproach. Gasping with shock she reached for the rifle, and the creature fled, its long body weaving sinuously as it scuttled away on three pairs of legs, so comical that her repugnance vanished and she began to laugh, still dazed with sleep, looked around for Arcady Kilczer and remembered what had happened.

Later, as she walked through the forest, between tall trees that were almost but not quite like the pine trees of Earth (but perhaps they were ancestors of the trees that cloaked the steep mountains of Thrace where she had worked for a brief, hot, thyme-scented week), she regretted having scared off the creature that had crept on to her while she had slept, out of need for warmth, perhaps even companionship . . . it would have been company for her. She, who had so often spurned company, yearned for it more and more during her solitary journey upward through the forest, missed Kilczer with a sense of loss that was not quite grief. Sometimes she imagined him to be walking a few paces behind her, nervous in the wilderness and impatient to be moving on, an impatience tempered with kindliness – and she would turn and the simple fact of her solitude would again be made apparent.

For the most part the climb through the forest was uneventful. She had long before lost track of the diurnal rhythms her timetab faithfully marked. She ate at no fixed interval but simply when she was hungry, first exhausting the store of jerky before beginning to hunt again – if that was the right word for it, for although animal life was sparse it was quite oblivious to the danger Dorthy represented: humanity, almost the destroyer of a world. Most often her quarry were small, short-haired creatures striped like bandicoot but with a long narrow head and spindly legs. They trotted across Dorthy's path quite fearlessly and she potted them without remorse, broiled their lean flesh over small fires she lit by exploding a strip of azide tape in a bed of crumbling bone-dry punk. Mostly she kept as close to the canyon as possible, twice having to ford white-water tributaries. As she climbed, the trees became smaller and more widely spaced, growing in definite clumps separated by open spaces or masses of coarse bush, a myriad thorny tendrils interwoven like tangled barbed wire, or massed conglomerations of bubbleplant, spheres of delicate tissue-thin octagonal panes as big as her head or larger piled one atop the other, trembling in the breeze. Sometimes she saw great flying creatures hanging in the wind from the rimwall peaks on double pinions a dozen metres across; superstitiously, she never shot at these huge wind-riders.

With no sense of time, she sometimes walked thirty kilometres between sleeps, sometimes managed less than five. Always, the rimwall was before her, rising into banked cloud. Sometimes she searched the dark sky for a sign of a thopter, knowing that she was being foolish but still nursing a faint hope. Sometimes she fantasised about abandoning the ascent, becoming an ascetic and chaste hermit in the alien forest, dressing in striped skins and finding some dry cave and carving texts from Shakespeare in rock so that the masters of this world, should they ever appear, might puzzle over the alien signs and her strangely shaped bones.

Dorthy saw the storm sweeping down upon her, a darkness covering the dark sky and the sullen face of the sun. The rain was a sudden deluge, a million silvery spears striking the ground, striking through the fanned branches of the trees where she sheltered so that within minutes she was as wet as she would have been had she remained in the open, and as cold. So she resumed walking, rain sluicing her face, plastering her coveralls to her skin. Thunder rolled low across the high sparse forest, and lightning leapt blue-white, making her squint; she had become used to the dim light of the sun. Wind rose, shaking the branches of the trees, blowing back her tangled hair. She laughed, suddenly exhilarated, and climbed on shouting quotations into the teeth of the wind. Blow winds, and crack your cheeks! Heigh, my hearts! cheerly, cheerly, my hearts! yare, yare! Take in the topsail! Tend to the master's whistle! Until, as suddenly as it had begun, the storm passed, rain becoming a hazy mist, faltering as the forest floor, drying, exhaled its own mist upward (Blow, till thou burst thy wind, if room enough!), a scent of pine resin, of the dead needles beneath her split, scuffing boots, bittersweet smell, honey and turpentine, of the barbed-wire bushes.

Higher and higher: the forest floor was more bare rock than carpet of needles now. She came to a bluff that rose above a turn in the river's canyon, and found that it looked out across the vast curving slope she'd climbed. The trees ran down dry slopes, becoming denser, serried armies of arrowheads bristling darkly, here and there slashed by the winding of the river. Small and far was the eye of the lake, a polished ruby dropped in the dark folds of the forest. And farther still, at the dim limits of vision, the red hem of the plain where she'd started her journey. I alone have survived . . .

She turned and went on, sometimes singing as she climbed, her small clear voice winging out across the great airy spaces.

In this manner she passed the treeline and ascended into the mists, the ground riven slopes of ash hardened into rock an age ago. Nothing grew there but low, wind-twisted clumps of paddle-leaved plants and great blotches like crusty lichens. The river ran among rough boulders in a wide shallow channel; the great sun swam above the thickening mists like a dulled mirror.

The river split, split again, as she followed its course backward. Usually it was obvious which was the main channel and which was the tributary, but at last she came to a confluence where two similarly sized streams joined. She spent a long time casting up and down before choosing the left-hand stream, but after she had followed it for more than half a dozen kilometres, the channel narrowing all the time, it was clear that it was not the river she remembered Andrews following in the thopter before flying through the pass into the caldera.

She sat on a flat slab of rock and stared off at the way she had come. Shaly rock littering a bleak landscape, the little stream chuckling away between moss-covered shelves of stone, subdued beneath the low ceiling of mist. 'What I need is a cup of coffee,' she said. 'I'm used to drinking three or four cups a day, a good, rich, bitter Java preferably. That's what I need, not all this fucking water!'

Her voice echoed and re-echoed, fading. 'Christ!' she said, and shivered. She could feel an ulcer in one corner of her mouth; she was suffering badly from sores and boils and bleeding gums; the meat that was the sole item of her diet (but she had no meat now, couldn't remember when she had last eaten) lacked the right combination of trace elements and probably most of the essential vitamins. Her feet were swollen in her boots – she was afraid to take off the boots in case she couldn't get them back on. And she stank, she knew, and was deathly tired. But she couldn't go to sleep, not here. Probably wouldn't wake up again. She could imagine Kilczer patiently suggesting that they walk a little more and nodded to herself, pushed up from the rock and began to retrace her steps.

When she reached the confluence, a fine rain was falling, little more than a clinging thickening of the mist. She trudged on beside the clear swift-running water with her head down, fine drops pricking her hand where it gripped the strap of the rifle up by her shoulder. The river swung away sharply, and Dorthy, half remembering, looked around.

A grey slope of bare stone ran up into the mist, towards a cliff that loomed up and up, vanishing as it rose. She left the river and clambered up the slope, and saw that the high cliff face was riven here, an enormous gap through which a warm wind blew, for all that the rock beneath the thin soles of her boots was icy cold.

The pass was so wide that, following one wall, stumbling among tumbled slabs of stone, Dorthy couldn't see the other side through swirling mist. Warm wind sighed in her ears; freezing rock stung her feet. She'd been following it for about ten minutes when she came across an ashy hearth, the remnant of a small fire tucked within a loose kerb of small boulders that protected it from the wind. She sifted ashes through her fingers; cold as the stone around her. The long rib cage of some cat-sized animal lay to one side. Blackened slivers of meat still clung to the curving bones, but despite her hunger she didn't dare scavenge from it.

Somewhere out there: herders.

As she walked on, the flakes of ash that clung to her fingers slowly blew away on the wind. She thought about taking a tablet of counteragent but decided against it because her Talent might slow down her reactions. So she walked with eyes straining to see through whirling white mist, the rifle loosely slung now.

The ground began to slope down, and the wind lessened. The mist was still around her, obliterating everything less than a dozen metres away; it wasn't until she saw the first of the trees that she realised that she had crossed the pass.

She was inside the caldera.

She had made it.

Still she continued to walk, descending the shallow slope among the trees, low and wind-sculpted, foliage a mare's nest of looped and relooped leathery belts with serrated edges, the inner strands lignified, rising from a broad stubby trunk covered with lapping palm-sized scales. There were not many of them. The mist was beginning to thin when she heard the sound, and she stopped walking.

It came from above, to her left. A soft quick thumping like a startled heart, the sound of a thopter. She saw the machine glitter through the mist and then its spotlight came on, white light burning through the mist and pinpointing her with uncanny precision, throwing her shadow backward across the shaly slope. It circled her once, the spotlight swivelling to keep her illuminated, then clapped its vanes as if in salute and dropped towards her.

She had climbed the rimwall and reached the caldera and won rescue. It had been sixteen days since the herd of critters had overrun the camp, down on the plain. The sun was only just beginning to decline from its noon station.

3
The Keep

They took Dorthy straight back to the high camp overlooking the keep, and without even asking her about Kilczer or the twins (she was too dazed and exhausted to volunteer anything) dumped her in the tank of an autodoc. Any halfway competent medical technician could have told them that there was nothing seriously wrong with her – electrolytes out of kilter, histamine reaction, malnutrition, scurvy – but the only medical technician in the survey team had been Kilczer, who was dead.

The autodoc was a military model. It bypassed her sensorium so that she drifted without sight or touch or taste or hearing, unable to lift even an eyebrow, and cut off her consciousness with Russian sleep while it replaced her blood with artificial plasma, cut in a liver bypass and began to dialyse the toxins that slowly leaked from her cells, flensed away skin and subcutaneous tissue around her many inflammations and stimulated regrowth. A civilian machine would have fed her a diet of soothing induced dreams, of the beach at Serenity, perhaps, or of Tallman's Scarp on Titan; but this model was efficient, no more. It sent her to sleep to stop her going insane from sensory deprivation while it worked, but it supplied no dreams; let her have her own.

Sometimes she was back with Kilczer on the other side of the hollow mountain, walking through pine forest with something shadowy behind them, something she couldn't get him to see, or she was in her little singleship out where comets traced their long cold orbits, and Kilczer's voice was crackling urgently from the receiver – but she couldn't understand because he was speaking Russian. Or she was in the little clearing above the waterfall, seeing the herder rush through the tall grass and smash into Kilczer, or she *was* Kilczer, as the impact spun her out over the drop, or the herder.

And sometimes she dreamed of hunting beneath a strange night sky, glowing with veils of frozen, luminous fog through which only a single, intensely bright star shone, the eye at the end of a long black rift. She was coming to understand that these latter visions might not be dreams at all, but something else, something trying to break through to her, when the machine decanted her.

All her senses rushed in on her at once. She was kneeling in a flood of blood-warm fluid, the same stuff stinging her nostrils as it ran out of them. Bright light rainbowed in the drops that clung to her lashes; beyond, someone reached out and gripped her arm at the elbow and helped her up. Cold tiles under her sticky feet. She coughed and coughed.

'Here, honey,' the tall woman, Angel Sutter, said, and guided her to a plastic mesh chair. 'How you feeling?'

It was a small, brightly lit room, half of it taken up by the auto-doc. A pump hummed somewhere, draining the amniotic fluid; the pallet that had tipped Dorthy out retracted into the machine's hard white façade with a smug *click*. The wall opposite curved in as it rose; the wall of a bubbletent.

Dorthy hunched on the chair, naked, her skin slick with long-chain silicones and fluorocarbons, glistening like tarnished bronze. All the stigmata of her journey had been flensed away.

'Like a critter coming out of its chrysalis,' she said, as Angel Sutter draped a huge towel around her.

'You look better anyhow,' Sutter said, patting her shoulders dry. 'When you came in I thought you weren't going to make it, like some dried-up mummy maybe a thousand years old.'

'That's how I felt,' Dorthy said. Then, shivering, 'Arcady Kilczer's dead.'

Sutter didn't pause as she patted down Dorthy's back. 'We guessed. The twins, too, huh?'

'They died when, when . . .'

'You don't have to talk right now, honey. Wait a while. You're lucky this thing was brought up here along with everything else. I don't think you would have made a flight back to Camp Zero. Been all sorts of changes going on here, not all of them to do with the keep.'

Dorthy touched the woman's arm. 'I have to talk with Duncan Andrews.'

Sutter stopped rubbing, disengaged herself from Dorthy's grip. 'There'll be time for that later. You should rest first.'

'I've been asleep for' – Dorthy looked at her timetab – 'for more than two days. There are things I have to tell him, things I've learned about the herders. What are you going to do, throw a hammerlock on me?'

'I couldn't throw a hammerlock on *anyone*. Look, okay, wait a minute. I'll get you something to wear.'

When Sutter returned, Dorthy had finished drying herself and had wrapped the huge towel around herself. The fluid spilled when she had been decanted from the autodoc had all drained away, leaving only a heavy cloying scent, just as her dreams had faded, leaving only a residue, the unsteady conviction that something, someone, was trying to tell her . . . tell her what?

Sutter handed Dorthy the bundle of clothing, holding back something else, a floppy sheaf of paper. As Dorthy pulled on crisp coveralls, Sutter said, 'You didn't have that thing with you, the Shakespeare book, so I had this printed out. Ramaro has a library about the size of that one in Rio, the Museum of Mankind? I had this printed.' She held it out, and Dorthy looked up from fastening her boots. It was The *Complete Plays*, in Portuguese.

'Thank you,' she said.

Sutter pulled at the puffball of her hair. Her regulation coveralls were belted with a nonregulation gold cincture. 'I read in some of it. It's not so bad when you get used to it. Pretty archaic though. Why do you like old stuff like this?'

'It has everything in it, if you look hard enough,' Dorthy said, taking the sheaf. 'Love, jealousy, avarice, loyalty, murder, madness . . . I find it reassuring that human nature is so constant.'

Sutter shrugged. 'Let's get something inside you anyhow, before you go see Andrews. Now don't argue, I'm doing my best to look after you.'

The bubbletent was more than twenty metres across, most of it taken up by the central commons, a scattering of tables and chairs and a complex treacher. Circling it like so many orange segments were small rooms divided by fibrechip panels. A man in uniform coveralls slept at one of the tables, his head resting on folded arms, but otherwise the commons was empty.

Dorthy lingered over her choice at the treacher. Strong black Java of course, but selection of food was more difficult; the screen blinked up almost a hundred pages. At last she settled for a bowl of *oyako donburi*, rice with mother and child. When she sat opposite Sutter, the woman stretched and said, 'So what have you got to tell Duncan, anyhow?'

'I think I can help him find out the truth about the herders.' For a moment the composite she'd built up from the mind of the captured herder lived again, and Sutter's long, full-lipped, dark-brown face seemed a frightening mask, somehow swollen and naked. Dorthy sipped scalding Java, and as familiar bitter oils flooded her tongue the moment passed, leaving her dizzy.

'Now, Duncan already knows *all* about the herders, or he thinks he does. You know they're coming up the side of the caldera, heading for the keep?'

Dorthy nodded, not trusting herself to speak.

'Duncan has abandoned his theory that herders are the savage descendants of the enemy. Now he thinks they're going to prepare the way for the true owners of this planet. Don't say anything about it to me, argue it out with him. But that's why this camp has become so important, the Navy is right behind him now, hoping to catch out the enemy just as they awake or whatever they're about to do.'

'They've already done it,' Dorthy said.

Sutter shrugged, 'You tell Duncan, I don't know too much about it to tell the truth, security and so on. But there's plenty else happening out there; we can all make our names here.'

Dorthy returned the other's smile. She didn't mind Sutter's enthusiasm; it was innocent, without guile. She asked, 'What's going on? I can tell that you're dying to tell me all about it.'

Sutter reared back in her chair, took a breath. 'Where do I begin? The thing I'm interested in is a change in the lake around the keep; the past few days its level had been going down and a causeway across it has become exposed. But what's really interesting is that stuff has begun growing in the water, a self-generating hydrocarbon just loaded with heavy-metal radicals, goddam weird stuff, let me tell you. It's phosphorescent, too; I think it gets the energy to replicate from the quantum change state of trapped photons. The principle isn't exactly new – we've maybe a dozen systems inherited from the Age of Waste. But those require a stable substrate, and can't replicate. And the stuff out there is damned efficient, has to be I guess, given the low input of the sun.' Sutter grinned. 'But you ask anyone else up here and they wouldn't give you ten seconds for it. Ramaro calls it pond scum.'

Dorthy set down her chopsticks and pushed away the bowl of stirred food. Apart from a slight rubberiness to the flecks of egg, the *oyako donburi* was remarkably authentic, but for all that her stomach was empty she wasn't particularly hungry. The autodoc had kept her blood sugar high. She asked, 'Do you know what that stuff is for?'

'Could be a food source, or maybe a base for manufacturing organics, like the alfalfa they grow on Novaya Zyemlya. But who the hell knows what anything really is out there?'

'And what else? What else has been going on?'

'I guess the main thing is that herders have been arriving, coming through the pass in the rimwall. That's how you were picked up so quickly, that area is saturated with remotes. Duncan Andrews calls the herders caretakers now, by the way.'

'I know what he means, but he's wrong.'

'*Anyway*, there's a bunch of them in the keep right now, seem to be working their way towards the top, although they're taking their time, reading every damn line of inscription as they go. They haven't got very far yet.' Sutter scratched her flat nose. 'That was when the crud started coming up, after they arrived.'

'There will be more arriving,' Dorthy said.

'Yeah,' Sutter said, 'there aren't any herds on the plain anymore. That's why everything has built up here. Ramaro's team has been doubled in size, and even so they're having trouble keeping track of the arrivals. The caretakers. Chung even came here, with the new batch of equipment and technicians. She'll be here again in a few days.' Her smile broadened. 'Oops. I gave away the good news.'

'Chung is coming here? I don't particularly care for the woman.'

'No, but you'll be able to go back to Camp Zero with her. How about that?'

'It's funny, but it doesn't mean a thing to me anymore.'

142

'You're still recovering. It'll catch up with you.' Sutter looked at the bulky but fashionable chronometer strapped to her wrist. 'I guess we can go see Duncan now, if you want.'

Dorthy drained the bitter dregs of her coffee and allowed herself to be led through the camp, nearly a dozen bubbletents in the wedge between high cliffs, with a landing body and a couple of thopters squatting to one side. Wind howled between the rock walls. 'Isn't the Navy worried about letting equipment fall into enemy hands?' Dorthy asked.

'We're hoping to get a bead on them before they get a bead on us,' Sutter said.

But Dorthy saw that that wasn't the whole truth. 'Come on, what else?'

'I guess it's no secret. There's a kiloton bomb buried here, enough yield to burn the caldera clean any time the computer controlling it decides it's being threatened. Pretty damned paranoid machine, too. Shit, I try not to think about it, you know, the price tag of knowledge. If it wasn't for the stuff in the lake down there, I'd be out with McCarthy's team, in the forest. Yeah, he finally got to come out here. Hussan, too. They're having the time of their lives out there. But I guess you know all about that.'

'I wish Arcady and I had run into them,' Dorthy said, and followed Sutter into the lock of the bubbletent.

Andrews was larger than she remembered, his red hair longer and in disarray, his coveralls rumpled, sleeves bunched high on his muscular, freckled arms. He kept scrubbing his hand over his face as he listened intently to Dorthy's description of how she and Kilczer and the twins had followed the herd, watched it merge with the others, how the camp had been overrun and only she and Kilczer had survived. Seated beside Andrews at the table, fat Major Luiz Ramaro scowled down at a sheaf of holograms, occasionally scribbling something on the grey screen of the memotablet and paying Dorthy only minimal attention. When she described how she and Kilczer had found the chrysalis, their realisation that the critters were the children of the herders and what the critters were turning into, Ramaro waved a hand languidly and said, 'But this is well known. I hope your other revelations are more original, Dr Yoshida. You forget we have many people working here now.'

'Let her tell it her own way,' Andrews said amiably. 'Go on, now, Dorthy.'

So she told about finding the new male herders, the caretakers in Andrews's terminology, building boats, how Kilczer had knocked out one of the males when they'd stolen a boat, her attempts at probing it.

Andrews questioned her closely on this, but again Ramaro was dismissive. 'To know their language would be useful, but this talk of hidden knowledge seems to me to be idle speculation.'

'It's there,' Dorthy said. 'It's real.'

'I do not doubt that you sensed something,' Ramaro said coldly, without looking up from the memotablet, 'but as for what it means, well, I must question your interpretation. Why are the caretakers even now reading their way around the spiral of the keep if they possess vast untapped wells of knowledge? What are they learning?'

'You tell me,' Dorthy said. 'Isn't that your department?'

'I wish it was so easy. The written language, at least, is very complicated. There are at least sixty-four graphemes, and I have catalogued more than a thousand ideograms as well. You are Japanese, so I do not have to tell you how difficult such a written language can be. Depending upon the context, a single ideogram may represent half a dozen disparate notions; and I have no Rosetta stone besides, only vague speculation on your part. I do not know what they read, down there in the keep, but I doubt that it is for entertainment. For knowledge, certainly. And if knowledge is hardwired into their heads, why do they read?' he allowed himself a little smile, his lips pushed out to make a little snout under his snub nose.

'I don't want to argue,' Dorthy said. The plastic surface of the little table was gritty under her sweating palms. Her dislike of Ramaro was at least as strong as his dislike of her. The touch of his mind was like immersing her hand in a pool murky with oil. She said, 'Large areas of the herder's mind – new male, caretaker, call it what you will – were locked away. Perhaps those in the keep are receiving the key. But it was there, all right. That's why I have to disagree with the consensus opinion about what the herders *are*. Maybe I should tell you the rest, so you understand.'

Ramaro shrugged. Andrews said, 'Please, Dr Yoshida. What happened to Arcady?' Behind him, technicians watched various consoles; screens softly glowed with red light, like windows on a furnace.

So Dorthy continued her tale. The travails of their journey up to the lake, the capture of the boat and the herder. The waterfall, where they had had to abandon the boat. The ascent. And the herder's sudden rush, the suicidal leap that had taken Kilczer, too.

Andrews shook his head. 'That's a terrible thing to happen, when you had come so far. I'm sorry, Dorthy.'

Ramaro said, 'He should not have entrusted the rifle to a woman, perhaps.'

Palms flat on gritty plastic, Dorthy pushed up from her chair, leaned across the table, and said, 'I can *use* a fucking rifle, and it happened so quickly no one could have done anything to stop it. Keep your nasty little judgements to yourself.'

'You really could not tell what the caretaker was about to do, with your Talent?' Ramaro did not lift his gaze to meet hers.

'The counteragent had worn off. No, I couldn't.' Dorthy sat back, her anger turning inside her like a smooth steel shaft.

'Dorthy, Luiz,' Andrews said. 'However it turned out, it is done with. But what else do you have to tell us, Dorthy? Why do you think we are wrong about the caretakers?'

'Because of what that one did, don't you see? Once it had decided that there was no way out of its predicament, it committed suicide. Just as the enemy do at BD twenty.'

Ramaro said, 'And that is all?'

'It does seem a little tenuous, Dorthy,' Andrews said, pinching the bridge of his large, shapeless nose between thumb and forefinger.

She saw that neither of them wanted to believe her. Too much depended upon the new male herders being no more than harbingers of the real owners of the planet. For if they were not, if they were the enemy, it would be too dangerous to remain so close to the keep, the survey team would be pulled out. 'It's what I felt,' she said stubbornly, knowing it was the wrong thing to say.

'You see, Duncan?' Ramaro said to Andrews. 'It is what I tell you. Women prefer feelings to facts. They pass judgements too easily.'

Dorthy ignored this. 'What you call the caretakers are the enemy. The new males have arisen because of us, and now they're learning all about their inheritance, down there in the keep. Once they come into it, how are you going to stop them?'

'There is a bomb,' Ramaro said, shuffling together the holograms. 'I have work, Duncan. Seyoura Yoshida, I wish you well on your journey back.' After picking up holograms and memotablet, he strolled off among the consoles crowded together in the dim circular space of the tent.

'He has a point,' Duncan Andrews said. 'I can't pull the plug on a programme this size on so little evidence.'

'How many herds were there, on the plain, before all this started?'

'Oh, perhaps a thousand.'

'And how many critters in each herd?'

'I know what you are going to say. The average was around a hundred, as I recall, so it makes a nice round figure of a hundred thousand potential caretakers.'

'Or enemy.'

'To be sure. Of course, not all the critters survive the change or the journey up here afterward.' He became animated, pulling at his elf-locked hair; it was growing out curly from the uniform crew cut. 'The change itself is an incredible thing, takes less than ten days. They spin their cocoon and then sort of liquefy inside. There are nodes of preadult cells all through this soup, and these form the new body. Damned quickly, like a speeded-up cancer. A lot simply don't make it, presumably because it is such a *forced* change. So let's say that twenty-five hundred will eventually arrive here. Suppose they are the enemy' – he held up a large hand – 'which of course I strenuously deny.' His smile was of old. 'However, let us assume that they are. It does not matter. If they initiate hostilities, there is a bomb—'

'I know. Angel Sutter told me about it.'

'A little crude, don't you think? But effective. You see, it does not matter if the caretakers *are* the enemy, or if they have arisen in order to revive the enemy. Either way, if they initiate hostilities – isn't that a lovely phrase? It is the way the people upstairs speak. Initiation of hostilities will set off the bomb, and that will flash-burn everything in the caldera. Bad luck on us, but we are volunteers, and you will be gone long before it becomes even a remote possibility.'

'And all the other holds? What's happening there?'

'We know only from satellite pictures, of course. But it seems that the herds are withdrawing from the plains, the various keeps are switching on in readiness, as here. I wish I knew how all this activity is coordinated.'

'If they all start trouble, you'll have more than a little local difficulty to deal with.'

'Ah, now, don't worry about that. The Navy has that in hand as well.'

Dorthy remembered the touch of fear she'd felt in Colonel Chung; this time it was not fear, precisely, but an uneasiness she couldn't quite pin down behind Andrews's smile.

He said, 'Look now, we must talk again, Dorthy.' His expression became solemn. 'I want you to tell me about your adventures, about poor Arcady, the twins.'

'Arcady buried Marta Ade; he couldn't find any trace of the other one.' She couldn't remember his name, plucked it from Andrews's mind. 'Jon Chavez.'

'We'll look for the bodies; I wouldn't like them left out there. That's no resting place. Yes, we will talk, when you are fully recovered. I'll find time, certainly. In the meanwhile, perhaps you could prepare a formal report, Dorthy. These things have to be gone through, I'm afraid.'

His concern was genuine, she saw, and there was tenderness, too, mixed with his scepticism about her belief that the herders were the enemy. It came to her, part pure intuition, part uncontrolled leakage of her Talent, that he was not truly ruthless; there was a streak of sentimentality that diluted his ambition. A helpless dreamer. That was why he got so involved, why he was down here when he could have overseen the whole thing from orbital command, safe above the atmosphere. His inability to delegate responsibility was not so much due to ruthless egotism, as she had first thought, but because he had been inculcated with the sort of idealist notions that the children of old, established money were taught, and one of these was that one should be able to do all that one expects one's underlings to do. It was because of this close involvement that he was unable to treat objectively any challenges to his ideas.

All this came to her in a moment, but Dorthy thought about Andrews and his concern and his closed mind off and on while she waited for Colonel Chung to arrive, while she waited for her release; and in the meantime dictated a formal report together with all she could recall of her two probe attempts, of the herder group, and of the captured male who had committed suicide. There was not much else to do. The technicians who guided and monitored the remotes kept away from her and she from them, and Angel Sutter descended into the caldera with Andrews for a couple of days, and then was busy with her specimens. But Andrews afterwards kept to his promise and found time to listen as Dorthy went over her climb through the forest again, again not mentioning that she and Arcady Kilczer had slept together despite the slow befuddlement brought on by a flask of illicit liquor that Andrews insisted they share, oily clear stuff that burned all the way down to the pit of her stomach. Dorthy had spent a little time in the command tent watching unattended screens despite Major Ramaro's disapproval, and one had shown the new males as they traced with painful slowness the cursive script that intagliated a high wall, dark as shadows in the bright red light of the keep. It was a scene that filled her with disquiet, a brooding dread, but she couldn't quite explain this to Andrews and he, good-humouredly and predictably, would have none of it. No one believed Dorthy, not even Angel Sutter.

So she waited for Colonel Chung, reading the plays Sutter had had printed, sometimes helping the biologist in her little laboratory, and, for a lot of the time, sleeping. She still had not fully recovered from her ordeal.

She was asleep when Colonel Chung finally arrived. Sutter woke her, and she dressed quickly and crossed the bare windy rock to the command tent. The colonel stood in a little knot of people, Ramaro and Andrews either side of her, studying a holostage as view after view of the keep blossomed there. Andrews smiled at Dorthy as she joined the group; Ramaro was explaining something to Colonel Chung. The stage showed a close-up of script that ran along a wall in a metre-wide band. Ramaro pointed. 'There, and there. We've a ninety per cent confidence limit now that Alea is the name of the species which planoformed P'thrsn.' He looked at Andrews, who merely raised an eyebrow.

'Meaning?' The colonel didn't acknowledge Dorthy's presence with so much as a glance. She had a brittle air of nervous impatience.

'Perhaps, *the people*,' Ramaro told her. 'It's our best guess, less than fifty per cent confidence there. You have to remember that many of the referents depend upon the context for translation, and in almost every case we are still unsure of the context. That much has not changed since your last visit, I'm afraid.' The red light of the hologram threw his round double chin into relief, made livid the seamed scar on his plump cheek. He was doing a good job of concealing his dislike of having to defer to the command of a mere woman. 'All in all,' he said, 'I'd consider we've done very well, Colonel. I wish I knew what the team upstairs is making of it all. It is frustrating.'

'I'll second that,' Andrews said.

Colonel Chung turned from the holostage. She looked tired, Dorthy thought. 'There can be no relaxation on security,' Chung said. 'It is perhaps unfortunate, but we must do our best down here.'

'Second-guessing what they want upstairs,' Andrews said.

'I would have thought you'd enjoy that,' Colonel Chung said. 'The brief reports I have received from orbital command have indicated no dissatisfaction with your work, at any rate. But I am alarmed to learn that activity in the keep continues to rise.'

'Those herders are no threat,' Andrews said. 'Believe me. They're not the enemy, just the caretakers. The enemy will come along, though, but I think we'll be ready for that.'

'One way or the other,' Colonel Chung said. 'Before this change you believed them to be, what, the ragged barbarian descendants of the enemy? And now you have had to alter your theory.'

'Well,' Andrews said, smiling, 'that's science.'

'Because,' Colonel Chung continued implacably, 'you have learned a little more. There is still much that is not understood. Major Ramaro is able to assign probabilities to the few translations he has made. What probability do you give this caretaker theory, Andrews?'

'It isn't that kind of theory, simply a best guess. These creatures have shown no sign of deploying any kind of advanced technology despite the time they've spent in the keep. If they *were* the enemy, they surely would have moved against this camp by now. But from what you tell me, the equatorial hold would appear to be a quite different matter.'

Colonel Chung nodded. 'It is indeed. Let us discuss it.' She reached into her uniform coveralls and pulled out a data cube. Addressing everyone in the group, she said, 'This was transmitted yesterday from orbital command. After Dr Yoshida apparently scanned or sensed the mind of something immensely intelligent as she descended in a dropcapsule, something to the east of Camp Zero, orbital command redeployed one of the mapping satellites to cover all the holds in that direction. One is located precisely on the equator; originally it had nothing in it analogous to the structures found in this and most of the other holds – no keep, nothing at all. Until five days ago.'

'Christ,' someone said.

Ramaro glanced around sternly, then took the data cube from Chung and plugged it in.

Dorthy craned forward.

A dark-textured circle on the red desert surface, seemingly ringing a black hole. 'This was made from ninety klicks up, and the transit velocity was considerable. Nevertheless, the detail is fascinating.' Colonel Chung reached out and with one finger, its long nail scraping plastic, pressed a pair of keys on the holostage terminal. *Flick.* Now the circle was larger, clearly a forested crater, its centre perfectly circular, perfectly black. 'I will not show the infrared scans at the moment. The signature of the slopes is the same as that of the forests in the other holds.' *Flick.* Not a hole at all, but a deep bowl ringed by forest, a deep, symmetrical, black bowl with something small and white at its centre.

It was tantalisingly, impossibly familiar to Dorthy, a dizzying moment of *déjà vu*. And then she remembered. 'Arecibo!' she explained.

Everyone looked at her.

She explained, 'On Earth. There's nothing left of it now; it dated from the Age of Waste and was destroyed in one of the wars. But it was a big, fixed radio telescope built in a natural valley.'

Colonel Chung cleared her throat. 'Precisely,' she said. 'A radio telescope. There appear to be buildings close by, in a canyon or cleft in the rim of the crater' – she poked a long-nailed finger into the hologram – 'but resolution is not good enough to show any detail and they are mostly obscured by trees, which is perhaps the reason why they did not show up on the long-range scans that were made for mapping purposes.'

'How do we know it's a radio telescope?' one of the technicians objected. She thrust a pen into the loose net that bundled her long fair hair. 'It could be anything, maybe a solar power generator—'

'Or a sports field,' someone else said, to general laughter.

'Please,' Ramaro said. 'It should be obvious that a radio telescope built by the enemy would look like one we ourselves built. Basic physics demands conservation of form.' He looked around, sternly disapproving of the sudden outburst of hilarity, the release of tension.

Andrews pulled at his nose, his habitual gesture of contained excitement. 'Has this convinced the people upstairs that we should be investigating that particular hold rather than continue to fool around here?'

'We must proceed cautiously,' Colonel Chung said. 'For now, no further attempt will be made to explore any hold but this. The events here will have to provide you with sufficient stimulation, Andrews.'

'I'm not interested in filling in details; I want to get to the bottom of all this. Look, we don't know why the enemy chose to planoform a world of such an impoverished sun, nor where they came from, nor how widespread they are through this arm of the Galaxy.' As he enunciated each point he pressed down a finger of his left hand with the forefinger of his right. 'Nor why the colony around BD twenty is so hostile, not even what the enemy really is: I will bet that it is not the herders in any shape or form, however. We've made no steps to contact whatever is living at this other hold. Perhaps they are as hostile as anything around BD twenty. Perhaps that goes for any technologically active colony we might run into. But so far we have not *tried*. Until we do, we can sit around making guesses, but we cannot substantiate them.'

'You are not here to make contact,' Colonel Chung said. 'You are here to study, that is all. Please, Andrews, leave the logistics of this expedition to those in charge of it. I have received no indication that this discovery will change the direction or pace of research here on the surface. We must be cautious. If hostilities are initiated, I need hardly remind you that it will be most difficult to study anything at all here.'

For a moment, Dorthy almost grasped what it was that orbital command could do if it chose, a general vision of burning, gone in an eyeblink. Were they planning to bomb every hold if hostilities broke out? It would be their style.

'Please, Duncan,' Ramaro said. 'Calm yourself. Have patience.'

Andrews smiled. 'You know very well that I'm short of that particular grace, Luiz. But I'll abide by the decision – what other choice do I have?' He didn't really mean it, Dorthy saw. 'Now let's get a proper look at this thing,' he said, and tapped at the holostage's terminal, shifting through various false-colour shots. Around him, the group broke into an unfocused discussion of what the telescope could be for, communication or listening, why it was fixed instead of movable, how much of the sky it could scan.

Colonel Chung drew Dorthy aside. 'You must be glad to have done your job, Dr Yoshida. There will be room to ride back with me. Perhaps you can find something to turn your hand to at the camp.'

'What do you mean? Wait. You're telling me that I can't get off this planet?'

'No one can get off, at least for the moment. Until the situation is secure, orbital command will not risk sending down anything that could be used by the enemy to get into orbit.'

There was a hollow roaring in Dorthy's head. 'This is some kind of mistake. You told me that when I had finished here I could go.'

'I'm sorry, Dr Yoshida, it's out of my hands. I cannot *make* orbital command send a shuttle down, I can only follow orders. If it is of any comfort, we are all in the same situation down here. Provided that you are occupied, I am sure that the time will pass quickly. You are an astronomer, are you not? Perhaps you could study this latest discovery.'

'No,' Dorthy said. Her throat hurt. 'No,' she said again, loudly, aware of the technicians and scientists turning to look at her all around the cluttered, dimly lit space. She couldn't give up now, not after all the days of desperate danger and deprivation tramping through the wilderness of the hold, not after the farcical tragedy of Arcady Kilczer's death . . . again Dorthy saw his mild face, felt the flow of his patient, inexhaustably inquiring mind. He wouldn't have chosen to sit in limbo at Camp Zero with the puzzle still to be solved. 'If I can't get off this world I'd rather stay here,' Dorthy said.

'You want to find out about the enemy – I'll use my Talent. All right?' She saw that Andrews was staring at her, his face expressionless. She couldn't tell what he was thinking.

'I would strongly suggest that you return with me,' Colonel Chung said.

'No!' Dorthy had the satisfaction of sensing surprise behind Chung's cold mask. 'It isn't me you want to protect, it's my Talent. That and the scandal the Navy wants to avoid if I'm killed. Well, the hell with that. I'll stay here unless you knock me on the head and carry me out.'

'Very well,' Colonel Chung said impassively. Although she was angered by Dorthy's rebellion, she would lose face if she showed it. 'But I hope you will not regret this, Dr Yoshida.'

Dorthy turned away, and saw that Andrews was smiling now, a quick wry flicker, whether of approval or amusement she couldn't tell. Then he bent towards the hologram of the radio telescope again, talking in a quiet voice to Ramaro. Dorthy held the edge of a console and thought: trapped.

Almost every day a group of new male herders emerged from the high pass through the rimwall. Never fewer than three, sometimes as many as a dozen, they carried tall staffs that, with their hoods of naked skin and dark fur, made them resemble robed medieval pilgrims as they strode down the rocky, misty slopes. When they came in sight of the keep they often stopped and built a campfire that they lit with a spark carried in a clay ball, and sometimes spent several days there, hunting small game and joined by other groups before at last moving on, descending the forested inner slope of the caldera by a well-trampled path through the low trees, crossing the straight causeway and dwindling into insignificance against the high shoulders of the keep's buttresses, its soaring peaks strung with a galaxy of lights. Squatting before the wall bordering the road or pathway that spiralled to the top of the keep, patiently tracing the lines of text there, the new males did not look like an army preparing to repel invaders, a point Andrews made much of. They looked like innocent unhurried scholars. The first group to have arrived were only now, two weeks later, halfway up the long spiral, where the text covered the wall from top to bottom.

Dorthy spent the next two weeks trying to fathom these strange creatures, studying the patterns of their arrival (but finding nothing that couldn't be explained by simple Poisson distribution) and venturing out to probe them with her Talent. She wanted to prove her point to Andrews, show the herders for what they were, not precursors of some greater glory but prodigal sons slowly coming into their own. She couldn't explain her sudden outburst against the offer of safety at Camp Zero. Before her adventure she would have railed against the broken promise, to be sure, but she would have accepted it with the same resignation with which, as a child, she had accepted her father's sequestration of her earnings during her indenture at the Kamali-Silver Institute. Angel Sutter thought that she was crazy, had said so the very next day.

'Maybe you're right,' Dorthy said, with a small smile.

'If I was in your position I'd have left like that.' Sutter snapped her fingers. 'I thought you were for getting out right from the beginning, the fuss you were making in the camp.'

'Things have changed,' Dorthy said uncomfortably. She looked away from Sutter's frank, probing gaze, at the table where half a dozen technicians were eating on the other side of the brightly lit commons. It was change of shift on the round-the-clock watch of the keep.

'Things sure have,' Sutter said.

'I don't know exactly why,' Dorthy confessed. 'I'd like to convince Andrews that he's wrong about the new males, the caretakers, but I could just as easily walk away from it, to hell with him, to hell with all of you, right? Except, what else could I do?'

'Changing Duncan's mind once he's fixed on something isn't easy, honey.'

'Perhaps I'm trying to justify what happened to me down there, the deaths of the twins, of Arcady . . .' It sounded silly when she said it, trivialising those deaths, and she blushed. Besides, at bottom she felt that it was not precisely the truth – that it was instead the portal to a deep, darker, as yet unfathomed truth.

Sutter pressed her lips together. 'Listen,' she said, 'I don't mean anything by this, but I'd guess you and Arcady slept together. You don't have to say anything if you don't want to . . .'

For a frozen moment Dorthy felt as if everything was falling away from her in every direction. She said slowly, 'Yes, it's true, but I don't think it meant anything to either of us. We were simply thrown together, that's all. It didn't happen until we reached the lake, you know, where the camp was. I suppose we both thought we were going to die, not make it across the rimwall. Things didn't seem to matter.'

'Oh, honey, don't mind me. I'm just plain damned nosy, that's all. I don't know if it's good, for you to stay here after all this. Even Duncan isn't completely happy about it, much as he likes having you and your Talent working for him again.'

'Running away from it didn't seem like much of a solution either, especially as I couldn't get any farther than Camp Zero. I'd still be on the damned planet, and I wouldn't be able to *do* anything there except sit with my thumb up my ass, under Chung's frosty eye.' Dorthy sipped her bitter coffee and added, 'You won't tell anyone about what I said, will you?'

'I may be nosy, but I don't go running my mouth off,' Sutter said, smiling. 'Except when I feel I have to. The way we're shut in here, gossip is like a poison, you know?'

And it came to Dorthy clearly then, the thing, the obvious thing that despite her Talent she hadn't seen before, that Sutter and Andrews were lovers, had been ever since Sutter had arrived at the lost lakeside camp.

If Dorthy had not already guessed, it would have become quickly obvious, for both Angel Sutter and Duncan Andrews accompanied her on the expeditions across the slopes of the caldera, and within the circle of the alarm system they rigged to give at least nominal protection against the new male herders there was not very much privacy. Dorthy found that she did not much mind their discreet lovemaking only a few metres from where she lay; for all that she valued her own privacy she had long been used to eavesdropping unintentionally on others, was able to look away from it. Nor was she particularly jealous, as she had been of the twins. That nerve had been dulled.

Besides, she was glad to be out of the camp, away from the cramped commons and the imposition of other minds on her own, the continual feathering brush of emotions as distracting as a moth beating at a light. And there were the long inner slopes of the caldera to explore, the scrub forest of trees, tangled loops never rising more than half a dozen metres above their stubby trunks, which in their obvious otherness were less disturbing than the pine forest through which she and Arcady Kilczer had had to climb. She remembered him with a qualified wistfulness not substantial enough to tip into mourning. He had not touched her deeply enough to draw on those wells (twice, they had only made love twice). She was beginning to wonder if anyone ever would.

She walked the caldera forest with a continual edge of adrenalin thrilling her blood, buoyed by Andrews's jaunty confidence, Sutter's keen awareness of the interconnections everywhere, the patterns of the patchwork ecosystem slowly unravelling. There was always the danger that, as they stalked the arriving parties, they would blunder into a new male that had gone off hunting. The belt-trees did not grow closely together, but the spaces between them, on the lower slopes, were colonised by tangles of thorny bushes or stands of tall grass, or stuff like pulpy organ pipes that gave off a faint blue phosphorescence and a cutting whiff of ketones. A herder could easily stalk the trio of humans, if it had a mind to. Although they hunted the lower slopes, the new male herders usually camped at the edge of the forest, high among mist and tumbled bare rock, and Dorthy had to make her way slowly and cautiously on her belly until she was close enough to begin probing the creatures, Andrews behind her with a rifle as welcome insurance – he had abandoned all pretence of obeying the guidelines laid down by orbital command, insisting that, after all, the caretakers were no more than dumb servant brutes.

And despite all her attempts, Dorthy found nothing that contradicted him. The minds of the new arrivals were little different from the mind of the new male she and Kilczer had captured, with the exception that the blinding compulsion to climb to the keep, the geas that had been the centre of every impulse, was purged, vanished as a pricked soap bubble vanishes, leaving only a faint residue. Calm, almost fulfilled after having crossed the rimwall, the new male herders lounged quietly around their campfires, the thin skim of their conscious minds still and placid over tantalising depths Dorthy could only strainingly glimpse, too deep and dark to be reflected clearly at her centre. She would surface from *Sessan Amakuki* with an aching sense of frustration and make her way back to where Andrews waited, shake her head and tell him that there was nothing new to report.

He took this with equanimity. Although he would have liked to have learned more, each of Dorthy's failures made his hypothesis stronger, aided his campaign to break orbital command's interdict and have the new males who were painstakingly reading their way around the keep's spiral more thoroughly investigated.

Angel Sutter, less patient than her lover and less experienced in the complex dominance games of the Navy, couldn't understand why Andrews didn't simply order opening of the keep to full exploration. 'Ramaro might be in nominal charge, but you're senior to him, you outrank him.'

Andrews smiled gently. He was sprawled on trampled grass, looking up through the braided loops of the tree that marked the centre of the camp – Dorthy's sleeping bag on one side, his and Sutter's on the other. He had hung the little box of the alarm system caster on one serrated loop, and it winked quick green light over his face, indicating that the perimeter was undisturbed. He said slowly, 'To be sure, I could flatly tell him that I was going to walk into the keep, but as soon as I left he'd make a panic call to orbital command and request permission to shoot me for violating contact procedure. They'd allow it, too.'

'Come on,' Angel Sutter said.

'It's true enough,' Andrews said. 'Don't you agree, Dorthy?'

On the other side of the little heating unit on which Sutter was simmering a stew of honeyed chicken and black beans made from raw ingredients she'd specially dialled up from the treacher in the camp, Dorthy said, 'Why not? But you know that I'm biased against that fat, prejudiced bastard.'

'My,' Andrews said, and raised an eyebrow. 'Assuming all that to be an accurate assessment of his character, it's not why Ramaro would have me shot without compunction. The reason is that he is a career man. When the Navy was created he simply moved sideways from the Greater Brazilian Peace Corps, and he sees it as an opportunity to advance himself. The thing of it is, he likes hierarchies, feels comfortable in a defined position. The youngest son of minor aristocracy – I know the type well, we have enough of them on Elysium, heaven knows. You don't believe me, Angel.'

'I'm from the Guild, which has just as rigid a hierarchy as the C.P.G.B.,' the tall woman said, 'but I'm not about to have you shot. Not yet, anyhow.'

'Ah, but you were in the survey arm, a scientist. What do you hope for, after this?'

Sutter tipped back her head and loosed her low, rough laugh. 'What a question! I don't know, maybe section head. That would be nice. I get kind of tired sometimes, doing the shit-work of collecting.'

Andrews smiled, 'You see, no ambition to speak of. Now Ramaro' – he raised a hand when Sutter good-humouredly started to object – 'Ramaro has a gut full of ambition, although in the end it too is limited. He will stay in the Navy, even if he gets to the top of it, God forbid the thought.'

'And what about you, Duncan,' Dorthy asked, 'what are the limits of *your* ambition?'

'Why, to conquer the galaxy, of course. I had thought I'd made that plain.'

'Sometimes I get the feeling you're not joking when you say that,' Sutter said. 'What about it, Dorthy? What are this guy's innermost thoughts? Go on, put that Talent to good use.'

Dorthy, crosslegged on her silvery sleeping bag, said, 'He's too shifty even for me to work out.'

She had actually asked Andrews about this on a previous trip, while they were waiting for Sutter to return from collecting specimens, asked him why he was so fired up, why he drove himself as he did. For he worked harder than anyone else in the camp, reading reports when he wasn't out in the field, with Angel Sutter or with McCarthy's team on the other side of the mountain, or running sample tests in the laboratory. Absorbing it all. He drove himself hard, yes, and expected as much from others. Only Sutter seemed impervious to his demands, shrugging them off casually, wickedly deflating his more grandiose claims.

When Dorthy had asked the question, he'd said, 'Because I'm rich, you mean?' They were sitting next to the grounded thopter in weak red sunlight, the sun near the edge of the rimwall now, close to setting, but because of the high mountain border its light still slanting down from a high angle. Andrews tipped his head back, dull light like dried blood on his red hair, in mock consideration. Dorthy, her Talent almost faded after another useless session, couldn't follow his thoughts. At last he said, 'The funny thing about money is that you own it, but it also owns you, once you have a certain amount. Poor people always think that they're slaves to money, but they have little enough to lose; really, they're slaves to habit. Past a certain amount, a very high limit of course, it demands more from you than you demand of it. That's the situation my father is in. He's possessed by it – although he enjoys all the stuff that goes with it, the meetings, strategies, wars. To be sure, wars. Corporate raids, that kind of thing. People even get killed. I am the eldest son, I get to inherit all that, but not for a long time. Maybe another century, maybe two. We have any amount of agatherin, and we have *very* good medical programmes. In the meantime . . . Well, you know of what they're beginning to call the Golden, on Earth?'

Dorthy nodded, but he was looking off through the low tangled trees. 'Yes,' she said. 'I've even met some.'

'The heirs waiting impatiently in the wings, most of them, although one is my old friend Talbeck Barlstilkin, who should spend more time running his part of the Combine than he does. The young rich – agatherin has more or less rendered that a tautology. They are perpetually in search of something else, some new thrill . . . Travelling with a group of them is like living in a perpetual party, do you know.'

Dorthy, who had once done just that down the ragged curve of the Barrier Reef (she had ended up going off on her own, high as a kite on a skin-contact psychedelic from Serenity, and for a week had been stranded on a little island after her skiff had broken down), nodded, but Andrews was caught up now in his explanation.

'Seen at sunrise on the peak of Arul Terrek on Novaya Rosya; skiing on the Glacier of Worlds on New America; climbing the rim mountains of the Taryshcheena on Novaya Zyemlya; trekking through the Philippine Preserve on Earth; seen at sunset by the Crystal Sea on Ruby. A hundred evershifting groups of hedonists. Oh, some have responsibility to which they now and again have to make obeisance; a few, like my friend Talbeck, are on the run from their wealth. I was quoting, by the way – a novel, *All That Summer*.'

'I didn't think people read novels anymore.'

'Not on Earth, perhaps. But on Elysium it has become a revived artform. There is even talk of printing actual books, like that one of yours. But the point is that that kind of life isn't my way. A lot of people sneer at science these days, say there's nothing new to be discovered that's worth the work of discovery; and besides, look what science did in the Age of Waste. Well, I studied biology because all my family's money stems from agatherin, which in the raw state is mostly a plant disease, after all. We are very much diversified these days, but back then agatherin and a tumbledown castle were all we had. Stay in anything long enough and you will gain some power, if only through inertia. And I suppose my family's name has not hurt. That is how I bluffed my way into heading the scientific arm of this expedition, crossing over from the survey arm of the Guild like a lot of people here, when the Navy was created to deal with the enemy.'

But he hadn't explained why he had forsaken his family for the Guild, and Sutter had returned before Dorthy had had a chance to ask. Watching him now, green light winking over his face as he sprawled like a prince at ease in his seraglio, Dorthy pondered his subtle devious ways – his strategy was to appear a plain man of action while carefully laying complex plans to entangle his opponents.

'We can eat in half an hour or so,' Sutter said, sitting back after stirring the stew. She looked up at the sun, the rimwall peaks that clawed its huge, soft disc. 'We're not going to make any more trips, anyway. I'm not about to go blundering around this forest in the dark.'

'I'll have to keep trying with the new males, though,' Dorthy said. 'I'm sure that there's something there.' But she wasn't, not after four failed attempts. She couldn't admit it, though. To do so would be also to admit that she had made a mistake in staying.

'In the dark, when those things are prowling around? You're crazier than I thought.' Sutter grinned. 'Nearly as crazy as Duncan.'

'I can catch them before they cross the pass,' Dorthy said. 'The sun won't set on that side for another week or so.'

'Have patience,' Andrews said. 'If I can work it, we can go and read the minds of the caretakers as they read their precious text. Think how that will upstage Ramaro.'

'I take it back. No one can be as crazy as you, Duncan. You go in there at *night?*'

'Why not? It's all lit up; brighter than the sun, in fact.'

'Oh, yeah. Still, rather you than me. Those things could gobble you down inside half an hour, boots and all.'

'No one has seen them eat since they entered the keep,' Andrews said. He added, 'Chung brought a summary of the findings of the translation team upstairs in orbital command. It turns out that the script is set out as a kind of musical notation; that's why Ramaro was having so much trouble with it. And it *does* form a coherent text, a whole, interconnected entity. Most of it is still incomprehensible, and it all seems to be mixed up with a weird cosmology, dragons or creatures with properties like dragons, stars having an effect on fate, all sorts of patent nonsense. It is as if someone had blended the Upanishads with Einstein's special theory of relativity and complete instructions for building a phase graffle. God alone knows what else is in there. Perhaps you'll be able to tell us, Dorthy.'

Dorthy shrugged. She was thinking of her bloodthirsty dreams of hunting beneath a night sky where only a single baleful star shone through winding interstellar gas clouds. Andrews's description of the text seemed to chime with the feeling, the *texture* of those dreams. But, just as each dream faded upon awakening, the explanation for that connection vanished as she strained to understand it. And she hadn't told anyone about the dreams, anyway. She said, 'It might be better to wait until they start acting on what they've learned. I can understand general concepts when I probe, action versus intention, but I can hardly translate a strange language as something equally strange reads it.'

'When they reach the top,' Andrews said comfortably, 'they'll have learned the song they need to sing to call up their masters. Believe it, Dorthy, you must. God alone knows what will happen then.'

'That damned bomb will probably decide it's had enough of this world and blow,' Sutter said.

'Well, you need not worry about that. Before the caretakers reach the top of the keep we will have moved the camp fifty klicks or so out on to the plain. That mapping satellite which orbital command moved over this area is always above the horizon, so Ramaro can bounce signals to and from his probes off it. Not much of a time lag to contend with.'

'That's really the plan?' Sutter grinned. 'You bastard, you never tell me *anything!*'

'That's unfair, Angel. You ask me a question and I do my best to answer it.' Andrews grinned sideways at his lover, then one-handedly fended off the cushion she threw at him.

After a moment Sutter laughed. 'You're *such* a bastard, Duncan!'

'Really? I think of myself as a moral man, on the whole.'

It was true, but it was not the complete truth, like so much of his talk. It was certainly true that he passionately believed in his vision of humanity's destiny, a vision founded on the humanist ideal of man's essential goodness . . . but at the same time he fought in any way he could to sustain that ideal, fair or not. To see him badgering Major Luiz Ramaro for permission to enter the keep was like watching a singleship ambushing an asteroid. Dorthy, witnessing one or two of these encounters, found them amusing. Ramaro was outgunned and knew it, yet put up a stubborn struggle to maintain the status quo.

'Come on,' Andrews said, one time in the commons, 'it isn't very much to ask, Luiz. You know we've been having no luck with the new arrivals. This whole thing is bogging down in detail. We might just as well pull out if we don't push it further.'

'You heard what Colonel Chung said, that upstairs is satisfied with our progress here.' Ramaro sucked the juice from a sweetstick, dropped it on his plate. Andrews had surprised him at his dinner. 'Look,' the fat major said, selecting another sweetstick, 'if upstairs wanted us to start manned expeditions in the keep, they would certainly rescind the directive about contact. As they have not, I must assume they don't want it. Besides, what use would such an expedition be? Are you dissatisfied with the results the remotes have been producing?'

'Of course not. Your people have done a fantastic job. But there are some things that require hands-on investigation.'

'Meaning your pet Talent, I suppose,' Ramaro said, looking at Dorthy who sat at the neighbouring table, pretending to read in the *Plays* but actually shamelessly eavesdropping.

'How else are we going to find out the caretakers' intentions?' Andrews said. 'For all their work, the language team upstairs haven't produced a very comprehensible picture of the meaning of all that writing. Of course, now that they have the notation, things may go more quickly. Has it helped you any?'

'If I had their resources,' Ramaro said, scowling, 'I would have a complete translation for you, perhaps. That discovery was blind luck, really.'

'But you do have a resource, if you'd only let me use it,' Andrews said. 'Think of the boost it would give you to have a report of what the caretakers are thinking as they peruse that text of theirs.'

'I don't know, Andrews. She hasn't had much success with the new arrivals.'

'That's because they haven't a thought in their heads beyond getting to the keep. It's all down there, Luiz, if we but had the key. The identity of the enemy, perhaps where they came from, all of it. Think on it. I have work to do.'

Later Dorthy told Andrews, 'You know very well that a mind isn't a text. I couldn't translate one word of that stuff, even if it was being read aloud by all of them at once.'

'To be sure, but Ramaro doesn't know that. Besides, you may be able to furnish some sort of clue that would help him.'

'I don't know, Duncan. I don't even know if I *want* to go down there.'

'Well now, you haven't had much success with the new arrivals, after all, and we can't move around out there in safety anymore.'

It was true. The sun had set behind the rimwall, and the only light in the bowl of the caldera was that cast by the myriad phosphors of the keep and the glimmer of the stars in the patch of sky above, hardly dimmed by the faint sky-scattering of the sunlight beyond the rimwall. Unable to stalk the newly arrived males within the caldera, Dorthy had once persuaded Andrews to take her to the other side of the pass, where the sun still shed level, horizontal light on the broken, mist-shrouded slopes. Strange to tread where once she had almost died. The stone stung her flesh as she sat zazen, its cold piercing her homeothermic coveralls. She knew now that it was artificially generated by a heat pump driven by geothermal energy, the same source that powered the strange processes of the keep. The cold condensed moisture out of the warm air and fed the rivers that irrigated the plains. The mountain made its own weather.

She and Andrews had located a group of new male herders in the eternal mists that hung on that side of the rimwall, by their infrared signatures, and she was able to probe them for ten minutes as they passed less than a hundred metres away, invisible in the fog. There was nothing in their minds but the labour of the climb and the blinding imperative impulse, the vision of the keep rising dark out of dark water, its many towers and pinnacles dividing upward as they rose, a strange fantastic crown. Then they were gone, and once more she knew only the taste of failure.

Dorthy didn't go out again. She spent a lot of the next week asleep, after jimmying the autodoc, on the pretence of checking her implant, so that it gave her a potent narcoleptic drug. She suspected that most of the technicians were abusing the machine as well; the strain of continually monitoring the keep with the primed paranoid bomb beneath their feet hung in the close air of the bubbletents like a suffocating gas, made Dorthy desperate enough to risk damaging her implant to escape it. Asleep, she lost the sensation of slowly being smothered and the continual pricking of the emotions of others. And, sleeping, her mind sank into the fantasies of hunting that had been with her since Kilczer's death, dreams she only vaguely remembered when awake, recalling their texture more than their content, potent and alien. Still she had told no one of them. Perhaps they were being broadcast by something, in the keep or elsewhere (that blinding glimpse, nova-bright, boiling up out of the planetscape spread beneath the plummeting dropcapsule, and out of the crude knotted ganglia of the penned critter); or perhaps she really was cracking up. It happened to Talents, one of the givens by which they lived. Once or twice, after particularly bad sessions, it had almost happened to her.

Dorthy slept sixteen or eighteen hours a day, emerging from her cramped cubicle only to use the toilet or to eat. She tried to get Sutter to teach her how to play triple-board chess – no longer able to collect material, Sutter was also at a loose end, and if not for her lover would have joined McCarthy's team on the other side of the rimwall – but the complexities eluded her. She investigated the library, finding little to her taste despite its size; spent an hour drinking a single cup of coffee. Mostly, she slept.

And was asleep when Andrews finally persuaded Ramaro to allow him to enter the keep, and didn't learn about it until Andrews himself came up to her in the commons and told her.

'Angel Sutter is right,' Dorthy said, 'you really are a bastard. Why didn't you tell me beforehand?'

'But you were asleep,' Andrews said with practised mock innocence. 'And besides, I went in a hurry before Luiz could change his mind. I didn't spend very long there, don't worry. Just peeked inside. That open space at the head of the causeway, what the technicians call the plaza. I did not even see a caretaker.'

'So what does it prove? What did you find that Ramaro's remotes have missed?'

'Nothing much. I chipped off a little of a wall, though. Here.'

He reached into the pocket of his coveralls, then held out his hand. A sharp-edged black chip rested on his creased palm, smaller than the topmost joint of his little finger.

'May I?' When he nodded, Dorthy reached out and pinched the chip between thumb and forefinger, felt the briefest tingle, static discharge of the strange.

'It's curious stuff,' Andrews said, as Dorthy turned it over and over: cold, hard, neither metal nor stone. 'For one thing it completely stops neutrinos – that's what has been frustrating Ramaro's attempts to find out what's behind all those walls. Resonance cavitation tells us that there are some pretty big spaces, and some pretty big things in those big spaces. But we can't tell what they are.'

'What is it made of?'

'Iron, mostly, just as the spectroscopy told us from the beginning. But not crystalline iron. Took me a hell of a time to get that little bit. The rest is carbon and hydrogen, oxygen and nitrogen, salted with a little sulphur and phosphorus. Mean anything to you?'

'Of course. Those are the elements associated with life. There are stony comets and CHON comets; some people say that the latter could sustain some sort of life, but nothing's been proved.'

'To be sure. Well now, there is a sort of organic lattice in among the iron. Which, by the way, is non-magnetic. No crystalline structure, do you see. It's all part of a whole.'

'You mean that the keep is alive in some way?' Dorthy laughed. 'Maybe *it* is the enemy. When the new males get to the top it wakes up and starts moving around, the stuff in the lake will be its food . . .'

Unsmiling, Andrews took back the little chip, put it in his pocket. 'It could be anything out there, really. Couldn't it?'

'That's what excites me,' he told her, for once an instance of unalloyed honesty. 'I will be going out again fairly soon, before Luiz Ramaro gets cold feet about the whole idea. Will you help me, Dorthy?'

So that was why he had sought her out. She felt the briefest touch of anger, of being used. Her Talent, not herself. But it quickly passed; after all, this was what she had stayed for. 'What do you want me to do?'

He was surprised. 'You will come? I shall warn you now, it will be very dangerous. There will be nowhere to run, should we be seen and chased.'

'Of course I'll go. I stayed here because I'd rather be working than rotting in Camp Zero. I should have known I would have to commit myself the whole way.'

'Do you know,' he said seriously, 'you have changed since I first met you. A few weeks ago you would not have volunteered.'

'Oh, I don't know,' Dorthy said, and at the same time wondered if it was true. Had she changed? And how could she tell if she had?

They left the thopter in Sutter's care, hidden at the edge of the forest, and walked across the wide meadow towards the moat and the towering constellations of the keep. Dorthy was struck anew by the sheer size of the structure. Its subsidiary spires, linked by flying buttresses and curved bridges or arches to the main part, were themselves as tall as the skyscrapers around the *Quadrado de Cinco Outubro*, some shaped like the thorns of roses, others rising sheer and needle-thin; and the main spire was so tall that, half a klick away, Dorthy had to tip her head back (a fold of the stiff chameleon cloak falling across her forehead) to see its summit, seemingly higher than the rimwall, against the starry sky. Lower down, irregular patterns of lights blazed a hot red.

'Come on,' Andrews said impatiently, and without waiting

hurried on across the carpet of interwoven tendrils, his own chameleon cloak instantly taking on their deep-textured violet. Dorthy flipped out a tablet of counteragent and swallowed it, then hastened after Andrews, seeing him more by his shadow than anything else.

As they neared the beginning of the causeway that ruled a straight line across the black water of the moat with its freight of slowly revolving, faintly glowing islands of photosynthetic scum, detail began to resolve out of the keep's soaring flanks. Sleek black buttresses with fine fluting; dark mounds of hanging vegetation; the spiralling way to the top, a delicate thread clinging to the terraced slope of the main spire, throwing off lesser spirals as it climbed.

Andrews asked Dorthy how she felt, and she confessed, 'Nervous as hell.' Even now his thoughts were beginning to nag at the edge of her Talent.

'But you have read them before.'

'That was before they had reached their goal, before they started on their text. This place dominated them just as it dominates the caldera. Inside . . . I don't know. Which is why I'm here, I suppose.'

Andrews, who'd been about to say that, said instead, 'How is your Talent coming on?'

'I'm ready.' She looked up, but now the central peak was hidden by the subsidiary spires that surrounded it. 'God, it's so big.'

'I feel like a knight come to rescue a maiden,' Andrews said. His face was just visible within the blurred outline of the cloak's hood: he was smiling.

The causeway was wide enough to take three crawlers side by side, its surface blackly reflective so that Dorthy had the illusion that she could see a little way into it; beneath her boots it felt grainy, slightly spongy. Either side of its black ribbon, phosphorescent rafts of scum ceaselessly washed.

Beyond the moat, the causeway rose, a wide ramp passing between two towers that divided and divided upward, studded with smears of red light glowing as fiercely as furnace mouths. Scylla and Charybdis, Dorthy thought, as she and Andrews passed between them. The ramp widened into a great concourse that gently sloped upward in a lazy curve. Twenty metres wide? Thirty? Smaller ramps spiralled off it like wood shavings, turning around subsidiary pinnacles that rose to different heights, some smoothly tapering, some flanged, some few bristling with sharp thorns. The keep did not look as if it had been planned and built, but instead sprung from some immense seed.

The ramp swept around a mass of dark vegetation, lines of light scribbled above, curved in to hug the wall again.

'There,' Andrews said. 'That's where the inscriptions begin.'

It was a single line, a flowing unbroken script like an incredibly complicated trace from an electroencephalogram, characters and ideograms flowing one into the other, clustered in groups of four, each group a single concept, each concept part of a greater group just as DNA codes for amino acids that, linked together, make a protein that in turn twists and coils, primary, secondary, tertiary spirals which determine its final functional form.

Andrews held up a little machine, intently watching its little screen; because his chameleon cloak blended indetectably with the wall, his face and the machine seemed to hang eerily in empty air. 'I'm picking up traces of the last group to enter this place,' he said. 'There's a probe watching them, a hundred, a hundred and fifty metres on up.'

'Wait here, then,' Dorthy said, and walked on alone, her palms pricking with anticipation, her cloak making her a mere shadow sliding across the wall. The line of script was at about waist-level, and as she walked she trailed a hand across it; but for all that the line looked slightly sunken into the surface, it felt as if there was nothing there at all. The stuff of the wall seemed to sting her fingertips, cold yet slightly flexible like the hide of a sleeping dragon. She wondered how old the keep was, if it was as old as the transformation of this world, and if it really was in some sense alive. No structure could resist the erosion of a million years unless it was self-replenishing. She thought of the complex molecules strung through the matrix of molecular iron, a nervous system that even now might be recording her footsteps. Then she sensed the by-now familiar trace of a new male's mind ahead of her and all speculation dropped away. But the trace grew no clearer as she walked on around the wide curve of the ramp, and she saw nothing.

Andrews's voice said in her ear, 'You should see the remote soon.'

Dorthy, concentrating on the tide of her breathing, the pulse washing her mind clear as she slowly climbed, didn't reply.

The trace was suddenly clearer, a distinct cloud of sensations but the sense of self somehow distorted, smothered, habitual frames overlaid with some unclear imperative. A fringe of fat vines covered with black scale-leaves spilled down the wall like monstrously magnified medusa's hair. As Dorthy passed this, the new male skittered around the curve ahead, almost falling over in its haste as it bounded towards her. She froze in panic, but just before it reached her the new male flung itself at the vines and began to swarm up them hand over hand, incredibly lithe considering the bulk of its darkly furred body. Then it scampered over some high edge and was gone.

'Christ,' Dorthy breathed.

Andrews's voice said in her ear, 'What was that?'

She had forgotten about the microphone that clung to the skin of her throat. 'Nothing,' she said. 'I'm just screwing my courage to the sticking place. Please, be quiet. I must concentrate.'

After a minute she was able to go on. She could sense more minds ahead, the communal purpose any group of new males shared, but shot through with a vivid current of informed yet unfinished intelligence, complex as sunlight on the restless sea's surface. Even as Dorthy approached, she felt herself submerging like a surfer racing through the toppling closing curl of a huge wave: she did not even have to prepare herself properly.

And suddenly the new males were revealed by the curve of the ramp, four of them crouched at the wall, running their oddly small, naked hands over the line of script, reading it with a plodding patience quite unlike the skittering haste of the average human reader whose eyes skip ahead of understanding, leapfrog passages perceived as banal. The new males read symbol by symbol by symbol . . . Dorthy could not understand precisely what they read, but its sense came to her as a line of melody rises out of the sullen dissonance of a Mahler symphony, as a dolphin breaches the mutinous waves. It was a slow unfolding perception of the entire ecology of the keep, all of it interwoven; the swift patterns of the animals, the slow weaving dance of growth of trees, of grass, the conjoined cycles of earth and air and water, all meshed: all. She saw that hunters must

169

understand the land in which they lived in a way only dimly grasped by those who were not dependent on its caprices. They did not subjugate it as farmers did, push it to balance at a single point and pump in energy to keep it at unstable equilibrium, but instead accepted and moved with the constant cycles that worked in slow stately pavane beneath the seethe of the little lives . . .

All this came to her in an instant, and for that moment she was overwhelmed: as if she had seen herself reflected in a funhouse mirror, and was held by the shattered gaze of her reflection.

The moment passed. Ahead of her the new males rose, their loose hoods suddenly flaring around their faces. There was no doubt that they could see her despite the chameleon cloak. New knowledge rammed into her forebrain like a spike. Trying to think around it, Dorthy turned to flee.

And something crushingly strong clamped an arm around her waist and hoisted her into the air, and seemingly without transition she was watching the curve of the ramp dwindle as her captor, holding her over his shoulder with one hand, swarmed up a vine using his feet as well as his free hand. Shock made everything seem clear and small and remote, as if seen through the wrong end of a telescope. The other new male: she'd forgotten about him, dismissed him when she'd seen him flee. He must have waited for her to pass before descending, come up behind her . . .

Softly she called to Andrews and he answered instantly. 'Are you done?'

'In a way. At the moment I'm hanging over the shoulder of a new male, a caretaker, while it carries me up. Hey, damn you! Watch out!' Because the new male had pulled itself over a terrace, bounded along the ramp beyond, and without pause begun to climb the vines that draped the next wall.

'You're okay?'

'Dizzy. It's a long way down.' At the back of her mind was the crazy thought that she'd seen something like this before.

'Do you know where you are? I'll break radio silence and Ramaro can have a remote on you within a minute.'

'Not—' She gasped as the new male swung sideways, continued to climb using another vine. Far below, the ramp was a thin line scribing the black vertical cliff; the other towers were a cluster of pencils seen end on. She could just make out the clotted phosphorescence in the moat. 'Not exactly,' she said. 'I have the feeling we're going all the way to the top.'

'Can't you tell what it wants?' It was Sutter's voice.

'I can't concentrate.' But although her Talent was blurred by the as-yet unassimilated knowledge she had garnered from the momentary contact with the other new males, she sensed that there was a bright edge to her captor's thoughts, as if it were driven by something else.

Sutter said, 'I can get the thopter pretty damn close in. If I can get above you there might be some way—'

'No,' Dorthy said. 'I don't think it intends to hurt me. And if you bring the thopter up here it might just let go.'

She had closed her eyes because the drop was making her dizzy. Now, as she felt the new male clamber over an edge, she opened them again. They were on another part of the ramp that spiralled from base to tip of the keep. Dorthy's captor squatted on its hams, gently but irresistibly holding her over its shoulder. Then she was lifted through the air and laid on the slightly rubbery surface of the ramp.

'I'm coming after you anyhow,' Andrews was saying. 'Keep the channel open, as long as possible. I'll follow the carrier wave.'

But Dorthy didn't reply, nervously watching the new male's narrow face above her, large eyes glinting darkly in the shadow of its flared hood, as it intently scrutinised her whole length. After a moment it pushed aside the chameleon cloak and began gently to manipulate her left arm, then her right. Dorthy tried to stay limp as it moved her joints; it was particularly interested in the rotation of her wrist. Huffing softly to itself, it started on her legs, bent her knee, then her ankle, again testing the rotation of each joint. It fingered the snaps of her boots, then came back up, pressing at her abdomen hard enough to make her cry out – then stopped as Andrews and Sutter said, 'What's happening?' in the same instant.

Dorthy said without moving her lips, the words humming in her throat, 'It's okay. Don't worry.'

'You are a long way up,' Andrews said. 'Look, there is a kind of ladder I'm following, but it seems to be taking me the wrong way. Tell me if you start moving again.'

And Sutter: 'Where the hell is that remote?'

Dorthy watched as the caretaker pulled at the belt of her coveralls, lifting one by one the knife and few tools that hung there, not detaching any but studying each closely before letting it fall. Dorthy's feeling of *déjà vu* was strong now, and then she had it: an old, flat, black-and-white trivia show she'd once seen – one of the students at Fra Mauro had had a whole collection of them, pre-Age of Waste stuff. *King Kong*, that was it. Dorthy stifled a laugh as the new male's face peered into her own, its breath sickly sweet but undercut by a whiff of acetone. Large eyes sunk in smooth black skin, no trace of lids but once, twice, nictitating membranes closed across the smeared horizontal black on black pupil.

What she sensed was a spark of self and reefs of newly acquired knowledge submerged by something simple and rigidly connected, the kind of thing she would have expected to sense had she been able to scan, say, a moderately complicated pocket computer. There was a programmed need to classify her within a rigid hierarchy of experience. Trying and failing.

And something else, flickering at the back of everything, something bright . . .

'What's going on?' Andrews asked in her ear, and the new male started back then peered closely again, puzzled by the faint sounds it could hear.

'Stay quiet,' Dorthy said softly. 'It's trying to figure out what I am.'

For a moment she feared that it would try to take off the microphone at her throat. But it simply fingered it, its touch hot and dry, then stood and bent and scooped her up, started along the gently rising spiral of the ramp until it came to more vines falling across the wall and the embedded script. It began to climb again, and Dorthy reported this.

Andrews said breathlessly, 'I very nearly ran into a bunch of them just now. I'm a level up, but you are perhaps two hundred metres above me. That thing is climbing fast.'

'I know,' Dorthy said. Now the moat was a thin stripe beyond the jumble of spires. She could see the wide meadow, the forest beyond rising into darkness.

'Are you sure you're all right, Dorthy?'

'I wouldn't put it like that, but unless it loses its grip I'm in no danger. Please, keep quiet. I don't want it disturbed.'

The vines ended at a narrow terrace where their roots spread like great flexed fingers. Ducking around these – one almost brained Dorthy – the new male nimbly sprinted the length of the terrace and leapt across a wide gap, landing – with a rush and a shock that knocked the breath out of Dorthy – on a ledge that hung out over a deep gulf. Dorthy looked straight down past the new male's furred back at a cluster of needle-pointed towers and closed her eyes, then opened them again as once more the new male leapt. She glimpsed something like a huge, slow bullet trawling the gap – Ramaro's remote – and then the new male gained the next spiral of the ramp. It was narrower here, and the braided script covered the wall from base to vegetation-shrouded top.

The new male shifted its grip on Dorthy's back, ambled on purposefully. She could sense a grouped mindset again, separate nodes of bright, dangerous intelligence within it.

The new male stopped, emitting a low, almost plaintive piping. Bright now, and close. After a moment Dorthy was lifted from the new male's shoulder and carefully set down. Her knees unhinged, she staggered against the wall, looked up.

Four new males, narrow faces within their cowls of skin compressed by the bulge of their foreheads, returned her gaze.

Dorthy stepped back, and her captor gripped her shoulder so hard that she cried out.

At once Andrews asked what was happening.

'Shut up! I'm trying to—'

And light split her apart like lightning leaping the gap between heaven and earth. Through a haze of tears she saw the four males back away. One was looking from side to side as if dazzled. She felt their fear and a complex incomprehensible jumble of images. In some part of her mind something alien was trying to hide.

As a child she had accepted the intrusion of other personalities, had allowed them to talk and weep and rant in the calm mirror at her centre while she asked questions of them, able somehow always to find the answers within the intruder. It had not seemed strange until after she had left the Institute and she had realised, newly arrived in the huge shuttle terminal at Melbourne, that the myriad minds around her were all closed to each other, a revelation that had loosed a sudden formless panic. That had been five years ago.

Now she felt that disorientation all over again.

Now she thought that she saw the stars stirred apart. Here was the danger, here! The danger that had awakened them was revealed, to be acted upon at once, too dangerous to be left alone now that it had penetrated so far.

Something was holding her back and impatiently she tried to pull away, but her captor slapped her down casually. On hands and knees on the resilient surface of the ramp she shook her head, thoughts jarred loose, drifting. Her captor was gesturing with both large and small pairs of arms to the other new males, slowly advancing on them, one naked hand slapping the wall and its tangled braids of script. It was trying to tell them that here was the danger, not in the stars but *here, now*. Dorthy was dazzled by its burning imperative. Nova-bright, yes, and oddly like the glimpses of planetary doom she'd glimpsed in the minds of Kilczer and Andrews and Colonel Chung. As if it *wanted* the world to burn . . . Piping, it slapped the script, gestured at Dorthy, slapped the wall again. For a frozen moment she thought that it wanted the others to kill her; but they simply turned and scampered away, gripped by subtle triggers of instinct.

Dorthy tried to stand, but something spasmed her joints and she collapsed, legs pushing weakly, helplessly. The unwelcome mindset at her centre had somehow meshed with her control, deep down at the crossing of the medulla. Not the ships of orbital command but the remotes; that was what they were going to destroy. The remotes and the driving force behind them.

She stuttered, 'S-switch off. Get off, off the, off the—'

The thing within clamped down. Calm, she thought, calm, concentrate on the centre, act out from the centre. She visualised the words she wanted to say, focused on them through the bucking welter of contrary alien impulses.

'Switch off your radios! They'll track you back and destroy you if you don't!'

'Dorthy, say again! What's happening up there?'

She rode the wave within her. Andrews's voice made it easier to focus. 'Switch off right now or they'll kill you!'

He didn't reply.

Something shifted within her mind, but she knew it now, could map its edges. It was no more than an analogue, a wave function locked in the electrochemical balance of her forebrain. What seemed to be deliberate behaviour were only pseudo-impulses parasitic on her own actions; it was a model of a consciousness, not a real personality. It could do no more than respond.

To know was to act. She rode it, cut through the channels that converted impulses to action, thought into deed. She breathed deeply. She was Dorthy Yoshida. She was herself.

After a moment she was able to reach up and switch off the microphone, the receiver in her ear.

Ahead, her captor turned, its vestigial arms clasping and unclasping their shrunken hands across its chest, and she understood that the bright-edged web that had overridden its mind was gone, leaving only a single fading impulse she barely had time to grasp before it vanished. The new male herder, unfettered, tracked her as she stood, opened its mouth to show wet ridges of sharp-edged horn. She saw its growing intention and stepped back as it stepped forward, then staggered as a wave of movement seemed to pass through the keep. All around, black walls seemed to glow slightly within the illusionary depths of their sheen. The scribbled script was shadowed against it. When the new male moved forward uncertainly, lines of light shimmered in the air around it as if drawn out by the movement. Something seemed to be crawling over Dorthy's head; it was every hair trying to stand apart from its fellows. The receiver in her ear howled, for all that she'd switched it off, and the new male wrapped its arms around its head and keened, rocking from one clawed foot to the other, its black fur bristling.

Dorthy slowly moved her hand to her belt, rested it on the knife.

Beyond the edge of the ramp, far below, a cluster of towers was limned in flowing colourless shimmer. Discharges snapped to and fro between the spikes of their tops, spinning faster and faster until a cradle of light nested there, blurring, widening. The howl of her receiver rose in pitch. Despite herself she cried out, as somewhere above delicate purpose moved into equilibrium. Poised, ready . . .

The new male charged her and she brought the knife up, its blade thrilling. Light flared everywhere as the creature fell on her; the blade entered its body easily, eagerly. Dorthy was knocked down, the weight of the herder pulling her wrist sideways, sharp pain merging with the great soundless nova that swelled through her clamped lids. Their thready blood vessels were for an instant outlined against vivid red light.

And then it was over.

She was lying twisted under the solid weight of the new male herder; its blood soaked her chameleon cloak from crotch to neck. Her wrist was bent at an angle and it hurt as she dragged the knife free. With an effort she pushed away from the body and scrambled to her feet. Poor Kong.

The light was nothing but the red light of the scattered phosphors. Far below, the towers stood in shadow again.

Cries and hoots resonated all through the great structure of the keep, distress calls and messages from one group of new males to another, inquiring, suggesting, informing. Dorthy almost blundered into half a dozen of the creatures, but they were so spooked that as soon as they saw her they all precipitately fled, some running away down the long curve of the ramp, others swinging up through tangled black vines, lithe for all their confusion. Twice Dorthy took to the network of vines herself to avoid other new males as they communed with their fellows across the high gulfs.

Her wrist still hurt, and her hand was covered in drying blood. But the analogue within her mind was slowly seeping away, water into sand. Her fear that it would become fixed and dominate her own self – the technical term was breakout – slowly receded as she descended. Belatedly she thought to switch on her receiver, and instantly Andrews was yelling in her ear.

'I'm here,' she said. 'I'm all right.'

He said, 'You're maybe a level above me. Do you want me to come up?'

'No. Wait there.' Dorthy walked the edge of the ramp until she saw a terrace a few metres below and worked her way down, dropping among angled roots. As she clambered down the thick rope of a vine, Andrews said, 'That was some fireworks display. The whole structure lit up from top to bottom.'

'I know. I was right in the middle of it.'

'What did they do?'

'I—' but the knowledge eluded her, or at least the precise reason. 'I think that they had learned enough to use the keep, and my presence triggered their instincts. Was a threat. Danger, preservation . . . I'm sorry. It was *clear*, now it keeps slipping away when I try to think about it. It was too different to last.'

'We must sort it out later,' Andrews said. 'Let's get off this thing before you set off something else.'

'That's just what I'm doing,' Dorthy said, sliding the last metre to the ramp. Just at the point where it swung out of sight Duncan Andrews, his chameleon cloak thrown back, waved to her. He and Dorthy met halfway.

As they went on down, Andrews said that he'd seen some of the new males running upward. 'You understand that I kept out of sight. What happened, exactly?'

'They don't like being invaded.'

'But they didn't object to Ramaro's remotes,' Andrews said. 'I've been trying to raise him. Angel isn't answering either. Do you think they've blown the communications net?'

'Yes, if it wasn't shut down. The new males, your caretakers, used the carrier wave to drive an impulse against anything working outside the keep. That's why I asked you to switch off your radios. I don't know what else they did.' She began to explain about the new male that had captured her, the thrall it had laboured under.

Andrews was incredulous. 'Something was controlling it? As if it were a remote? And *what* was controlling it? Ah, of course, the intelligence you sensed.'

'Yes,' she said. 'Yes, I think it was.'

Andrews scratched the top of his head. 'But why—'

He stopped, because one of the remotes had come into view. Or what was left of it. The burned hulk lay at the edge of the ramp, smoke still pouring out of the crumpled vane complex. The midsection had blown apart.

'Looks like the fuel cell blew,' Andrews said, after squatting to examine it. He straightened, said, 'I've a bad feeling about Ramaro and his crew. Come on.'

They followed the spiral down, meeting no more new males, crossed the wide plaza. The mindset that Dorthy had picked up was almost gone now, sunk with hardly a residue. She hurried after Andrews. The causeway stretched level before them.

'Organics,' Dorthy said, as they walked high above the scummed water.

'Huh?' Andrews was fiddling with his receiver. 'Why the hell doesn't Angel answer?'

'It mines iron from the bedrock, but it can't stockpile organic components. So when it needs them it has to farm them.'

'What are you talking about? Hell, I can't get *anything*.'

'The keep. It's growing, changing. Or the new males are changing it, shaping it. You were right; it is alive, in a way.'

But Andrews wasn't listening. He had stopped near the end of the causeway, was pointing up. Dorthy looked up, too, past the irregular forested terraces that rose to the sheer cliffs, the peaks of the rimwall black against the starry sky. Except for one point near the top, a ragged flower of fire as small as her thumbnail in the distance, red petals glowing around a dimming bloom of yellow.

Andrews set off across the meadow at a run, the lights of the keep throwing his shadow ahead of him. Dorthy, exhausted, trailed behind, her chameleon cloak flapping at her ankles; long before she reached the trees Andrews had vanished into them and she followed him through the near darkness beneath the forest canopy by use of her Talent as much as sight and sound and touch, finding him at the edge of the little glade where the thopter stood. He was embracing Angel Sutter.

The tall woman was saying, 'I didn't dare switch it on. You didn't see? You really didn't see?'

Dorthy said, 'It's the base, isn't it?' Exhaustion had loosened all her joints. Her throat tasted of iron.

Sutter half turned from Andrews. It was so dark that Dorthy couldn't see the woman's expression, but she felt her despairing fear clearly enough. Sutter said, 'I was watching through field-glasses, trying to see what you were doing. It was as if the whole place was stirred up, like a termite nest.' She was remembering the time when, a child, she had after much effort prised away one of the concrete-hard pinnacles. The furious creatures that had boiled out then, white, blind, alien. She said, 'Then there was this crazy fireworks display—'

'I saw some of that,' Andrews said.

'And then,' Sutter said, 'the place where the camp is, *was*, simply exploded. I saw the flash reflected on the towers of the keep, it was so bright. And when I looked around it was gone. There was just a kind of molten river where the ledge was. A laser, I think it was a laser; there were ionisation tracks spitting across the sky for maybe a minute afterward.'

'An X-ray laser,' Andrews said. 'A very big X-ray laser; maybe even gamma. Too fast for the bomb to react; it would have vaporised the camp in a picosecond. And at any rate, that damned computer was programmed to ignore light displays in the keep, otherwise we'd have gone up long ago.' He was looking over Sutter's shoulder, at the high cliff, the dimming fireflower. Abruptly he broke away and ducked into the thopter's bubblecabin, began to rummage through the dead channels. Dorthy cast off her bloody cloak and sat on the ground, picking at the flakes of dried blood that gloved her right hand. At last, his frustration clear and bright, Andrews switched off the set and sat still, a shadow in the shadowy curve of the cabin.

'We'd better go,' Sutter said quietly. 'Jesus Christos, it's like we opened Pandora's box.'

'Let me think,' Andrews said from within the cabin. 'Dorthy, did those caretakers know about the ships we have in orbit?'

The danger from the stars. 'I think so,' she said.

'Damn. I was hoping . . .' He ducked out of the cabin, began to pace around the little clearing. After a minute he said, 'It doesn't make sense. Why would they destroy the lesser danger? Even if it is closer to them. That laser could certainly pick off orbital command. Damn. It's as if the caretakers *wanted* to provoke us, bring an attack down on their heads.'

Dorthy remembered the brief glimpse she had had of her captor's burning imperative, the whole world aflame.

'Maybe they're crazy, Duncan. Maybe that's all there is to it,' Angel Sutter said.

He stopped pacing, sighed. 'It is hardly an elegant solution.'

179

'Whatever the truth is, we can't do anything,' Sutter said. 'It isn't our job to fight. That's what the fucking *Navy's* for.'

'Precisely why it is my fight,' Andrews said, 'because I know just what the Navy will do. Would you like to know a secret? Dorthy, do you know what I am going to say?'

'Why they built the blockhouse at Camp Zero? No, I don't exactly. My Talent is running down.'

'Listen then. Listen, both of you.' His voice was quiet in the darkness. 'The Navy has a contingency plan in case the enemy looks like they're breaking out of control here. The blockhouse is the bolt-hole should it go into effect, and after what happened here I think it's likely it will go into effect. And very soon. Those creatures out there aren't going to stop at this. They're building up the keep, changing it, finding out about us. Perhaps the destruction of the camp was a test, I don't know. We're their enemy, the invader: they are the response. Have I got it right, Dorthy?'

'You agree that they are the enemy, then,' Dorthy said.

'Does it matter?'

Sutter asked, 'Just what is this contingency plan?'

'They have a ship in close orbit around the sun, a stripped-down freighter, a robot. It has phase graffles on it.' When neither Dorthy nor Sutter said anything, Andrews continued drily, 'When a phase graffle is turned on inside a gravitational singularity, it doesn't hook a ship into contraspace; the differential is too great. What happens instead is a sort of blowout – for an instant the energy levels between urspace and contraspace are connected. This star happens to be a mite unstable – in fact there was a minor flare when we first arrived, nothing more than a half per cent increase in activity over five or six days though, a minor hiccough. But the graffles will rip up the star's structure. There'll be a big, nasty flare full of free radicals and hot particles. It'll lick out across two million klicks, and it'll *sterilise* this world. The blockhouse is the funkhole, do you see. Chung and everyone else will sit there until the flare dies down. Fifty days, maybe sixty. Long enough to roast the entire surface. Then the ships will come down and take everyone off.'

Dorthy said, 'And the Navy really thinks that that will deal with the enemy?'

'To be sure. But look at that thing out there. The caretakers have had a couple of weeks in it, learning, finding out. In two more, what will they be able to do? You tell me. We don't even know all of what they can do *now*. That's no city, I was wrong about that. It's a weapon. The whole thing is a fucking weapon.'

Angel Sutter laughed. 'So they have to be dealt with straight away, isn't that how it should be? Jesus Christos, Dorthy's right. The herders are the enemy.'

'I don't know if I am right,' Dorthy said.

'I don't want to stand around here debating it,' Sutter said. 'Duncan, we should clear out of here before they realise they've overlooked us. Damn you, come *on*! We're too close here.'

'Just over the rim,' Andrews said. 'I still haven't said all I want to say.'

Andrews took the controls and flew the thopter low over the dark forest towards the rimwall. Dorthy, squeezed into the back, watched the lights of the keep diminish, waiting for something to happen. Nothing did.

Ahead and above, the rimwall's ragged edge seemed softened, and as the thopter rose Dorthy saw that rivers of mist were beginning to pour down the cliffs, and felt, as they passed into this blurred whiteness, the taut wire of Angel Sutter's anxiety relax a little. Andrews hunched over the stick, flying by radar. After a while he said, 'We're across. I'm setting us down.'

'Just keep flying, Duncan,' Sutter said. 'There's nothing we can do.'

'Not here, perhaps,' Andrews said, and in that instant Dorthy remembered what she had seen in her captor's mind after it had been freed from its thrall. The residue: the clue.

The thopter settled near the source-stream of the river that Dorthy had followed back to the pass in the rimwall. So long ago now. Mist hung low over wet, shaly rock; the setting sun was a blurred colourless eye far below. Wind fluted around the bubble-cabin as Andrews called up the biological team in the forest farther down the outer slope and told Jose McCarthy what had happened. 'You're to go back at once, tell Chung,' he said, and cut off the man's crackling protest. 'There is nothing you can do, truly. I wish to God that there were. We will return to Camp Zero in two days. Make sure

Chung understands that. Two days.' He switched off the radio and Sutter punched the clear plastic beside her.

'Jesus Christos, what *is* this shit?' Her voice cracked with disbelief.

'I'm going to eat something,' Andrews said flatly, and opened the hatch. Cold wet air blew in as he climbed out.

Sutter jerked around, fixed Dorthy with her fierce glare. 'You know what this is about, right?'

'You won't change his mind,' Dorthy said.

'Jesus Christos, don't I know *that*. Maybe I should just take the thopter up now, you think?' But after a moment she followed her lover out.

Dorthy turned the heating element of her coveralls all the way up, slapped her arms across her chest in the freezing wind. Most of the dried blood on her right hand had scaled off, but there was a black rim around the ragged end of each fingernail. Beside her, Andrews seemed not to notice the cold; he'd been born on a cold shore, after all. Wind tugged at his sandy hair as he ate emergency rations from a self-heating can. Hazed by mist, Sutter prowled the barren slope above the thopter. Dorthy watched her and picked at the blood crusted under her fingernails, around her fingerjoints. After a while Andrews said, 'Come on. Try a sip of this.'

Dorthy sucked on the metal straw. The little flask held oily bootleg rum; it burned her throat and she coughed and spluttered. 'Thanks,' she managed to say.

'How are you feeling?'

She held up her blood-flecked hand. 'Wishing a little water would clear me of this deed.'

'You can still pull out now, if you want. Really.'

She asked, 'Why are you doing this?'

'You know, when the Federation came into being, it was supposed to be for the advancement of everyone.' His face had a pinched, pensive look. 'I suppose you're too young to remember. There was a lot of sentiment in those days; Earth had helped Elysium out of the barbarism we'd fallen into – well, in Namerika, at least. I'm old enough, you know, to remember the tail end of the Inter-regnum, when we'd lost all contact with Earth for more than four hundred years. And it was mostly the same with the other colony worlds. And then the ships came from Earth, and here was the Universe suddenly open before us because of the phase graffle; of course we were grateful. No need to sleep away a dozen years or more on a one-way ticket: here was a way open for commerce, for real exploration. Sentiment, idealism, birth of the Federation for Co-Prosperity of Worlds: those were great days, Dorthy, great days. But it began to wear pretty quickly, soon became clear that the Federation mostly benefited Earth, and Greater Brazil in particular. We had the raw materials and Earth took them in, gave precious little back. And as for the Universe . . . well, here we are on the cutting edge of exploration, and we're no farther from Earth than Earth is from Elysium. Two new worlds colonised, that's all, two in fifty years. The Americans and Russians managed more with their rinky-dink arks and colonyboats crawling along at less than lightspeed. I hear a lot about moderation, about caution. Usually the Age of Waste is brought up as an example. But the real reason is that if people started diving off the edge of known space in all directions, setting up wherever they found acceptable real estate, Earth would lose control.' He smiled. 'I would guess that you are hardly in the mood for a lecture on politics. I apologise.'

'I didn't know that you were into politics.'

'Anyone with money has to be. Real money, I mean. Even criminals need to keep a politician in their pockets these days. I am treading water, as it were, but my father is a long way down indeed. Anyway, here I am, hoping to prise up the lid that the Navy has clamped down, hoping to let out whatever the enemy has. Shake up the system, see what falls out. They want to contain it, seal it off. I want revelation. And you?'

'You'll need my Talent, even if you don't need me.'

He laughed. 'I need anyone I can get.'

'I've never really believed that people are wholly explicable, you know. Even though that's my job.' Not since Hiroko, and what she did after she had been rescued from the ranch. After Dorthy had rescued her . . . or at least that's what she thought she had been doing at the time, crouched in the bush in the hot night, evading her father's search parties, slipping through the net. On the cold alien mountainside she said, 'Besides, there's something I haven't told you, something I saw in the mind of the new male that captured me. This was after it had been released from whatever was controlling it; the control had gone, but it had left an image. I think that it meant me to find it.'

'Go on,' he said, wholly attentive.

'You want to go to the equatorial hold, the one that built the radio telescope. Well, that's what I saw. I think that's where I'm wanted.'

'Damn,' Andrews said, 'I knew—' He punched at the cold air, grinning. 'It's nice to be proven right. You think this is something to do with that intelligence or whatever it was you spotted while you were coming down in the dropcapsule?'

'Perhaps,' Dorthy said. That bright edge to the simple net that had bound the new male's mind. Had it been trying to break through to her, in her dreams? Or were the dreams a residue of some deep tampering? The thought struck her coldly: why did it want her to go to its lair? Hadn't it wanted her dead, down there in the keep? She shivered and looked away from Andrews.

On the slope above, Angel Sutter had been watching them talk. When Dorthy's abstracted gaze fell on her she stalked down, took the flask from Andrews, and sipped. Droplets glittered in her bushy hair as she bent to the straw. When she had finished, she blew out her breath and said, 'I guess I'll have to ask what crack I've got my ass into. Come clean, Duncan. Where the hell *are* we going?'

'To the equatorial hold. At least, as far as the edge. Only Dorthy and I are going in. It seems that there's something out there, Angel; maybe the thread that will unravel this whole knot. I want to find out what it is.'

Sutter looked at Dorthy. 'You found this out in the keep?'

Dorthy nodded.

'Then it's not likely to be very friendly.'

'Perhaps not. On the other hand, there is still so much to learn. A million years old, Angel, imagine. We still don't know how they spun this world, we still don't know where they came from, what their history is. If they are truly dangerous,' Andrews said, 'isn't that worth finding out? And if this whole thing is simply a misunderstanding, wouldn't it be best to set it all straight, and end the war at BD twenty?'

'Well, I think you're a little crazy, if you don't mind me saying so. You think Chung will wait until you come back? She's always been on your case, man. The button's there, she won't wait on you. She'll *press* it.'

'I don't think so. It would be politically unacceptable.'

Angel Sutter sighed, accepting the inevitable. 'I still think you're crazy. You're just walking in there?'

'Perhaps that is what will save us,' Andrews said.

They rested for half a dozen hours before setting off. Huddled in the back of the bubblecabin, Sutter's fear and Andrews's eager impatience nagging at her equally, and the wind howling outside, Dorthy got little enough sleep. What there was was shot through with dreams. Over and over she jerked awake from walking alongside Kilczer through red-lit pine forest. In one of those dreams he said, 'I will be with you, Dorthy. You have no need to worry. It is an invitation, is it not?' When he turned to her to hear her answer, she saw that he had her mother's tired brown eyes. And awoke, dry-mouthed, to feel the thopter shaking beneath her – but it was not just the thopter, it was the whole side of the mountain. The mist had lifted somewhat, a wrinkling ceiling suffused with brilliant red light, as restless as the underside of the surface of the sea.

Sutter and Andrews were already awake, and as Dorthy asked what was happening the thopter's twin vanes thumped above the bubblecabin. She asked again, and Andrews said, 'I don't know, but I'm not sitting around to find out.'

His last words were almost drowned by the roar of collapsing rocks farther down the slope. Dorthy saw that the stream had run dry.

Sutter said, 'Duncan, come on, *make* this thing *go!*' As if in reply the vanes clapped, pushed down, and the thopter hopped into the air, rising through mist and turning away from the rimwall as it rose so that Dorthy had to twist in the cramped space behind the seats to see, as the thopter cleared the mist, the ragged rimwall peaks silhouetted against a glare that filled the cabin with red light. Andrews swore; Sutter said, almost reverentially, 'Jesus Christos . . .'

It's as if the whole caldera is on fire, Dorthy thought, squinting against the light, has to be. But she felt no heat against her face. The column filled the embrace of the rimwall, rising and rising like an immense search-light beam probing the stars. Flickering nodes of gold qualified its pellucid red, seeming to swarm upward like spermatozoa.

'What the hell *is* it?' Light ran like oil on Sutter's dark skin.

'Whatever it is, it isn't affecting the instruments,' Andrews said. 'Just light, perhaps.'

Just light . . . If only it were as simple as that, Dorthy thought, watching the enormous column recede as the thopter fled out, from mystery into mystery.

4
At The Core

The site of the radio telescope rose in the eastern sky, a low symmetrical cone silhouetted against drifts of stars whose cold light outshone the setting sun. Andrews flew the thopter low and fast over the dead land towards it; unlike Sutter, he was quite unafraid, or his fear was buried beneath the surge of his anticipatory excitement. As for herself, Dorthy felt nothing; her hands trembled lightly if she unclasped them, but perhaps that was no more than exhaustion. At least, that was what she told herself. Andrews had downed a stimtab halfway through the two-hour flight (without an autodoc to advise her what it would do to the biochemistry of her implant, Dorthy didn't dare to follow his example), and as he flew he monotonously tapped the edge of the tiller with his thumb, overflow of nervous energy, flicked his gaze back and forth between the dark landscape and the radar screen with eager expectation.

At last he throttled down the vanes and began a long glide in, pointing out the sinuous edge of a canyon on the radar screen. 'There's a rise that'll screen the thopter from the hold as we come in. Perhaps two klicks before the beginning of the slope. Are you up to a long climb, Dorthy?'

'I'd rather you carried me, but I'll do my best.'

'Take it in as far as you want,' Sutter said. 'I'll be waiting for you a *long* way from here, you can believe it.'

'Thank you, Angel,' Andrews said. And to Dorthy, 'You can still back out. No shame.'

'That's nothing to do with why I'm going.'

'Glad to hear it.' He made minute adjustments, feathering the vanes to kill speed as they glided in. Still, he stalled the thopter at the last moment and it abruptly flopped down, raising slow clouds of dust, bloody veils in the sun's last, level light.

Angel Sutter winced but said nothing and remained uncharacteristically quiet until they had unloaded what little equipment Andrews and Dorthy needed. It only took a few minutes. 'Good luck,' Sutter said then. 'Look after him, Dorthy. I'll see you in thirty hours, no more. It's a long haul back to Camp Zero.'

'Of course,' Andrews said. He handed Dorthy a signal flare, clipped another to his belt. 'Watch out for us, Angel. Don't fall asleep now.'

'Out here? Are you kidding? I won't even *blink*. Just keep to the schedule, or you'll have to walk back!'

'Keep your head down,' Andrews said, then embraced her, whispering something Dorthy didn't catch.

After a moment Angel Sutter folded her arms around his broad back. 'Goddamn it,' she said, her face muffled against his neck, 'be careful.'

Embarrassed, Dorthy turned to look up at the profile of the hold. She could just make out the line where vegetation started, a long way up the slope. It was so much smaller than the hold from which they had fled, no more than a shallow forested crater.

'Come on,' Andrews told her, and Dorthy followed him, glancing back once and seeing Sutter standing still beside the thopter, unable to tell in the twilight whether or not the woman was looking after them.

Andrews took the lead, the rifle that against Dorthy's objection he had insisted on bringing slung over one shoulder. He didn't look back at all, not even when the thopter finally took off and sped out across the desert in search of a safe hiding place.

The slope that had seemed gradual and smooth from the air turned out to be a rough, broken terrain, punctuated with steep banks of sliding stones and sudden crevasses, a difficult climb made worse by the fading light. Dorthy and Duncan Andrews kept setting off little avalanches that rattled loudly in the stillness. Nothing else moved but the shadows of the boulders, and those imperceptibly, as the vast sun slowly shrank towards the horizon, bleeding into a long hazy line of light that girdled half the world's rim.

By Dorthy's timetab it was past noon when she and Andrews reached the first vegetation, a sprinkling of ridged woody growths clinging to pockets of bone-dry soil that had gathered in ancient lava ridges. They rested a few minutes, chewing sweet concentrate and sipping from their canteens. Looking up at the dark line of the forest, Dorthy wondered if she should take the counteragent. No, not yet. Patience. Patience and calm. Stalking her greatest, most dangerous subject, she would need plenty of both.

Andrews asked, 'How are you feeling?'

'I think you really *should* be carrying me.'

'I am glad that you came, Dorthy, but not that glad. Do you think it's up there?'

She understood what he meant. 'I haven't taken my counteragent. I'll wait until I'm sure I need to.'

'You managed without it before, and from a good deal farther away, too.'

'Of course, but I was in some kind of tranced, hyped-up state then. I don't think I've ever been that sensitive before. Nor, I hope, will I ever be again. It was like trying to stand naked on the surface of the sun.'

Andrews peered at her; he was a shadow perched on an outthrust rock, the star-flecked sky behind him. She could only just make out his smile. 'You really do not like your Talent.'

'I suppose not.'

'Yet it isn't you who is exposed: it's us. We're all of us open to you.'

'Oh no, I'm the one who is exposed. Bombarded. It hammers down on me like information from a dozen hypaedia tapes playing at once. Without the discipline to enable me to concentrate on only one source, to focus, I'd go crazy. Some of the Talents do anyway.' Once with bleach, once with a sharpened table knife . . . But she'd been so much younger then.

'I've known one or two Talents,' Andrews said. 'They *were* pretty damned odd.'

'And me?' She regretted asking that question on the instant.

'Well now,' he said, 'you stand away from it all, don't you? You won't let anything hurt you. That's why I appreciate you coming with me. It was a human kind of thing to do. Unselfish, if you follow me.'

He was trying to be kind, but it still fell hard on her when once it would have simply bounced off her armour of practised indifference.

She remembered that Arcady Kilczer had once said something similar, and for a moment saw his soft weary smile, his characteristic gesture of pushing back his unruly fringe from his forehead. She bit her lip and said, 'We should get on.'

'All right. But I mean what I say. I am glad you are here.'

They began to climb again, and soon were walking beneath low trees with tangled beltlike foliage, like the trees in the caldera around the keep. Long roots clutched the shallow stony soil, criss-crossed by a network of woody vines. Then the slope gentled, and the trees gave out on to a kind of meadow of the by-now familiar tendrilled groundcover.

It curved away on either side, encircling the rim of the crater whose symmetrical bowl was lined with material of a depthless black that no doubt was radioreflective. It was perhaps a kilometre across, but distance was difficult to estimate in the chancy light. Something that had to be the antenna complex hung above the centre, supported by cables strung from three angled towers.

Andrews walked to the edge. Dorthy followed cautiously, feeling exposed. Somewhere, she was sure, something was watching her, measuring her, biding its time. Andrews pointed to the cleft that split the far side of the crater; it glowed in the red light of the setting sun. 'The orbital survey suggested that there's something down there,' he said, and took out his field-glasses. After a minute he handed them to Dorthy.

The view was grainy because the amplification circuit was turned all the way up. 'Under the trees, to the right,' Andrews said. 'See it?'

'I see it.'

A complex of low walls that followed the contours of the steep ground, mostly obscured by groves of trees. Here and there stunted flat-topped towers rose to various heights. It looked like a long-deserted, overgrown ruin.

'No wonder we didn't see much from orbit,' Andrews said, when Dorthy returned the field-glasses. 'Do you sense anything?'

'As if I'm being watched.'

'Hell,' he said, 'even I feel something like that, it's only natural. This is it, Dorthy, this is the core of things on this planet. Come on, I want to look at that tower.'

They set off towards the nearest of the three support towers,

Andrews jittery with excitement but Dorthy more circumspect, oppressed by the heavy sense of something watching. For all that Andrews dismissed it, it was real. But they saw no herders, no sign of any animal life at all.

The support tower jutted out from the abrupt edge of the drop that swept down into the bowl: a thick, curved backbone supported by ridged buttresses, black against the dark sky. Andrews scraped at one of the buttresses with his knife and the blade sank into it easily; when he hit it with the knife-butt, it sounded dully. 'Not metal, anyway,' he said, flaking a sample into a pouch before testing his weight on the barbed ridges that spiralled around the spine.

Dorthy watched as he clambered out to the end, her palms sweating. The drop was a long one. He clung to the end for a long time, fiddling with the cable that seemingly without transition ran down from the tower's spiked end in a smooth arc to the irregular shape of the antenna complex, a raft of irregularly stacked polyhedra hung out there above the centre of the bowl. At last Andrews worked his way back, and Dorthy helped him swing down. His face was slick with sweat, but he smiled at her with boyish enthusiasm. 'Damndest thing. It seems all of one piece, cable and tower.'

'Is that all you found out?' She was angry at Andrews for exposing himself in such a way: exposing himself to the risk of falling, to the risk of being spotted. Except she was sure that they had already been spotted. She forced herself to speak calmly, for all that her hands were shaking with the effort of control. 'Obviously, they'd have to adjust the position of the antenna, there must be some mechanism to move it. The focus of the receiving bowl is fixed, so the antenna must move to detect radiation reflected at different angles, from different parts of the sky.'

'Well, maybe the machinery for that is in the antenna itself. Don't worry, I'm not going to crawl out there to look.'

'I don't see what's so important about knowing *how* it's moved, that's all.' Dorthy touched one of the barbed, curving buttresses: it was warm beneath her fingers and sensuously smooth, like rigid silk.

'I don't know what's important, so I have to assume that everything is,' Andrews said, adding as he stepped back, 'Stay there.' Quickly he took half a dozen holos; Dorthy blinked back the dazzle of laser light.

Andrews put the little camera away. 'I'll give you one when we get back; it will make a fine souvenir.' Then he said seriously, 'Perhaps you had better make ready your Talent, Dorthy. I think that we must go down there' – he jerked a thumb towards the cleft – 'to learn anything else.'

This was the mouth of the deed, then. Everything else, the ride down in the dropcapsule, the long trek up the slope of the caldera, the adventure in the keep, had simply been a prologue. Dorthy took out the dispenser and clicked a tablet into her palm, swallowed it dry. She could feel it going down, slipping into the private darkness of her metabolism.

Done.

They had reached the edge of the cleft when Dorthy felt her Talent begin to come on, the texture of Andrews's thoughts blurred and disconnected at first but becoming clearer with each step, a skimming counterpoint to her own thoughts, like jottings in the margin of a text. She had to stop at last, sat zazen some way from the edge in a kind of shelter made by two slabs of rock tilted one against the other, breathing in and holding, breathing out, feeling her pulse gentle as she sank away from the outer world. Andrews prowled about restlessly, squinting into the vast slow sunset framed by the cleft, the wedge of tawny desert spreading beyond the dry ravine of which the cleft was the mouth. Thick vines climbed the cliff, looping over the edge and fanning out into the undergrowth beyond, into the stunted forest. Andrews squatted at the node of a junction, then unsheathed his machete and hacked, hacked again. The wood split easily and suddenly water spurted, pumping from the wound in diminishing gouts that mockingly counterpointed Dorthy's slowing breath and pulse, disrupting her entry into the trance state.

She stood and crossed the tilted rock to where Andrews stood, hands on hips, watching water chuckle away down a dry channel, spill down the face of the cliff. 'Will you look at that,' he said.

Dorthy asked, 'Are you trying to have us caught?'

'If something really is watching us,' Andrews said, pressing down with the tip of his machete and prising the node apart, 'it must already know about us. Have you found out what it is yet?'

'I was doing my best, but you're awfully distracting.'

'Sorry,' he said abstractedly. 'Look here, this is a kind of pump.' He had dissected out a fibrous membrane; others flexed impotently within the ruined node. The water was only a trickle now. 'I'll be damned. A living irrigation system. These vines are pumping it up from somewhere. Artesian, perhaps? It can't all flow back down, unless the trees back there don't transpire when they photosynthesise.'

'Look,' Dorthy said, angry now, 'you wanted me here, you said that you were pleased when I volunteered to come, but I can't concentrate if you don't keep quiet.' She was angry because he hadn't been taking her seriously; his fiddling around suggested that for all he had seen of the workings of her Talent he still thought it inconsequential, a tool secondary to the razor edge of scientific inquiry.

He said, 'It seems to be an awful time in coming, is all. I was simply passing the time.'

Dorthy looked off at the trees down on the other side of the cleft; glimpses of the walls that snaked up and down the slopes beneath the thin canopy, the scattered towers. She could sense something down there, a stirring, an unfocused glow. Andrews started to say something else and she asked him to be quiet: surprisingly, he was.

She concentrated, sinking into her centre, away from the seethe of Andrews's thoughts. And it came on her in a rush even before she was fully prepared, a wave of burning intelligence that touched her only for a moment before it turned away and vanished, like a lamp carried around a nighttime corner.

Out of darkness, a voice.

A dry, male voice with an edge of metal to it, mechanically reciting times and destinations of departing shuttles. Then, filling the space beneath it, the ceaseless murmur of the crowd all around her, minds like little candles each flickering in a cupped hand, all closed, all unaware . . .

Shouldering her day bag, Dorthy fled through the jostling crowd of strangers. Overhead, huge holographic signs rippled beneath the green panes of the high roof; the sourceless voice began to repeat its list. Green panes pulled away from sheaves of aluminium blades that cascaded towards the exit. And then she was outside. Hot dry sunlight fell on her from the empty sky. On one side, traffic glittered on a high overpass. On the other, people moved among the ranked cabs and buses and thopters, and other vehicles rose or settled towards the concourse like bees swarming about a hive, a hive of silver aluminium and green glass flashing in the sunlight. Beyond, the dense maze of fluxbarriers and bafflesquares of the spaceport proper stretched to the hazy horizon, the tops of only the largest ships visible.

After the years in the Kamali-Silver Institute the vast perspectives were dizzying. Dorthy managed to flag a cab and rode it to her hotel, watching the cityscape, rambling white buildings in an endless grid of tree-lined streets, flow beneath the vehicle's keel. From that height it all seemed safely unreal, like a trivia show.

Unreal, she thought, but the feeling died. She went through the registration procedure mechanically, and in her room showered and then stood on the balcony, salt seabreeze smoothing her wrap against her legs as she watched the little sailboats tack back and forth across the huge blue bay. Earth.

The journey down from orbit and the drag of gravity, almost twice that of the Institute, had exhausted all wonder. Dorthy sprawled on the huge suspensor bed and flicked through trivia channels, finding nothing much to stay her: it was all reassuringly familiar. During a segment of some space opera – a woman captured by something like a cross between a monk and a bear that carried her to the summit of a vast indistinct tower – she fell asleep, and slept deeply, all unaware of the trivia's self-obsessed mumble and flicker, waking the next day at noon. She showered again, ate breakfast and dressed, slotted her credit disc and left. She hadn't even unpacked her bag.

The mono lay like a ruled line across the random geometry of the Outback. Dorthy watched the desertscape trawl past, draws silted with fine dust, eroded circles of meteorite craters, long slopes of rubble, all the colour of dried blood beneath the depthless blue sky. She felt no anticipatory excitement: all feeling was suspended in the train's silent headlong rush. Besides, it was not as if she was coming home. Home had been the little apt in the whaling town on the coast, not a cattle ranch in the Outback. She slept, ate an indifferent meal, slept again, and was awakened as the train lurched, slowing as it swept into the little town.

Dorthy was the only passenger to alight on the baking concrete platform. The town, a sparse sprawl of homesteads each lushly green within its transparent dome, a processing plant and clustered silvery silos on the outskirts, seemed to be asleep, stunned by the vertical fall of sunlight.

The driver of the groundcar Dorthy managed to hire was a gruff, gaunt woman, bleached hair swept back from her baked, red complexion. Dust boiled behind the groundcar as she steered it down the unmetalled track towards the ranch. Scrubby bushes were scattered over the brown threadbare grassland: no trees. Once Dorthy saw the desiccated corpse of a cow, looking as if it had been caught in some searing blast at the moment it had been gathering form from the dry ground.

The driver jerked her chin and said, 'Bad drought. Can't afford to bring in rain, see.'

Later they passed a group of emaciated cattle at a shrunken waterhole, the remaining water like a viridescent mirror set in the broad circle of cracked mud. Ahead, trees clustered on the horizon, the black gleam of a solar array among them.

'You kin?' the woman asked.

'My father owns this,' Dorthy said, and at last felt a stirring of the curiosity that had brought her here. Her father had bought the ranch with the money she had earned at the Institute before she had attained her majority, but he had never told her anything about it in his brief, infrequent communications, not so much as a holo.

The woman said, 'Never been out here, right? Take my advice, girl, and don't bother. They're a bad lot altogether.'

Remembering Seyoura Yep, Dorthy stiffened.

The driver drew up by the first stand of eucalyptus. 'Luck now,' she said, as Dorthy climbed out into the heat, then spun her vehicle on its cushion of air and barrelled away. Hefting her sack, Dorthy went on.

The house was an extended single-story structure fronted by a deep, shaded veranda. It had once been painted white, but most of the paint had flaked away, and the composite beneath had weathered to a tired grey. A couple of battered ground-trucks were parked among the rubbish in the front yard; the stripped skeletons of three more stood in a corner, their skirts rotting around them. What has he done? Dorthy thought. Is this all? As she neared the house a chained dog rose, growling obscenities as she picked her way to the veranda; rotting steps creaked under her slippers.

As she gained the top, half a dozen children, almost all naked, careered around the corner into the yard and halted in a ragged semicircle a few metres from the veranda, looking up at Dorthy. She asked where the papa-san was, speaking Japanese for the first time in a dozen years, and after a flurry of exchanged glances and shuffles and nudges, the eldest girl came forward, brushing at the flies that clustered around her seeping, crusted eyes. She led Dorthy through a squalid hall to the kitchen in the back of the house, woke a fat, slatternly woman who had been dozing in a corner.

Again, Dorthy asked for her father, for her sister, her disbelief now as unsettling as panic. Flustered, the woman half bowed, saying 'Gomen nasai, gomen nasai, I am sorry. You are the daughter, such an honour, if only we had known when you come. They are all asleep, you understand, it is the heat, we sleep during the day. Sit, please,' she added, and told the child to run and fetch Dorthy's father.

Dorthy sat on a filthy cushion while the woman fussed about, preparing a bowl of *misoshuri*; for of course, an honoured guest must be fed. Dorthy felt a sinking heaviness: it was becoming real for her, and far worse than anything she could have imagined. The bean soup was lukewarm and gritty, but she politely forced down a few mouthfuls. The woman, watching her, cocked her head, said, 'He comes,' and scurried off. Dorthy turned, then scrambled to her feet.

Naked to the waist, his hair tangled around his face, her father caught the door frame with one hand, rubbing his eyes with the heel of the other. His face was seamed with dirt; his bare feet were black. 'I am glad to find you, daughter,' he said hoarsely. 'I had hoped to prepare a proper welcome; you must forgive me for not foreseeing that you would arrive so soon. As you see, there have been difficulties . . .'

Where before she had felt disbelief sinking into helplessness, now she felt a mixture of anger and contempt. 'This is all you have to show for my work?' she said.

196

Taken aback by her directness, her father muttered something about a drought, several droughts, began a stumbling litany of complaints about prejudice and harassment, disease of cattle and crops. He was half drunk, reeked of rice wine. Slowly he became belligerent. 'How poor things are I know. They must seem poorer to you, coming from where you do,' he said, 'but it is your home, and you are as a *chonan* to me, Dorthy-san. More a son than a daughter in the honour you have done your family. This is your *uchi*, where you belong. We must all work hard.'

'To me this is no honour,' Dorthy said coldly, her anger tight in her chest. 'To me this is not *uchi*. It is *onbu*, it is all on my back, and you have wasted it all.'

'You don't know how it is . . .' Her father shuffled to the standing tap in the corner, drank from it and wiped his wet hands over his face. He said, 'After the *okaa-san* died, I have been a broken-hearted man, daughter.' He fumbled at his chest as if to show her this ruptured organ.

'To me it seems that it was you that broke my mother's heart,' Dorthy said. 'You and your impossible demands and dreams. You didn't even tell me when she died!'

'Quiet, daughter!' For a moment a measure of his old sternness returned. 'You do not come here to criticise. This is my house!'

But Dorthy had outgrown his bullying. 'It is all paid for on my back! *Onbu!* You fill it with hangers-on, strangers who drink the sweat of my childhood and piss it away. There is no house here, Father.'

She sensed his intent and danced away as he clumsily swung at her. His fist slammed into the wall and he clutched it, suddenly contrite. 'It is fate,' he said, 'it is fate.' His almond-shaped eyes were screwed shut, tears glittering in their black lashes. He added weakly, 'Forgive me, daughter.'

For a moment, only a moment, Dorthy felt a loathsome wave of pity, like a maggot squirming in her gullet. 'Where is my sister?' she demanded. 'Where is Hiroko?'

'She sleeps, we are all asleep now.' Then, 'Wait, daughter, wait!'

But Dorthy had already pushed past him.

She hurried down the long corridor that was the spine of the house, opening door after door. Most of the rooms were dustily empty. In one, heavy furniture was piled as high as the ceiling; in another, a dozen people slept on overlapping futons, the air close and fetid. Next to this room, a door hung half open, and Dorthy pushed it back.

Dressed in a soiled *yukata*, her Uncle Mishio looked up, his single good eye glinting in the dimness. Beside him, the naked girl looked at Dorthy and then pressed her hands over her mouth. It was Hiroko.

After the shock, a cold calm. Dorthy ordered her sister to dress, ignoring Mishio's wheedling drunken explanations, turning away from him and pulling Hiroko with her along the corridor. Mishio began to shout. By the time Dorthy and Hiroko had gained the veranda people were stirring all through the house.

'Where are we going?' Still half asleep, Hiroko brushed back long straight hair from her pinched face as they started across the junk-strewn yard. The dog eyed them but did not speak.

'Oh, Hiroko!'

'He kept the other men from me,' the girl said.

There were shouts behind them. Dorthy turned and saw half a dozen people spill on to the veranda, and felt their intention like a gathering thunderstorm. She grabbed her sister's thin wrist and they ran through the gate, plunged into a thick stand of eucalyptus. Within five minutes they were at the edge of the dry bush. The sun was setting, and each scrubby bush seemed touched with flame. Distantly, there was the whine of a starting motor.

'They will look for us,' Hiroko said, clutching the dress around herself. 'Oh, Dorthy, we should not run away!'

'Which way is the town?'

Hiroko pointed, and Dorthy struck off at a right angle to that direction. 'We'll hide until it's dark, then we'll get away. Don't worry, I can tell if anyone comes close; I'm good at hiding.'

'I remember how you found that little boy. I sometimes wish I were like you, Dorthy-san.'

'We've both been unlucky, I think.'

They were soon out of sight of the house. Far off, the dog voiced some complaint; a trail of dust boiled down the track behind one of the trucks. Hiroko led Dorthy to a dry shallow ravine, and they crouched there as the sky darkened. Dorthy, calmer now, remembered that she had left her day bag behind; well, there was nothing in it that she needed. That part of her life was over. All around, insects sawed and creaked and hummed. Dorthy tried and failed to cast her Talent wide, wishing that she had brought tablets of counteragent, while Hiroko told her the history of the ranch, their father's hopes of setting up a centre of Japanese culture that had foundered beneath the heavy indifference and indolence of the drifters and layabouts, most of them Uncle Mishio's friends, who had battened on to him. 'After Mother died, he gave up,' Hiroko said. 'He no longer used the farming machines, and all the crops died. The cattle grew thin and the solar power does not work, but he does not care. He does not even care about Uncle Mishio and me.'

She began to cry, and Dorthy held her, comforted her. 'I'll find a place for us to live, I've a little money left. Oh, Hiroko, what a homecoming.'

The stars hung soft and shimmering in the hot night sky when they began to walk towards the town. Once Dorthy sensed a group of men working towards them, but their search was noisy and only desultory, and in the darkness and with her Talent it was easy to evade. As they walked, she told Hiroko about the Institute, about her plans to study astronomy.

'That is why you can understand. As you must understand.' It was not Hiroko's voice, no human voice at all.

Dorthy stopped. The shadowy figure beside her was too tall to be her sister, but in the darkness she could not see just what it was. It said, 'Do not be afraid,' and gestured upward at the frozen, luminous billows of interstellar dust clouds that shrouded the sky, at the rift where a single star shone: so bright it threw their mingled shadows behind them. 'That was the way we first went,' the figure said. 'Inward, searching for stars like our own.'

And for a moment Dorthy felt a wrenching dizzy sensation as if she were toppling into the sky.

The world came back to Dorthy piecemeal. She was lying on her back in a kind of bower hacked from a tangle of dense ropy growth. Above, a faint glow slanted between bulbous tree trunks, broken by looping belts of foliage, more shadow than light. Andrews lay a little way from her, breathing evenly and slowly, an arm across his face. She could feel the texture of his dreams: her Talent was still active. When she looked at her timetab she discovered that only an hour had passed.

She wet her mouth with a swig of flat-tasting water from her canteen and lay back, thinking of the dream. In some part of her mind she was still walking with her sister through the hot Australian night towards the town. She had found Hiroko an apt in Melbourne and had opened a credit line for her. The girl had insisted that she would be all right, could look after herself, and, reluctantly, Dorthy had left for Rio to take up her first contract as a freelance Talent. She had sent Hiroko money every week, but whenever she called on the phone her sister was not in, and during those three months in Greater Brazil Dorthy had fretted more and more; but she could not quit this first job – she needed the money. She had been only partly truthful with Hiroko, and setting up the apt had taken most of what little she had been able to save. Her father had taken all the rest. When Dorthy at last returned to Melbourne, Hiroko was gone; had left, it seemed, only a week after Dorthy had gone to Rio, had returned to the squalid, broken-down ranch in the desert, to their father, to Uncle Mishio. Her brief handwritten note explained nothing, a sphinx's riddle Dorthy had puzzled over for years afterward.

I cannot live among strangers.

Dorthy still did not entirely understand it.

And the rest of the dream, especially when it had turned sideways into nightmare, had that sprung from within herself? Dorthy, trained to detect the taint of otherness in her mind, suspected that it had not. It had been given to her, to prepare the way. But the way to what?

She left Andrews to his dreams and pushed through the tangled vegetation. The edge of the cleft was only a little way away, and she sat there and watched the trees that mostly hid the maze of walls and towers on the other side. She could not immediately sense anything, certainly not the bright, dangerous something that had brushed against her mind. Even the uneasy sense of being watched had vanished. She doubted that that was a coincidence.

Uneasily, reluctantly, she began to concentrate, losing first her sense of the world and then her sense of self, floating free at her centre. Slowly, slowly, faint lights of other minds came to her, like the lights of the little lives in the abyssal depths of the ocean. She was too far away to understand them, only that they were there, all touched by the rigidly linear pattern she had detected in the mind of the new male herder that had captured her back at the keep.

She had not been studying them for long when she felt Andrews coming towards her and reluctantly disengaged, felt her self pour through the shape of her body. She rose stiffly, saw his shadowy figure approaching over the stony, shadow-lapped ground, his rifle slung at his shoulder. 'Why didn't you wake me?' he said angrily. 'I didn't know where you were!'

'But you found me easily enough, so no harm is done.' His anger dazzled her, a pyrotechnic flare of thwarted ego. She said, 'There are herders down there; I'm not sure how many, nor what they are doing. I will have to go down. Alone.'

'Herder, but not the Grand Boojum, eh?'

'Pardon me?'

'The intelligence. The enemy.'

'I still don't know if it is the enemy. But it isn't there now.'

Andrews's anger melted into concern. 'But it *was* there, wasn't it? Was that why you fainted?'

'I think so. But I haven't learned anything new. Look, Andrews, I'm still too far away up here. I will have to go down. Alone.'

For a moment he debated whether or not to argue. 'So be it, Dr Yoshida. Desperate times call for desperate measures, eh? I shall do some scouting of my own. We will find each other in the shelter I hacked out in the forest. All right?'

She could only just make out his grin; it was that dark now. 'All right.'

'You are recovered from your attack?'

'I think so.'

'Good. But please, do not think of going under the trees down there, into those buildings or whatever they are. It's not worth finding out anything if you cannot return to tell me about it.'

'Oh, I can take care of myself. I hope you can, too.'

Dorthy knew better than to say anything else, to make clear the danger they were in, the trap that might already have closed about them. This was too important to Andrews, to his pride, to be aborted; but he might prevent her from using her own initiative and, obscurely, she also desired to search out the core of the mystery here. As she turned to begin her descent Andrews called after her softly, 'Good luck, now.' And was gone before she could reply.

After a punishing climb down rubble-strewn slopes in red half-light, Dorthy squatted, some twenty minutes later, behind a crumbling ridge of lava. Below was a little dry riverbed – dry how many thousand of years? – mostly covered in tangled creeper, and then the beginning of the trees that climbed the opposite slope, and the long dark walls that ramified with no discernible pattern beneath them.

Within those walls were the herders.

There was no trace of the single-minded association Dorthy had encountered in the keep and in the forest beside the lake. Instead, each mind was overlain by an ordered grid of routine, a rigid hierarchy of separate units. Now that she was closer, she could detect differences, see how some of the sparks of individuality amounted to little more than the stamped limits of their thrall, how others were intelligences only lightly held. But where was the singular intelligence that ruled this place?

She swallowed another tablet of counteragent and waited, chaffing her hands and shivering in the breeze that blew ceaselessly from the desert through the ravine. As she scanned and rescanned the quilted pattern of the herders' minds superficially reflected within herself – she had not truly submerged, reluctant to scan any individual herder in case this was all a trap – the sun sank by imperceptible degrees.

Nearby a single tower rose out of the treetops, windowless and flat-roofed. Whatever it was for, there were no herders inside it – they were all in the maze under the trees – but Dorthy was jerked out of her skimming contemplation when it suddenly flashed red. A queer flaw twisted the air above it, lensing the last light of the setting sun. A moment later the air all around Dorthy was filled with a lurid blush as a shaft of light poured through the cleft into the bowl of the radio telescope. For an instant the antenna complex seemed to burst into flame. Then the sun sank fractionally lower. The finger of light declined, draining the black bowl; the antenna complex went out as, behind Dorthy, the airy lens flickered and untwisted.

Beyond the trees, tiny figures were climbing the far edge of the cleft, highlighted by residual glow. Dorthy fumbled out her field-glasses and made out four of them, mounting a narrow stair cut into the lavic rock.

She began to work her way around the trees, keeping close to the edge of the bowl, where bedrock seamlessly met matt black lining. For all that this path dipped out of sight of the mazy walls beneath the trees, Dorthy once again had the uneasy sense that she was being watched, almost a physical sensation of the weight of some other at her back.

It stayed with her when she reached the stairway and began to climb. The treads were broad and high and mirror-smooth, and there was no guardrail to prevent her tumbling over the edge should she slip; more often than not she climbed on hands and knees, and reached the top sweating and out of breath. A cold chaste purpose was moving away from her around the rim.

She followed in the shadow of the trees, pulling the bulbous lenses of her nightsights over her eyes, everything grainy and fading into darkness so that she felt objects as much as saw them, the crook of a root, a tree trunk, leathery strands of foliage materialising centimetres from her face in grainy chiaroscuro as she groped her way, acutely aware that the creatures she was stalking were night-hunting carnivores. Certainly *they* could clearly see where they were going as they trod the tangled groundcover of the rim-meadow. Dorthy, stumbling behind, was guided mostly by her Talent.

But the herders remained unaware of her and when at last they stopped, Dorthy was able to crawl through undergrowth to the edge of the rim-meadow, where one of the supporting towers of the antenna complex stood – the very one, indeed, that Andrews had shimmied up hours before. Dorthy could scarcely make out its curved skeletal shape against the darkness, despite her nightsights. Beside it, four herders – male herders but not new males, and curiously placid, *chaste* – squatted, each one corner of a square, a square centred on light.

Light flickeringly played over their black fur, the hood of naked skin that flared out around their narrow faces, glinted in their large eyes as they intently watched its source, long strings of curdled red and orange along which nodes of brilliant blue travelled up and down, all hung eerily in nothing, painfully intense in Dorthy's amplified vision. Sometimes little spinning lights appeared, rising rapidly and popping out of existence as abruptly as they had formed.

Once one of the herders reached forward and waved a heavy arm through the lights; they froze for a moment, then twisted into a slightly altered pattern, blue nodes clustering to one side. Out in the centre of the bowl, smoothly, silently, the shadow of the antenna complex moved against the starry sky, the cable that linked it with the tower seeming to contract rather than wind in. Dorthy watched until it had stopped moving, then traced the constellations hung overhead, not much different from those of Earth. Andrews had said it: fifteen light-years is no great distance in the vastness of the Galaxy. There, the sketched kite of Cygnus, and the long line of Serpens Cauda leading into the river of milky dust that spilled the sky from edge to edge . . . of course.

The herders settled on their haunches as they steadily watched the rippling construct of light. Dorthy was drawn into their communion as a plant, slowly, irresistibly, turns to the sun.

And came to herself almost an hour later, her legs knotted with cramps. Like the herders, she had not moved in all that time. Now they were flitting silently past the skeletal tower, towards the cleft. No lights, only the faint frost of starlight on the carpeting ground-cover. She knew, along with much else, that the herders would return: and that the next time their master would be there, too.

She did not have to go far to find the bower Andrews had hacked in a tangled brake, and she sprawled in it gratefully, pushed back the uncomfortable nightsights, and rubbed her sore legs. The unfamiliar concepts she had absorbed from the herders seemed to hang like afterimages in the darkness, and she was so intent on picking them over that she did not realise that Andrews was returning until she heard him pushing through the tangle. Something was very wrong.

He squatted before her, a solid shadow in the darkness of the bower. 'I saw you follow those herders up here,' he said. 'Did you find out what this place is for?'

Dorthy slipped the loop of her nightsights over her head, settled the goggles. Andrews and the tangle behind him showed in grainy black and white. Nervously she told him, 'Those were just servants, males but not new males. I think they are neutered in some way. They were running a start-up operation, aligning the antenna, as a matter of fact. Whatever runs this place, your Grand Boojum, will be up there later on.' She hesitated, but it could not be denied. 'I know what you did.'

It was the first time she had truly revealed that she knew his thoughts, and despite his overwrought, excited state, Andrews was taken aback.

She asked, 'Why did you kill it?'

'I thought you could read my mind.'

'Now you're deliberately jumbling your thoughts. Just tell me.'

'I'm not trying to keep it secret. It was doing something to that groundvine I broke, came up when I was hiding at the edge of the forest and watching after you. Any moment it could have seen me and raised the alarm, so I shot it. I hid the body, you need not worry about our being discovered.'

'The Grand Boojum has known about us since we left the thopter, I think.'

'Well, it does not matter, because I've found out all that I need to know. The complex of buildings down there in the trees is all above ground, so it can be easily cauterized.'

'Cauterized?'

'Taken out. Bombed. A small fast-neutron emitter will not harm the telescope or the buildings, only the herders. And the Grand Boojum, if it exists.'

'I see. And what happened to your rhetoric about the need to find out the truth, about saving the scientific programme?'

'It will be saved. This is the centre of the disturbances, you think as much yourself. That intelligence, the Grand Boojum, is the nexus of hostility on this world. Take it out and the Navy will be satisfied, I believe. Really, the Navy is quite primitive, you know, but it has had so little time to evolve. Make a threat and it will respond quite predictably, and then, after the spasm, when the nerve has been discharged, it will become quiescent again. We will be able to complete our work.'

'But you don't know what you're destroying! You can't sacrifice this, not when I can find out about the Alea, why they came here, where they came from – everything you need to know.'

'There is not time, Dr Yoshida. We cannot stay here forever. It is too dangerous, and besides, eventually Colonel Chung will assume that we are dead, and will act accordingly. Angel won't wait out in the desert forever, you know. No, there has to a sacrifice, and which would you rather? The hold here, or the whole planet? Because that is what it comes down to.'

'But there is still a little time. Everything will be revealed soon, I *know*.'

'You know,' he said flatly, mockingly.

'Yes, I know. It's been laying down hints in my dream. I think it wants—'

'Dreams are of no value, Dr Yoshida. The Navy does not believe in them. The intelligence is here, that much is known. You passed out because it brushed against you. That is all you have certainly found out, although I admit that I was hoping for more. But politics is the art of the possible, and it is not so important. Whatever we need to learn from the herders themselves will be in the other holds – did not that fireworks display convince you? It certainly changed my mind. And I rather think that the herders, the caretakers, are servants of the thing down there, and will be rendered harmless once it has been removed.'

Andrews had spoken with such smooth cold plausibility – for he truly believed that this was the right thing to do, *had* to believe – that he had held Dorthy in a kind of spell. Now she said weakly, 'You kept this from me.'

She had to imagine his smile in the sketch of his face revealed by the nightsights. 'That is what angers you most, I think, that you could not pluck it from my head at will. Ah, Dr Yoshida, Dorthy, I told you once that I know Talents, and they taught me one or two tricks. So I was able to fool you, my ordinary un-Talented mind managed to keep a secret from you. Never mind.' He reached for her, but she had already anticipated him – he could hide a thought or two perhaps, but he couldn't disguise the gross muscular impulses that fire up ahead of any movement. Even as he reached for her, Dorthy plunged into the tangled vegetation. Andrews swore and blundered after her as she wriggled out into the open beneath the trees, everything grainy black and white and oddly two dimensional, a lithographed maze whose dimensions became apparent only as she plunged through it. Andrews's voice called faintly behind her, called her name. But Dorthy ran on, dodging among trees, tripping over roots and scrambling up and running on. She was smaller than he, and could move more easily through the forest; and of course she always knew where he was and roughly what his intentions were, where he would be next. His voice grew fainter, anger mixed now with fear, as she went on. Soon even the trace of his thoughts had faded. She was alone.

Later, hiding at the edge of the rim-meadow by the support tower, waiting for the herders to return, Dorthy lay on her back looking up at the scape of stars that spanned the sky from the horizon to horizon. Directly overhead was Sagittarius and the centre of the Galaxy's stately slow-turning starswarm, the hub of a wheel of four hundred billion suns. Suns and suns and suns. And this was only one galaxy in the local group, by no means the largest of the thousand or so strung along one of the many infolded ripples of space-time that had been flung out by the explosion of the Monobloc . . . and in turn the local group was by no means the largest of the millions of groups of galaxies in the known Universe. What was any human endeavour, any single human life, against that? Nothing, of course. And yet, precious. Stars were stars, but no more: a woman was greater because she had the potential to transcend herself, even as a bacterium was greater, for bacteria had evolved into women and men, every one a unique node of being . . . Andrews took precisely the opposite view: that the human race was all, the individual a replaceable cell in the blind outward urge, spreading like some weed through the stars. Dorthy remembered one week on the Great Barrier Reef, pulling starfish from the coral banks with gloved hands, voracious, destructive bundles of stiff barbed spines. Crown of thorns. Andrews's vision was of mankind battening on the reefs of the Galaxy, using it regardless of its own worth. For blind matter seeks form just as life does, following the laws woven in the very heart of atoms, the spiral of a galaxy duplicated in the ring of tentacles around the mouth of one of the coral animacules that, billion upon billion, blindly build the vast coral reefs in unknowing cooperation. That forms of matter were simpler to predict than the quirky forms of life was the only difference, one of the reasons why Dorthy had been attracted to astronomy. *I cannot live among strangers.* Perhaps she was beginning to understand that now. And she remembered what Arcady Kilczer had said, that she had cut herself off because she resisted integration with others and the relaxation of the borders of self that integration required. She rolled over on to her belly. She didn't want to think about Arcady or Hiroko right then.

Feeble lights were glimmering now among the trees in the cleft that split the black bowl, skeins of pinprick illumination that here outlined the sweep of a wall, there the pinnacle of a tower, a mocking counterpoint to the stars above. Dorthy wondered if Andrews had gone down there again, to salvage some measure of his pride, and hoped not. And what if he had returned to Angel Sutter, what if they had abandoned her? What price knowledge then?

But in her own way Dorthy was as stubborn as Andrews – although he was certainly braver, foolishly brave, with only the standard human equipment to help him. Dorthy had so often felt that her Talent was a curse; a mark she had tried to expunge when she had become an astronomy student (and because she had not exploited her Talent she had lacked the political contacts necessary to avoid the draft that had sent her here). But she felt now, in the darkness at the edge of the alien forest, how much she needed it, for all that she had deliberately allowed it to wither, fearful of meeting that terrible singular mind with it in full flower. And then she stopped musing and pulled her nightsights over her eyes. For with the dregs of her Talent she could sense that the herders were coming to their trysting place.

She recognised the enthralled neuter males from before. But now their leader was in their midst, a mind burning like a laser among candles, brilliantly dangerous for all that it was not directed towards Dorthy, for all that her Talent was almost exhausted. And at last Dorthy understood why technology had survived here.

The leader was a neuter female.

A bloated shadow in the strip of starlit meadow, supported by two of the males, the neuter female moved slowly and painfully, grunting as she slowly settled to the ground. The males squatted respectfully behind her as rods of orange and red light unfurled in the air. Now Dorthy could see the female's face: a bulging forehead shadowing huge eyes, a small mouth constantly moving as if mumbling a wad of cud, the hood of skin swollen and wrinkled, falling in thick folds over broad, furred shoulders.

Out over the bowl, black against black, the antenna complex began to move slowly and smoothly, until it was aimed just as Dorthy had guessed it would be, aimed straight at zenith. At Sagittarius, the heart of the Galaxy. Belatedly she realised that the ceremony must already have begun and carefully, lightly, brought her diminished Talent to bear on the group beside the support tower.

And, almost at once, was thrown into a maelstrom.

It was as if her skull had been torn apart and all the Universe stuffed inside. Stars bombarded her, incandescent specks exploding upward from an unravelling centre, whirling past and gone even as more rose up to meet her. Then she was sweeping through the veils of dust that hung before the core. There was something beyond, a watchful presence, and she was falling towards it along compressed geodesics of space-time. No more dust. Swollen stars glowered around her, their fusion burning oddly, a flux of heavy atoms contaminating the pure piping song *hydrogen to helium, hydrogen to helium*, atoms thrown out by novas and supernovas and swept up by the close-packed stars that glared with spiteful red or blue or white light. Brown and red dwarfs danced attendance; quintuple and septuple systems whirling complicated gavottes were common in the close-packed reaches. So few had worlds, yet the implacable search was tireless, the endlessly unfulfilled appetite of the worm at the core, somehow devouring its own self even as its gaze roved out and out.

Dorthy flinched, recoiling among drifting suns. Was fixed. And felt herself shrink beneath that deadly gaze, the jewelled core spinning away among shrouds of interstellar dust, ordinary suns flying backward as she shrank to her self, to the familiar limits of her body.

Red light pressed on her eyelids. The dull pain of a headache, a rich spice in her nostrils. Dorthy gagged and opened her eyes.

And scrambled back, panic thrilling in every muscle. On the other side of the small, round room, a herder squatted on its hams, watching her impassively. His black eyes glinted like huge, unfaceted opals in the shadow cast by his hood of deeply folded skin; flakes of red light lay along every hair of his black pelt.

Dorthy was locked in her skull. In the interval before her return to consciousness, the counteragent had finally worn off. She still had her coveralls, and nothing seemed to have been taken from her belt or her pockets, yet she had no weapon but a knife, nothing that could help her but her own wit and knowledge.

When the herder saw that she was awake, he turned and quickly squirmed through a low opening. Dorthy understood that she was in a kind of cell, smooth-walled and almost spherical, lit by sourceless red light. It was like being inside the shell of a blown egg.

After a minute the herder, or another just like it, came back. With long stiff fingers – three, all opposable, set around its naked palm – it urged her out through the small opening. She had to duck; at her back, the herder scrambled through on hands and knees. Around them, streaks of light wavered at the tops of smooth walls, shedding a glow that seemed to seal the air above into an impenetrable black ceiling; Dorthy was the focus of many faint truncated shadows.

The herder prodded her again.

She shook off its touch and said, 'All right, damn you. Show me where to go.'

As if it understood, the herder loped off for a few steps, turned and made sure that she was following before setting off again, leading her up narrow, steeply sloping passages between smooth walls. Trees grew from the resilient black floor without seam, and where the strips of red light were more widely spaced than usual Dorthy could see interwoven branches beyond the tops of the walls. She saw no other herders, but here and there groups of monkey-sized creatures with long bifurcated tails and silky pelts clung to high ledges and watched her pass, their small solemn faces cupped in long fingers as if they were scholars contemplating some unexpected wonder that had erupted into their closeted studies.

Then the passage turned a corner and Dorthy followed the herder into a kind of plaza, a round, flat-topped tower at each corner. On the far side, a crowd of herders formed a rough crescent, some squatting, some standing on splayed legs with both pairs of arms, small under large, folded across the kegs of their chests. All watched Dorthy as, her heart beating quickly, lightly, she followed her jailer into the centre of the plaza, where the neuter female reclined, as motionless as an enormous stuffed toy. One of the monkey-things was perched on her shoulder, combing her black fur with crooked fingers.

For all that Dorthy's Talent was suborned by her implant, for all that she was alive in her every mundane sense and not concentrating on her still centre at all, it seemed to her that a kind of aura hung around the neuter female, as restless as the corona of a star, made up of hundreds of sources that whirled in double lobes that pulled apart from a common centre.

No signal was made, but one of the herders behind the huge female hopped forward awkwardly. He looked ill used, his pelt dull and matted, his hood of skin loose as an old man's wattles. Shivering, he looked back and forth between Dorthy and the neuter female. And then he spoke. His voice was high-pitched, blurring and scrambling the consonants, but the speech was human, pure, unaccented Portuguese.

'I will speak to you through this servant. He has learned your ways, although at the cost of his sanity. But he will suffice. Welcome to my hold. I understand that you are an astronomer. Perhaps we have much to learn from each other, in the time we have together. Please understand that I know about you.'

'Then you must understand that we mean you no harm,' Dorthy said, as steadily as she could. She had always thought that death would be welcome when it came, a blissful eternity of silence, but she had discovered now how much she wanted to live.

The neuter female regarded her. Although she was sprawled on the ground, propped on one crooked arm, and Dorthy was standing, their eyes were level. The creature that had been grooming the female clung to her swollen cowl of skin by one hand, its large eyes watching Dorthy, too.

The female said, 'You do not, perhaps.' If irony had been intended, it was lost in translation.

'We tried to establish contact at another hold.'

The bifurcated cloud wobbled wide for a moment. 'I know this.

Of course, my brothers and sisters would have nothing to do with you, because they could not understand you. And their changed children, understanding you, would wish you destroyed.'

'But you know about us. You understand us. May I ask how—'

Abruptly, a cat's cradle of orange light flickered in the air before the neuter female. She waved a three-fingered hand through it and a shocking cacophony of human voices echoed around the plaza. The translator shivered. Now the orange web was studded with flickering blue lights; the female pointed at one and it pulsed more brightly as the babble faded to a single woman's voice crisply enunciating a string of numbers, pausing to say 'No, point two oh three on the azimuth, or you'll have it most of the way around the dayside, don't you see?' before resuming her recitation. The neuter female reached out and the web flickered off; the voice died in midsyllable.

The translator said, 'Long ago, one of my sisters built analytical engines to watch the sky. They were saved for a reason I cannot be bothered to remember, and since your fleet arrived I have set them the task of studying your speech: my poor brother here has absorbed the results. You understand that your communications are not closed to me. The movement of one electron instantaneously displaces the orbit of a myriad others throughout the Universe. In that way I gained much understanding, yes, but I was able to obtain a religious document that gave me the key to your kind.'

'Religious . . . ?'

'If blasphemy has been done by my reading, I apologise. But it was necessary to understand you. The communications were mere data. Now I return it to you.' Again there was no signal, but a herder loped forward and placed something at Dorthy's feet.

As he returned to his place among his fellows, Dorthy picked it up. A book. Her book, the book of sonnets that she had lost when the critters had overrun the camp. But it was not *the* book, she realised: it was instead some cleverly detailed facsimile, its pages not ancient brittle paper but some slick stuff grained to imitate pressed wood pulp, ornate type not printed but seemingly burned into the sheets, the cover harder than leather yet marked with an imitation of the stain where, three years ago at Fra Mauro, she had once spilled white wine on it. *The Sonnets. William Shakespeare.*

Dorthy said, 'You gained understanding through this?'

'I understand now a little of what you humans strive for, perhaps. It is a mystical tale, of course, but the analytical engines were able to unravel its meaning.' Sprawled with her massive, hooded head propped on one hand, lesser arms clasped across her chest, the neuter female looked like one of the cheap images of Buddha that streetsellers hawked in most cities of Earth. Smug. Obliviously complacent.

Dorthy asked, 'Why did you want me to come here? It was you who gave me those dreams, wasn't it? And made that new male in the keep capture me – you wanted me dead, and now you want me to live. What *do* you want of me? Are there others like you?'

'No longer. I am the last of a line of guardians of this world. Soon it will need no more.' The fragmented cloudy aura split again, the myriad orbiting specks dancing like dust motes disturbed by a breath.

'The last of a line? You have a family? Are the herders your relations?'

The translator threw up its head and howled, a sibilant keening. The neuter female did not move, except her vestigial pair of hands now clutched at the fur of her chest. The translator lowered its head, shivering, said, ' "New male" is the term you humans use for the changed children, I believe. Yes, I overrode the consciousness of one, I wished the children to see you for what you are; a danger, yes, a danger greater than any this world has faced before.'

Beside Dorthy, the herder who had acted as her jailer scrambled to his feet and gripped her arm, gently but irresistibly began to turn her while the translator said, 'There is knowledge to be given. Accept it.'

'Wait,' Dorthy said as she was dragged away, 'you haven't told me! What do you want of me?'

But the translator hung its head and said no more, and Dorthy was borne out of the plaza into the maze of passageways beneath the forest canopy. She wondered what the female had meant when she had called the sonnets a mystical tale. For of course they were nothing of the kind, in fact were the most autobiographical of Shakespeare's writings, concerning his feelings about his patron, the Earl of Southampton, and the woman Shakespeare had been charged with urging Southampton to marry, the courtesan Emilia Lanier,

Shakespeare's own dark young mistress. This triangular relationship, with its shifting geometries of love and power and responsibility, had generated the finest love poetry of the lost nation of England. Despite all, it had endured, its flashing images eternal reflections of the depths of one human mind. But mystical . . . ? Dorthy could think of nothing that could be mistaken for that: even the meditations on the inevitability of mortality and the end of love were couched in small, human concerns. *Thus in his cheek the map of days outworn, When beauty liv'd and died as flowers do now . . .*

Dorthy's jailer pushed at the top of her head, urged her to stoop and enter the cell, following at her heels and rearing up within the red-lit hollow. It opened one hand, and Dorthy glimpsed a wadding of fine wire. Then, casually, the herder flung it at her face.

It clung to her skin and she instantly collapsed, all her muscles unstrung. Out of the corner of her unfocused vision she saw the wire unfolding, felt it crawl over her head, felt a myriad pinpricks over her scalp. And then the herder and the cell seemed to recede to an infinite distance.

This time she was the centre of the vision, the stuff that shaped it spinning out of some hidden part of her mind, knowledge and images rising simultaneously. To see was to understand, every object its own text.

To begin with, there was a sun.

It was a red supergiant three thousand times the diameter of an ordinary dwarf star like Sol, so tenuous that it was little more than a local vortex of angular momentum in dust clouds that fluoresced for a light-year with its radiation. Within a few tens of millions of years after its ignition, it should have become a variable Cepheid, as its outer layers burned up their hydrogen and became opaque to radiation generated beneath, explosive pressure finally blowing them away to start the whole cycle over. But it was billions, not millions, of years old: for the dust clouds in which it traced its lonely path were those that shrouded the Galaxy's heart, laced with radial belts of hydrogen sufficiently compressed by the shockwaves of core supernovas to overcome the outward light-pressure of the supergiant, and so continually renew it. It was a flare star, yes, but the flares were localized, and storms in which ordinary stars would have instantly vanished were no more than pimples on its insubstantial surface.

Over the eons, the supergiant had gathered a motley family of planets, as well as a marginal brown dwarf that was little more than an oversized gas giant, its core collapsed and sluggishly fusing, radiating infrared light and a welter of hard radiation. Among its host of moons circled an Earth-sized world bearing a thin scum of liquid water, an oxygen atmosphere, life. It was the homeworld of the herders, the Alea, the People.

In her vision, Dorthy saw strange fierce civilisations rise each time the supergiant passed through a local compression in the dust clouds, the herders' children metamorphosing into intelligent males in response to the increase in background radiation, surviving only long enough to preserve their indolent parents during flare-time. And then civilisation and the brief territorial wars faded, and the herders returned to their usual way of life, shepherding their flocks of children – of which only one in a hundred would survive the rigorous culling by which mutants were eliminated – and hunting beneath the dark eye of the brown dwarf and the hot red light of the giant sun that, although more than half a light year distant, dominated the sky. Its vast bleary disc glowered against the dust clouds, frozen violet banners that shrouded all other stars except, occasionally, a nova or supernova that flickered briefly through the general glow.

And then it all changed.

Dorthy saw a baleful point of light grow in the luminous sky, a supernova less than a dozen light years from the perimeter of the dust clouds. With visible light came hard radiation, and a fraction behind that, and more deadly, came heavy nuclei stripped of electrons and accelerated almost to light-speed. Even in daytime the sky was painted with lurid salmon and green and cyan streaks as the clouds of interstellar matter fluoresced, and the supergiant's disc was spotted with flares as its thin substance was perturbed by the onslaught. As ever, the herder children metamorphosised as the level of radiation increased, but this time they determined that the instabilities might last centuries, might eventually tear apart the great star. Reluctantly they began to evacuate the planet, mobilising a swarm of asteroids that had gathered in the trailing Trojan point of the brown dwarf and bringing them into stationary orbit in its shadow. There, the asteroids were spun to provide gravity, hollowed, and equipped with the remnants of the homeworld's ecology – vanished now on the surface, nothing left alive but a few hardy species in the ocean deeps. By then the onslaught of the supernova had diminished, but the supergiant was pocked with flares across half its surface, and even the brown dwarf was showing signs of disturbance. One by one, the herder families decided to move out, heading in the only direction where they knew other stars existed, heading towards the core.

Dorthy felt a million years unreel in a few moments as one by one the asteroid arks completed their long sublight voyages, found new systems within the crowded reaches of the core, almost all of them systems of red dwarf stars – in the core's vast jewel box of stars only these were stable enough. Worlds were transformed and seeded and settled, and once the ecosystems stabilised the herders returned to their former ways. The children that survived culling changed only into other herders; civilisation died out. Forgotten, the asteroid arks circled in lonely parking orbits.

But one family, one of the last to leave the home system and thus more in need of exploration than most as it searched for a suitable uncolonised system, decided to create a new caste: neuter females, long-lived watchers over herders, preservers of civilisation. This family settled not one world but dozens; a slow wave-front of civilisation began to expand through the fringe of the core, towards the black hole that dominated half its reaches.

Neuter females of the newest colony of this family were the first to notice the altered pattern of flare activity among the red dwarf stars of the core, brief fierce increases in radiation of stars known to be stable, stars whose systems had been settled by other families. Expeditions set out from dozens of worlds to investigate, but only a few returned; and those in disarray, with reports of warps in the space-time continuum, of energy pouring out of the infolded structure of space itself, of freshly sterilised worlds guarded by fleets of small, heavily armed ships. On some worlds the neuter females, determined to fight back, raised armies of altered children; others decided to flee, also causing the children to change, but organising them to construct arks. One by one, hollowed asteroids dropped through the close-packed stars of the core, trailed by reports from the worlds that had chosen to defend themselves. One of the last of these to survive finally identified the marauders: no strangers after all, but a family of the People that had pirated the technology of a long-vanished race and was now bent on conquering all the known worlds of the Alea, scorching them clean by briefly destabilising the suns and then resettling them with their own kin.

Meanwhile, the arks fled outward, novas flaring in strings behind them as the war progressed and those resisting the marauders' advances were snuffed out one by one. By now the arks were travelling too fast in Einsteinian space to be ambushed. They fell through the circling dust clouds and to the astonishment of their crews emerged into the wide reaches of the Galaxy's spiral arms, the billions of suns previously hidden from view.

Like meteor fragments briefly scratching the vault of the night sky, the arks plunged into the ordinary reaches of the Galaxy, vanished among the myriad undistinguished stars.

Dorthy saw one such ark, a hollow, roughly cylindrical asteroid, reach the end of a voyage which had lasted longer than recorded human history, undergoing a centuries-long course change that eventually brought it into a wide orbit about a dim red dwarf. The planet chosen for colonisation orbited so close that long ago it had come to rest with one face towards its primary, almost all of its atmosphere frozen out on the side which permanently faced the interstellar void. Temporary habitats were constructed close to the small weak sun as the ark was cannibalised. Under the guidance of the neuter females, the children spun a fragile web around the planet, essentially the dismantled drive of the ark. What it did was cancel mass – not simply weight, but rest mass. It shut off the Universe with respect to the object on which it was focused. The ark had been propelled to near light-speed by the equivalent of the energy needed to boil a few hundred litres of water (although operation of the mass-canceller required gigawatts of power, thus satisfying the first law of thermodynamics).

On moving day, then, the drive was activated and for a moment webs of light wrapped the planet. By the time they had faded, the planet was gone. All but a fraction of its mass cancelled – enough remaining to prevent it becoming a super-photon and leaving the system at uncontrollable lightspeed – but still possessed of the angular momentum with which it had swept out its orbit, the planet shot across the system on a carefully calculated trajectory, passing close to the largest of the half-dozen gas giants in the outer reaches. For a few moments the drive was switched off and gravity reasserted its hold, bending the planet's trajectory around the banded, blue-green gas giant; and in the transference of momentum the planet gained spin, driven now back to the sun and neatly injected into its old orbital path.

The rest of the transformation, although minor by comparison, took centuries to complete. Ice asteroids, culled from the gas giant's trailing Trojan points, rained down, pluming gigatons of steam into the atmosphere and starting a year-long deluge that filled the scars left by their impacts with shallow freshwater seas. Huge volcanoes spewed carbon dioxide and more water vapour into the atmosphere, and the seas were seeded with oxygen-generating photosynthetic bacteria; at last, the flora and fauna of the ark's ecosystem were introduced into their new home. Gradually, the once-dead world quickened.

But before the settlement of the planet was complete, a dispute broke out amongst the neuter females. Some of them were already dismayed by the careless expenditure of energy during planoform-ing, and at last they determined that the act of spinning up the planet had left an immutable signature which could, theoretically, be detected by the marauding Alea family which had stormed the Galactic core so long ago. And in the newly created paradise, their own family would return to the ancient pattern of hunting and herding; if the marauders arrived, it would take too long to prepare a defence.

This discovery precipitated a brief but fierce war. The neuter females and those children who had already descended to the gardens of the new world were bombarded by metal-rich asteroids, long ago brought into orbit to provide construction materials, which were flung to the planet's surface using the dismantled drive. Their fiery impacts decimated the fragile new ecosystem and shrouded the entire planet in dust. In the confusion which followed, the rebels captured the ark and with no time to rebuild its propulsion system drifted off at low velocity to seek a system without planets to use as a

218

base, where the children would remain intelligent because of the need for technology to sustain their family, a perpetually alert army . . .

There was more, but the dream snapped sideways and vanished even before it had ceased its spinning out. Unwelcome consciousness rushed back. A hand was over Dorthy's mouth; another held her arms behind her back.

'Be still,' Andrews whispered.

A space of silence stretched. Still disorientated, Dorthy tasted the sweat of Andrews's palm, salty stench like soured butter: *gaijin* sweat. With the vestige of her Talent she could sense the edge of his fear, a kind of wild desperation.

At last he released her, whispering, 'We have to go now. Come on.'

'You're crazy,' she whispered back, rubbing her wrists. The delicate web which had fed her the saga of the herders, the Alea, the People, lay crumpled on the floor of the cell, its strands feebly stirring.

Standing over her, Andrews asked, 'What have they done to you?'

'They were telling me where they came from, and why. I know, now. But for you I would have learned everything you came here to find. They're hiding here, Andrews, hiding from some of their own kind who usurped some great, terrible power. I haven't figured it all out yet, but I've met their leader, and I think there's something wrong with her, as if there are two factions fighting in her mind. If you hadn't pulled that wire off me I might have discovered why she's behaving as she is.'

Andrews picked up his rifle. 'I would have expected a little gratitude, perhaps. I risked my life to rescue you, and if we do not move now it may well be in vain. Can you walk?'

She could, although when she stood blood rushed into her head and for a moment her vision was washed with dizzy red. When she staggered, Andrews moved forward solicitously and helped her through the low doorway. But once outside she shook off his grip and said, 'What did – Why . . . ?'

'That, I would have thought, is quite obvious,' Andrews said coolly.

Dorthy stepped around the body of the herder, pushing back her hair. The tips of her fingers came away stickily, smeared with blood from wounds caused when Andrews had torn the wire from her scalp. She was still in the grip of the induced trance, as if the real world was merely an overlay to a deeper reality where explanation surfaced with perception. She said, 'You killed it.' But no explanation came.

He pulled at her arm, pulled harder when she resisted.

She said, 'I told you that I met your Grand Boojum, that she's not all that she should be. I think that I might be able to find out why. Look, if we can understand the Alea we can communicate with them, and they with us. Isn't that better than destroying them?'

'Don't be naïve. You cannot change the Navy. These things are already responsible for the death of a dozen men and women, remember? You're under their influence, the Lord knows what they were feeding you with that thing. You've gone in too deeply. You're not thinking properly.' He gripped her arm again, gave it an angry shake. 'Now come on!'

'It's too late,' Dorthy told him, sensing herders, four, five, six, coming along the sloping passage even before they turned the corner. Andrews raised his rifle and in that instant everything came together in Dorthy's head. Just as he fired she knocked up the rifle with doubled fists, and the shot pattered away harmlessly through the canopy overhead. Andrews didn't have time to swear, much less push Dorthy aside, before the herders were upon them, whirling them apart, plucking the rifle from Andrews's grasp and cuffing him to the ground when he tried to resist.

Dorthy and Andrews were marched in close formation through the passages, herders pressing behind them as they stumbled on the heels of those in front. Dorthy tried to convince Andrews of the importance of talking to the neuter female, telling him of what she had learned in the trance, and of the dichotomy she had observed in the neuter female's mind, the way her thoughts seemed to be pulled in two directions, as if she knew that what she was planning was wrong.

'And what is she planning?' Andrews had lost his cockiness now, and nervously eyed a group of the little split-tailed monkeys.

'I don't know that, but I think she's going to tell me. I was shown how they planoformed this world, Andrews, how it was spun up!' Remembering, she wondered what had happened to the ark's drive, and asked, 'When the Navy arrived here, did they find anything in orbit?'

'In orbit? No, I don't think so. Look now,' he said, 'I suppose that you're not to blame. They've brainwashed you and of course you can't see that. Well, it doesn't matter. Whatever this neuter female is planning, the Navy will act in, oh, fifteen hours from now, and that will be that for her and for us, if we're still alive.'

'There's still a chance,' Dorthy insisted; but now she was less sure. Suppose some subtle change *had* been wrought on her when she had been under the wire? And suppose she was overestimating her ability to plumb the depth of the neuter female's psyche, as in her childhood she had dissected the neuroses and psychoses of the subjects presented to her at the Institute. But there was no other chance. They were nearing the plaza now, and she took out the dispenser, popped out a tablet of counteragent, and swallowed it.

Andrews saw this, but made no move to stop her. He said, 'If I see a way to get us out of this, I'm going to take it. This time restrain yourself if you feel the impulse to stop me.'

Dorthy didn't reply. He was still afraid, she saw, but his fear was not as deep as hers, and neither was his uncertainty. At bottom he was like all the Golden she had known, quite unafraid of death because he was unable to imagine it. Stay the same and after a while you come to think that nothing will ever change. Even now, as they were marched out into the plaza, this belief flooded Andrews, and his fear was only a superficial skim glittering like drops of oil on a sunlit sea.

While Andrews looked around, the translator shambled forward, head hunched so that the hood of naked skin almost hid his narrow face, and said, 'I trust that you learned enough, before you were . . . interrupted.'

Andrews stepped forward defiantly, hiding his shock at the scene. When he spoke, Dorthy for a moment saw it through his eyes: the dark menacing crowd of herders behind the gross, reclining figure of the neuter female, the looming red-lit walls and the black air above: Minos in judgement at the gate of Dis. Andrews said, 'I understand that you want to explain yourself. To begin with, perhaps you can explain about the behaviour of your people in the keep. Are they under your control?'

He had addressed the translator, who cringed and shied back, glancing sidelong at his leader. Dorthy pointed to the neuter female and explained that she was speaking through the translator, and without a pause Andrews turned and repeated his question.

'Once I could affect them in a gross way, but now that they have gained in knowledge it is very difficult.'

Dorthy watched the neuter female with new perception. Not a Buddha, no, not calm and indifferent at all, but a lonely half-crazed queen feeling the reins of power fraying in her grip. She asked, 'Where are your sisters? The others like you?'

'I am the last lineage.'

'What's this about sisters?' Andrews asked. 'There are others like her?'

'Neuter females,' Dorthy said. 'Remember what I told you? She is the last of them, a cloned descendant of one of the crew of the ark that settled this world.'

Through the translator, the neuter female said, 'In me live my ancestors,' and at last Dorthy understood the nature of the aura or cloud of frantically whirling psychotrophic nodes that seemingly hung about the neuter female: they were the fragmented traces of past lives decayed to a last furious obsession. But why were they split, as if into opposing camps?

Impatiently Andrews said to the neuter female, 'I must ask what your intentions are.'

'I will do nothing now. It is all set in motion.'

'What do you mean?' Dorthy felt the first tingling intimation of her Talent; the flickering aura around the neuter female seemed to be growing brighter, resolving as a cloudy fleck in a telescope's field of view becomes, with the smallest motion of the focusing screw, the starry spiral of a galaxy. When there was no reply, Dorthy said, 'Well, if you won't tell me that, explain your conclusions about us, the myth you see explicated in the book.' She drew it from the pouch-pocket of her coveralls and tossed it to Andrews, who turned it over and read the cover, then looked at her askance.

The neuter female, seeming to gain a kind of smug confidence, said through the translator, 'It is a tale of supplication and revelation. As a changeling child might approach me, so the narrator approaches a savant and flatters him into revealing religious secrets by virtue of his mastery of language, promising immortality in the written word so that generations to come will marvel at his learning.'

' "So long as men can breathe, or eyes can see," ' Dorthy murmured. ' "So long lives this, and gives life to thee." '

The neuter female said, 'Your species is space-and-time-binding, ambitious in its grasp yet helpless in the shadow of individual mortality. Again and again in this writing the dark goddess is evoked, the darkness of nonexistence. It is against that you strive.' The light about her seemed brilliant now, the dwindled personae of lost ancestors like sparks whirling through the general glare. The neuter female's intellect burned even brighter in their midst: Dorthy found that it was not overwhelming as long as she did not resist it but let it fall cleanly through her, as light falls through a pane of glass. No longer terrible, but tragically flawed. Dorthy knew that if she could understand that dark knot in the centre of the light, unravel it, all might yet be saved, the new male herders' hostility subdued, the Navy's fear calmed.

Andrews said, 'And what about you? What do your . . . relatives, the herders, achieve by staying hidden here?' He stepped forward, hands on hips; the herders around the neuter female stirred uneasily and those behind Andrews moved to flank him on either side. Dorthy saw their naked hands flex, claws sliding from blunt fingertips. Andrews glanced at them, his fear quite evaporated by the heat of his proud anger.

It was a long time before the neuter female replied. At last the translator stirred and said in its flawless Portuguese, 'They survive.'

'Ah yes, survive. And achieve nothing to deserve it.'

'The only meaning of life, if it can be said to have meaning, is to survive. My brothers and sisters, herding their children on the plains, find meaning in the simple pattern of their lives and need nothing more. They are immersed in the processes of the world: all is one. That is their religion. They seek no other meaning.

'Your race, now, believes that expansion is all. You think to outrace your dark destiny, believe that the whole Universe is yours when you understand so little of it.'

'And you,' Dorthy asked, 'is that what you believe?'

'I serve my family,' the neuter female said, and although she seemed as calm as ever, Dorthy sensed the turmoil within the double cloud, sparks of ancient selves whirling like gnats in a windstorm, struggling for dominance in the battleground of the neuter female's mind just as the two factions of the Alea family had once fought for dominance before taking their separate ways.

Andrews said, 'You are hiding from those of your race who stole technology from some civilisation, is that right? They are still there, at the core?'

'It is wise to assume so.'

'There is only one way to find out: and that is to confront them. If you allied yourself to the Federation—'

'You have no imagination, and less understanding. The weapons used when the marauders fought against the other families are beyond your comprehension. I possess a device that can perturb the sun – in fact, that is how I stimulated the children to change into the new males – but the family that found the ancient technology would count that as the least of their powers. They are able to snuff the fusion pathways of a star as you might pinch out a flame between your fingers. This memory has been passed down the chain of my ancestors, and so, too, I remember that as we fled the core we observed vast structures orbiting the black hole there, remnants of the technology that the marauder family had pirated. Structures a light-year or more across, how old I dare not guess.

'We are a slow, conservative species. Perhaps even stupid, compared to others who briefly establish themselves among the stars. We left our homeworld because we were forced to do so by a cosmic accident. Before that, we had lived there for millions of years . . . how many is not known, for the changeling children never concerned themselves with history. Of course, except in time of need, few of us are technologically manipulative, but perhaps that is why we have survived for so long. Technology is destabilising. Often, after a flare, the changeling children of different families fought destructive wars before they died out, each seeking to enlarge their territory just as the marauding family, using pirated technology, has vastly enlarged its own. In all the time we spent travelling from star to star in the core, and when we fled, we did not discover the principle of the phase graffle, as you call it. We did not realise that faster-than-light travel was possible until the marauders demonstrated it – stupidly perhaps, but also luckily, for a phase graffle leaves an indelible signal in space-time that can be read and traced to its source.'

And Dorthy thought, there, there is the knot, the flaw. There.

Andrews asked, 'The marauders, as you call them, can trace phase graffles? You mean that they might know about us?'

'You have signalled your presence and they will come for you, from the core. It will take time, but they will come.'

The seeking eye. Dorthy remembered the fear that she had felt in her first dream about the homeworld of the Alea, and saw that fear at the core about which the divided cloud of the little lost selves flickered.

'If it is that inevitable,' Andrews said stubbornly, belligerently, still not wholly believing it, 'then it is all the more urgent that you join us.'

'No. When I first contacted the mind of this female' – as awkward as a puppet, the translator threw up an arm, gesturing towards Dorthy – 'I saw through her how you are. Later, when the book was captured by one of my brothers, this was confirmed to me. Your people are all locked inside themselves. There is no sense of belonging, of loyalty—' The translator shook his head and whimpered. Then he said, 'My servant cannot find the right term. That your speech does not have it is indicative.'

'*Uchi*,' Dorthy said.

Andrews turned to look at her, raising an eyebrow.

To him, to the neuter female, Dorthy explained, 'In the language of my father's people it means one household, the sense of belonging to the place where you live. Of belonging to a family.' *I cannot live among strangers.* Yes.

'Look,' Andrews said, 'we are not so different. You have your loyalty to your family. Mine is more general, to my species. Yet there is also a particular instance: to the place where I was born, the place of *my* family. My hold, if you like. Can you not see that?'

And Dorthy did indeed see an ill-defined image in his mind, the picture of a high-walled castle atop a rocky promontory overlooking a surging grey ocean. But she also saw the flaw twisted in the luminous mind of the neuter female, worm at the core. She said, 'It's no good, Andrews. Don't you see? She wants the war to happen. If she hadn't stirred up changes in the herder children there would have been no hostilities; they didn't arise because of us but because of the radiation of the flare. She caused it to happen. She *wants* the war.'

The translator said, 'Your people fight mine, of this I am certain, at the other star we settled, in the asteroid system. The children there may have at first mistaken you for the marauders, but once engaged with you that mistake would not matter. As long as you remain in their territory they will fight you. It is their instinct. So be it. After so long, they are not my concern.'

'And here?' Andrews asked.

'If you left the surface of the planet, the changeling children would have no reason to follow you. Eventually they would die out.'

Andrews looked at Dorthy, then said, 'Then let that be the basis of our first cooperation. I can agree to have the base on the surface dismantled, the people there evacuated. We can arrange some link with you.' He was lying of course, simply trying to buy time; perhaps he even harboured the hope that the female would agree, let them go . . . and then the Navy would destroy her. Dorthy said nothing.

The neuter female said through the translator, 'You misunderstand. I do not wish peace. That is why I wished this female killed, for she could have guessed the truth of the changeling children before they began their defence of their parents. Twice I tried to arrange her death, twice I failed. But she came here anyway.'

Dorthy remembered the vision that had been planted in her mind at the keep and said, 'You wanted me to come here.'

'And now I have you, and the war will proceed.'

Andrews said stubbornly, 'But there doesn't have to be a war! Together, your people and mine could fight these marauders, if they come.'

'It would be better if you ran, as we did. But you will not. Your species is like so many that have gone before, seeking to bestride the Galaxy. This has already happened, from the evidence of the technology captured and perverted by the marauders. Perhaps many times. We live in the ruins of history. This family may be destroyed by your people, *must* be destroyed. Before the marauders come, as they will come. Yes, yes. And others in the refuges scattered among the small stars will all uncomprehending see the flashes of light in their skies that show the destruction of the suns of your worlds.'

'And of yours,' Dorthy said.

There was a pause. The female's vestigial arms fidgeted with her pelt, and the monkey-like creature dropped her shoulder and bounded away, its bifurcated tail high in the air. Two herders followed it through an archway. The others continued to watch the humans, faces impassive within cowls of folded skin.

Watching the neuter female's aura and the flaw within it, Dorthy thought, it's like an upwelling, an eruption from some deep vent that is dispersed by strong currents before it reaches the surface. If I knew its source . . .

At last the translator raised his head. 'It is necessary,' he said. 'If we survive, we will be found by the marauders when they track down the traces left by your ships. Finding this world, they will know to search all the other insignificant stars for the other refuges.'

'Nothing would go to such lengths,' Andrews said.

'It is truth.'

Andrews worried at his hair and said with explosive exasperation, 'Then you're crazy! Keep us here and you will surely die. Everything on the planet will die.'

'It is necessary,' the neuter female said, as the cloud surged about the knot, the flaw, that split it. She was lying, Dorthy saw, lying. Her only loyalty was to her own immediate kin, those of her family living on this planet, not other colonies sundered by more than a million years. She had said as much herself.

'Will you discharge your duty by sacrificing your family?' Dorthy ventured.

'For the greater good of the species,' the neuter female said.

A lie, a lie. Dorthy tried to look into the outpouring light, like trying to glimpse the ghost of a snowflake whirling in a nova. For a moment her entire self was open to the light; the only way she could capture the knot and resolve it was to take it into herself, regardless of the danger of breakout. From a long way away she heard Andrews shout, 'What are you doing to her? Stop it, fucking *stop*—' And without interval, it seemed, she was lying on the ground, looking up at Andrews's anxious face, framed by the black sky beyond. For a moment it was like seeing double, his familiar features overlaid by a weird alien mask, a wrongness. And then she felt the pattern of the neuter female's multiple persona fade, and she was herself again. And understood the flaw, the knot, the terrible thing that had had to be done so long ago to keep this world hidden, keep it safe from the core.

'Christ,' Andrews said. 'Say something, Dorthy. Are you all right? It was as if you had a fit.'

'I'm okay,' she said, and tasted blood: she'd bitten her tongue. When she sat up she discovered that she'd wet herself, too. Petit mal. But she knew.

Andrews helped her stand, and she said in English, 'Don't try anything, I know why she wants to die now . . . and perhaps how I can convince her not to die.'

'She didn't do that to you?'

'Not exactly. I looked into her mind. I *saw*.' Dorthy grinned, and felt a thread of blood roll down her chin. 'I thought I'd given up therapy long ago.'

'Use your Talent if you like, but there is only an hour until we must rendezvous with Angel. If we stay here any longer she'll go without us, and the Navy will trigger the sun. If you can do something, do it quick.'

'Trust me,' Dorthy said, and turned to the neuter female – who, if she knew what had been done, showed no sign of it. In Portuguese Dorthy said, 'I should have guessed you wanted to die when you gave that ridiculous explication of the *Sonnets*.'

'This was wrong?'

'The dark lady was no God; she was only an ordinary woman, a female. The poet was urging his master to marry her, the woman he also loved. There is the dichotomy from which the themes of the *Sonnets* sprang. There is flattery, yes, but also the discharging of a duty, no matter how painful, and the promise of the poet's undying love, as undying as his art. You saw only what you wanted to see, an obsession with death, the path your sisters took from shame so long ago. But the shame is not yours; it is your ancestor's, the one who acted to preserve this world. It was wrong, yes, but you cannot allow your family to die now. It will not wipe away the shame. Because I know now. I know what was done.'

'I knew that you were dangerous. Yes, I knew.' The neuter female watched Dorthy with great, lambent eyes. Behind her, the herders shuffled in confusion, the grip of the webs of routine slackened.

Andrews said, 'What is all this? What guilt?'

'Half a million years ago,' Dorthy said steadily, returning the female's gaze, 'more or less, a civilisation arose on a world of a nearby star: Epsilon Eridani.'

'Novaya Rosya,' Andrews said. 'So that was what almost destroyed it.'

'Yes. In the same way that they moved this planet, some of the neuter females altered the orbit of one of the moons of one of the gas giants, sent it careering towards Epsilon Eridani. I wondered why the drive system of the ark was no longer in orbit around this planet; now I know. It went with the moon. Only a small, insignificant rock, all that the drive could move after millennia of disuse, but when it struck Novaya Rosya it was travelling at close to the speed of light. It didn't quite destroy the planet, but it came close. And destroyed the civilisation which had just begun to explore the nearby stars, which would have soon betrayed themselves to the marauders; and perhaps betrayed this world, too. Poor Arcady! His zithsa hunters were right after all! The other neuter females tried to prevent the genocide. There was a power struggle; you can guess who won—' Dorthy stopped, because the neuter female had begun to move.

Grunting, she rolled her great bulk on to bended knees, then pushed with shaggy arms, shadows weaving around her as she reared up, almost twice as tall as the herders ranked behind her.

'Goddamn,' Andrews said, and Dorthy caught his hand, reminded him to be still.

He shook off her grip and stepped forward. He had gone beyond fear. 'Is what Dorthy said true?' he demanded. 'You destroyed a world to keep your secret here?'

'Let her talk to me,' Dorthy said.

'You and your goddamn pride,' Andrews said fiercely. 'Your damned Talent can't do everything.'

'It happened long ago, so long ago,' Dorthy said to the female. 'Why does it still torment you?'

'Because I am many, not one, and many remember. When the new civilisation arose, so close to our hiding place, we remembered how this world had been harmed by a few small asteroids when our rebellious sisters had stolen the ark. Afterward, we had to scour nearby systems to replace all that had been lost of the life we had brought here. Yes, we remembered that, when the new civilisation was discovered. We were the oldest of our kind then, and only we remembered. Only we knew what had to be done. Some of our sisters did not understand, and resisted us. They are gone, so long ago now. Even those of our sisters who helped us are gone. Only we are left. Only we remember.'

How old she was, Dorthy saw, how singular and alone, how tired of living! The lineages of the other neuter females who had helped the act of genocide had died out long ago; those who had resisted it had been destroyed. She alone was left, still gripped by the urge to protect the herders. This instinct, which had driven her to genocide and murder and left her ridden with guilt, had also sustained her through the millennia . . . until the humans had come. She had not been able to repeat her act, but in their coming she had seen a chance to rest, to bring an end to her guilt, the collective guilt of her ancestors. That that end would also mean the end of her family was the paradox which Dorthy had seen knotted at the core of the neuter female, the pivot on which she might be turned.

Dorthy said, 'Will you discharge your guilt by sacrificing your family? They know nothing of it. How can they? You told us of their innocence, their ignorance. Why should they also die?'

The neuter female said nothing, her gaze still locked with Dorthy's. But the translator threw up his head and howled, clutching at his hood with clawed fingers so that blood ran along the folded skin. Behind the female's still figure the other herders clutched their heads, too.

And in that long still moment Andrews made his move.

Dorthy realised what he was about to do and whirled; but too late. He triggered the signal flare and white light scorched among the herders behind them, searingly bright. One whirled, afire, its panic breaking the weakened thrall of command. Frantically slashing at its burning pelt, it stumbled into two of its companions. The flare screamed into the far wall and skittered off in a shower of sparks as Andrews ran forward, scooped up the rifle that one of the herders had dropped. When he turned, Dorthy caught the hard edge of his purpose: he thought that he was doing right, destroying something before it destroyed him, unable to imagine any motivation on the neuter female's part other than those he himself possessed. Kill or be killed.

All this in the moment as he brought up the rifle.

The first shot kicked fragments of black flooring around the female's clawed feet. She did not even flinch, watching Andrews as if calmly resigned, the cloud of her aura united at last, as he steadied his nervous grip and fired again.

In the moment of her fall, the herders were still. Then the translator collapsed like an unstrung puppet, and the others began to shuffle forward. Andrews struck Dorthy's shoulder, turning her and pushing her back.

'Run,' he said. 'Run, you little fool,' and turned to face his enemy.

Dorthy ran.

5
Four Hundred Billion Suns

Later.

A stone disturbed by her feet chuckled away over some unseen edge and Dorthy stopped, listening to the diminishing echoes. She was still afraid that one or more of the herders had followed her through the vegetation-choked dry riverbed of the ravine, around the slopes of the hold; still half expected that Andrews would walk up to her, smiling his easy smile.

But he was dead; as dead as Arcady Kilczer, as dead as the twins and the people in the high camp in the keep. All dead. The desert circled Dorthy, quiet and immense beneath the starry sky.

She went on, stumbling through chalky shadows until at last the homing compass settled to a steady glow. She threw it away, its little light vanishing silently into darkness, pushed up the goggles of her nightsights and rubbed the pinched bridge of her nose. Now all she had to do was await Angel's return. No more than a few minutes.

And afterward?

She would tell her story, explain all that she had learned. If she was persuasive enough perhaps she could convince the Navy to withdraw from BD twenty and so end the war; but she was certain that this world at least would not be scorched clean. Once the Navy learned that the enemy was, at bottom, cowardly, the risk of exploration would seem small beside the potential rewards. P'thrsn would be blockaded until the changeling children died out, but it would not be destroyed.

And if the marauders still lived at the core, they would not come in Dorthy's lifetime. From the residue of the neuter female's mindset she knew that the signals which betrayed phase graffles propagated through contraspace at the same relative velocity as the ships they powered. It would be at least two hundred years before anything arrived in the vicinity of Sol; the very size of the Galaxy would protect her. Unless Andrews had been right after all, unless human-kind went out to challenge the marauders in their own territory . . .

Well, the future was, as always, unguessable. But Dorthy knew at least that when her part was done, when she was released, she could no longer hide as the herders, the Alea, hid among the marginal suns. Poor little monsters fearful of the sky, of the light of four hundred billion suns.

No, she could no longer deny her birthright. She would go out at last among the burning mysterious minds of her people.

Contemplating this resolution, Dorthy sat on a slab of freezing rock and hugged her meagre warmth to herself, too tired to wonder if she had missed the rendezvous. But at last she heard the thrum of the thopter, distant but already growing louder, nearer, a heartbeat winging over the still, dark desert. She stood and triggered her signal flare.

At the top of its brief erratic arc the white glare for a moment drowned out the stars.

ABOUT THE AUTHOR

A biologist by training, PAUL McAULEY is now a full-time writer of stunning hard SF and alternate reality novels. His first novel, *400 Billion Stars*, won the Philip K. Dick Award, while *Fairyland* won both the Arthur C. Clarke Award and the John W. Campbell Memorial Award for Best SF Novel. *Pasquale's Angel* won the Sidewise Award for Alternate History.

He lives and works in London. Visit his blog at http://unlikelyworlds.blogspot.com